A KING'S BARGAIN

BOOK I OF LEGEND OF TAL

J.D.L. ROSELL

Illustration © 2020 by René Aigner
Book design by J.D.L. Rosell
Map by Kaitlyn Clark

ISBN 978-1-952868-00-9 (hardback)
ISBN 978-1-952868-01-6 (paperback)
ISBN 978-1-952868-02-3 (ebook)

Published by JDL Rosell
jdlrosell.com

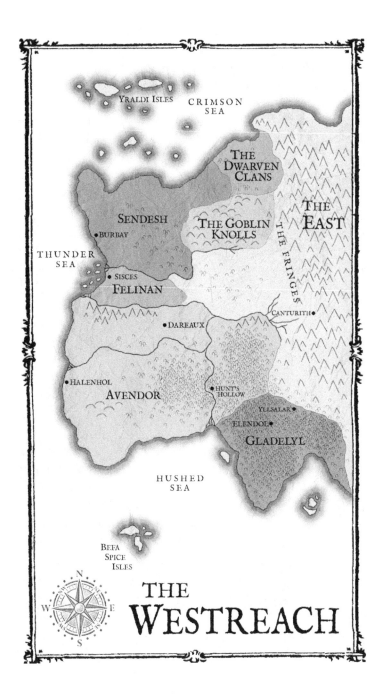

YRALDI ISLES

CRIMSON SEA

THE DWARVEN CLANS

SENDESH

BURBAY

THE GOBLIN KNOLLS

THUNDER SEA

SISCES

FELINAN

THE FRINGES

THE EAST

CANTURITH

DAREAUX

HALENHOL

AVENDOR

HUNT'S HOLLOW

YLLSALAR

ELENDOL

GLADELYL

HUSHED SEA

BEFA SPICE ISLES

N
W   E
S

THE WESTREACH

PROLOGUE
THE TRUTH OF LEGENDS

TAL HARRENFEL IS MORE LIE THAN LEGEND.

This is my conclusion regarding "the Man of a Thousand Names," and by the flagrant dishonesty of Falcon Sunstring, Harrenfel's minstrel, I must doubt all of the infamous adventurer's purported exploits.

Sunstring's opening ballad would have you believe:

> *He stole the Impervious Ring from the Queen of*
> > *Goblins*
> *He killed Yuldor's Demon and saved the Sanguine City*
> > *of Elendol*
> *He protected the Northern Shores and plumbed the*
> > *depths of the dwarven mines*
> *He stole the heart of a princess and the tongue from*
> > *a bard*
>
> *Ringthief — Devil Killer — Defender of the Westreach*
> *His name harkens back to the deeds of his youth*
> *His legend rings out from every throat in the West...*

Yet Sunstring fails to mention the darker stories also attributed to

Harrenfel. Magebutcher. Red Reaver. Khuldanaam'defarnaam —
*or, translated from the Clantongue of the Hardrog Dwarves, "He Who
Does Not Fear Death, For He Is Death's Hand."*

*The story is at best incomplete, at worst impossible. That one man
could be a swordsman, sorcerer, and mercenary as well as an accomplished poet, diplomat — and, if the rumors hold true, lover —
stretches the limits of belief.*

*And how could any of the legend be believed, when Harrenfel
himself was recorded saying to His Majesty, Aldric Rexall the Fourth:*

"I've never claimed to be more than a man."

*As a historian and a scholar, I will gather the witnesses, collect the
accounts, and piece together the true story behind this modern fable.
Then, fraud or impossibly true, I will expose Tal Harrenfel for the
charlatan I suspect — nay, I know him to be.*

- Brother Causticus of the Order of Ataraxis

THE CALL OF THE CONSTELLATIONS

FAR FROM THE HEART OF CIVILIZATION, COWLED IN A GLOOM barely lifted by the moons, rests the town of Hunt's Hollow, all still and shadowed — all save a candle flickering into flame.

A man, hunched over a rough-hewn table in a cramped room, stares at the swaying flame. Dark planes fall over his face, and lines of age and old injury fall into deeper shadow. A beard, tan speckled with red, is barely kept at bay, and long, tawny hair streaked with gray and white falls around his face.

The candle's flame dances in a breeze that claws through the boards, and the light reflects in the man's eyes, black as a devil's heart and wide with a wolf's hunger, as he shifts his gaze down to the object before him.

A book, its pages worn around the edges and yellowed with age, lays open on the table. His gaze does not shift, his eyes do not read the words, but he stares as if to see beyond what the pages can offer.

He is still for a long moment, then his eyes dart up to the swaying flame, and one calloused hand stretches forward. As his hand passes over the candle, the flame sputters and blows out, and the night sweeps into the room once more.

Sleep — sleep is all he dreams of. Sleep that comes as easily as extinguishing a candle, that banishes the thoughts of all he's lost. Only asleep can he lose himself in remembrances of fine wine and unwarranted fame, of palaces with mirror-bright halls and sly-eyed gentlefolk at balls. Even memories of the dark towers filled with murder and fury where he'd been hunted by beasts and black-hearted warlocks — even those nightmares would be preferred.

For, while awake, no dream can be real.

The wind whistles through the cracks, and the tired wood groans. Another mumbled word, and the candle flickers to life again, the hand falling back to the table to rest next to the book's frayed binding.

His eyes wander down to the tome again, and his fingers stretch toward it to brush across the rough, aged paper. He whispers, "Would that you'd reveal the truth of your secrets."

Then, he might know the face of him named the Enemy of the Westreach. Then, he could end this war, this farce.

Then, he could finally rest.

Far from the heart of civilization, cowled in a gloom barely lifted by the moons, rests the town of Hunt's Hollow, all still and shadowed — all save a man filled with memories of what once was and dreams of what could never be.

Both near and far away, lost in a solitude of his own, a boy just becoming a man stares up at the ceiling of his shared bedroom, listening to the sounds of his sleeping brothers and remembering the stories of the stars.

The bed, stuffed with straw, is hard and lumpy and scratchy, but he barely feels it. He is strolling down shining rooms with ceilings as high as the sky, and a woman, as lovely as a sunset's glow, holds tightly to his arm. A sword is belted at his hip, and a smile plays on his lips. As they pass a group of people, he hears their whispers: *There he strides! Isn't he glorious, the Hero of Avendor?*

A brother snores, and the youth jerks back into the dark, stuffy room, the lumpy bed beneath. He shifts, tries to get comfortable, fails, and finally settles back.

He can see and feel it all so clearly. He can taste the wine, sweeter than any freshly picked autumn apple. He can smell the air, perfumed with roses and mysterious spices. He can see the famed bastion of the King of Avendor, salmon-colored towers rising into the clouds. And he can see himself among it all.

But when he breathes in, only the stench of stale sweat and manure fills his nose.

The youth sighs and stretches out on the bed long grown too small for him. He's never seen a castle, never tasted wine, never smelled a perfume the surrounding forest couldn't provide. All he knows of the World, he has learned from stories told around the fire. Every imagining he has, he steals from the tales of the legends.

Markus Bredley, the roguish adventurer who delved into the treasure troves the dwarves keep hidden beneath their mountains and came out a rich man. Gendil of Candor, the warlock who learned the names of the moons and ascended to dwell with the Whispering Gods. General Tussilus, who led the charge that drove back the Eastern Horde during their last incursion two centuries past. And Tal Harrenfel, the Man of a Thousand Names, the living legend who disappeared into the barbaric East seven years before and was never seen again.

But more treasured still are the tales his brothers have told of their father, a captain who left to serve the King and died in his service, so long ago now he can scarcely remember his face.

"I'll earn my own name," he whispers to the night sky, hidden beyond the thatched roof. "I'll earn my stars."

One of his brothers mutters, and the youth falls silent. In the darkness, his dreams are safe. Only in silence can he hear the call of the constellations, whispering, beckoning him onward.

THE GREATEST CHICKEN FARMER

As Garin watched the man dart back and forth across the muddy yard, half-bent like a raccoon, trying over and over to snag one of the hens and failing, he couldn't say he'd ever seen a better chicken farmer.

"Come here, damn you!" the man cursed as he chased the chickens. As they scattered, he made a grab, missed, tried again, and nearly fell face-first into the mud.

"Try approaching slower," Garin said, a twitch to his lips. "Not that an old man like you could go anything but slow."

The would-be chicken herder straightened and stretched his back with a groan. "Tried that. Still don't have a chicken roasting on a spit." He eyed Garin. "Maybe if a certain lad helped me chase them, we might both be chewing on succulent meat before the hour's up."

Garin pretended not to notice as his gaze wandered up to the sky. "Best hurry about it. Looks set to rain at any moment."

The man sighed. "Maybe the mud will stop them. Yuldor's prick, but chickens are degenerate birds, aren't they? What kind of bird can't even fly?"

The farmer stalked after the hens, a hand pressed to his

side. He often touched that spot, Garin had noticed, like one might pick at a scab that refused to heal.

Garin shook his head and looked off toward the main muddy road through the town. The chicken farmer, incompetent as he might be at his chosen profession, had been the most exciting thing to happen to Hunt's Hollow in the last five years. Little else changed in their village. The seasons came and went; rains fell, and fields dried up; youths coupled against their parents' wishes and established their own farms. Life was trapped in amber, the same cycle repeated for every man, woman, and child in the village. The only thing to change in the last five years was the lack of deaths, for though the Nightkin beasts that came down from the Fringes had still been sighted, none had stayed long enough to attack.

His eyes turned toward the western tree line. Garin had traveled to all the other villages in the East Marsh, taking every opportunity he could get, but found them all the same, and Hunt's Hollow the largest of them, with its own forge and sharing its mill with only one other town. The World, he knew, lay with the rest of the Westreach.

I'll see it all and make my name, he promised himself. *Someday.*

His unfocused eyes were drawn by a figure approaching down the road. As the man drew closer, it became apparent he wasn't from any of the surrounding towns, or even the East Marsh. *No wagon or horse — can't be a peddler. A wandering tradesman?* But where he kept the tools of his trade, Garin hadn't the faintest idea, for his pack was small and slight.

As he came closer still, he observed how oddly dressed the traveler was. His hat, made of stiff cloth that was worn and gray and notched on the rim, was pointed and bent at the top. The long braid of hair draped over the front of his shoulder was black as a winter night. His chin was completely smooth and so sharp Garin reckoned he could cut a wheel of cheese with it. His clothes, like his hat, were well-used, but despite the many patches, they spoke of quality not too far gone.

A man of means, Garin wagered. *Always best to be polite to a man of means.*

"Welcome, traveler!" he called cheerily as the man came within earshot. "Welcome to Hunt's Hollow!"

"I read the sign on the way in."

He sounded somewhat irritable. But then, Garin reasoned, he must have traveled a long way. Opening his mouth to respond, he found the words caught in his throat. The traveler's eyes were shadowed by the wide brim of his hat, but he could detect a shining quality to them. *Like staring into a forge,* Garin thought before he could banish the boyish notion.

"Rain's blessing to you this day, stranger," he finally said. "A lonely corner of the World the roads have taken you to today."

The man cocked his head, the floppy tip of the hat tilting with it. "Not for long, I hope."

Garin kept his face carefully smooth. He was quite good at it, having had plenty of practice with Crazy Ean, who drank too much marsh whiskey and said things that could stiffen even an old man's beard.

"You'll be looking for a place to stay, I reckon?"

The stranger's gaze shifted past him, and Garin glanced back to see the chicken farmer approaching them. Somehow, he seemed changed, his shoulders back and posture upright despite his earlier defeat, and an unfamiliar hardness in his eyes.

"No," the stranger said. "I won't."

"Garin! Who's this you're keeping inhospitably in the mud?" The chicken farmer had reached his fence and leaned against it, wearing an amicable smile. But that smile… something about it made Garin suddenly feel he'd gotten in the way of two hogs who had their sights on the same sow.

"The boy has been accommodating," the stranger said before

Garin could answer. "Silence pray that others in this town are just as kind."

"Oh, Hunt's Hollow is a fine town," the chicken farmer replied. "Peaceful and quiet. We like it to stay that way."

Garin swallowed and edged back along the fence.

The stranger turned his gaze on him. "Boy, I may yet take you up on your offer. Stay close by."

"No, that's alright," the chicken farmer said with his smile wider still. "I'm sure I could put you up if it comes to it. You get along now, boy."

If nothing else had his hairs on end, the chicken farmer calling him "boy" did. In the five years since he'd settled in Hunt's Hollow, the man had never been anything less than respectful to him, treating him as a man grown — which, at fifteen, he damned well was. A boy would run, he knew, but a man would stay.

"I'll stay. You might need someone to help you chase down chickens, Bran."

The stranger's eyes seemed more molten than ever as they turned back to the chicken farmer. "Bran, is it?"

"It is." Bran straightened, one foot still on the fence. "But I must have missed your name."

"I very much doubt that."

Man or boy, Garin was starting to think he ought to run for someone. Smith wouldn't be a bad man to have around if this came to blows. Though to look at these two, a bout wouldn't take long to settle.

Bran looked to have forty summers to him, from the crinkles around his eyes, and the dark tan-going-leather of his skin. But he had broad shoulders for a man of his middling height, and a chest and arms to rival Smith's, which Garin guessed he hadn't earned through chasing chickens. Then there were his tattoos, and the scars they covered. Bran always wore long shirts, even in the heat of the day, but Garin had glimpsed them: the bright colors, the strange, scrawling patterns, the puckered skin running beneath them all. The scar on his side looked the worst of them, and he often caught Bran clutching at it as if it pained him still. And his hair was streaked with white and gray so that Garin had occasionally teased him by calling him "Skunk."

Bran had been a soldier once, Garin had no doubt. Though, if his swordwork was as good as his chicken herding, he wondered how the man had survived.

The stranger, meanwhile, was slight as a scribe, and though tall and weathered, he didn't have a visible weapon. The match, he decided, could only sway in one direction. Except he couldn't quite shake the feeling that things didn't cut as straight as that.

Bran, quick as a snake in the brush, leaped over the fence to stand before the stranger. He tilted his head up to meet the other man's gaze, a slight, crooked smile still on his lips. Garin tensed, waiting for the strike that must come.

"Well, Aelyn Cloudtouched, He-Who-Sees-Fire, I'd hoped I'd never see you again. But since you're here, how 'bout I offer you a glass of marsh whiskey and we talk like old friends?"

"Like old friends," the stranger replied. "Or old enemies."

Bran shrugged. "Conversation is only interesting with animosity or amorousness — or so the bards sing. Follow me, it's not far."

Bran turned his back on the man. From the look in the stranger's eyes, Garin half-expected him to strike at the farmer's back. But instead, he followed him down the fence toward the small house at the end.

"You too, Garin," Bran called behind him. "If you've seen this much, our guest will want you to witness the rest."

"As if I'd have done anything else," Garin muttered as he tailed behind.

Bran settled in a chair across from his guest and smiled like they were old friends.

The house was nothing to look at, he well knew: two rooms large, with a ragged curtain separating them; a small wood stove settled behind him, and a well-used pot and pan, travel-ready, hanging above it. As rain began to patter against the roof, the usual leaks started up in the corners.

He didn't care to impress folks, not anymore, and this man least of all. But he'd helped his guest over the stoop like a nobleman might usher a lady into his bedroom, and ignored the man's protests that he needed no assistance in a similarly lofty manner.

Gallantry, he'd often found, suited a liar like a cape fit a king.

Garin squirmed in the seat next to them, but Bran paid him no mind as he took his glass and threw it back. He sighed as the liquid burned its way down his throat to settle a steady warmth in his gut. "Say what you want about Crazy Ean, but he makes a damn fine whiskey."

"So says anyone mad enough to try it," Garin muttered.

Bran grinned at him. "Life is short and dark as it is. May as well brighten it with a few glorious risks."

The youth shrugged.

He turned his gaze to the guest again, who hadn't touched his glass. "I know your name, Aelyn, and you know ours. The table is set. Now lay out what you want, or we'll have to settle on beans and roots for dinner."

Aelyn hadn't removed his hat, but even with his eyes shadowed, they seemed to gleam. "You know what I want. I'm not idly used as a messenger. But I obey my commands."

He lifted his hand to reveal a small, shining band resting in his palm, then set it on the table. Garin stared at it, mouth open wide. Bran found he was unable to resist looking himself, though he knew its kind well. Not a ring of silver or gold or copper, but milky white crystal, with a steady glow from within its clouded center.

"What is it?" Garin asked, sounding as if he wished he hadn't spoken but was unable to resist.

Aelyn didn't answer but kept his steady, orange gaze on Bran, like a raptor on a hare.

Bran sighed. "It's a Binding Ring. An artifact of oaths that holds the wearer to a promise."

Garin might be a man grown to the villagers, but he looked a boy at that moment, his eyes wide, his mouth forming a small "o."

"Like… a magic ring?" the youth ventured.

"Enough of this!" Aelyn snapped. "Take it and put it on. We must be returning immediately."

"Off so soon? But you haven't touched your drink."

The man snorted. "If I wished to poison myself, I have a thousand better ways than that human swill. Don that ring. Now." His fiery eyes slid over to Garin. "Or do you want the boy to know your true name?"

Bran studied him. A feeling, hard as flint, was starting behind his eyes. A feeling familiar as a distant memory. A feeling he'd hoped to have dug a deep grave and buried in the past. As it rose, a warmth unconnected to the whiskey began coursing through his body. *Dread?* he mocked himself. *Or anticipation?*

He reached a hand forward, finger brushing the crystal. It was warm to the touch. From past experience, he knew it remained warm most of the time. So long as the wearer kept to what he was bound. If he didn't, a mountain peak in winter would be preferable punishment.

Aelyn's eyes watched. Wary. Waiting.

Bran scooped up the ring, vaulted across the table, and shouted, "*Heshidal bauchdid!*"

The man jerked, then stiffened in his chair, eyes wide with surprise, hat knocked askew. Bran took his moment, snatching one of the smooth hands and slipping the ring over a long finger.

As Aelyn shivered free of the binding, his mouth stuttered, "Bastard of a pig-blooded whore—!"

"Quiet down!" Bran shouted over him. "This I bind you to: That you will wear this ring until I am safely back in Hunt's Hollow. That you will tell no one that you wear this ring instead of me. That you will tell no one my true name unless I bid it. And that you won't harm the boy Garin or myself in that time."

The ring shone brightly for a moment, and Aelyn shuddered, eyes squeezed shut, teeth braced in a grimace. A moment later, the ring dimmed, and Bran released his guest's hand. As he settled into his chair, brushing back the hairs that had worked loose of his tail, his blood began to cool again.

"Now," he said as he reached for the whiskey bottle, which had fallen over in the struggle, and pulled out the stopper. "You sure you don't want any of this human swill?"

The man raised his hand and stared at the crystal ring, horror spreading across his face. "She told you, didn't she? She told you my true name."

Bran poured a glass, then proffered it to the youth, who stared at him as if he were the stranger. "Feeling mad enough yet?"

Garin took the glass, threw it back, and promptly coughed half of it back up.

"There you are, Garin, there you are," Bran said, thumping his back. "You'll learn to swallow it all before long."

THE BLADE THAT RUSTS

"This changes nothing," the stranger hissed from across the table.

Garin stared at him through watering eyes. His stomach swirled and turned like a basket caught in a river, and not only from the whiskey. The ring, those *words*, and all this business about Bran's "true name"...

He was beginning to wonder if there were two strangers in the room.

"To the contrary," Bran said brightly. "This flips the negotiation. Why else would I risk getting blasted across the room?"

"Your binding — it shouldn't have worked. I wore a charm —" The man called Aelyn pulled back his sleeve, then hissed, "It's gone!"

Bran held up a hand, and hanging from his finger was a delicate, silver bracelet that looked as if it had been threaded together from fish scales. "You mean this?"

"When?"

"Helping you over the threshold. Pays to have a pile of dung in front of your door on rare occasion."

Aelyn's jaw hung open for a moment, then snapped shut. After a long moment, he spoke, "I am bound to your oath — I won't pretend that I can break free of such an artifact. But you said my binding lasts until we return to this hogwash village — which means you intend to come on my errand."

"Yes, I did say that." Bran leaned back, hands folded behind his head. "That was the clever bit."

"I don't see how."

Bran shrugged. "We can't return to Hunt's Hollow if we never leave, can we?"

Aelyn's eyes narrowed. "You mean to tell me you plan to stay in this backwater swamp for the rest of your days?"

Garin finally roused; he didn't know about bindings and magic, but he knew his home. "You don't know what you're talking about. Hunt's Hollow is the finest town east of Halenhol — there's naught a better place to live!"

He looked at Bran, hoping to find the same fire in his eyes, but he saw only calm consideration.

Aelyn stared at him like he were a stinkbug in his bed. "Finest, indeed. How many other towns have you been to, boy?"

Garin could count them on one hand, and he had a feeling that wouldn't impress this strange traveler. "Enough."

Aelyn raised one thin eyebrow, then looked back at Bran. "So, this is the sort of company you keep these days?"

"Indeed, it is." Bran hadn't shifted from his easy recline. "After all, it's the finest company east of Halenhol."

Garin had to grin at that.

"Enough!" Aelyn snapped. "Enough of this charade! I cannot say your real name, but you know it as well as I do. Is this really where your name ends? Forgotten, a failed chicken farmer in a provincial village, meaning nothing to those he'd fought and cared for?"

The smile had slipped from Bran's mouth, and his hands came to rest on the table. "Why not?" he asked quietly. "It's where I began."

Garin blinked, seeing Bran anew. "You were born here?"

The man stood, not meeting his eyes. "You could say that."

He glanced at the visitor. "There's a fine bit of hay in the barn. Day's winding down, and if the patter on the roof is any indication, the rain won't let up soon."

Aelyn stood, stiff as a board. "Much as I revile it, I won't leave until you come with me."

Bran smiled at that, but the joy behind it had dulled. "Then I hope you're not as bad at chicken farming as I am."

The traveler had run, muttering under his breath, for the barn through the streaking rain, while Bran watched from within his hovel. Garin stood behind him, scuffing his shoes until he stopped himself. He was a man, not a boy. High time he started acting like one. He cleared his throat.

"All that man said," he started. "About your 'true name'... what did he mean?"

Bran remained facing the open door and the rain. "You're a man now, Garin, but still young. You can't know how the past, no matter how much you wish it gone, clings to you no matter where you go. Like a phantom fist clenched around your heart, squeezing and choking when you least expect it. But even still, when you've gone astray, there comes a time when you have to try and separate yourself from it. You have to change who you are."

Garin couldn't help a little snort escaping him.

Bran met his gaze now, his lips twisted. "Something amusing?"

"I may be a young man, but I've seen enough of people to know they don't change, not really. Oh, they put on new faces — sometimes literally, like Aunt Helan with her elven paints. But underneath, they're still the same."

Bran shook his head and looked back out at the rain. "I hope you're wrong. But I suspect you're not."

Garin stepped closer. He wasn't sure if it was the whiskey or something else, but his stomach had set to a nervous tumbling, like he was on the verge of something, but didn't yet know what.

"You said to me earlier that life is short and dull, and you have to find the sparks to light the way. Back there, when you tricked that Aelyn fellow — you were more alive than in the five years I've known you. More... you." He scratched his head. "If that makes any sense."

"Unfortunately, it does."

"I don't know you as anyone but Bran. But whoever you were before, I'm guessing those same things are still in you. And I'm guessing you haven't succeeded in cutting away the past."

Bran studied him in silence for so long Garin started to wonder if he'd gone too far. He'd only known Bran five years, after all, and he had the scars of a soldier and tattoos of wild folk, or hedge mages, or something foreign and strange. He had no idea what he was capable of.

But the man's lips curled into a familiar, lopsided smile. "You know, you're a lot wiser than I was at your age. But I'm going to guess you're not as wise as you should be."

Garin frowned. "How's that?"

"Because when I ask you to leave Hunt's Hollow, I suspect you'll say yes."

Garin's pulse quickened. He remembered Aelyn's contempt as he boasted about Hunt's Hollow. He could count the number of villages he'd seen on one hand.

And there was the whole World out there.

Garin shrugged. "What else could I say?"

The chicken farmer threw back his head in a laugh. "We'll let our companion stew for a bit first. But I suspect in a few days' time, the easterly winds will blow in more autumn rain and carry three travelers away."

Garin smiled uncertainly.

As the mirth left him, Bran eyed Garin. "Go. Think it over

carefully. Be sure this is your time. And if it is, be ready to leave at a penny's drop."

"When?" he asked, hardly believing this was happening, hardly believing he was going along with it.

"Soon. I'll come for you."

Bran wiped the rain from his face as he stepped into the barn.

Orange eyes, like the eyes of a stalking cat, gleamed from the shadows. As if he'd been waiting for his approach, Aelyn stepped forward holding a long object wrapped in a sack. In the fading blue light, Bran could see clumps of dirt still clinging to the cloth.

"You found it quickly," he observed.

"It was shallowly buried. Though I can't see what use a chicken farmer would have for a sword."

The traveler held out the swaddled item, and Bran stepped forward, took it, then stepped quickly back. Aelyn had been ensorcelled not to harm him, but, as his mother had often lectured him, *Only a clod-wit trusts a sure thing.*

Aelyn's lips curled in a mocking smile. Even inside the barn, he hadn't taken off his hat.

"You can remove that now," Bran observed. "Others won't see you in here, though I doubt they'd take offense even if they did. We aren't far from Gladelyl, after all."

Aelyn flashed a thin smile and ignored him. "I had hoped we would leave sooner rather than later."

"We'll leave when it's time."

He scowled, then gestured at the package. "You'll be needing that."

Bran ignored him, his concentration shifting to the object in his hands. Slowly, he unwound the leather bindings of the package, slipped it free of the sack, then of the oilskin wrappings under. An ornately decorated scabbard rested in his hands, silver-blue script spiraling up the dark leather, slightly blurring before his eyes as he followed their lines. The hilt that protruded from it was plain black steel with a worn leather grip. It was a bastard sword, fitting in one hand, but just long enough for two. The crossguard was straight and short but would catch a blade from sliding down on his hands.

Velori, he thought, and the blade hummed in response, knowing its name even in his thoughts.

He placed a hand on its grip, then pulled it free. The sword vibrated as it whispered free of the scabbard; but in Bran's ears, it carried a reverberating ring that sang of glory and honor and fame. The silver steel gleamed even in the dim light as if it couldn't help but gather light to its polished edge.

But though he heard the glory-song, other murmurs had crept into the sword's hum over the years. Desperate screams. Grunts of hard contests. The song of splattering blood and splintering bone and dying men.

Bran sheathed the blade again, eyes downcast.

"You've kept it sharp," Aelyn said. Bran could feel his eyes burning into him. "And not a spot of rust on the steel."

"We're in the far reaches of civilization, close to the East. Here, the war never ends. Besides, it's said the blade that rusts is borne by a fool."

"A quotation from one of the famed generals?"

Bran glanced up. "From myself."

Aelyn gave him a smile full of biting knowledge. "How humble you are, Magebutcher."

Bran winced. "I know we're not on the best of terms right now; I'll take the blame for that. And, unfortunately, I've only oath-bound you to not say my true name and not the rest. But if you could not mention those other titles to the boy…"

Aelyn watched him, the smile remaining. "That depends on your good behavior. But what name do you fear the most, I wonder? Bran the Bastard? The boy fathered by a warlock who seduced his mother and left him to a childhood of loneliness and ridicule? The boy who was forgotten even as he returned as a man?"

Old wounds, he told himself. But Bran knew better than anyone that old wounds could always pull open and bleed.

"Or perhaps Red Reaver," the traveler continued. "I think there are many sins attached to that epithet that haunt you still."

Bran looked sharply at Aelyn then. *How much does he know? How much could he?* His words came too close to the mark to be randomly thrown.

Aelyn only smiled wider. "But that evokes the question — why bring the boy? He can only be a hindrance to us and a danger to himself."

Hoping only he knew the connection between those thoughts, Bran let the sheathed blade fall to his side and kept his voice even. "Better that he's endangered in my care than left here for whatever comes down from the East. The World is a hard place, and these marshlands some of the hardest. The people here have only had five years of peace, and already they forget that."

"Five years. Strange — that's as long as you've been here, isn't it?"

Bran smiled despite the horrid memories that came to mind. "I fear they'll remember soon enough. And hopefully, the boy can help them keep the darkness at bay when we return."

Aelyn held his gaze. "You do not even know why we go."

Bran shook his head. "Not the details. I trust you'll tell me what I need to know along the way. But I know the important thing: when a king gives a command, you do your damndest to comply."

It was Aelyn's turn to smile. "Best you'd remember that. And remember it's not Bran the Chicken Farmer he's commanding."

Bran turned away, wrapping the sword in the oilskin again. "I never let my blade rust, did I?"

EASTERLY WINDS

THE DAY HAD NEVER DRAGGED ON FOR SO LONG.

Garin set down the bucket of slop and leaned against their boundary fence, staring off toward where the sun was setting behind the trees. Next to him, the pigs squealed and jostled each other to knock over the slop bucket and claim their portion of the windfall.

A chance to travel to Halenhol. To leave Hunt's Hollow, to see the World, to make a name for himself.

Isn't this the chance I've always dreamed of? he thought. *Shouldn't I be excited, ecstatic?*

A breeze rustled his clothes and blew his hair flat against his head. *A man wouldn't feel so torn. A man knows his own mind.* And, fifteen summers old, wasn't he a man grown?

He snorted, spat to the side, and watched the squall carry it out of sight behind him.

"That nearly hit me."

As his sister leaned on the fence next to him, Garin tried for a smile and fell short. "Shouldn't sneak up on me then."

Lenora's gaze was calm and placid. *Father's calmness,* he recognized. In many ways, she was far more like their father than him. He wondered morosely what that said for him as a man.

Yet as he looked back over to the woods, he couldn't help his thoughts wandering back to all that lay beyond them.

"You've let the pigs get at the leftover slop."

"Then they'll fatten quicker."

"Garin. Look at me."

Reluctantly, he complied. Her eyes were an unremarkable, flat brown, and her features were, while pretty, a bit plain. Yet something about the way his sister held herself was compelling all the same. *No wonder Hunt's Hollow's young men are scrambling for the chance to court her,* he thought, and despite the weight on his shoulders, he felt a flush of pride.

Lenora looked between his eyes for a long moment. "Did something happen?"

"Not yet. But it could."

"Bad?"

"Good. I think."

She frowned. "We've never kept secrets from each other before."

Garin shrugged. "Might not be anything to tell."

"Does this have something to do with that stranger visiting Bran yesterday?"

No secrets in a village — he'd always known that. "Something like that."

Lenora sighed and reached over to put an arm around him, leaning her head on his shoulder, offering in silence what words could never convey.

"I'm trying to decide," he found himself saying.

"Decide between?"

"Staying or going."

She went very still. "Leaving Hunt's Hollow, you mean?"

He tried to say it, but the word caught in his throat, so he nodded instead. "Just for a while," he added quickly. "I don't know how long. But it won't be forever."

When Lenora remained silent, words pressed out of him once again. "I've always told myself I would see the World, sis. That I wouldn't just be content to stay here and split Father's plot in quarters with our brothers. I've lain awake nights, staring at the stars, imagining my stories will be written in them."

He stopped just short of the most embarrassing, boyish admittance of them all. *I've imagined myself as Markus Bredley stealing into those dwarven vaults. I've pretended I'm Tal Harrenfel in all his deeds. Stealing the Ring of Thalkuun. Killing the northern marauders and burning their black-sailed ships. Kneeling before the King as he heaps praise on my shoulders.*

Lenora lifted her head from his shoulder but kept their arms twined together. "The youngest son often flies the coop," she said quietly. "I guess I always knew you would, too, some-day. I just didn't think someday would come so soon."

"You knew I'd leave?"

She nodded. "Honry has put down deep roots and has a family of his own now. Corbun and Naten both have girls from the surrounding countryside. But you've chosen to spend every free moment you had with a man who moved here from the wide World and barely lived here for five years."

Garin brushed absentmindedly at his hair, uncomfortable under his sister's sharp scrutiny. "I suppose that's true."

"But it's not just that. You've a fire in you, Garin. You need to feed it with all the World has to offer. If not, if you stay here without venturing away…" She shrugged. "I'd be afraid of that fire burning you up inside."

He briefly met her gaze, then looked away again. "So you think I should go."

"I think you should do whatever is right for you."

"But is that what Father would have done? Is it a man's decision, or a boy's?"

Lenora rarely snorted, so it took him by surprise when one escaped her. "That's the last thing you should be worried about.

Men are often boys, and women are sometimes girls. We are what we are."

Garin frowned, not sure he agreed, but unable to refute it.

"But if it's us you're worried about," she continued, "we'll be fine. Corbun and Naten are still around, and even when they start their own families, all three of them will be close by." She grinned suddenly. "And don't forget that I can take care of myself and Ma both if I need to."

He sighed. "I suppose so."

She squeezed him tight. "Take the night; think about it. You can always make the decision tomorrow. And, no matter what you decide, I promise Father would be proud of you."

She pulled away and headed back toward the house.

His eyes stung for a moment. Wiping at them, he bent to pick up the bucket from among the pigs and followed after her.

The traveler glared across the table. "You can't keep me bound here forever."

Bran smiled back at him, all of his teeth on display. By some stroke of luck, he'd managed to keep most of them through the long years. "To the contrary. The terms of the Binding Ring very much say I could."

Aelyn's eyes narrowed further still. "I can't harm you. But I could bundle you up and transport you across the kingdom if I have to."

"If you think you could manage it."

Bran took the bottle and raised an eyebrow. Aelyn's lips curled in a sneer, but he held his glass forward yet again, and Bran splashed in another helping of the marsh whiskey, then refilled his own.

"Say what you will about Hunt's Hollow," he opined, "but you can't deny we have the finest whiskey in the whole of the Westreach that's made with swamp water."

Aelyn coughed and dribbled the whiskey he'd been drinking back into his cup.

Bran smiled again and drank his down, sighing as the fire crawled into his belly. His smile was coming looser the further into the bottle he went, and he was almost starting to enjoy his surly company.

"So, my old acquaintance, what brings you to Hunt's Hollow?"

The traveler wiped at his mouth with the back of his hand, eyes glimmering as he looked up. "You know very well what. I've come to fetch you for King Aldric."

"Why? You're Gladelysh. You're not his subject. You serve at Queen Geminia's pleasure."

"It is, shall we say, a convoluted chain of command."

"It always is in the courts of royals."

Aelyn exhaled in a sharp huff. "I serve as Gladelyl's emissary to Avendor."

Bran raised an eyebrow. "That does little to elucidate the present situation. But an emissary — surely that's a waste of your varied talents."

"Strange to hear you speak of wasted talent."

Ignoring the barbed comment, Bran drank back his mug of whiskey, then poured himself another. "Hunt's Hollow has a hallowed history," he said, swirling the golden liquid in his cup. "Do you know how the town earned its name?"

It was Aelyn's turn to raise an eyebrow. "I barely knew what it was called before this journey. But I'd guess a man stumbled upon a meadow and found it adequate for hunting." He shrugged. "Most names lack artistry."

"This isn't one of them. There's a tale told by the elders of the times before the village began, before any of the Bloodlines had settled these wildlands. Then, this was only marshland, and considered a place best avoided."

"As it still is," the traveler muttered.

"Yet its few visitors told tales of marvelous things, and chief among them, one prey worthy of only the greatest hunter: the Phantom Doe."

Aelyn snorted. "As likely a folk tale as any I've heard."

"The Phantom Doe was a legendary beast, said to be as clear a blue as a glacial peak. The hunter was young and eager to prove himself, and he'd tracked the tales across the Westreach to these very swamps. At times, he thought he'd glimpsed his quarry, but mostly, there were only ordinary beasts and the stinking mire."

"A fact sadly still relevant."

"But with every mile, he grew nearer to the eastern mountains, and the danger grew. So it was that the hunter wasn't caught unawares when he came upon a clearing and saw the greatest of all beasts the East has to offer."

"Let me guess," Aelyn said drily. "A dragon."

Bran grinned. "The dragon was longer than a seaworthy ship, and its head went higher than the tallest tower. Each talon was as long as a spear and as sharp as a sword. His mane of spikes bristled with each movement of his flat head as he tasted the air with his flickering, forked tongue. Dragons hunt by taste like snakes, and this one had tasted prey on the wind."

"A dragon." The traveler shook his head. "As if this tale could grow more unbelievable. The ancients might write of such beasts, but no one has seen one in generations. More likely, our ancestors were having a laugh at their descendants' expense."

Bran shrugged. "The dragon was real to the hunter. He crouched in the hollow of a tree, quivering and trying to remain still and silent, for a dragon's hearing and sight are almost as keen as its sense of taste. But the dragon knew he was there. Slowly, it crept toward the hunter, and no tree would be able to hide or protect him once the dragon caught wind of him.

"But as the dragon loomed over the hunter's hiding place, something darted through the brush at the other end of the clearing. The hunter watched in amazement as a doe, shining the brilliant blue of a cloudless sky, leaped over the tall grass to dart into the woods. The dragon, hearing the doe, whipped its head around and roared as it set off in pursuit. The hunter yearned to follow the doe himself, but fear kept him behind the tree until long after the beat of the dragon's wings had faded away.

"When both beasts were gone, the hunter exited the hollow and looked around. No longer did he wish to hunt the Phantom Doe, for he had realized it was a spirit sent by Mother World to protect this place. So he decided to settle a town in that clearing, the place that would later become the very town we sit in." Bran spread his arms and grinned. "Hunt's Hollow."

Aelyn shook his head. "A diverting tale to explain a backwater town. Now, was there a point to my torment?"

"The point is, you came here seeking a legend and found a man." Bran held up his hands helplessly. "And sometimes, that's all you get."

Aelyn leaned close. "Maybe you're just a man. But your name is bigger than you, and it's time you remembered that. The King of Avendor has need of *you*, not Brannen Cairn."

"Even kings can be disappointed. And disappointment is nothing I'm not used to."

The traveler cocked his head, a small smile on his lips. *I never liked when he smiled,* Bran thought.

"And what of the disappointment of your long-lost lover?" Aelyn asked softly.

He stiffened. "What does she have to do with this?"

The traveler's smile grew, like an angler feeling the hook set in a fish. "Nothing directly. But wouldn't she be sad to hear what you've become? A drunken old chicken farmer, hiding from his name and deeds."

Bran sat back, staring up through a hole in his roof at the fading light. "The past never dies, does it?" he spoke softly. "It only sleeps, then one day drags you back in."

Aelyn set his cup down, then withdrew a hand from below the table. Bran's throat tightened, and his body went rigid as the man placed a leather-bound book on the table, just outside of a small puddle of spilled whiskey.

"Only if you let it," Aelyn said quietly. "And what, pray tell, is this piece of the past you've dredged up?"

He didn't shift his position, but every muscle in his body had tensed. "Hand that to me, Aelyn."

"Did you not think I would recognize the Darktongue? Did you think my studies in the Gray Tower had faded from my memory?" Aelyn's molten eyes searched his. "Now, tell me: what are you doing with such a fell book?"

"Have you read it?" Bran asked quietly.

"Only the title. *A Fable of Song and Blood.* Meaningless drivel, from what I can tell."

"You don't know the half of it. Now, hand it over, or I'll be forced to take it from you."

Aelyn's eyes narrowed. A long moment passed. One of Bran's hands below the table inched toward his belt knife.

Then Aelyn released the book with a thump and sat back, crossing his arms. "Have you become one of them?"

Bran took up the book and only exhaled as he tucked it under his arm. "You know me better than that, Aelyn. That book is the one weapon we might have against the Enemy. Promise me, if anything should happen to me, that you'll protect it."

That seemed to take the traveler back. But after a moment, he nodded. "Very well."

The inevitable had come. Bran rose to his feet, silently cursing his swaying vision. "Make any preparations you still have — we leave in the morning. I just have one more loose end to tie up tonight."

Without waiting for a response, he turned from the house, taking the book with him.

———

Garin was still awake when he heard the tapping at the window. His heart, already racing over the decision, began to pound.

"What's that?" Naten asked sleepily from across their shared room.

"Nothing. Just getting up for a piss." Garin scrambled out of bed and pulled on his clothes, then half-walked, half-stumbled his way out of the door.

Bran leaned against the fence post of their front gate, only just recognizable by the twin moons' light. Though he wore the same sweat-stained, homespun clothes as usual, something about his stance looked different, more like the man Garin had glimpsed with the traveler. Tucked under one arm was a book, a rare enough sight in Hunt's Hollow, but hardly the strangest thing about Brannen Cairn.

"You were awake still," Bran observed when Garin was close enough.

"Been thinking."

"Good. It's time to make a decision."

Garin's heart was like a prisoner banging on the wall of his cell. "Now?"

The farmer smiled, his teeth gleaming in the moonlight. "Once you decide to do a thing, best to get it over with. So what do you say? Are you ready to see more towns and cities than you can count on both hands?"

Garin found his gaze wandering up. Even with both moons ablaze, the night sky was littered with stars, and his eyes immediately picked out the familiar constellations telling his favorite stories.

Markus Bredley wouldn't hesitate to go, he thought. *And Father went when it was time.* Not an easy decision to make — but grown men make hard decisions, and it was time Garin made his.

He lowered his gaze to meet Bran's. "I'm ready. When do we go?"

Bran grinned. "I knew you'd come, lad. We depart before first light tomorrow. I'd tell your family before you leave, though. Avoiding farewells is like ignoring an arrow in your side. Best to pull it out and let it bleed now rather than have it fester for a long time yet."

Garin nodded, though when he imagined his mother's face upon hearing his news, he wasn't sure he agreed. "Before first light then."

He turned to enter his home for what he knew would be the last time in a long time.

PASSAGE I

I commence this writing in the tongue of the source of all magic, the tongue of Yuldor's Heart itself. But though it may seem arrogance to do so, I do it but from caution. Only those with the iron will required to wield Mother World's treacherous power should be privy to the secrets I herein inscribe. For, if they bear any truth, they have the potential to wrought destruction not only on our Glorious Empire, but all the lands to the West and South.

These secrets I allude to relate to a rare and curious phenomenon. All have heard the tales — of those who, despite giving no supplication to a patron god, nor descending from a race naturally inclined toward witchery, are able to summon magic.

Many have proposed theories for this phenomenon. Even as I compose this treatise, I cannot confirm many of my suspicions. But the ideas alone are evocative enough to threaten sacrosanctity against our Savior, the Peacebringer, that I must exercise all caution.

Perhaps this book will never feel the touch of light. Perhaps I will not have the courage to complete it. Nevertheless, I must write it, and not only for the sake of the truth. If my theory proves correct, there will come those of Song and Blood, whom I will call Founts, powerful enough that they will rip the World asunder as we know it.

And we must be ready.

- A Fable of Song and Blood, *by Hellexa Yoreseer of the Blue Moon Obelisk, translated by Tal Harrenfel*

THE TRAVELER'S HOME

BEFORE THE SUN HAD EMERGED FROM THE EAST MARSH'S horizon, three figures — two upright, one slumped — walked under the town's welcome archway and down the road leading away from Hunt's Hollow.

Despite the mage's grumblings, they had no horses or mules. King Aldric's constant requisition for their use along the Fringes made them scarce in the East Marsh at the best of times, and all the more since a disease had recently taken many more. Aelyn insisted he had the seal of the King and they could seize any beasts they found, but Bran flatly refused, saying he'd have to drag him if he wanted to ride. And though Aelyn looked perfectly willing to do so, the traveler only huffed and turned away.

Garin kept looking at the two men from the corner of his eye as he battled with his overpacked rucksack. Their packs were smaller except for Bran's weapons. The chicken farmer carried a bow and quiver of arrows, and had tucked a scabbarded sword under his bag.

But it wasn't their possessions that drew his eye; there seemed a brightness to their steps, a liveliness to their faces, that spoke of who they were. This was their home, this winding road. All other places were waystones and resting places, the sojourn the only place they could be at peace.

He looked back as the last of the buildings faded behind him and wondered if he'd become the same as these two travelers.

Then his mother's face came to mind, and he cringed. He hadn't had the courage to say goodbye, no more than leaving a brief note. He hadn't had the courage, either, to tell that to Bran. Though Bran thought Garin was wiser than he'd been at his age, he'd still ignored his advice.

He resolutely put her face from mind, imagining instead all the wonders waiting ahead of them. Halenhol, capital of the Kingdom of Avendor, was said to have buildings that touched the stars, and knights in shining silver armor that rode through the streets, and peoples of every Bloodline, color, and shape. Elves, dwarves, and even goblins living beside humans in the greatest city in all of the Westreach — even the World.

Maybe.

The truth was, he didn't know how much of it was a crock of crap made up by bored old men to entertain young children, and how much was real.

He glanced nervously at Bran, wanting to ask his endless questions, but the look of the man's face stopped him. A solemn expression had claimed his features, and with the morning sun behind them and his hood pulled low, his face was cast in shadow. More and more, he wondered how he'd ever thought Bran a hapless chicken rancher.

"You have a question."

Garin startled at Bran addressing him, but said with forced calm, "What makes you say that?"

"Because curious young men always have questions." Bran glanced sidelong at him, and the solemnity had been replaced by fey humor. "And feathers that float alike know their flock."

Garin glanced at Aelyn on Bran's other side. Even if he was inclined to ask his questions of Bran, Silence knew he wasn't going to ask them in front of that mage.

So he plastered on a crooked smile. "I do have a question. How do you old men expect to keep up with my young legs?"

Bran laughed. "Oh, you need not concern yourself with that. Young or old, a traveler's legs will go further than a farmer's."

Garin started to retort, then paused. "I suppose I'll be a traveler soon myself."

"Yes. I suppose you will."

The day grew brighter as the sun rose, but Garin's thoughts fell into deeper shadows. What had he done? He was no traveler. And now that he thought about it, it had been a damned foolish notion, running off with two strange men he barely knew. A boy's idea of adventure, he saw now all too clearly.

He scrunched up his brow. What would a man do? Would he stay to his word? Or would he think better of it and go home?

As they walked mile after mile, he mulled over his dilemma. The longer he took to decide, the further from home he went. *A man should be decisive* — his father had always told him that before he'd been conscripted for one of Avendor's endless wars. His older brothers had certainly listened to him.

But Garin had always let others make his choices. His daily chores, his meals, his clothes — his mother and brothers had overshadowed what he thought and said. The decision to leave off his duties early to spend time with Bran had been his one rebellion. And this, going on the journey, had been his first, real resolution. Going back on that now would show them all he wasn't a man after all, but just a boy.

Evening began to fall, and still they walked on, only briefly breaking for food and other necessities. The day had grown late enough that other travelers had thinned out on the road. Ahead, the Winegulch Bridge came into view, the river flowing sluggishly below, never smelling of the fruity sweetness that Garin had been told was wine's aroma, but stinking instead.

Garin's heart began to pound harder like they were approaching a bear's den rather than a bridge. He'd never crossed the Winegulch before, never been so far west of Hunt's Hollow. Even if it made him a boy, he had to speak — to turn back or to seek assurance, he didn't know.

"Bran—" Garin started to say, but he cut off as a sudden whoop filled the air.

"Hold there!"

His companions stopped mid-step onto the bridge, and Garin stumbled to a halt after them. Whipping his head around, he saw three men step out from the brush. A glance forward showed another two stomping across the bridge, hard frowns worked into their faces. His heart began to pound harder, like Smith's hammer working out a particularly tough piece of iron.

Dusk, Garin's mother had well instructed him, was the time of day that brigands liked best.

And these were brigands, without a doubt. Their hair hung in greasy locks. Pimples dotted their skin, and wiry, untamed beards grew from their chins. Most of them looked half-starved, faces gaunt and eyes hollow, but for one big fellow, who was bloated enough for the rest of them, if no less healthy looking. In all of their hands, some manner of weapon was clutched: knives, axes, and in the big man's hands, a warhammer.

It was the large fellow who spoke. "You!" he said, his voice not as deep as Garin had expected, but plenty loud enough to send his legs wobbling like a newborn calf. "You'll give us your coin. Now. And everything that man is wearing." The big man pointed one sausage-like finger at Aelyn.

The mage narrowed his eyes, and Garin noticed he had delved his hands deep into his mysterious pockets. He wasn't sure if he was more nervous about the highwaymen or whatever his companion had in store for them.

"Now, now, wait a moment." Bran wore an amiable smile and raised his empty hands. "I can tell from your accent that you're not from around here, and from your clothes, that you were conscripted not long ago."

Their assailants exchanged glances that Garin would have thought apprehensive if they hadn't had them surrounded with sharp steel.

The big man stared at Bran, unmoved. "Then you know we mean business."

"I know you're running away," Bran corrected. "And I know exactly why. I, too, ran from war once. I'm a deserter, as surely as you are."

Garin stared in astonishment. He'd guessed Bran had been a warrior — but a deserter? The King's wars might be many, but men didn't run from their duty. It put his companion in a new, uneasy light.

"What of it?" the brigand barked. "So people think you're a coward like us. Don't mean we won't rob you!"

"Of course not," Bran said, speaking as if he were trying to soothe a horse. "We'll give over our gear in just a moment. But I just want you to be fully aware of what you're doing."

The highwayman took a step forward, and his companions followed his lead. Garin was sure he'd start sweating through his tunic, and jerkin besides. He gripped his belt knife tightly as if the small blade meant for cutting meat would be much help against former soldiers with proper weapons.

"We know what we're doing," the big man sneered. "Now, I'll give you to the count of five. One—"

"You really don't know what you're doing, I assure you." Bran, far from seeming uneasy, jabbed a thumb at Aelyn. "For example, did you know he's an elven mage?"

The brigands, ready for blood a moment before, all stumbled back, though their weapons raised higher. Garin was ready to run himself. He'd accepted Aelyn was a mage — but an elf besides?

The big man, however, narrowed his eyes. "Show me your ears!" he commanded Aelyn.

The mage didn't move, his molten eyes leveled at the big man. Under that stare, Garin would have turned tail, but the deserter seemed unmoved. In a swift motion, however, Bran swept the hat from Aelyn's head, and pointed ears sprang up from beneath the ink-black hair.

The mage hissed at him, but Bran hardly seemed to notice. "See?" he said pleasantly. "An elf. And everyone knows elves possess magic."

The deserters backed away another step, and even the big man seemed to be having second thoughts. Garin recognized him now for a bully. Small as Hunt's Hollow was, it had its fair share of bullies. But as Garin knew from experience, until a bully broke, he didn't back down.

"Then I'll break him first!" the large man growled. "Forget the counting! Hand over the bags now, or I'll smash your head in!"

"But you don't even know who *I* am yet," Bran said pleasantly. "See, in addition to a deserter, I'm a bit of a sorcerer myself. I'll warn you once — drop that hammer."

Far from dropping it, the big man raised the big weapon, and Garin stepped back, wincing as he waited for Bran's head to cave in.

"*Kald!*"

The hammer's shaft burst into flames.

The brigand stiffened in surprise, then howled and threw his hammer to the ground, staring at his charred hands. "Yuldor's fucking balls!"

Bran shrugged, not seeming the least alarmed. "I warned you, didn't I? Now, I only ever mastered a few cantrips. Imagine what this fellow next to me will do if you stick around. Let's see... How about I give you until five? One—"

The brigands were bolting before he'd finished the first count, disappearing back into the forest. Only the big brigand remained.

"Same goes for you," Bran reminded him. "Two—"

The man eyed his still-burning hammer on the road, then growled a curse and made for the forest at a lumbering run.

Garin stared, open-mouthed, at his companions. "Who are you?" he whispered.

The chicken farmer — who was no chicken farmer, Garin knew all too well now — had gathered a solemn look again. "Exactly as I said. A deserter. A failed warlock. And many more half-realized roles." He glanced at Aelyn. "Sorry about the hat."

The mage had bent to retrieve his pointed hat and was brushing irritably at a bit of horse dung that had crusted onto it. "I very much doubt you are," he snapped as he fixed the hat back on his head, ears tucked into it.

Bran shrugged. "I'd be lying if I said I wasn't also amused."

"Why did you let them go?" The question burst from Garin.

Aelyn eyed Bran as well.

The man looked between them. "Many reasons. In my experience, violence should always be a last resort. Men who use it too quickly, like our would-be smith here—" he gestured at the hammer "—get themselves in far more trouble than out of it. But more pertinent here..." He looked off down the road. "Acting the brigand, too, I can claim in my past."

Something was stirring in Garin's stomach. Hunger, yes, and a bit of the need to relieve himself. But under that, the warm glow of awe, and the cold shiver of fear.

"Who are you?" he asked again.

"You'll learn soon enough, and regret that you did."

"Enough," Aelyn cut in. "We must walk miles yet before we make camp to be sure we're far from those fools."

Garin's stomach grumbled, but he followed as the elven mage set a quick pace across the bridge. He was tired, and scared, and still had to piss. But one thing had left, he realized. No longer did he wonder if he should stay or go.

For better or worse, he'd made his decision to follow the road where it willed him. Even if he still didn't know the first thing about those he traveled with.

THE RUINS OF ERLODAN

When the evening of the sixth day began to fade, Aelyn glanced at Bran with his strange, copper eyes. "We must make a detour here."

Bran looked away, studying Garin to buy time. After their run-in with the brigands, the young man had taken to doing his part by setting up camp with an avidity that puzzled him. Perhaps, he mused, that fire cantrip had done a little magic for the boy's doubts as well as the big bandit.

He turned back to find Aelyn still watching him and reluctantly answered. "I thought you'd want to make all haste for Halenhol. The King's summons and all that bilge."

"This is in the spirit of the King's orders, as I'm sure you've guessed."

"Perhaps I have."

But though he hadn't, the truth came to him a moment later, and his stomach clenched. "Are we traveling a day north to the top of an abandoned hill?"

Aelyn nodded. "The Ruins of Erlodan, they call it these days. A high name for a low place."

"That's the truth behind most high names, in my experience."

The elf narrowed his eyes. "All elven places possess high names."

Bran flashed him a smile. "I couldn't mean those, surely."

Anger flared in the mage's eyes, and Bran's grin grew wider. *A prickly lot, elves, and mages the thorniest of the lot.*

"Why didn't you go on the way to picking me up?"

Aelyn's eyes had tempered down to their usual subdued bronze. "I wouldn't have had the requisite sacrifice then, would I?"

They stared at each other in silence.

Bran cracked a grin. "For a moment, I thought you were serious."

The elf still didn't smile. "Perhaps I am."

"In that case, I have the perfect candidate. I hear from the Creed that the more rotten a person's heart, the hotter they burn when they descend to Night's Pyres."

Aelyn shook his head. "Jest while you still can. You won't feel so jovial once we reach the ruins."

Bran turned away. "I wouldn't count on it."

The trek, however, proved Aelyn right. Bran's mood took a dip as they slogged through bog after sticking bog, his boots filling with muddy, cold water and his nose full of the swamp's stink.

Beside him, Garin looked yet more miserable, for though he was adjusting to the rigors of the road, he was far from adapted.

As much to take his mind off the misery as Garin's, Bran asked, "Doing alright, lad?"

The youth glanced over with a raised eyebrow. "What do you think?"

"Nothing like a detour through a swamp, eh?"

"What are we going here for, anyway?"

Bran shrugged. "You'll have to ask our fearless leader."

Garin glared at Aelyn's back, twenty strides ahead of them. "What's he about, anyway? I know he's the Gladelysh emissary to King Aldric and serving the Avendoran Crown on his Queen's orders. But why's he so...?" The youth seemed to be hunting for the right word.

"Foul?" Bran suggested.

He grinned sheepishly. "More or less."

Bran glanced toward the mage. "I'm the last person who would make excuses for him, but... he's had a hard life."

Garin's eyebrows raised.

"When he was a babe," Bran continued, "a rival kinhouse claimed a brutal revenge for an old vendetta. His parents, his siblings, everyone in his extended family were killed, and he was left an orphan."

"How did he survive?"

"Elves have different ways of doing things than us. A child is given many different 'mothers,' we'll call them — not only for their benefit but to strengthen the ties between kinhouses. At the time of his family's murders, Aelyn was in the care of an allied family, and so he avoided their fate."

Garin was looking at the back of the mage with a different expression now. "What happened to him?"

"That family chose to foster him, as good as adopting him, though in the elven way, Aelyn kept his name."

"Cloudtouched?"

"That's the translation into Reachtongue. In Gladelyshi, it's Belnuure."

Garin shrugged. "No worse than my family name, Dunford, I suppose."

And mine, Bran thought. "But Aelyn's woes don't end there. Though he was raised by allies, the oldest brother of the family didn't appreciate an outsider suddenly adopted as kin. Thus, he made sure to make Aelyn constantly feel an outsider in his own home, and despite the sister's efforts otherwise, his childhood was full of strife."

"It's almost enough to make you pity him."

Bran grinned. "Almost."

Garin yelped as his foot stuck in a bog, then grunted as he pulled it out, boot hanging precariously off his foot. "Damned swamp," he muttered as he pulled it back on and staggered upright again. "How do you know all this, anyway?"

Bran's smile froze on his lips. After a moment's hesitation, he found himself able to speak. "We both loved the same woman, though in different ways."

Garin's brow was furrowed, but sensing Bran's change in mood, he asked no further questions.

They reached the base of the hill that marked their destination as the day's light began to fade.

"Aren't we going up?" Garin asked when Bran and Aelyn set down their packs.

Bran shook his head. "Up there's a foul place to be when night falls. We'll ascend in the morning."

Garin set his pack down as well, though he cast a dubious glance up the hill. "Why's that?"

Bran glanced at Aelyn to find him watching him from another one of the magically formed chairs that he'd taken to shaping each night at camp. The mage had a bad habit of staring. Not for the first time, he wondered just what the King of Avendor had in mind for him.

But soon enough, he'd have to sit with the knowledge of it. And he'd had enough poor tasks put before him to know that rushing into the next one wouldn't make it settle any easier.

Looking back to their young companion, Bran gestured to a nearby fallen tree. "Sit."

Garin's eyes darted to the mage as if sitting in his presence might offend the elf, but he obliged.

Bran mounted a foot on the end of the tree, leaning into his leg as he scrunched up his face like he were in deep thought. "Once, a long time ago, a great and powerful warlock lived in those ruins, celebrated as the foremost of the followers of Jalduaen — the Revered Spirit of Knowledge, to all human warlocks. This warlock went by the name of... Hm, let me see..."

"Was it Erlodan?" Garin asked drily.

Bran snapped his fingers. "That's the one! But in Erlodan's day, those ruins were a magnificent castle, with a plethora of halls for his many distinguished visitors and an army of servants to serve them. Erlodan occupied the highest tower, the better to look over his domain and work his wonders.

"The warlock was respected and trusted, but not widely loved. With great power comes a great many enemies, and Erlodan was proof of the saying. But wise as he was, the warlock kept his defenses tight and had lived for centuries insulated against those who sought to do him harm.

"But there was one enemy that Erlodan could not prevail against. For though Jalduaen is a fierce patron god, the warlocks of the East had a mightier deity still: the Night itself, as manifested in Yuldor, the Prince of Devils. And so it came to pass that one of the East's mages finally decided to challenge the Warlock of the East Marsh and overtake his dominion."

"You're talking about the Extinguished, aren't you?"

Bran lowered his gaze to find Garin's eyebrows raised in skepticism. "Perhaps I am."

The youth rolled his eyes. "The Extinguished are fairy tale enemies, just like Yuldor — they're used to scare children into staying in bed. They don't *actually* exist."

"What makes you say that?"

"Because if they did, and they were as powerful as the stories say they are, why wouldn't they rule not just the Eastern Empire, but all of the Westreach?"

Bran glanced at Aelyn, but he had his back to them as he bent over something. Working some kind of devilry, he didn't doubt.

Looking back to the youth, he suppressed a sigh. "Power

isn't enough to reign supreme, Garin, and the Extinguished are far too clever to rely only on their strength. They crush their enemies when they have to, but far more often, they use their deviousness and wits to bring about the ends they desire."

The youth's brow creased. "You speak as if they exist, here and today."

A frozen moment. Then Bran forced the wolfish grin again. "A story isn't right without urgency, is it? But back to the point — and no more interruptions!

"As I was saying, one of the Extinguished took the guise of a servant and found a reason to go up that high tower, intending to ambush the old wizard. But for all the skill the Soulstealers wield in illusory magic, no sooner had the Extinguished opened the door than did Erlodan recognize him for what he was.

"The old warlock rose with all the power possessed to him, and the Extinguished threw off the servant's skin and attacked. For a full day, the two pitted their wills against each other, their sorcery crashing together like two great waves, both tiring, but neither of them faltering. Both had such a towering degree of sorcery that no single effort on the other's part could break him, but they had to be worn down as slow as a river wearing on rock.

"But the eldritch spirit behind the Extinguished had no such patience. Yuldor, the Night's Savior, forced his way into his servant and took the battle into his own hands. With complete disregard for his warlock, he channeled his god-given power against Erlodan."

Bran fell silent, looking down at the ground as if thinking. He felt Garin's gaze on him, avid and curious.

"And?" the youth demanded. "What happened then?"

Looking back at his captive audience, Bran grinned. Few things gave him as much pleasure as hooking a hapless listener on their curiosity. He pointed up the hill to the castle, hidden at the moment by trees.

"That. The castle was marred, broken, dashed to pieces. Erlodan's high tower, which could see to the far reaches of his lands, was completely obliterated. Neither contestant survived, the life of the devil's servant weighed a fair cost for Erlodan's destruction, and all of Erlodan's staff and guests were killed as well."

"Huh." Garin looked up the hill. "No wonder you don't want to go up there. Is it haunted by ghosts, or ghouls maybe?"

Bran shook his head. "No ghosts or ghouls. But the Ruins of Erlodan deserve their reputation nevertheless. Yuldor's touch still lingers there, a hint of the East's evils, waiting to seize a hapless wanderer to turn to his cause. A single turn of the day in those ruins could corrupt the best of men or women into willing servants of the Night."

Garin shuddered. "Why must we go there at all?"

Bran's smile had slipped away, and he looked at the elven mage, who had finished whatever he'd been doing and now sat, listening to the story from afar, a small, knowing smile curling his lips.

He stood. "I'm sure our guide will inform us when he wishes to. Now, where was that fire?"

Garin startled and leaped to his feet. Looking between the men, both of whom were idle, his mouth started to open. A moment later, though, he seemed to think better of what he'd been about to say and bent to strike up a flame.

Bran grinned at Aelyn, but knew the humor was lost on him as the mage stared stonily back. As he turned away and bent to gather kindling, the smile slipped off his face.

"What do you want, you knife-eared marsh monkey?" he muttered as he picked up small branches. "Why would you risk us entering that evil place?"

But he already knew. There could be only one answer when a king and his immortal enemies were involved.

A TOUCH OF NIGHT

GARIN WEARILY SHOULDERED HIS PACK AS HE FOLLOWED THE older men up the hill.

He'd barely slept a wink the night before. Howls had sounded somewhere in the forest — coyotes, probably, but he'd imagined them to be a pack of wolves, circling and hunting them. Worse still, when twigs and leaves had rustled in the dark, he'd opened his eyes and thought he'd glimpsed the shapes of men. How long he'd stared wide-eyed into the darkness after that, he couldn't say.

But it was the thoughts of what lay ahead in the Ruins of Erlodan that sent the deepest shivers through him.

Garin shook his head as he huffed behind the men. Young he might be, but they set a grueling pace, and he found himself hard-pressed to keep up. But he'd be damned if he let himself fall behind in a place like this.

Yuldor himself had cursed the derelict castle and broken apart the stones, and if Bran's story was to be believed, the Night's evil lingered there still. By visiting such a place, the Puppeteer could seize Garin for his own to make him dance to his malevolent designs.

He forced a grin. As if he believed such childish tales.

Garin had visited no more villages than he could count, but he knew a thing or two about devils. Monsters wandered down into the East Marsh from the Fringes — he'd even seen one or two himself: a runty harpy, a four-foot-tall, womanish bird who screeched at them until a hunter put it down; and a crag boar, nine feet long with tusks that could gore three men each at a thrust. The boar had taken much longer to kill.

There were monsters, and now he'd seen there was magic. But Garin wasn't so naive as to believe devils and demons existed, plotting their domination of the Westreach from their fortresses deep within the mountainous East.

"Keep up, Garin!"

At Bran's call, he looked up and found he'd fallen behind. Clenching his jaw, he pushed his leaden legs faster.

The men had stopped by the time he caught up, standing just above a treeless crest. Taking the last switchback, Garin turned the corner and stopped in his tracks, breathing heavily as he stared above him.

Erlodan's castle was in ruins, but it was undeniably a castle, and far grander than anything he'd ever seen. He'd considered the inn in one of the neighboring villages tall at three stories high, but even the shortest of the ruined, black walls reached four times the inn's height. The citadel was as large as all of Hunt's Hollow — larger, maybe. Garin couldn't imagine the wealth one must possess to fund building such a thing. More coins than had ever passed through his hometown, he knew that much, or any of the towns he'd been to.

He found Bran looking over at him from the corner of his eye. "Grand, isn't it?"

Garin found his jaw hanging open and snapped it shut. "Doesn't blow me away," he said casually.

Bran grinned, but the smile seemed strained. "Listen, Garin. Aelyn and I are going to enter the ruins, but I think you should stay here. You'll be safer."

It shamed him to admit, but a shiver of fear went through

him at the thought of staying there alone. "You don't have to worry about me," he said quickly. "I won't be a bother. I just want to see more of the ruins you've told me so much about."

On Bran's other side, Aelyn's mouth tightened.

Bran glanced at the mage, then sighed. "I suppose we'll be able to keep an eye on you this way. Very well. But no falling behind."

Garin nodded. "I'll keep up."

"If that's settled," Aelyn said impatiently. He pulled out something from beneath his collar, and Garin peered closer. It glinted faintly in the morning light, dull gray metal that had never seen polish, and scrawled along its face were red lines in shapes like a script. The lines seemed strangely familiar, though Garin was sure he'd never seen the symbols before. He found Aelyn's gaze intently on him and quickly looked away.

"What's that?" he asked, not meeting the mage's eyes.

It was Bran who answered. "A glyph ward. Our friend here was kind enough to provide us all protection from the East's corruption. Or... wait, there's only one."

The mage's expression grew sourer still. "I'm the only one who would be of any real danger if I were turned. The Named has no use for mere men like you two."

Bran clutched a hand to his chest. "Ah! Is there any wound so dire as insignificance to a man's pride?"

Garin smiled, but it was a weak, limp thing, like a fish pulled from a river already dead.

"The Named?" he asked, as much to distract himself as out of curiosity.

"What the elves call our devil friend," Bran said, dropping his maudlin act. "Whose name, by the way, you shouldn't say here."

"You mean Yul—"

Garin found his arm in Aelyn's hard grip. "Silence!" he hissed. "Or do you wish to bring him down upon us?"

Stunned, he stared back at the mage. "Could saying his name do that?"

Bran moved forward and extricated him from the elf's grasp. "Mind your binding, Aelyn. No harm to the youth, or you'll experience it in equal measures."

The elf hissed, then turned and stalked away.

Bran nodded after him. "Come on, then. We'd best stick close to him. No matter what the puffed up cock thinks, the Prince of Devils has a use for anyone who wanders into his grasp. Best not take any chances."

Head spinning, Garin found he could do nothing but nod.

As they passed under yet another broken archway, Bran pretended to watch his footing and glanced back at Garin. As promised, the youth was sticking close to his and the mage's heels. He put a brave face on, but from his wide eyes and slightly parted mouth, Bran knew that the Ruins of Erlodan had worked its cold fingers far under his skin.

And little wonder why. Bran felt it himself: how the shadows clung like cobwebs when they passed through them; how every precariously positioned boulder seemed poised to crush them; how eyes seemed to watch them from under collapsed floors and walls, then disappear the moment he turned toward them.

Something lingered in these ruins, that was clear enough. And Bran had been around the Night's corruption enough times to know it for what it was.

He leaned close to Aelyn beside him. "What exactly am I supposed to be looking for?"

"All out of clever quips, are you?" the elf mocked him. "No more knowing smiles tucked away? Perhaps this place has you frightened as well as the boy."

"If it doesn't scare you, I can't think what does."

Aelyn gave him a thin smile and said nothing.

"But since you didn't answer my question, I'm guessing you don't know yourself."

The mage was silent a moment longer. "Perhaps not. But you and I both know we'll recognize it when we find it."

"How, precisely? A foul, sulfuric stench? Our enemies are unsavory, but I imagine they still bathe." Bran paused as if thinking for a moment. "Though I can't exactly picture those bastards in a bath."

"Must you always play the fool?"

"You say that as if I have a choice."

Bran, who had kept his gaze warily about them despite his easy manner, turned back to check on Garin.

And found no one behind them.

He spun and stared into the long shadows cast by the morning sun. But in no dim corner could he find the boy.

Despite his better judgment, he took a deep breath and yelled at the top of his voice. "Garin! *Garin!*"

"Quiet!" Aelyn hissed. "You'll rouse things better left undisturbed!"

Bran ignored him. "Garin, you damned fool! Where are you?"

Garin stared, slack-jawed, at the object on the pedestal.

Even in the dimly lit chamber, the necklace seemed to sparkle. Gold chain; black gems; an intricate pattern of interwoven snakes holding it together. He might have seen all the towns in the East Marsh, but he'd never seen anything — no horse, no distant mountain peak, no steaming piece of meat — that was half as beautiful as this necklace.

He began to reach for it, then hesitated. How he'd arrived in the chamber, he suddenly couldn't recall. He'd been following Bran and the mage, and then…

He blinked into the darkness. Nothing. He couldn't remember when he'd turned aside.

Yet here he was.

Glancing behind him, he saw the faint glow of distant light, and a faint breeze tickled his skin. Outside — it wasn't far away.

He found his eyes wandering again to the stone pedestal. How odd, that a pendant would be waiting here for him. How very right. After all, how could it be waiting for anyone else?

Again, he reached for it, and again, he stopped, fingers inches from the necklace.

He puffed up his cheeks and blew out the air slowly. It cost him all of his resolve not to move his hand forward to grasp the pendant. But why should he stop? It ought to be his — he'd found it. These ruins belonged to no one anymore. The necklace was his. His. He ought to take it.

His fingers stretched closer, closer.

But a bell seemed to be ringing frantically in the back of his mind like the ringer was having a fit. There was some reason not to take it — if only he could remember it. But he felt as if he were a man clawing his way through a misty field, unable to see in any direction around him. Memory, thought even, hardly seemed worth the bother.

Seeing as he couldn't remember why he ought not to, why not take it?

He closed the distance between the chain and his fingers and lifted it from the stone.

It weighed almost nothing. Garin held it before his eyes, letting it sway slowly back and forth, the pendant the only thing he had eyes for. The gems were black, but there was a molten light hidden in them. He peered closer, closer, trying to see what set it aflame.

Put it on.

Garin slipped the chain over his neck and sighed. A good thought to wear it, a very good thought. He was already feeling warm from the top of his head to the tips of his toes, a pleasant sensation amongst the cold ruins.

Hide it, Listener.

An even better thought. What if someone saw it? They'd see how beautiful it was. They'd want it for themselves. Garin tucked it inside his collar, as quickly as if someone were sneaking up on him while he took a leak.

Once it was secured under his shirt and pressed warm against his chest, he breathed another sigh. Safe at last.

"Garin! Damn you, lad, I told you to stay close!"

Garin blinked. Bran. He'd told Bran he'd stay close. But somehow, he'd lost track of him.

"In here!" he called, voice cracking, but he didn't even care. Relief flooded over him, though he hadn't known he'd been frightened. "I'm in here!"

Bran ran for the doorway from which the youth's voice had echoed. As soon as he reached it, Garin himself stepped out. Bran seized him by the shoulders, shaking him before he knew what he was doing.

"I told you to stay close!" he roared.

Garin was stiff in his hands, eyes wide, but his mouth was hard-set. "I went to take a leak. Is that not allowed?"

Bran had spouted enough foolish lines not to be put off. "I don't tell you to do much, Garin. But when I tell you to do something, I mean for you to do it. Didn't I warn you? Didn't I tell you to stay close?"

The youth's mouth was twisting into a sneer. "You think you can protect me. But you can't. You're a failed chicken farmer — what could you ever do against what lurks here?" Garin snorted disdainfully. "If anything does."

His anger drained away as suddenly as it had come, and

Bran released him, staring. Never in the years that he'd known the boy had he seen him in such a foul temper.

But never had Bran allowed him to see his rage, either.

"I'm sorry, lad," he said softly. "I shouldn't have done that."

Garin just walked around him to face Aelyn. "Are you going to yell at me too, elf?"

The mage had stood silently behind them, and Bran turned guiltily back toward him. He'd expected to see smugness in his expression, but Aelyn looked thoughtful.

"Did you find anything in there, boy?" he asked.

Garin's mouth set harder. "I'm not a boy," he said, though the statement was undermined by his voice cracking. Clearing it, he continued, angrier than before, "I've had my fifteenth yearsday. I'm a man, the same as you."

Aelyn seemed not to hear him as he walked around him toward the shadowed entrance.

"Don't step in his piss," Bran offered weakly.

The mage ignored him, too, as he was lost to the shadows within.

Bran glanced back at the youth, then jerked his head. "Guess we'd best follow him."

"And I'd best obey you, hadn't I?" Garin said sarcastically.

But when Bran turned into the doorway, he heard the youth following.

———

Garin stared at the back of Bran's head as they reentered the chamber. The mage had a light dancing at the end of his fingertips, a pure white light that shone so brightly the whole room was illuminated. Peeling his eyes away and trying — and failing — to stifle his anger, Garin looked around and saw the place for the first time.

The chamber was larger than he'd expected. When just the glow of the black-gemmed necklace had illuminated it, he'd felt like the walls and ceiling pressed in close on him. Now he saw the roof was domed and rose three times his height, and the walls stretched to either side, the space empty up to them, only a thick layer of dust that rose to make beams of the light as they walked. Garin stared at the walls and the intricate etchings on them. Under the fey light, the shapes seemed to gather a glow, the pale green of fresh moss. They were like the runes on Aelyn's glyph ward, but sharper somehow, so sharp it seemed they could cut his eyes by staring at them too long.

The mage stood over the pedestal, glaring down at it like he was reading a book. Like a moth drawn to a flame, Garin found himself drawing closer.

Dispose of him.

Garin's breath caught in his throat, and he stumbled to a halt, frozen like a hare before a fox, not daring to move lest he act on the mad thought.

"Something was here," Aelyn muttered.

Bran had wandered over from examining the walls to peer at the pedestal. "Amazed as I am to say it, but you're right. The dust has been disturbed."

"You can see its shape," the elf continued, ignoring Bran's comment. "A medallion, it looks to me. Or a pendant."

As if by some hidden cue, both men turned to look at him.

Stop them. Kill them, if you must.

Blood filled his mouth — he'd bitten his tongue. His hands clenched in fists at his side, and he wasn't sure if it was to stop himself from acting on the inclination or to throw himself at them.

"Garin," Bran said, voice calm as if he were speaking to a spooked horse, "did you see what was here?"

"No." The word burst from him, sore tongue eager to spout the lie.

"Boy," Aelyn said sharply, "don't lie to us. Fell magic has preserved this place for a purpose. What did you take?"

Garin found himself backing away so that he bumped into

the wall. "Nothing! I told you that! What has gotten into you two? You're acting like I'm a thief!"

The men exchanged a look, then both began slowly advancing.

Flee, Listener!

Garin bolted.

The mage shouted something, and Garin cried out as the pendant burned against his chest. But despite the mage's spell, he continued forward unimpeded.

Then something rammed into him and carried him to the floor. Garin wheezed, then coughed as dust choked him.

"Got him," he heard Bran say over him, his voice hoarse as well.

"The necklace!" the elf hissed.

Hands grappled with the collar of Garin's tunic, and he squirmed and struck back with an elbow. Bran grunted but pressed him harder into the dust. Garin was coughing, writhing, cursing, then the heat of the necklace slipped from his skin, and all of the fight suddenly drained from him.

He felt the weight lift from his back. "Got it," Bran said above him.

Slowly, wracked with sneezes, Garin turned onto his back and sat up. He thought he'd be angry for the rough treatment, but all he felt was tired. "I found that. It's mine," he protested feebly.

Bran held up the necklace in the werelight, the chain clutched in his bunched up sleeve. Aelyn stooped before it, squinting at the black gems.

"One of theirs," the mage said, then smiled. "Hold it a moment longer. A silver-spun sack ought to contain it."

The elf fished in his cloak for a moment, then drew out a small, shining sack. Garin stared at it dully. Before he'd laid eyes on the pendant, he might have thought it a marvelous thing, shimmering like a silver fish darting in a stream. Now, it seemed as dun as sackcloth.

Aelyn held it under the necklace, and Bran dropped it in. The mage quickly tied it off and secured it back within his cloak.

Then both of them turned toward him, mouths parting to speak.

"I know," Garin said before they could chastise him. "I wasn't supposed to wander off. And I'm sorry, I didn't mean to, honest. One moment, I was behind you, and the next—"

Bran knelt before him. "It's alright, lad. You were ensorcelled."

"A touch of Night fell upon your mind," the mage said with a good deal less sympathy. "You hadn't the strength to resist it. I knew it was foolishness to allow him here."

"He hasn't been trained against it," Bran shot over his shoulder. "Give him time."

"Nevertheless," the mage continued, ignoring him, "we have what we came for, and the boy is free of the artifact's influence. We should leave and be down the hill before nightfall."

"Give him a moment." Bran extended a hand. "You alright, Garin?"

His arm felt leaden, but he managed to lift it and grip his hand, letting the man pull him to his feet. "Sorry," he muttered as he swayed.

Bran gripped his shoulder. "It's alright. Don't mind the mage. He has thorns, but he's all rose beneath. Even if he doesn't smell like it."

"Careful," Aelyn said as he passed. "You might prick your tongue on one of those thorns."

A grin split the man's face. "Look at that! Coming around already, isn't he? Evil artifacts always did put him in high spirits." Bran gave his shoulder a squeeze. "But he's right — best be on our way. And if you don't mind, I'll take up the rear this time."

Garin gave him a weak smile. "Can't say I blame you."

Though his legs felt wobbly beneath him, they held as he took one step forward, then another.

Never tell.

He stumbled, his dragging foot catching on a piece of rubble.

Bran was there in a moment, a hand on his arm steadying him. "You alright? That necklace took a lot out of you."

"Fine," Garin muttered. His heart hammered in his chest. His stomach swirled like he'd be sick. But he managed to straighten and walk quickly after the retreating sorcerous light, eager to leave the bewitched chamber far, far behind.

THE WOLF IN SHEEPSKIN

In the days that followed, Bran strove to ensure Garin would get no rest from dawn to dusk. While they walked, he spoke of all he had learned in nearly three decades of travel. He told stories of the World, tales of ancient times where every man, woman, and child had magic on their fingertips, and demons ran rampant like mice in a barn. He told of the founding of the Reach Realms, of the kings and queens responsible for the rise and fall of the states. He spoke of the recent politics, or as recent as he was privy to; but, after one too many smirks from their elven companion, he moved quickly on to other subjects.

But Bran didn't stop there. He spoke of essential facts on the beasts that came down from the East that one must known to hunt them. He pointed to plants they passed by, indicating which could be eaten and which should be avoided. He talked of how to care for a horse for travel rather than farm work, and, for good measure, how best to saddle one for war.

It was astounding, Bran mused, how much ground could be covered while walking — metaphorically and otherwise.

In the face of his indefatigable instruction, Garin proved to be a far more diligent student than Bran ever had in his youth. Though he occasionally caught him staring glassy-eyed down the road, as if his mind had traveled far away, he would always bring his attention back as soon as Bran prompted him with a teasing remark. And when Bran broke off in the middle of a lecture on the different weights and balances of swords to ask what the Second King of Avendor said to the Queen of the Gladelysh elves when they broke ties, Garin answered before he'd finished asking the question, with the proper intonation and all — "Then fare thee well, you pig-nosed bitch!"

The boy was as sharp as a scythe before harvest, that much was certain. But, even so, there were gaping deficiencies in the boy's education, especially for where they were headed.

"Lad," Bran said as they stopped the tenth evening, "there's no way around it. You'll have to learn your letters sooner or later."

He'd seen less fear in Garin's eyes when they'd been surrounded by bandits. "Do I? Gotten by this long, haven't I?"

"But you're not in Hunt's Hollow anymore — you're going to the Coral Castle. Even the servants know their letters."

The youth's eyes narrowed suspiciously. "What for? Servants don't need to read."

"In a king's service, anyone might need to read. And more importantly, in your pursuits, you most certainly will have need."

Instead of weakening Garin's reluctance, his arguments seemed to strengthen it. "What do I need books for when tending a horse? Or hunting a chimera?" He got a sly look. "Didn't seem to help you much when herding your chickens."

Bran laughed. "Some things just have to come naturally, I suppose. Unfortunately for you, literacy isn't one of them."

But, lacking the materials to make an honest attempt at teaching the lad, and the one book he carried being wholly inadequate for the job, he let the argument lie.

On occasion, the lad would introduce the subject. But even

knowing Garin's prodigious curiosity, Bran couldn't anticipate every question.

"How does it work, anyway? Magic, that is."

Bran tried to hide his dismay behind a sly smile. "You think I would explain a thing as mysterious, as powerful, as *dangerous* as sorcery to you?"

"You took me into the Ruins of Erlodan," the youth pointed out.

"Fair enough. What do you want to know? You've already seen it done."

"So you speak a strange word and... that's it?"

"A word of the Worldtongue, yes. But there are several other factors, what the elves call 'the Four Roots.' The First Root is you must possess an affinity for magic. That is, you must either be of the Eldritch Bloodline — in other words, an elf — or, if you're human, you must have sworn an oath to a patron god, like the Warlocks' Circle worship Jalduean."

"Who's your patron god?"

Bran grinned. "I don't think any would want me."

"Then..."

He quickly moved on. "The Second Root is speaking the word of the Worldtongue. Each word corresponds with a resulting effect. For example, '*kald*,' which I used on that big bandit back there, means 'fire.'"

Garin stared at his hands. "But saying *kald* didn't summon fire now."

"No, because I didn't implement the final two Roots." He held up a third finger. "Sorcery also requires an energy transfer. For small cantrips like *kald*, your body is sufficient for the transfer. *Kald*, fire, draws a scant amount of your body's heat, then multiplies the effect tenfold. But even though each casting only takes a little energy, a sorcerer must be careful when using their body as a conduit. Expel or draw too much energy, and you'll find yourself a corpse.

"But, if there's a need to cast a cantrip many times in a row — say, you have a particularly wet pile of sticks—"

"Or a monster to kill," Garin added with a grin.

"—there's a way around this, a technique mages call 'balanced casting.' Instead of just casting *kald* and draining themselves of heat, the sorcerer would also cast *lisk,* 'ice,' which draws heat into the caster's body to create cold. The sorcerer then alternates between the two cantrips, and the amount of heat added and subtracted more or less evens out."

Garin's brow furrowed. "So if you use balanced casting, you could do magic for... forever?"

Bran shook his head. "The Fourth Root would eventually stop you — proper concentration and imagination."

"Imagination?"

"Imagination." Bran grinned. "Think about it. Your imagination can create wondrous and terrible things, dreams and nightmares. It has the power to chain a man to his past and yoke a woman to her future. Every time you picture something you cannot know with your senses, it is with imagination that you see, smell, hear, touch."

As if summoned, a familiar scent drifted by his nose, and Bran breathed it in hungrily. He knew it must be his imagination; the white mangrove flower bloomed far and away from the road they walked. But all the same, the honey-sweet scent filled him, bringing with it memories worn with being remembered so often. A touch of skin, impossibly soft. Chestnut eyes laced with tendrils of cerulean fire, deep as forest pools. The essence of the white mangrove flower she washed through her golden hair.

He cleared his throat, suddenly coming back to himself. The only thing he smelled was the stench of the road clinging to him. *A trick of memory,* he mused. *Nothing more.* Glancing at his would-be apprentice, he saw Garin was just as lost in thought. *Who do you remember? A Hunt's Hollow sweetheart? Or the father you lost long ago?*

Bran cleared his throat again and waited to speak until Garin glanced over at him. "But unlike becoming lost in your thoughts or an idle remembrance," he said with a sly smile, "imagination for magic requires knife-honed concentration. You must be able to imagine with all your senses the spell you wish to cast. When summoning fire, there is the smell of it, the heat washing over your skin, the mesmerizing sway, the gradients of color. If you imagine it vividly enough, speak its word in the Worldtongue, and draw upon a source, then fire will appear."

"If you're an elf," Garin said. "Or a warlock."

Bran inclined his head.

"But not all magic is just summoning fire and such — cantrips, like you said," Garin continued. "The magic you hear about in stories, the terrors and wonders... how does that work?"

"Similarly, but with much greater stakes. Spells of more than one word usually require an energy source beyond the caster's body, and mages often use catalysts like powders and oils, or prisms and other magnifying elements, to draw power from chemical reactions or sunlight. But even with such aids, with each added word, the consequences of failure magnify exponentially. A miscast spell of just two words could kill an inexperienced magician."

They walked in silence for a few moments, the youth considering his words.

"So that's how all magic is done? Like..." Garin hesitated, then spoke reluctantly, as if his curiosity compelled him. "Like the Extinguished in the stories. They're said to be all-powerful, to form illusions that people lose themselves in for the rest of their lives, and able to take on other people's faces." Garin grinned. "But that's all hogwash, isn't it?"

Bran echoed his smile, though only slightly. "Not completely. But they are far from all-powerful."

Garin's smile faded. "Again, you speak like they exist."

Bran stared off ahead for a long moment. Birds chirped from the trees around them.

"What have you heard of the Extinguished?" he asked finally.

"Only what everyone has heard. There are four of them, just like the Devil's Stars show. They serve the Night and Yuldor, as the Night's Chosen, in attempting to conquer the Westreach and all the other lands of Mother World." Garin shrugged. "That they're all-powerful, but held at bay by the lingering power of the Whispering Gods."

Bran shook his head. "They weave their illusions in more than just magic. Yes, there are four of them, and yes, they serve Yuldor. They have incredible powers, including near-immortality, the same as the Night has bestowed upon Yuldor. But they are not all-powerful. They can be killed, if only for a time. They can steal souls, and wear others' faces, and cast powerful illusions that can warp a person's reality.

"But they work in illusions for a reason — their magic must abide by the same rules as any others, with the same costs and consequences. Remember the story of Erlodan? A talented magician can match the Extinguished in power, and though those are few in the Westreach, there are more than four. And though Yuldor sends down the Nightkin, they've never yet overwhelmed the defenses of the Reach Realms. Thus, to accomplish their goals, Yuldor and his servants work in subterfuge, weaving a web of lies and deceit, and threatening more often with secrets and incentives than magic."

Another silence fell between them. Garin stared down the road, seeming lost in thought. Bran wondered how much he had accepted. Seeing fire summoned before him was one thing; it was another entirely to believe in fairy tales.

The youth glanced over, eyes again alight with curiosity. "Where did you learn sorcery?"

Bran pretended to study something in the distance. "That's enough on magic for now," he said without taking his eyes away. "We can't neglect your knowledge of castle cutlery, can we? Now, in the dining hall, there are three spoons, two forks, and two knives..."

The youth patiently listened to the explanation of proper dinner etiquette that followed, though his raised eyebrow let Bran know that the deflection wasn't lost on him.

At the end of the long days, when the boy's head was soaked as thickly with knowledge as an oilcloth, only one thing could provoke him from his bedroll.

"Are you a coward?" Bran would taunt, then toss him a long branch, or however long they could find that day.

The youth would scramble up, grab the end of the branch, and brandish it like it were real steel. "Come and see!"

Even the mage's molten eyes watching them couldn't dampen their fun.

During their sparring sessions, Garin seemed to truly come alive. Curious as he was, tales of long-dead generals and heroes didn't have the same appeal as the blood-pumping work of slamming a stick against your opponent.

Though he failed more than he succeeded in hitting Bran at all. Not one to go easy on an opponent, Bran would sidestep, roll, and block every attempt Garin made at getting through his defenses, then beat him back and tell him his mistakes, piecing out proper technique bit by bit. Only one in a hundred strikes found him, and most of those were when his back was turned.

"What did you expect?" Bran said one time when Garin slumped to the ground, rubbing at fresh welts after another failed assault.

"I expected these to be lessons in the sword, not dancing," the youth grumbled.

Bran laughed. "Every fight is a dance, and the one who knows the choreography will sweep the performance." He extended a hand. "Let's make sure you're not the partner with two left feet, shall we?"

Grumbling under his breath, Garin took his hand and let him pull him upright.

On the twelfth night since they'd left Hunt's Hollow, after Garin had slumped into his bedroll and immediately fallen asleep, Bran joined Aelyn at the fire. The mage had magicked himself a rough stool from nearby deadwood and sat staring into the flames.

"I'd ask what you see there," Bran said, "if I didn't know better."

Aelyn turned his gaze on him, and the flames reflected in his eyes made them seem even more fiery than usual. "I'm to assume you disbelieve infernal divination?"

"Have you met those channelers? Kooky, the lot of them." Bran shook his head. "No, any kind of forecasting into the future is a fool's errand. Each man and woman forges their path."

He didn't like the look of the elf's smile as he shifted his eyes back to the flames, and his silence even less.

"You're too fond of the boy," Aelyn said as if they'd been speaking of it the whole time.

Bran hesitated. "I've an interest in his growth. But only a cold snake like you would see harm in that."

"You let your guard down around him. Like in the ruins. You allowed the darkness that possessed him to infect you as well. Or do you deny it?"

Shame rose in him. "I don't know about that, Aelyn. I have demons enough of my own for a tantrum like that."

"Perhaps so. But the catalyst was our Enemy's enchantment, not what the boy had done. Because you care for him, you allowed the Night to touch your mind as well."

"Then what would you suggest? Walk silently the whole way to Halenhol? Teach him nothing of fighting and the World so that he can stumble his way through it? I suppose that's the way you were raised — playing with magic until you learned it?" Bran snorted. "A grown man's blindest spots are in his own past, and that's even truer of the long-lived elves."

Aelyn set his gaze flatly on him. "You have accepted him as your apprentice, that much is clear. Though what he's apprenticing in is far from certain. But, student or not, you cannot protect him from the evils of the East. No matter how much you teach him, when he inevitably comes in contact with the Enemy, it will be his will pitted against the boy's, and he will be found wanting."

Bran found his fists were clenched and loosened them. "I don't see why he needs to come against the Night again. Not if elven mages don't lead us into fell ruins."

"With the company you keep, how could you doubt it?" Aelyn waved a lazy hand. "Do as you will. But heed my warning, Magebutcher. We need your legend, not the man behind it."

Bran forced a smile onto his lips. "Whatever I've done and been, I've never claimed to be more than a man."

Not waiting for an answer, he stood and walked away from the firelight.

Only when the darkness surrounded him did he allow the tight smile to drop. Staring up at the yellow moon Cressalia, he let his mind slowly turn. He had thought himself safe for a time. Over the past five years, he had secretly protected Hunt's Hollow and the East Marsh from the encroaching East. Defender of the Westreach — hadn't he been given that title for a reason? If he could protect all of civilization, could he not protect a single boy?

A moonsinger didn't need to croon the answers for him to know them. *Magebutcher, Ringthief, Red Reaver* — those were his true names, honestly earned through his own immoral and bloody actions. He'd be a fool to believe he could ever live up to the royally conferred, pompous title "Defender of the Westreach."

He'd been accused of many things, a fool the most common

among them. But he'd more often than not proved them wrong.

"I must remember who I am," he murmured to the moon. "I must remember I am no chicken herder, and never have been. I must remember that though I was born Brannen Cairn of Hunt's Hollow, he died when I left for war. I must remember—"

He stopped short. Soon enough, others would remember his name. For a little while longer, he would remain the Bran whom Garin thought he knew.

Before the World pulled back the wool and revealed the sheep to be the wolf.

A NASTY FLOCK OF CHICKENS

Sixteen days on the road, four towns passed — and still no horses for sale.

Garin's feet dragged through the muddy street, freshly moistened by the morning's rain. Sixteen days of endless walking and ceaseless speaking. He'd now seen more towns than he could count on his hands, but he didn't feel any excitement for it.

Traveling, he decided, wasn't all it had promised to be.

But however disappointed he might feel, Aelyn's irritation eclipsed it. "King's coin," the mage grated as they left the fourth village. "What good is a king's coin if it can't buy horses?"

He glared at Bran, who was whistling rather cheerfully. Garin didn't know how he could be so nonchalant under the elven mage's stare.

"This is your fault," the mage pointed out.

"It is," Bran agreed heartily. "Just because you *can* take anyone's horse by the King's seal doesn't mean you *should*. And what's the rush? It's a marvelous day!"

Garin and Aelyn shared a look before Garin quickly looked away. He and the elf didn't share much in common, but on this, they were in agreement.

"I wouldn't mind horses," Garin muttered.

"But how would we conduct our lessons? We'd be 'hoarse' halfway through the day!" Bran grinned at him. "If you take my meaning."

Garin rolled his eyes. "*You* would be, anyway."

"Besides, not only do those folks need their horses, but didn't you see those skinny beasts? I wouldn't have been surprised if they collapsed halfway to Halenhol — and then what good would they do us?"

"They'd get us halfway there," Aelyn snapped.

Halfway. Weren't they halfway there yet? Sixteen days they'd been walking, and they had many more miles ahead of them. As much as Garin enjoyed learning more of the World from Bran, the would-be chicken herder never stopped lecturing and quizzing him. Even swordplay was growing dull amidst the rest of the drudgery.

He was realizing just how much of traveling was the long, boring moments in between the stories folks told.

But even more than what he had to face was what he no longer had. He missed kicking his feet up by the hearth at the end of a hard day's work. He missed the teasing from his older brothers and sister, and his mother's fond smile and tight hug. He missed the freshly baked bread to the stale hardtack they ate now; the tender meats to their tough, salted pork; potatoes and cabbage rather than whatever bitter roots and foul-tasting mushrooms they could find in the surrounding forest.

He'd never admit it to his companions, but he missed home.

After the town faded from sight, Bran walked up next to him again. "Where was I? Ah, yes — the Siege of Halenhol. Now, Queen Jalenna had fair warning of warlocks among her enemy's ranks. To counteract these, she sent out the Mute Monks to silence them—"

"Why don't you ever tell stories from your life?"

The question seemed to come from nowhere, but he realized it had been simmering inside him for a long time. As he lifted his gaze from the road, he found not only Bran's eyes on him but Aelyn's as well.

When Bran didn't answer, Garin barreled on. "You had a different name before — both you and Aelyn said so. You've been a deserter and a highwayman according to what you told those brigands. You know magic and magical artifacts, and say you've trained as a warlock. And to hear you talk, you've seen the Extinguished firsthand."

Bran gave him a small smile, though his eyes looked flat and sad. "Not much slips by you, I see."

"I can't figure you out. You must be a madman or a myth, but you seem as grounded as a man could be. But I don't know you at all, do I? How could I, when I don't even know your name?"

Aelyn had drifted closer and flashed him a sharp smile. "A brave thing, to run off with a man you don't know. A brave thing — or a stupid one."

Garin stubbornly kept his gaze on Bran, who had averted his eyes. "Who are you, Bran? Or whatever your name is?"

Bran stared at the muddy road for several long moments longer. In the gray light, with his shoulders slouched forward and his eyes hooded, he looked a worn and defeated man, like a farmer after he'd watched all his crops gone to rot.

"When we reach Halenhol," he said quietly, "you'll hear many stories about me. That I'm a hero. That I'm a murderer and a traitor. Some good things, but many more of them bad, and all of them exaggerated." He finally lifted his gaze, but only to stare down the road. "I suppose, by not telling you, I wanted to preserve this simple guise I've worn in Hunt's Hollow. The chicken farmer, friendly and helpful, his past buried and dead behind him, ready to settle down into a quiet life in the far country. I wanted to inhabit again the realm of my childhood before it was torn away from me."

Bran looked at him finally. "My name is not a lie, Garin. I was born Brannen Cairn, but all the children knew me as Bran the Bastard. So you see, it's not my current name that is the lie, but the one I adopted upon leaving. The one all the World came to know."

Garin stiffened his jaw. It wasn't an answer, not like he wanted. More than ever, he burned to know the stories behind the man next to him. It wasn't even that he distrusted him — especially as he'd been using his birth name all along.

"Birth name or not, if the other name is the one everyone else knows you by, I want to know it. And if I'll hear it in Halenhol anyway, why not tell me now? If the stories they tell about you are lies, why not tell me the truth?"

"Because you'll never look at him the same, boy," Aelyn spoke from Bran's other side. "Because he knows that once you are privy to all his sins, you'll go running back to your little mud-road town and shudder to think you ever traveled with the likes of him."

Garin felt his face flush. But though he wanted to lash back, he held his tongue. Theoretically, the elven mage couldn't harm him as long as that ring was on his finger. Yet provoking Aelyn would be like poking a stick at a caged bear.

And what if he was right?

Bran suddenly stopped, and Garin stumbled to a halt, watching as the man stood stock still.

"It seems our mysterious companion is having second thoughts as it is," Aelyn taunted.

"Shh!"

The intensity in Bran's shushing quieted Aelyn instantly, and he, too, looked around, alert. Garin strained his senses, but he saw nothing in the encroaching woods, could hear nothing but the wind stirring through the leaves, and the birds—

He frowned. The birds had stopped singing.

They come, little Listener.

Garin's heart lurched into a gallop, and he whipped his head around as if he could find the speaker. As if the words hadn't come from within his mind.

"Wings!" Aelyn hissed as his gaze turned upward. "Death on wings!"

Bran gripped Garin's arm tightly and pulled him off the road. "Get into the trees and find cover — a gully, a cave, anything."

Garin stumbled to keep his feet under him. "Why? What's coming?"

The man's eyes were on the road behind them as they slipped into the forest. "Quetzals. A whole tangle of them from the sound of it."

"Quetzals?"

"Winged, feathered serpents. They're small, but they attack with perfect coordination. A tangle can take down a chimera if they're hungry enough."

Garin imagined the sight and shuddered. He'd never seen a chimera, but he'd heard they were bigger than bulls and much deadlier. Besides, he wasn't fond of snakes, and snakes flying through the air were even worse than slithering on the ground.

"Feathered serpents?" Garin mustered a laugh. "No worse than a nasty flock of chickens, right?"

Bran flashed him a wolfish grin. "Exactly. Now go! Leave them to a professional herder."

Releasing him, the man spun, hands untying the straps across his back and letting both scabbard and pack fall to the ground as he drew the sword.

Despite the danger, Garin paused and stared at the weapon. Even in the shadowed forest, its silver blade gleamed, and strange blue symbols, like on the walls of the dark pendant's chamber, squirmed across the steel.

Bran shouted over his shoulder. "Run, Garin!"

He stumbled through the brush, blood hammering in his ears, knowing he was a coward and scarcely caring.

Bran scanned the forest surrounding him. Big trees, spread out, with little undergrowth to speak of. Not good ground to fight a swarm of flying beasts.

But when it came to killing quetzals, there never was good ground.

He heard the buzz of their wings churning the air as they swiftly approached. No point in being quiet now. Quetzals hunted by smell, and they would have already caught theirs.

Though, he suspected, it was by another sense that they had tracked them this far.

Aelyn slipped from the shadows to stand by him. In one hand, he clutched a pouch with its drawstring slightly loosened to show a yellow powder within, while in the other, he held a slender, iron rod that resembled a fire poker but for how intricately it was forged.

"They've come for the pendant," the elf said. "They'll focus their attacks on me."

"I knew I'd brought you along for something."

An idea occurring to him, Bran shrugged off his cloak and, setting down his blade, began to wind the cloth around his left arm. Aelyn watched him wordlessly. As he stood, arm wrapped and sword in hand again, the buzzing had grown so loud he knew they must almost be upon them.

"When I throw this powder," Aelyn said as the leaves above them began to shake violently, "try not to be in the way."

Before he could respond, the canopy burst open.

Even in the dim light, the quetzals were dazzling. Wings sprouted all down their spines, a dozen pairs to each, their long bodies undulating through the air as the wings flapped in a rippling pattern. The feathers were brilliantly colored: the green-blue of glacial lakes, the bright red of arterial blood, the yellow of freshly husked corn.

But for all their beauty, the twisting, hissing ball of them swiftly descending toward them stirred in his gut nothing but fear.

With famed synchrony, the quetzals dove as one, like fifty arrows streaming toward their targets. Bran darted for a nearby trunk and spun around. Aelyn, unmoved, pointed the iron rod up at the tangle, then shouted. The words boomed through the clearing like a thunderclap, and the rod sparked.

Bran squeezed his eyes shut, but even behind his lids, it flashed a brilliant white. A roar filled his ears, and energy crackled around him, then a wall of wind sent him stumbling backward.

Opening his eyes, he squinted through the light dotting his vision at the mage. He stood, hat blown off, revealing his dark hair sticking out from its braid, his fiery eyes staring up in defiance. Around him, the dead bodies of seven quetzals lay blackened and crisp. Bran was surprised when his stomach rumbled at the smell.

"Not now, you insatiable animal," he muttered.

The quetzals had scattered before the lightning, but they'd already regrouped at the canopy and readied another attack. This time, instead of diving straight at the mage, they spread out like a noblewoman's skirts around him, then arced in from all angles.

Aelyn dropped the rod, tossed the powder in a circle around him, and withdrew a glass orb the size of an apple. "Now would be a fine time for aid!" he shouted above the tangle's hissing.

Bran was already moving forward, sword a blur as he chopped at a passing quetzal. "*Kald!*" he shouted as the steel met the serpent, and for a moment, the blade flared in brilliant flames. The snake shrieked as its tail severed, blood spraying over Bran, but even as it flew away, the sorcerous flames greedily ate at its body.

Recognizing the second threat, six of the quetzals veered off from their dive at the mage and flew shrieking toward him.

"Yuldor's flaming balls," Bran muttered, lifting his left arm.

Behind the approaching snakes, he saw the rest of the

tangle descend on Aelyn, then twist away. As the quetzals scattered, he saw not the elf's mangled corpse left behind, but an orb of blue light surrounding the mage, a protective barrier that had warded the serpent's attacks away, and the yellow powder rising in flames around it.

But instead of giving up, the rest of the tangle turned toward Bran.

"Thanks for that!" he shouted, but there was no time to say more as the first half dozen reached him. Thrusting his cloak-wrapped arm out, he felt the snakes latch into it, one after another, their fangs just long enough to prick his skin. Grunting, he spun the blade up, and six limp bodies fell to the ground, their heads still lodged in his arm, their blood spraying into his face.

But the rest of the tangle was there, and they seemed less intent on his arm. Hastily wiping his eyes, Bran suddenly found himself in a dizzying, whirling dance, *kald* a mantra on his lips, *Velori* flashing with flames, the hilt growing unbearably hot beneath his glove.

But even as others fell or flew off, screaming and burning, the remaining score was wearing him down. Some he warded off with his protected arm, but others darted in, tearing at his legs, his shoulders, some even scraping his head. Bran dove into a roll and swept flames overhead, but still they came, harassing him as mercilessly as crows at carrion.

"Over here!" a youthful voice suddenly called.

One of the quetzals spasmed, then darted off into the woods. Three more followed it, then another two. Then the rest of the tangle, deciding there was easier prey, fled after the others.

Even as Bran chopped into one of the last serpents still attacking him and cried out as the second bit into his backside, he groaned. "You Night-touched fool, Garin!"

Awkwardly beheading the serpent that had lodged in his

rump and prying it loose, he limped off in the direction that the tangle had flown.

Garin had never cared much for running.

In Hunt's Hollow, boys had little to occupy them but what they could find outside. Most of their games involved a physical contest of one kind or another — wrestling, archery, and slingshotting numbered among Garin's personal favorites. Races, however, never had. As often as not, he wouldn't even try but would pretend to give it an honest effort, then jog along at his leisure.

But now, with a tangle of quetzals in pursuit, he'd finally found a race he cared to win.

His heart hammered fast in his chest, wild as an unbroken stallion. His tortured lungs hardly seemed to pull in any air and screamed for more. His legs, leaden and clumsy, tripped over the brush.

But with winged death flying behind him, he had no choice but to push on.

He'd just thought to distract them when he'd flung the stones at the quetzals. He hadn't imagined the whole flock would turn and give chase. Now, he wished he'd remained a coward and done as Bran had bid him.

He didn't even know where he ran but took whichever course was easiest. When a ravine appeared in front of him, he veered and followed its edge. When the slope became steep after that, he searched for level ground. He heard the quetzals gaining on him, some flying overhead now, no doubt readying for a coordinated attack.

Garin's wind-teared eyes wandered to the ravine on his left. The only place safe from them.

But as much as he didn't want to be torn apart by flying snakes, he couldn't force himself to jump. The stream was thirty feet down, and shallow from the looks of it. Maybe if he lay down, he might escape the quetzals underwater, at least for a little while. But when he had to come up for air, what then?

And that was assuming he survived the jump.

The quetzals were circling all around him now, so many he couldn't count them at a glance. His feet edged toward the cliff-side. He wanted to collapse with exhaustion and fear.

Command them.

Even with death surrounding him, a deeper terror stabbed through him. Garin scarcely dared to breathe, wondering if he'd imagined the dark whisper in his head, wondering what it meant if he hadn't.

Command them, little Listener. They will obey.

Unmistakable that time. Though the words were soft, they were sharp, cutting through his mind as if they might draw blood. Garin stared up at the winged serpents, mouth opening, dry tongue working around his mouth.

"Go away," he said weakly. Then, stronger, "Go away!"

Young fool — in their own tongue!

"I don't know how!"

Cede control to me.

Garin swallowed hard. The quetzals were circling in, closer, closer, barely ten feet away on any side. Their hissing surrounded him, their fangs flashing as they bared them, their wings buffeting him with reptilian musk.

"Alright," he said in a small voice.

He felt his muscles seize, and his tongue lashed in his mouth. Head jerking back, his eyes stared up into the churning mass of feathers. His lips moved, and from his throat ushered forth sounds so guttural and harsh he could scarcely believe he made them.

The quetzals scattered.

His muscles slackened, and his knees buckled. Unable to keep upright, consciousness slipping away, he collapsed, falling backward.

Back into the ravine.

———

Bran lunged and seized Garin's jerkin while digging his sword into the earth behind him. The boy was slight but growing tall, and it took all of his effort to haul him back from the cliff edge and onto solid ground.

There he collapsed next to the boy, laughing weakly, though nothing that afternoon had been amusing, and the old wound in his side throbbed painfully. He leaned over the youth, looking down into his half-lidded eyes and pale face.

"Oh, lad," he said softly. "What have I gotten you into?"

HAGGLING WITH A KING

"Is that it?" Garin said as he stood in his stirrups. "Is that Halenhol?"

Bran nodded. "The Last Refuge of Civilization. The city that has never been conquered since the Eternal Animus began between the Eastern Empire and the Reach Realms, not even during the worst of the Nightkin incursions. Or so the historians claim."

The youth seemed well-inclined to believe anything as he stared, wide-eyed, at the white-walled city, and Bran was content to let him. His burst of enthusiasm was a welcome change from the week before. After the quetzals had so strangely fled, Garin had been so weak he could barely walk. Three days later, he'd regained strength enough to ride the horses Aelyn finally found available for purchase. Bran had kept watch over the youth to make sure he didn't slide from the saddle, and often had to pry open his eyes with a ribald joke or a teasing remark. But finally, as they arrived at their destination, he seemed to be himself again.

Bran's eyes wandered over to their other companion, who had also been watching the youth, but now pretended to observe the city. His gaze had often been on Garin since the quetzal attack. The mage had come upon them as they lay exhausted by the ravine and demanded to know what happened. Bran had lied through his teeth, though it had hardly been his best story — bleeding from a dozen small wounds, he'd only had the wit to say he'd come just in time to ward them off from the boy. In the state he'd been in, he knew it seemed unlikely, particularly as they both knew quetzals were famed for hunting until the whole tangle was dead. But Aelyn hadn't questioned him further, and Bran had no intention of bringing it up again.

He looked toward Halenhol again, and his stomach turned in that familiar mix of emotions. *Here is where it ends.* The thin squall of peace of the past five years would blow away as soon as he entered the gates. The weight of who he had been and who others believed him to be still would hang from his neck, dragging his spirits down into the morass he'd risen from.

At least, he thought, *there'll be feather beds and foaming baths as a consolation gift.*

Aelyn drew his horse a little ahead of them, blocking the way. "Remember," he said imperiously, "speak nothing to the guards and allow me to do the talking. Times are hard, and even for emissaries to the King, entering the Refuge can be a tricky business."

But the guardsmen gave less trouble than Aelyn had warned. Though they cast them hard looks, a flash of a scroll with the King's seal — a hawk with a crown clutched in its talons — was enough for them to cut the queue and clop their way into the city.

As they set down the main thoroughfare, people parting before their horses, Bran glanced over at Garin and smiled at his expression. "Nothing like Hunt's Hollow, eh?"

The youth looked back at him, eyes wide. "I didn't think there was anything like this in the World." His gaze swept around. "The buildings — you could stack three barns and still not be as tall. What do they need them so tall for?"

Bran grinned wider. "To pack the people in. The more you can get in one place, the more money the landlords earn from rent."

That made his expression falter. "It's about commerce?"

"In a city, lad, it's always about commerce."

But Garin's amazement waxed again as the city unfolded around them. The youth didn't see the mud-smeared walls, the dust and smoke clogging the air, the beggars putting all their tricks and wiles toward earning a single coin from an uncaring passerby.

No — he saw Halenhol as grandeur incarnate, as a mythical city from a fireside tale. Edifices rising so high they cast the streets in shadow. Manors as large as the whole of Hunt's Hollow, and tenement houses with the village's population living in a single building. And in the public squares, the magnificent marble archways, the fountains, and the Undying Flames, said to have been burning since the beginning of the Rexall reign, mounted above statues of the old kings and queens.

Watching the youth brought a smile to Bran's lips. Perhaps the ugliness of Halenhol didn't drown out the beauty. Perhaps it was worth looking past the grime to see the shine lying beneath it. But then again, as his commander, the first of his many mentors, had always said, *Pays to know what shit smells like when you're wading through it.*

Soon, the greatest that Halenhol could offer rose before them. The Coral Castle, so-named for the pink tint of the rose limestone it was built from, perched on the highest point in the city. *All the better for a king to look down on his subjects,* Bran thought, *and for his subjects to look up to him.*

At the gates, Aelyn scarcely needed the King's seal to be granted entry. In a matter of minutes, their horses had been taken away to the stables and the elf was leading them through the tall double doors, under the carved edifice of the Whispering Gods, and into the grand atrium. Bran hid a smile at

Garin's unrelenting gape as he stared at the ceiling a hundred feet above and hurried the youth after the mage.

His smile was short-lived. With every step, the weight of what he walked toward pressed down on him. His heart thumped like a servant pounding the dust out of a rug. His breathing grew shallow as an apprentice pumping at a forge's bellows. His cast-off name, repressed for so many years, burned in his mind like a curse.

Garin leaned close to him and whispered, "Are we really seeing the King now?"

"Yes."

The youth's eyes were as wide as if he were eight summers old rather than nearly twice that age. "Aldric Rexall the Fourth, King of Avendor... I can't believe I'm about to meet him."

"I wouldn't grow too eager. Aldric, like most kings and queens, is a man best avoided whenever possible and handled like a crag boar when you cannot."

Garin's brow furrowed. "What do you mean?"

Bran glanced to either side at the guards flanking them and spoke loudly enough for them to hear. "When Aldric came into power eleven years ago, he faced opposition from within and without. His father's power had been slowly crumbling away during his reign, and the nobility were claiming more for themselves. They even began demanding a Peers' House in the fashion of the Gladelysh so they might weigh in on the making of the law and the ruling of the kingdom. Twenty-two years old at the time of his coronation, Aldric seemed an impressionable boy to the nobility, a puppet by which they could take yet more power from the throne."

The guards wore frowns, but neither interrupted as Bran continued.

"But Aldric was far from a puppet. Knowing he needed to consolidate power, he manufactured an affront from Jakad and invaded their small kingdom. Typically, an act of war would be protested by the nobility, but Aldric was clever, promising to reward key houses with significant lands from the kingdom once it was won, and keep little of it for the crown. It played on both the nobility's petty politics, allowing some to lord their promised winnings over their rivals, and their greed, for Jakadi vineyards and the wine they produce are favored across the Westreach.

"But Sendesh, as Avendor's balancing power, couldn't ignore such an aggressive act. Believing Avendor overcommitted to the Jakadi front, the Sendeshi Protector declared war in defense of their ally and began to march south. But Aldric had known Sendesh would come and had set a plan in motion. While his armies swept through Jakad, he sent ships to Nemenport, a Sendeshi town important for trade along the northern coast. Yet Aldric didn't sail his warships, nor fly the flags of Avendor, but instead commandeered fishing vessels and trade boats and raised the black sails of the northern marauders, the Yraldi. Oddly enough, it became the foreshadowing of the summer that would follow, where the Yraldi came down in greater force than they ever had before."

The guards were nodding now, eyes gleaming as they basked in the reflected glory of their King's butchery. *Though I'm the last man who can condemn another's massacre,* Bran mused.

"Burning and pillaging Nemenport, Aldric's self-fashioned marauders swept east along the coast, razing three other Sendeshi towns as they went. It was enough to force Sendesh to split its forces into two, with half the army continuing to march south and the other returning to deal with the incursions. But by the time Sendesh had reached Avendor's border, Jakad had been conquered, and King Aldric extended them a claim they couldn't refuse, granting them the best of the Jakadi vineyards and castles. The Sendeshi Protector, seeming to have lost his appetite for blood and gained one for wine, accepted the offer after only minor skirmishes. Ever since, it has established an uneasy peace between our nations, but one long enough that the Annexation of Jakad has been touted as a victory."

For a youth walking through a castle for the first time, Garin looked strangely somber. "My father must have died in one of those wars," he murmured. "In Jakad, or Sendesh. I thought he went to the Fringes. But it was eleven years ago that he went to serve the King and never came back."

How well I know it. Bran found he couldn't look at the youth. "Must have," he muttered.

It was almost a relief when they reached the throne room. A pair of doors nearly as impressive as the ones at the castle's entrance were cracked open in the middle so that Bran could see glances of the glimmering gold room beyond. The youth's mood had sobered since his story, his thoughts no doubt on his long-lost father, and the King he believed had sacrificed him for his own gain, but he perked up at this fresh glimpse of grandeur.

The guards at the doors took their weapons while their escort motioned them toward the entrance. As they stepped through, the room opened up into a dazzling, airy atmosphere. Sunlight from high windows filled the room with an ethereal glow, and everywhere gold and silver gleamed in complement to the apple red and sunset orange of the Rexall crest. On either side of the room, guards lined the walls, and between them, brown-robed monks stood similarly at attention.

Though their simple, coarse clothing looked out of place among the opulence of the room, Bran wasn't surprised to find them present. Monks of the Order of Ataraxis — or Mutes, as most called them — were often used by the monarchs of the Westreach to utilize to their peculiar power of Quietude. Assumedly attained through their oath of silence to the Whispering Gods, Quietude allowed Mutes to produce a barrier of silence around them when they chanted, ensuring that undesired ears would not overhear the proceedings. That the monks themselves might hear was of little concern; between their chanting and their magic, their eavesdropping was unlikely, and their silence assured. At the moment, the monks were quiet, and they watched the newcomers with demure stares.

Turning his gaze from the monks, Bran looked to the far end of the long, red carpet on which they stood to the golden throne and the man sitting atop it. His face was a mixture of annoyance and boredom as he stared at the half-circle of other richly dressed folk around him. *As every king should look*, Bran reflected.

Before they had taken more than a few steps toward the King, however, a herald approached them with an expectant look. Aelyn turned to Bran, one eyebrow arched, a cold smile twisting his lips. Garin watched Bran as well, seeming to realize something was about to happen, curiosity alight in his eyes.

Bran met Aelyn's gaze and knew then that Bran the Chicken Farmer would soon be just another chapter in his past.

He sighed. "I'll tell him myself — if he doesn't remember."

The mage, still smirking, waved the herald back and began leading Bran and Garin down the pristine carpet, ignoring the monks and guards to either side of them. Garin seemed nervous even to walk on the rich fabric, but followed a step behind Bran.

As they approached, the King glanced up from the men and women surrounding his throne to stare at them. "Emissary Aelyn," he said in a thin, nasally voice. "I expected you to return last week."

The King's gaze fell on Bran, and he tried not to flinch. King Aldric Rexall the Fourth was not an intimidating man in looks. He had pudgy cheeks, a weak chin, and large, watery eyes that made him seem a large babe sitting the throne, never mind having nearly three and a half decades to his age. But looks were a mask, as Bran had long ago learned during his time in an acting troupe, and though he wasn't a gambling man — at least, not anymore — he would have wagered gold that Avendor had never seen a more ruthless king.

"Your Majesty," Aelyn said as he swept off his hat and gave a low bow. His voice had gathered a sycophantic air that had been distinctly absent from any words he'd uttered to his companions. "My deepest and sincerest apologies. I would have come sooner, but a tragic lack of horses delayed my errand."

At this, the mage flashed a nasty look at Bran.

"Never mind, never mind." King Aldric wrinkled his nose and waved a hand as if trying to banish a particularly persistent flatulence. "Councilors, I bid you leave us. You guards as well. But stay close — this won't take long."

The guards bowed, then led the arc of councilors from the throne room. As the most powerful men and women of Avendor passed, eyeing them curiously, Bran kept his gaze solidly forward, forcing an insolent smile onto his lips. *Let them think of that,* he thought. *A man who would dare smile before a private audience with the King.* No doubt they'd consider him a fool, and that was all the better — a fool was permitted to do what a wise man never could.

As the door to the throne room closed behind the councilors with an echoing rumble, the Ataraxis monks began chanting. King Aldric screwed up his eyes at Bran, and over the monks' indecipherable words, he said, loud and clear in his nasal voice, "I never again thought to see you standing before me alive, Tal Harrenfel."

Garin turned his wide-eyed stare from the King to the man standing next to him.

A chicken farmer, he'd thought him. Brannen Cairn had a few mysteries about him, but he'd been a chicken farmer when it came down to it. But now, with his true name revealed,

Garin realized he'd been traveling with, training with, *saved by* none other than Tal Harrenfel himself.

All the names the man had earned streamed through his head. Red Reaver. Ringthief. Defender of the Westreach. The man who had stolen a magic ring from the Hoarseer Queen and lost it to the Warlock of Canturith. The man who had led the charge that drove back the marauders from the Northern Isles. The man declared by King Aldric Rexall, the very king they stood before, to be a living legend, the hero of Avendor, and the foremost champion of civilization against the evils of the East. Songs were sung about him in the taverns, tales told of his deeds around fires on wintery nights. Garin had dreamed of being him during more than one discontented night.

And here he'd been, standing next to him the whole time. Tal Harrenfel, the same man who had lived as his neighbor for five years, and was terrible at herding chickens.

The man he'd known as Bran looked over at him. Even knowing who he was, Garin found it hard not to see his neighbor in those eyes. *How could he be both Bran Cairn and Tal Harrenfel?* he asked himself, and could find no answer.

"Well?" King Aldric barked, and Garin startled, remembering with a jolt that they stood before the King himself. Frantically, he wondered if he should have already bowed, or if he was supposed to wait for some signal. But the King's eyes were on Bran — or Tal, he supposed he should call him now.

Tal turned his gaze to meet the King's. "You called. I came."

"That much I gathered myself," the King snapped. "If I needed a parrot, I would have called a menagerie. If I needed a fool, I would have called on your friend Falcon. I need neither, Tal Harrenfel." King Aldric leaned forward in his throne, almost as if it pained him to remain seated on it. "I need you."

"And what do you need me for?"

King Aldric whipped his head toward Aelyn. "You didn't tell him?"

If Garin hadn't known better, he would have thought the mage cringed.

"I tried to tell him," the mage said, a hint of a whine to his voice. "He wouldn't listen."

The King snorted and looked back to Tal. "Sounds like him. Yuldor's prick, man — time is short, and the Mutes' Quietude won't go unnoticed. Do the corner callers venture out to that bilgewater town where you've been living?"

"Few enough would listen if they did."

"Then allow your King to tell you the copper news. War is coming, Harrenfel. A great war. The East sends its monsters down from the mountains in such numbers that the Fringe Guard cannot hold them. It's gotten so bad the smallfolk are claiming to see dragons roaming the sky. Dragons!" King Aldric snorted, his derision plain.

"But that's just the beginning. Gladelyl is heading toward civil war. Sendesh is marshaling its forces, looking to take advantage of any weakness. And we of Avendor are expected to hold both lines, as usual."

"Little of that is different from before."

"You think so?" The King leaned forward. "Then here's a bit of news you won't have heard: not all of the Westreach remain filial to the Bloodlines. Some want to join the so-called Empire of the Rising Sun."

For the first time, Tal seemed to flinch. "Who?"

The King of Avendor irritably waved a hand. "Most everyone else, it seems! The Dwarven Clans have delved too deep for too long in their mines and seemed to have found a darkness they cannot shake. The Goblin Knolls, as all know, have long been sympathetic to the Eastern cause. The Elves of Gladelyl are split in their allegiances and squabble among themselves for the honor to bow and scrape at the feet of the 'Peacebringer.'"

At this, King Aldric spared Aelyn a sneer. The Gladelysh emissary's mouth twitched.

"And among us humans," the King continued, "Sendesh always plots to best us, using whatever means Protector Unne deems appropriate."

The man who had been Bran seemed utterly different now. A slight sneer perched on his lips, and his eyes looked sharp and incisive. Garin knew little of the ways of the court, but he knew that a man who didn't bow to royalty, who smiled in the face of an angry king, was a force to be reckoned with.

But then, Garin realized, neither had he bowed. Should he now? Or, if he did, would it draw attention and risk punishment? And if he didn't, would he face the King's wrath?

As the King's gaze turned on him, he was sure he'd noticed. But all the King of Avendor said was, "What's the boy doing here?"

"Never mind him," Tal said. "He's with us."

"Never mind?" The King's eyes looked ready to bulge from his head. "You dare to tell me what to mind?"

"Yes. I do."

The King stared a moment longer, and Garin was sure he was going to order them all executed. Then a shriek erupted from him.

"I'd forgotten how bold you were, Tal Harrenfel! Very well, he stays. But it's his silence or your head, Harrenfel."

Tal glanced at Garin. "He stays."

With his tongue glued to the roof of his mouth, Garin wasn't about to object.

"As you will. Now, to our true business. The threat of war is not relevant for your task. Why I have called you here, Tal Harrenfel, is for the traitor in our midst."

Aelyn's expression spasmed. Tal's eyes flickered to him, then back to the King. "Why do you believe that?"

"Too much has gone wrong!" King Aldric was suddenly enraged, spittle flying from his lips. "Supply lines bungled! War rations spoiled! Rumors and scandals sprout in my city like boils on Duke Vandon's cock!"

Garin hid his astonishment at the King's turn of phrase, more suitable for a tavern than a throne room. *Though couldn't anything be considered kingly when done by a king?*

"Perhaps these were simply mistakes," Tal replied. "Perhaps there is no traitor. Maybe you have simply surrounded yourself with a council of fools."

"I daily suspect this myself. But there is one piece of evidence that I cannot attribute to their incompetence." He gestured impatiently at Aelyn. "Tell them."

The mage's ears twitched as if uncomfortable at being exposed. "A handmirror was discovered among the King's possessions that no servant could recall placing there. When I took it for inspection and looked within its glass, I divined on the other side a face of fire and smoke suddenly dissipating. Further spells revealed what I suspected." Aelyn glanced at the King. "The handmirror was cursed."

King Aldric leaned forward, eyes bright and moist. "Someone was spying on me, Harrenfel. In my bedroom. Every time I performed my kingly duties for my wife and sated my manly needs with a whore, they were watching. And if the elf is right, that damned mirror was capable of plenty more besides. Now tell me — does that sound like incompetence to you?"

Tal's smile was gone. "No. It doesn't."

The King leaned back again, wearing Tal's stolen smile. "Then you know why you're here. I've always been a great admirer of your work, Harrenfel — the greatest, I imagine. But it's the achievements that few know of that have been your finest, have they not, Magebutcher?"

A wince crossed Tal's face, and Garin's mind began to race. *Magebutcher?* He'd never heard that name in any of the stories. From Aelyn's sour expression and Tal's paleness, the tale promised to be far from heroic. But how could this kindly, joking neighbor of his, who was renowned as a hero throughout the Westreach, do anything less than honorable?

"Yes," Tal said slowly. "I know what you want. But you have yet to hear what I require in return."

King Aldric's eyebrows, thin as they were, reached toward the thin golden circlet on his head, while his lip quivered like a child about to have a tantrum. "Are we merchants sitting down to squawk? I'm a king, Harrenfel! I. Don't. Fucking. *Barter!*"

Garin's heart hammered, and he thought he might collapse. Standing before a king had almost been enough to make him faint; standing before a furious king promised to finish the job.

But Tal didn't back down. "You made that clear when you called me back here, Aldric. We made a deal when I left this room nine years ago, a deal I've never violated. I was to have a quiet life on the frontier of your kingdom in exchange for what I gave you." His gaze shifted to Aelyn. "Then he showed up on my doorstep, and I knew that was as much a dream as it had always seemed."

Garin's head spun. What deal had he made? And why would a man like Tal give up anything to spend years in Hunt's Hollow, much less something valuable enough to interest a king?

Though he'd seemed in a right fury just a moment before, and his face was still flushed red, King Aldric smiled without even a tremble. "Nine years is a much longer promise than most a king makes."

Tal laughed, the sound hollow. "Those might be the truest words you've ever spoken."

The King still wore a smile as he reached over and grasped a goblet from a small table next to him and lifted it to his lips. A trickle of red dribbled down his chin as he drained the goblet and set it down with a rattle, wiping carelessly at the spill with the back of his hand.

"I'll tell you what, Harrenfel. I'll hear you out. You get one chance to ask for whatever you wish. And if it's reasonable, you have my word, I'll give it to you — once you've done my job."

Tal stared, motionless, at the King. Then he nodded. "It's as much as I could ask for. But as your task has at stake not just a kingdom, but the whole of civilization, I'll make my wish three in part."

The King's eyes narrowed, though his smile never slipped. "Careful," he said in a low, singsong voice. "You wouldn't want to overdraw on my generosity."

"Can't overdraw on a thing that doesn't exist."

While the King's mouth worked, Tal skipped ahead. "The first thing: I'll have words with my old friend Falcon. Considering you broke your end of our deal, I believe it's only fair that I break mine."

The smile finally fell from King Aldric's lips. "Fine," he growled, or as near as he could with his high-pitched voice. "And the other two requests?"

"Second — upon completing your task, I'll be free, truly free, to go wherever I please, and never be called upon again for one of your jobs."

The King snorted. "Done. You're getting too old for my jobs as it is. Like as not you'll be pushing up flowers next time it's necessary. And the last?"

Tal gestured at Garin, and as the King turned his gaze on him, he felt as if his heart would stop. "Lastly, that you'll provide for this boy in whatever manner I see fit, be that an apprenticeship, knighting, or duchy."

King Aldric narrowed his eyes at Garin. "Him? Who's this boy to you — your bastard?"

"No," Tal said quickly, a touch of his cool air lost. "Never mind that. Those are my terms. Tell me, Aldric — are they reasonable?"

The King looked a moment longer at him. Only when his gaze pulled from him did Garin dare breathe again.

"Deal," King Aldric said, not sounding pleased for it. "So long as you don't try and give the boy my crown."

"I wouldn't dream of cursing him with it."

Tal inclined his head in what looked like, even to Garin's

untrained eye, an insincere bow. But he rushed to follow his lead all the same. Rising, he saw the King's amused eyes on him.

"A king's bargain!" King Aldric shouted, banging his fist on the arm of his throne and shrieking a laugh. "Words I never thought I'd string together! Now, find my traitor, Harrenfel, and do it quickly. Else, legend or no, I'll have your head — and the boy's — mounted on my wall."

"I'd expect nothing less of a king," Tal said, and he turned on his heels, Garin following uncertainly after him.

THE MAGEBUTCHER AND THE
MINSTREL

AS THE CHANTING OF THE MONKS FADED BEHIND THEM, AND THE
gazes of the councilors in the foyer were lost from sight, he
glanced furtively at Garin.

The youth seemed remarkably calm for all the revelations
he'd been privy to. He seemed more interested in their
surroundings as a servant led them down the coral-colored
halls toward, he hoped, their rooms.

Garin's eyes went everywhere but at the man walking next
to him.

The man, he mused. Who was he to him now? Bran the
Chicken Farmer, Bran his neighbor and friend?

Or Ringthief. Red Reaver. Magebutcher.

He sighed. He knew who he was, even if he'd told himself
otherwise for five years. He was Tal Harrenfel and had been
ever since he'd first left Hunt's Hollow all those decades ago,
more a boy than Garin was now, and hungry for blood and
glory.

"Well then," Tal started, then cleared his throat. Little
made him feel awkward, and the unfamiliarity of the feeling
made it all the more uncomfortable. "You've met your first
king, eh?"

Garin glanced over at him, eyes crinkled. "That's the first thing you have to say?"

"Should I have said something else?"

"How about starting with you being Tal Harrenfel, a living legend, and never bothering to tell me?"

A living legend. He winced. "We could start there, I suppose."

"Yeah, I'll bet we could." The youth's eyes were fully on him now, and it was Tal who found himself unable to meet his gaze.

"What's there to tell? My name is as the King said." He looked at Garin, almost meeting his eyes. "But I'll say one thing in my defense. Not all the stories are true about me. The originator of them took certain artistic liberties with the truth."

The youth snorted a laugh. "You think I wouldn't know that? In my experience, most stories are more fantasy than fact."

Tal repressed a smile. *The lad learns quickly.*

"But that doesn't answer my questions," Garin continued. "What I mean is, how could you hide that from all of us in Hunt's Hollow? I came around your farm for five years! And you never let slip even a hint that you were a hero."

"Hero? I'm no hero." He said it more sharply than he intended, but found himself hard-pressed to regret it. "I've done some good things, true enough, but usually for the wrong reasons, and I've done plenty bad besides. But those deeds didn't make it into the songs."

Garin leaned closer, eyes bright. "I won't judge you for anything. I just want to know the truth."

A smile twisted his lips. *The truth.* Did he even know it himself?

"I'll tell you everything," he promised. "In time."

The youth couldn't hide his disappointment as he looked away.

"I could tell you a story or two about Tal Harrenfel that would put hair on your chest, lad!"

At the end of the hall, a man suddenly stepped into view

and leaned against the wall. Garin startled, but Tal's chest leaped like a child at the sight of a new toy. He strode forward, a grin tugging his mouth wide, and spread his arms.

"Falcon Sunstring! I should kill you for all you've done to my good name!"

"Murder is a strange form of thanks." The minstrel grinned as well and stepped into the embrace, hugging him tightly back. "Good to see you, my friend," he murmured in his ear.

"You too."

Stepping away, Falcon looked at Garin. "And who is this strapping young fellow?"

Tal almost set a hand on the lad's shoulder, as he had done before as Bran, but held himself back. "This is Garin. Garin, meet Falcon, my very old friend."

Garin stuck out a hand, though his expression was far from certain. Falcon, however, took the hand and pulled the youth into a hug, laughing at his expression. "I don't know about being *very* old, but a friend of Tal's is a friend of mine!"

As Garin extricated himself from the bard, Tal looked Falcon up and down. Life in the King's court seemed to have treated him well. He wore a wide-brimmed black hat with a yellow feather that billowed a full foot over his head. His charcoal-dark hair stretched down his neck, and still had the shine of a prized mare despite his advancing years. His doublet was finely tailored, even if a burgeoning belly pressed at the seams, and was black lined with silver and yellow. A dark metal bracelet peeked out from beneath one sleeve, seeming in blunt contrast to the rest of the finery. His stockings were a bumblebee motley as well. But most alive were his eyes, green swirling with amber, one of the tells of his partial elven blood.

"What do you see, my roguish friend?" Falcon watched his observations with a wry twist to his lips, and as Tal's gaze had wandered over the bracelet, he'd tugged his sleeve down almost self-consciously.

"You look as if you're well," Tal observed. "Or well-fed, at least."

He tittered a laugh. "Your tongue is still sharp! I'm glad that much hasn't changed." He leaned confidentially toward Garin. "He's easily flattered — I would use it to your advantage, were I you!"

The youth smiled uncertainly.

"Garin is well-used to pulling my strings," Tal said. "He's been my neighbor for the past five years."

Falcon's thin eyebrows shot up. "Has he indeed? In that small, provincial town where you'd shut yourself away?"

"Hunt's Hollow is its name, and it's the finest town in all the East Marsh." The smile had disappeared from Garin's expression as he stared at Falcon.

The minstrel held up both hands with a laugh. "I meant no offense, young master! I only speak out of hurt abandonment. You see, Tal and I were brothers-in-arms once."

It was Garin's turn to raise his eyebrows. "You were soldiers together?"

"In a manner of speaking, quite!"

Tal rolled his eyes. "By which he means no. You've only just met him, but I imagine you can't see Falcon fighting with anything but words."

The bard gasped and clutched his heart as if struck. "You wound me, sir!"

"If words wound you, I can only imagine how you'd fare in a war camp."

As quickly as he'd donned it, Falcon lost the affect. "Miserably, I'm sure."

Garin looked between them, brow knitting together now. "What did you mean then? How do you two know each other?"

Falcon raised an eyebrow at Tal. "Will you tell him, or shall I?"

Tal sighed. "If you must."

The bard leaned toward Garin and said in a carrying whisper, "Once, Tal here was a player in my very own troupe!"

Garin's eyes widened as he looked at him, and Tal winced. But the youth just exclaimed, "I'd forgotten that part of the legend! The Dancing Feathers was *your* troupe?"

Falcon looked pleased. "Indeed, it was and still is! We were the finest in Felinan when we first started. So fine, in fact, that our own King Aldric had to poach us for his entertainment."

The memory cut as it rose from the depths of his past. "A fateful day, when he saw us first perform," Tal said quietly.

The bard's smile slipped. "Yes. I suppose it was."

Confusion had claimed Garin's expression again. "What do you mean?"

"Don't you remember the songs, young master? How Tal Harrenfel had to hide in plain sight before the Warlock of Canturith as he watched the performance as one of the old King's guests, then afterward flee to the north to escape his mortal enemy's wrath?"

"Kaleras is not my mortal enemy," Tal corrected.

"Of course not," Falcon said soothingly. "But my version of events had to claim as much. Every hero needs a nemesis, after all."

And who could be more of an ironic nemesis than that old warlock? Tal thought.

"And better still," Falcon continued, "for the warlock is here visiting, and the last thing you need is to reignite old quarrels."

For a moment, Tal found he couldn't speak. "He's here?" he choked out.

His friend smiled sympathetically, while Garin looked back and forth between them, brow furrowed.

"Been here for a week now," the bard said. "Nobody knows why exactly. But then again, nobody has dared ask."

Tal closed his eyes, trying and failing to stifle the swirl of emotions that had risen in him. When he'd forced them back under his skin, he opened his eyes and forced a smile. "Another old friend to greet, then. But before I forget, Falcon — you mentioned my legend. I should tell you Aldric has given me leave to make a few red-lined marks to your songs."

Falcon's smile turned to a pout. "Revise my songs? But your deal with the King!"

"We've made a new one." Tal clapped a hand on the bard's shoulder. "Think of it this way — you'll get to share many nights by the fire with an old friend."

"An old friend who wishes to destroy my life's work," Falcon grumbled. But the amber in his eyes stirred a little faster, betraying his true feelings.

Squeezing his shoulder, Tal released him and looked to Garin. "But that will have to save for later. We've had a long road, and should settle into our rooms. Kings wait for no man, and Aldric is nothing if not a king."

"Never were there truer words." Falcon folded his arms around Tal once more, then cavorted back with a grin. "I'll pry into your affairs when I've forced a glass or two of Jakadi wine down your throat, my Winter Stoat!"

Then as swiftly as he'd come, the minstrel disappeared around the corner.

Garin looked after the man, looking as perplexed as if the heavens had opened overhead and poured down rain. "Winter Stoat?" he muttered, then said louder, "You're truly friends with that strange man?"

Tal nodded with a smile. "Falcon is the truest friend I've had. He helped me through my blackest years and has stood by me ever since." *No matter what he learned about me and my past.*

His gaze slid sidelong to the youth, who only seemed more confused, and wondered if he could dare expect the same from him.

Garin laid back in the bed, sighed long and deep, and marveled that anything so soft and comfortable could exist, much less be his to sleep on.

Goose feathers, Tal had said it was stuffed with. Garin wondered how many gooses one would have to pluck to get enough feathers to fill a bed like this. One hundred? Two? It was a ridiculous thought for an absurd luxury.

He wagered he could get used to it.

His room — or rooms, rather — were every bit as extravagant as the bed. A closet was dedicated to his bodily needs, with servants to take out the chamberpot at intervals throughout the day. There was a room for "entertaining guests," as Tal had put it, and a room for sleeping. The bath had been in a common area, but he hadn't minded as he settled into steaming hot water, fragrant with rose and spices he'd never before smelled.

But now, his body clean and relaxed, his mind began to turn over the many mysteries surrounding him. Foremost among them was the man who had brought him here, the man who had pretended to be nothing more than a chicken farmer for five years, who was a hero of Avendor with enough clout to defy a king. Not Bran any longer, but Tal Harrenfel — Red Reaver of the Northern Coast, Ringthief of the Goblin Queen, Devil Killer of horned Heyl—

The Magebutcher.

The more he thought about it, the less he understood. What was the truth behind the names? Who was Tal Harrenfel? And why had he negotiated with King Aldric on Garin's behalf?

And the people from his past. That strange minstrel Falcon, so familiar with his touches and carefree with his smiles, who had written the songs of Tal Harrenfel, if Garin had understood the implications right. The Warlock of Canturith, who was supposed to be a long-time adversary, the one who stole the Ring of Thalkuun from Tal, then later drove him north into hiding. But that, too, seemed uncertain now.

And then there was the matter of their task, finding a traitor working on behalf of some unnamed enemy. Aelyn had ventured across the whole of Avendor to fetch Tal so that he could hunt this traitor. What made him so necessary for sniffing them out? Was it because he was a legend? Did it have to do with whatever enemy was behind the treachery?

Garin rubbed at his head. So many questions and so few answers. And the man who could answer them all was as forthcoming as a locked chest. The more he saw, the smaller Hunt's Hollow and even the East Marsh seemed.

But as much as the questions needled him, and despite it still being light outside, Garin found his worries drifting away. Questions could wait, he decided drowsily, until after he'd gotten his best night's sleep.

PASSAGE II

The first variety of Fount, those who possess the Blood, is cloaked in mystery, for the origins of their sorcery are still unknown.

Some have posited it is nothing more than the reemergence of a distant and forgotten ancestor of one of the Heart Races. Others suppose these individuals harbor secret religions to obscure deities. But I prefer the explanation of the Blood for several reasons.

Founts of the Blood can, for seemingly no reason, perform magic just as capably as any of the Heart Races. But while this might imply little more than an unknown ancestor, those of the Blood differentiate themselves as well through great and terrible accomplishments.

Aqada the Conqueror, for one, long boasted of being as capable of magic as any Obelisk sorcerer, and indeed proved it through defying our brethren's attempts to stop her — yet she was only a human, and showed no signs of any of the Heart Races. And another, Sage Hester, who invented many of the healing decoctions we still use three hundred years later — despite being a half-breed of the Dun Races, did he not claim never to have adopted a patron spirit, but worked magic of his own will?

- A Fable of Song and Blood, *by Hellexa Yoreseer of the Blue Moon Obelisk, translated by Tal Harrenfel*

TREACHERY'S DUE

Tal ghosted down the dark hallway, a small, heatless light balanced on his fingertips.

The castle was silent, most of its residents long ago asleep. The hour had been slow in arriving. *But I'm accomplished in nothing more than wasting time,* he mused.

He'd passed the daylight hours by eating, bathing, and sleeping, making sure to spend his idle hours in the public eye in complete and utter frivolity. He'd ordered clothes to be made from the King's tailors for both himself and Garin, then hounded the servants for Jakadi wine, making a grand scene in the great hall, where several knots of nobility lingered, of having the servants send a full tun to his room. By this point, everyone would be asking who this tasteless boar of a guest of the King's was, wholly convinced that, whoever he was, he was a provincial pig unworthy of a monarch's attention, and despising him all the more for it.

Now, creeping down the sleepy hallway, shoes left behind in favor of noiseless stockings, Tal played the unseen side of the coin he'd tossed: the conspirator in the night.

Reaching the door, he set his hand to the wood and gently pressed on it. The door swung silently open on well-oiled hinges, and Tal stepped inside, closing the door behind him with the greatest care.

"You're late," an irritable voice greeted him.

Tal extinguished the werelight as he walked into the flickering orange glow of the fireplace before him. "You would have said that even if I'd been early."

Aelyn smiled from the chair in which he sat by the fire, but there wasn't a trace of humor in it.

"To business," the mage said, gesturing at the chair opposite him.

Tal examined the seat and, finding it untainted, sat.

The mage had raised one eyebrow. "Do you think me a child to play a low prank on you?"

"Perhaps not a low prank. But certainly a high one after the one I played on you."

The elf's molten eyes swirled faster. "Your buffoonery never ends. And to think the King of Avendor would entrust this task to you."

"He couldn't just rely on you. You're not even his subject — you simply arrived at a convenient time, after all of this started, so he could be sure it wasn't you behind it all." He gave him a lazy smile. "To take this on alone, you'd need a folktale and a bard singing your praises."

But instead of his gibe rousing Aelyn further, the swirling in his eyes began to slow. "Do not make a fool of me before King Aldric again," he said in a low voice. "Or I will be sure to level the field."

Tal smiled, sharp and bright. "I wouldn't dream of it."

"I'm sure." The mage retreated into the darkness and returned with a small handmirror in hand. "This is the cursed object discovered in the King's room. Nothing more malignant than a scrying mirror, but in a king's room, that is a potent weapon indeed."

Tal extended a hand, and Aelyn handed it over. The metal

frame was cold, and as he turned it over, the glass appeared scratched and clouded on either side.

"If you had this, why the excursion into the Ruins of Erlodan?"

"Because the link is broken. I could no more use it to track our Enemy than a broom."

"Assuming the usual antagonist is behind this." Tal gave the mirror one last look over, then handed it back. "Aldric's court seems to contain enough vipers besides."

Putting away the mirror, Aelyn's eyes gleamed anew as he leaned into the firelight. "Every court has its scorpions. But I have already cleared the most obvious subjects. No councilor in the King's Circle nor other close advisor is our traitor here. The greatest of the noble houses, too, appear exempt. If any of them were aligned with the Enemy, it would already be too late."

Tal kept his doubts to himself. "What of a servant? Or an unknown Jahn?"

The mage shrugged. "Perhaps. But this is not the work of a little man. There have been other disturbances of unnatural origin. Some I've felt myself. Others have been witnessed. And you have seen how the Enemy extends his power. Or was that tangle of quetzals not as far inland as you've ever seen?"

The memory of the feathered serpents scattering from around Garin cut through his mind. "'Tis true, I'll admit. But alone, it's not enough."

"It's not the only sign. At least three cases of madness have been reported among the nobility. A whole party of young noblemen swears they saw ghouls in a courtyard on a full moon night. And then there were the matters of sabotage that the King mentioned."

Tal crossed his arms and leaned back, careful to avoid pressing on his side, still sore from the quetzal attack. "It's certainly enough to make you wonder. Alright — say I'm convinced. What did you have in mind?"

"The same as any hunter." Aelyn reached inside his cloak, now a formal one rather than the traveler's cloak he'd worn on the road, and withdrew the white, silken bag that contained the Night-touched pendant. "We'll follow their scent."

Tal stared at it for a long moment, eyes narrowed. "Won't work," he said finally.

"What won't work, precisely?"

"Your plan. It has one major flaw."

"And that would be?"

Tal held out his hands helplessly. "If the Enemy is behind these events, he'll see it coming. He'll feel you probing and have fair warning. Either the traitor will escape, or the Enemy will claim you."

A sneer worked its way onto Aelyn's lips. "The latter will never happen, I assure you."

"Why? Because you have your glyph ward?"

"Because, fool, I am always vigilant and never trusting."

A snort escaped from Tal. "Check your finger and tell me that again."

The mage's lips pressed tightly together. "I underestimated you. I won't make that mistake with the Prince of Devils or his servants."

Tal shrugged. "Either way, your plan doesn't accomplish what we want — finding the traitor rather than driving him off. And we must find him. Only by discovering his identity can we hope to stop all the mischief he's put into play."

Aelyn narrowed his eyes. "I suppose you have a better plan?"

"I believe I do." Tal leaned onto his elbows and flashed his wolf's smile. "We hunt this traitor down the old-fashioned way. Every prey leaves tracks, and we have several leads already."

The mage shook his head. "It's no better than using the pendant. If it's you doing the hunting, they'll see you coming from a mile away."

"Oh, I wouldn't say that. I'm rather adept at playing the fool when I wish."

"Perhaps because it comes naturally."

Tal laughed softly. "No doubt. Now, feel free to risk your sanity if you wish to pry at the necklace — that's your business, and I can't stop you. But tell me what you know first."

Aelyn shifted his legs, a wince showing through his rigid mask. "Very well. Where do you wish to start?"

"The sabotage. I want to know who all would have had access to that bungled supply line and missing war rations."

"I'll provide a list. But you'll be interviewing them for weeks."

Tal tapped the side of his nose. "Not to worry — I have a keen sense of smell when it comes to trouble. Then the ghouls — I'll need the names of those witnesses as well."

"And I suppose you'll want the same for the victims of madness?"

"Exactly." Tal reached over and patted the mage's arm. "See how well we're getting along already?"

Aelyn's fiery eyes swirled, but he didn't shift. "If you want a full list of suspects, you should add Kaleras the Impervious to the list as well."

Tal flinched before he could stop himself. "The Warlock of Canturith? He's Avendor's first line of defense against the East. Why would he be suspect?"

The mage had found his smile again. "If I can be claimed by the Enemy, then that old warlock certainly can. Your 'first line of defense' may very well be a thrall to Yuldor."

Tal had to keep his fists from clenching. "It's possible. But I heard he arrived here a week ago, and the incidents happened before that, did they not?"

Aelyn inclined his head. "They did. But accomplishing deeds from so far away would be no great feat for a magician of his renown. And there remains the question of why Kaleras abandoned the Fringes to come to Halenhol. Suspicious, is it not? It would be prudent to investigate him — just in case."

What do you know? If he could have ripped the elf's head

open and discovered the answer, he would have been sorely tempted. As it was, Tal painted on another smile. "Of course it would. I'll feel him out, just in case."

The mage rose from his chair. "Wait here a moment — I'll look up those names and give you that list."

"But aren't we searching for the traitor together?" Tal called softly after the mage as he disappeared into a dark doorway.

Aelyn didn't bother responding.

After several long minutes, Tal slowly eased from his chair and tiptoed across the fireplace to the shadowed table next to Aelyn's chair. There, he saw a bag sitting, as inviting to a thief's hands as a king's feast to a starving vagrant. Glancing at the doorway again, Tal reached inside the bag and pulled out the handmirror.

Little wonder it had been noticed — it wasn't a beautiful piece of work, but crude and roughly hewn, just sufficient for its job, as if it had been made with the brutal efficiency of goblins. Little more than a hand long, it wasn't difficult to find a pocket for it to slip into. Harder was the replacement object so that Aelyn wouldn't notice it missing. Tal hunted around the room before settling on a small journal that was roughly the same size, if a bit too rectangular for an exact match. But, with any luck, the mage wouldn't touch the mirror's bag again, having considered it useless for their hunt.

When Aelyn returned with the list of names, he was again lounging in the chair, a goblet of wine in hand, every bit the bored dandy. The elf's lips curled in distaste, but he made no comment as he handed over the lists.

His poor opinion suited Tal just fine. After all, a fool could do what a wise man never could, and he intended to do a great deal.

LESSONS FOR A LEGEND

As the door slammed open, Garin shot upright from his bed and stared wide-eyed at the entrance, heart sprinting like a startled doe.

"A fair morning to you, my young friend!" Tal said cheerily as he entered, a tray balanced in one hand. "Can I interest you in breakfast?"

Garin stared mutely at him a moment longer before sucking in a ragged breath. "Did you have to enter like that?"

"Of course not! But I'm an inconsiderate, ignorant, and irrelevant ignoble who doesn't care a whit for others' feelings. Or so I must act now." He winked as he sat on the edge of the bed, sliding the tray toward Garin.

Despite his annoyance, he found his stomach grumbling at the aromatic richness of the food. Bacon, thick slabs cooked to golden crispness, sat next to lard-fried potatoes and leeks, and a small mound of gleaming red berries beside. The plate looked large enough to feed a small family.

"Is all of this for me?" he asked hopefully.

Tal snorted and snatched a slice of bacon. "Not a chance. But half of it is."

Without complaint, Garin seized a fork and began to carve out the larger half.

"Now," Tal said around mouthfuls of food, "to begin your day of lessons — a lesson in perception."

Garin nearly choked trying to respond. "My day of lessons?"

"Of course! You didn't think your education would stop once we reached Halenhol, did you? No, don't interrupt. When playing the game of the court, you must establish a character for yourself and always maintain it. In this way, you maintain your influence over others' opinions of you. If you do not, others will begin to form ideas for themselves, and this is the very last thing you want."

Garin stared at him, chewing as placidly as a cow.

Tal sighed. "You're supposed to ask me why."

"You told me not to interrupt!"

"Your second lesson: Never obey the spirit of any law, and only oblige by its letter when it suits you."

Garin just shook his head.

"Your other lessons," Tal continued, "will begin after you've finished scarfing that food down. I should warn you, though — you may not want to stuff yourself. Getting whacked in the stomach is unpleasant enough when it's empty."

He nearly spat out the food in his mouth. "Does that mean... sword training?"

"Of course! An adventurer ought to know how to fight. But I should warn you: it won't be as simple as thrashing other young lads with a stick. Others may approach you, seeking to coax information out of you."

Garin sighed, wishing a morning of swordplay could be only about that. But here in the Coral Castle, that promised to be as unlikely a wish as a goose feather bed had seemed back in Hunt's Hollow. "Information about what?" he relented.

"About me. Possibly about you as well. But you can't flat out refuse them." Tal cocked his head. "So, we must invent a story for you."

"A story?"

"Yes. Hmm..." He put his hand to his chin as if thinking deeply, though Garin guessed he'd thought this through already. "How about this: You're my distant cousin, recently orphaned, and from a far-off town in the East Marsh. Out of the goodness of my heart, I've decided to take you on and bring you here to Halenhol to afford you every opportunity. Though you resent me and know me for a fool, you're going along with my plans as you want what I can provide." Tal beamed at him. "How's that?"

Garin swallowed his mouthful and shrugged. "Kind of weak."

"You wound me." Tal rose suddenly from the bed, almost causing the whole breakfast tray to slide off. "I'll come by after the sword lesson to take you to your next one."

"Which is?"

The man grinned. "It's a surprise."

Garin doubted that portended anything good.

Once he'd dressed in a simple set of tunic and trousers — or as simple as the wardrobe Tal had provided allowed for — Garin followed him down the winding hallways of the castle. Now that he'd eaten and dressed, he felt eager and nervous. How would he compare to the other young men in training? He doubted any of them would have come from a place as small and far away as Hunt's Hollow. Small — it was strange to think of his hometown that way, but he'd seen it was true as soon as he'd entered the gates to Halenhol. Hunt's Hollow had been the World for most of his life. Now, it was quickly becoming one small part of it.

He set his jaw, pushing the thoughts away.

Coral Castle was sparsely populated at the early hour of the morning, only a few people bustling back and forth down the salmon-colored corridors. Back in Hunt's Hollow, their immaculate clothes would have deemed them as well-to-do at least. But having glimpsed how the nobility dressed, much less the King, and from the respectful nods and bows Tal received as they passed, Garin could tell these were simply servants. And with a startle, he realized they weren't just bowing to Tal — they were bowing to *him*.

A long way from Hunt's Hollow, indeed, he marveled in a daze.

But when they arrived at the courtyard, all thoughts of heightened status were quickly dashed away. At first, Garin thought six boys were standing there, all younger than himself. But as he came closer, he saw that though one of them stood at the same height as the others, he was far from a boy.

The Master-at-Arms was bald and wore a long, gray beard bound into two tails with leather cords. Two swords, one on each side, were belted to his waist, and he wore a scowl that was even more intimidating. As if to make up for his diminutive stature, he was built broadly, a stockiness that suggested strength and endurance far beyond an ordinary man.

"Is he a dwarf?" Garin whispered to Tal.

He glanced back at him with a wry smile. "Half-dwarf, actually. If he had full dwarven blood, he'd be one foot shorter and two feet wider."

Garin shook his head. When he'd set out from Hunt's Hollow, he'd hoped to see more of the World. But he'd never imagined how all the stories would come alive before his eyes.

"Fresh blood?" the Master-at-Arms bellowed as they stepped onto the courtyard. "Come here, boy! You're late!"

Garin clenched his jaw at being called "boy," but talking back to the weaponsmaster didn't seem likely to make a good first impression.

As he walked over to join the other boys, Tal grabbed his arm, stopping him. "Remember, this is the game of the King's court," he said in a low voice. "You must watch what you say, even here. As far as we're concerned, anyone can be a traitor."

"Got it." Garin pulled away.

"Enjoy hitting other boys with sticks!" Tal called at his back.

Garin hunched his shoulders and hurried away, hoping his face didn't look as hot as it felt.

The Master-at-Arms was staring severely at him when he reached the others. Garin was the tallest by far among them, but he doubted it would play to his favor. Odds were that all of them had been "hitting other boys with sticks" much longer than he had.

"Finally," the Master growled. "But next time I tell you to hurry, you run. Understood?"

Garin opened his mouth uncertainly, then nodded.

"That's good. What's your name, boy?"

"Garin. Garin Dunford." His eyes flickered to the others, wondering what distinguished names they had. He doubted anyone as provincial as himself usually received lessons from the Master-at-Arms to the King.

"Garin. Let me tell you something." The weaponsmaster stepped within inches of him, staring up into Garin's face, though his glare made it feel as if he were staring down at him. "Your name doesn't matter here. Be you a sweeper's son or a duke's daughter, you're one and the same to me. And you know what that is, Garin?"

"No, sir."

The half-dwarf squinted up into his face for a moment that stretched out long and brought a trickle of sweat to Garin's brow. "Clay!" the Master barked, making Garin jump before he turned to look at the others. "Clay to be molded as it suits me! Understood?"

Now, the other pupils joined Garin in saying, "Yes, sir!"

"That's good!" The Master began jabbing his finger at the pupils like he meant to spear them. "Jad, you pair with Kendall. Petier, with Haruld. Wren, you're with the fresh blood."

"As you wish, Master," the last pupil said, turning toward him.

Garin stared. Five boys, he'd thought them. But between the name and a second look, he saw without a doubt his partner was a girl. Her black hair was cut short, but her features were petite and decidedly feminine, and beneath the tunic and trousers showed the beginning of curves.

"What are you staring at?" Wren snapped. "Are we sparring or picking our noses?"

Garin flushed. "Sparring, I suppose. But don't we need sticks to spar?"

"Sticks!" The girl snorted and turned away. "Come on. I'll show you where we keep the swords. But keep your stick put away, or I'll snap it off."

As he babbled a reply, Wren cast him a disdainful look and stalked toward the other end of the courtyard. Red-faced, Garin set to follow at a distance, but an iron grip seized his arm.

"Mind you treat her the same as the others," the Master-at-Arms growled in his ear. "Wren is one of us and has the same right as you to train here. Understood?"

"Yes, sir." Though he didn't know what he meant, Garin figured she had far more of a right than him.

"That's good." The half-dwarf released him, and Garin scuttled after Wren.

He caught up to her at the racks. The other pairs had already grabbed wooden swords and shields, but Wren waited, expression bored. "You took your time."

"The master just—" he started, then stopped.

Her eyes narrowed as she looked back at him. "What? He give you the talk?"

"No, no, nothing like that! …At least, I don't think so?"

"Gah!" The girl turned to the rack, then tossed a practice sword at him so swiftly Garin nearly fumbled it. When he'd managed to secure it in his hands, he found Wren standing inches away from his face. He wondered if his breath smelled of his breakfast, and held it just in case.

"Look," Wren said in a low whisper, "I know it's strange for a girl to learn the sword. But you know what? I'm not going to let you or any other moronic boy stop me. My father couldn't stop me — so don't dream that you could."

He had to let out his breath to respond. Had there been garlic in the potatoes? He thought he tasted garlic. "I wasn't trying to stop you," he said weakly.

"Good." Suddenly, she grinned, and he found himself even more frightened than before. "We'll get along well, then. Grab a shield and follow me."

Feeling as if he had two left feet, he staggered over to the racks, grabbed a shield, and hurried after his strange sparring partner.

———

The sun beat down from high noon by the time the Master-at-Arms demanded they return the equipment to the racks. Garin's head felt swollen, and not just from the beatings he'd endured from his partner. They'd received instruction on every manner of form: the proper grip for varying lengths of swords; the ideal footwork for different styles and intents; how to watch your opponent and judge their next movement before they knew it themselves — and a hundred other considerations.

Swordplay, he was beginning to realize, was not like the freeform contests between the boys of Hunt's Hollow, but was as exacting and unforgiving as a courtly dance.

"You did well," Wren said, holding out a hand to Garin. "For fresh blood."

Wearily, Garin accepted it, as he had every time she'd knocked him flat on his backside. "I'm nothing. You're brilliant."

"Truer words were never spoken." Wren flashed him another of those grins that made his insides turn and tumble as he had for the last three hours.

The Master-at-Arms suddenly stood at their elbows, roaring, "Didn't I say it was over? Get those arms back to the racks!"

"Yes, sir!" they chorused as they ran.

When they'd returned the swords and shields, Wren glanced over at him. "Thanks for giving it your all," she muttered. "None of the other boys do. That's why Krador paired you with me."

Garin blinked, taken aback. "For all the good it did me. I couldn't have scratched you if you had both eyes closed."

She snorted. "Flattery will do you well. But don't take it too far."

"Alright." He ran a hand through his sweat-soaked hair.

With a last curious smile, she walked past him without a backward glance. Garin stared after her, dumbfounded, before realizing he had to follow.

Tal was waiting for him at the other end of the courtyard, one eyebrow arched. "Who was that?"

"Don't ask," Garin mumbled, walking past him.

"A girl, sparring in the Coral courtyard?" Tal nodded with a small smile. "I'm impressed. That's one forward-thinking nobleman allowing her here, and I don't say that lightly."

"Can we stop talking about Wren?"

"Wren?" His smile turned to a frown, and he peered after her. "Her ears are right…"

"Her ears are right for what?"

Tal just shook his head. "We'll check before I start spreading rumors. In any case, we must hurry to your next lesson."

"My next one?" Garin groaned. "But Master Krador has already worked me to the bone!"

"Oh, you won't have to move from your chair for this one — it's your mind that's in peril."

Tal swept through the Coral Castle, and Garin struggled to keep up with his leaden legs. He had a bad feeling he knew what was coming but didn't know if he could refuse. In Hunt's Hollow, it had been acceptable to be illiterate; but here, surrounded by Avendoran nobility, he found himself wanting to know and be able to do just as much as they could.

Sure enough, Tal led him to a dim, dusty room from which an older woman emerged. "Is this him?" she asked with a tender smile. "Oh, and look at that growth on his lip! Almost a man, aren't you?"

Garin shifted uncomfortably, wondering if it would be too obvious to cover his mouth.

"Sister Pond is going to teach you reading and writing, Garin," Tal said. "She's a nun, but she hasn't taken any vow of silence so that she could be a teacher."

"And I do so love doing it!" Sister Pond simpered. "Teaching that is. Silence has ever been a struggle for me." She tittered a laugh.

"Thanks," Garin muttered, casting a rebellious look at Tal. The man grinned back.

"Now, my dear, shall we get started? So much to learn for a boy your age! Come in, sit down, grab a quill…"

With a heavy heart and drooping eyelids, Garin followed the old nun into the room.

It felt far longer than the morning's practice by the time Tal returned for him.

"And how was it?" his mentor asked with a grin.

Garin gave him a mutinous look. "Miserable. First, she had me on my letters, sounding them out one by one — I felt like a mooing cow, drawing each vowel out. Then she spoke about the Creed and the Whispering Gods, and how important it was to listen for Silence, Solemnity, and Serenity in every quiet moment. Only, I couldn't figure how she thought there'd be a quiet moment with her around."

"Sounds like you're learning already. Keep at it, and you'll be composing religious manifestos in no time."

"Manifestos?"

Tal waved a hand. "Lengthy, self-indulgent ramblings that gather mad folks to them."

"Like 'The Legend of Tal' songs?"

Tal grinned over at him. "Nearly. But written down."

"Then you've described the Creed. She had me repeat the First Creed about a thousand times."

"Let's hear it once more."

Garin faked another scowl, then obliged, taking on the droning tone Sister Pond had used:

"In Silence, we hear their Song.
In Solemnity, we understand their Song.
In Serenity, we accept their Song."

Tal paused, a thoughtful look on his face. The next moment, though, he masked it with a smile. "I about fell asleep just listening to it once. One problem you won't have in your next lesson."

Garin wondered at that look, but aloud, he groaned. "Will they never end?"

"Yes, in fact — this is the last one. But mind that you pay attention." Tal's expression had gone uncharacteristically serious. "This more than the others taught me things that would have served me well in my younger years. Had I known what you are about to learn, I might have avoided many of the mistakes that led me to where I am today."

"To what? Being a hero?"

Tal smiled, but there was no humor in it. "To being a legend. Which is far from the same thing."

They walked silently to the far end of the castle, far away from the gatherings of nobility or the bustlings of the kitchen. Garin, who hadn't eaten since breakfast, found his stomach rumbling, but curiosity reigned supreme for the moment.

Finally, they stopped at an unadorned door. Beyond it,

laughter and loud voices rang through, jarring against the silence that had fallen between the two of them. Tal glanced at him.

"Ready?"

Garin raised an eyebrow. "How could I be? You haven't told me why we're here."

"All part of the fun."

Then he pushed the door open and stepped inside.

As Garin followed him, a cornucopia of sound, light, and color flooded his senses. Every high-mounted window seemed to beam with delight at the eclectic array of sight and sound. People of every size and Bloodline, dressed in more colors than a rainbow, spoke loudly at each other, or tumbled, or held mock sword fights that were far from the displays Garin had seen earlier that morning.

A man who could only be a goblin — with his short stature, wrinkled, grayish skin, pointed ears, and black, beady eyes — blared a familiar, bawdy pub tune. A big man with skin as dark as coal leaned next to a milky pale elf with blazing blue eyes. Two of the squattest of the company resembled Master Krador, but their girth was broader and their height shorter. He knew they must be dwarves, and one of them a woman, from the pink dress she wore. Garin was vaguely surprised she didn't have a beard, as he thought female dwarves were supposed to.

He wanted to run and hide. For him, this room held far more fear than the Master-at-Arms or even the quill and ink had. Even if there were lessons fit for a legend here, he wasn't sure he wanted to give them a try. But for Tal's sake, after all he'd done for him, he knew he had to.

Swallowing, Garin followed Tal within.

"Ah! The Three-Faced Rogue himself!" Falcon emerged from seemingly nowhere, arms spread, his grin stretching nearly as wide. Drawing up short of them, he made a mocking bow. "Your Great Smelliness!"

Tal put him upright again with a smile of his own. "And I

even cleaned yesterday for you! Never enough for a trouper's sensitive nose. But no matter — I didn't come for a social calling." Tal jabbed a thumb back at Garin. "I need you to turn him into an actor."

"Him?" Falcon's smile slipped as the bard peered at him. "Hm… Even worse off than when you began. You're sure you want to put the poor boy through this?"

"He has a clever tongue and an ear for pitch, though he rarely uses them. With some training, he might make a passable troubadour in a pinch."

That, Garin decided, was going too far. "I don't want to be a troubadour."

They both turned to him, astonishment writ large across their expressions. The room fell silent as everyone turned to stare. Garin felt his face flush an even deeper red than it had before Wren.

"You don't?" Falcon gasped.

"Garin!" Tal thundered. "How could you say such a thing?!"

He was frozen, unable to move, unable to speak, barely able to breathe. He didn't know if he should run or start babbling excuses, but he felt he had to do *something*…

"Kidding," he gasped with a weak smile. "Just kidding."

Everyone in the room stared at him for a moment longer. Then, as one, they burst out laughing.

"Well done, lad!" Tal clapped him on the back. "You passed the test!"

Garin looked from Tal's beaming expression to Falcon's grin to the rest of the laughing troupe. "Test?" he asked dumbly.

"Of course!" Falcon gestured expansively to the room. "A test to see how you would react in an unexpected situation. And you played a role! If that's not passing, then all of us are doing it wrong."

While Garin chewed on that, Falcon suddenly bowed, sweeping his feathered hat from his head. "Falcon Sunstring welcomes you to his acting troupe for His Highness, King Aldric Rexall the Fourth — the Dancing Feathers!"

The troupe gave a cheer. Then, all at once, they were pressing forward, everyone wanting to hug or shake his hand. Names were exchanged so quickly he could hardly keep track of any of them, and though he felt like a juggler who'd dropped all of his balls, he grasped at them all the same. Ox, the big man with an even bigger laugh; Jonn, the pale, blue-eyed elf who stayed closed by Ox's side; Yelda, the dwarfess, a stern-looking actress who told him straight-off she always played the lead female roles; Mikael, the goblin, who seemed to think everything was a joke, funny or not—

Finally, Tal extricated him from the mass of over-friendly players and pulled him close. "I think there's at least one person you'll be pleased to see."

Head still spinning, it took Garin a moment to notice a slight, short-haired girl leaning in the corner, an eyebrow arched and a quirk to her lips. His mouth went dry.

"Wren Sunstring," Tal said with a chuckle, "is Falcon's daughter. So I imagine she'll be teaching you how to act as well as how to use a sword. Sounds like a lot of time together to my ear."

Garin had no responses left but stared dumbly at her. He only knew it for a mistake when she pushed away from the wall and stalked over toward him.

"My surname isn't Sunstring," Wren said to Tal. "If my father can make up his name, why can't I?" She looked at Garin next. "And you. Are you tailing me?"

"Wren, Wren," Falcon said, placing a hand on her shoulder. "We've already had our fun with him."

Now that he saw the father and daughter side by side, the resemblance was unmistakable, down to the green-gold eyes — though Wren's colors swirled so slightly, and her ears were so lightly pointed, he could barely tell she had any elf in her at all.

She shrugged off his hand. "You can never have too much fun."

"Spoken like a true trouper," Tal said approvingly.

That she gave him, a living legend, as cool a glance as she had Garin, made him feel better — if only slightly.

She glanced at Garin again. "Come on. I'll show you the ropes since they're going to ask me to do it anyway."

Looking at Falcon, who nodded, then Tal, who raised an eyebrow as if to say *What are you waiting for?* Garin hurried after her. He had to hide a grin.

A day of lessons could turn out to be not so bad after all.

STORIES UNDER THE STARS

Falcon leaned back and sighed. "Ah, is there any fairer feeling than a rooftop under a clear sky paired with a glass of Jakadi wine?"

Tal smiled and lifted his wine to his lips. Though neither of them could be called young anymore, he'd felt a boy as he followed the bard out of one of the castle's windows and onto an obscure open rooftop. If the space had been meant for any purpose, he couldn't divine it, but it suited their purposes well enough: two old friends, drinking together, and reminiscing over days gone by.

"Perhaps a warm bed with a wily woman waiting in it," Tal posited. "Paired with a glass of Jakadi wine, of course."

"Perhaps for me, old friend. But I know there is only one woman for you, and she's quite cold." The bard patted his arm consolingly.

Tal arched an eyebrow, hiding the depth of feeling awakened by his words. "You make it sound as if she's dead."

"Dead of affection, perhaps." Falcon's eyes found his. "She has a son now."

For a moment, he was as still as the night-shrouded castle

below them. Then he sucked in a ragged breath and laughed. "Well. That's put to rest, then."

"If only," Falcon said wistfully.

They drank.

"Your daughter seems hale and healthy," Tal said, following the first change of topic he could invent, as he poured them each a second glass, finishing off the bottle. "If not quite happy."

The minstrel sighed. "She's restless, that one. And damned stubborn. Sometimes, I wonder if she missed the influence of a mother, and that's why she's as hard as a soldier."

"Then you told Wren of her mother?"

"You know I've always believed in telling the truth. When it matters," Falcon added at Tal's raised eyebrows.

"How did she take the news?"

"With a biting retort, like she takes most things. Sometimes, you'd think she was Aelyn's daughter more than mine."

"Oh, I wouldn't go that far. The only thing Aelyn could father is a thorn bush."

They both laughed and drank.

"But she's young," Falcon mused. "She's at that age, you know. When you think you need to prove something to the World — or to yourself, at least."

Tal leaned his head back, idly finding the constellations of the three Whispering Gods among the stars. "I know the feeling well."

"Ah, but you would. The old feelings of inadequacy from being a warlock's bastard, I imagine?"

He looked around sharply at his old friend, wondering what had provoked that barb, but Falcon's smile was guileless. *A callous remark, nothing more*, he told himself, and let it pass.

"Your Garin seems to be faring fine," Falcon continued, not noticing Tal's reaction. "What exactly is he to you, anyway? I heard a rumor — that you wrested him a duchy from the King. But that's fanciful even for my stories."

"That might be true. If it's what the boy wishes."

Privately, he held his doubts. Duchies never brought much happiness to any of the dukes he'd met, but they did bring their share of misery. And Garin had been adapting well to the traveler's life before they arrived at the castle. *Perhaps you've been more influential of a mentor than you realized,* he mused. *Or perhaps it's who he's meant to be.*

A breeze, cold at their altitude, stirred through the silence, and Tal's wandering gaze found Yoldur's constellation and the four serpents coiling from his back, one for each of the Extinguished, symbolizing their eternal servitude to the Prince of Devils.

Glancing back at his friend, he found Falcon had been touching the dark bracelet he kept under his sleeve but pulled his hand away at Tal's gaze. "That only makes my question as to who Garin is to you all the more intriguing," he noted.

Tal closed his eyes. *I cannot tell you all of my stories, my old friend. Especially not this one.*

Aloud, he said, "Garin came around my little farm in Hunt's Hollow before anyone else. He accepted me into their community for all that I seemed an outsider. He'd listen to the stories I told — believing them all to be lies, to be sure, but he listened. And he has a sharp, curious mind and an unsettled spirit."

"Sounds like a certain man I knew in his youth."

"But maybe he doesn't have to end the same way," Tal said softly. "Maybe he can be different. Better."

"Happier?" the bard suggested.

Tal raised his glass in answer, and they drank together again.

When they lowered their goblets, he glanced inside. "We're going to need more wine."

Falcon leaned over his chair, then righted himself with a grin, a bottle in his hands. "A good trouper always comes prepared."

"Another Jakadi? The King has been generous with his royal actors."

The bard shrugged as he uncorked the bottle and topped off their glasses. "He and the other nobility."

After he set the bottle down, he looked back at Tal, good humor fading. "Why did you come out of retirement, Tal? I thought you were done with all this."

Tal forced a smile. "I thought you might need more material. What have you been up to since you finished my songs anyway?"

Falcon raised an eyebrow, letting him know the deflection hadn't been lost on him. But he answered, "For a time, I didn't write anything. After your legend, tales of lovers twining together in lonely gardens or knights and their glorious deeds in battle had lost their appeal. But then I began to dig deeper." He leaned closer, the gold in his eyes turning quicker. "I began to look into myths of the Worldheart."

"The Worldheart?" His gut clenched. *Perhaps*, he mused, *my old gut has had too much fine wine.* But when he'd only read hints of that word in one other place, far removed from the Coral Castle and the Dancing Feathers, he had a feeling the wine couldn't be blamed.

"You know it, surely? All the power of the World, coalesced into a single stone? And the bearer of it becoming the Sovereign of All, the Master of Time and Material, able to weave the fabric of reality to their designs?"

How well I know it. He thought of the old tome he'd lugged from Hunt's Hollow, *A Fable of Song and Blood,* and the secrets entombed in its yellowed pages. "It was used by the Whispering Gods to create the Bloodlines," Tal murmured. "Each with their measure of time and capacity for magic."

Falcon nodded. "I knew you, of all people, must know its tales."

"But why the Worldheart? It's one of the oldest tales, true, but surely there is little enough about it these days. If it existed at all, it must have been thousands of years ago."

"Ah, but you have not heard all that I have. Drink up, old friend. You'll want a hearty spin in your head for this story."

Tal obliged, the spicy sweetness tickling his throat.

Falcon sat up, his poise adjusting minutely, an actor preparing to give a monologue. "The Worldheart is a stone misplaced. Once, during the Age of Clamor, it rested inside the World, a font of magic that spread to all the creatures living on its surface. Yet it was not to last. During the Ancients' War, the deities we know as the Whispering Gods needed a way to overcome their antagonist, the one known now as the Night. And so they stole from the World its Heart, the source of all magic, and used it to cage their foe into the sky.

"But though their adversary was defeated, the Whispering Gods found their desperate act had reaped dire consequences. All across the World's surface, those who had depended on the World's magic began to suffer and die. The Whispering Gods searched for a way to return the Worldheart to its proper place, but it was a task beyond even divinity.

"Consumed by guilt, they sought to right their mistakes and performed one last feat with the Worldheart. The stone in hand, they enacted the Severing and thereby formed the Bloodlines we know today. Elves, with long lives and sorcery born within them, but slow to change and few seeds in their wombs. Humans, possessing shorter lives, but with ambition bred in their bones, and magic attainable by those with the drive to pursue it. Dwarves, no magic accessible to them but resistant to its allures, and long of lives and stout of heart and body. And goblins, with short lives and twisted bodies, but with clever minds, endless initiative, and the ability to forge mystical artifacts."

Tal snorted. "Why they thought creating the Bloodlines was a good idea, I'll never know."

Falcon raised an eyebrow. "They believed it the only way to secure the future of the World. And who's to question the workings of gods?"

"Everyone forced to live with their acts, I'd say."

The bard grinned. "But our story doesn't end there. After the Severing, the Whispering Gods deemed their work done and the World's future secure, and so they retreated to the sky to continue their eternal war and bring light to match the Night. They left behind the Worldheart, for though they couldn't replace it, they thought it wrong to rob Mother World of such a font of power. But long after the gods went silent, another seized the Worldheart for himself." Falcon glanced sidelong at him. "I believe you can guess who."

Tal found himself leaning toward his friend. "I can guess. But is this tale true, Falcon? These aren't the fanciful imaginings of a bored bard?"

His friend smiled back, but it lacked the wild enthusiasm it usually held. "I wish it were. But I heard this among the Gladelysh elves, from an elder who was as stiff as an old root and could claim over three centuries to his life. If anyone knows the truth of the past, it would be him."

"But it can't be true. Yuldor cannot have the Worldheart."

Falcon shrugged helplessly. "It is what he said."

"If the Prince of Devils has the Worldheart, then how are we still fighting a war against him? Why has he not used its full power to make all bow to him and his cult?"

"Ah, my friend, but you don't know Yuldor as I do." Falcon's eyes seemed almost to glow for a moment. "We've always believed Yuldor a god, like the Whispering Gods, or Jalduaen, patron spirit of the Warlocks' Circle. But I am beginning to understand that might not be true. What if instead Yuldor were a mortal, just like us, before he seized the Worldheart?"

Tal leaned back and closed his eyes. "Then he would not have almighty power even with it."

"Exactly. The Gladelysh elder told me of Yuldor before the Eternal Animus began, of Yuldor the mortal. Seven hundred years ago, Yuldor was a powerful elven sorcerer and well-renowned throughout all of Gladelyl for his power and wit.

But when he delved too far into the workings of the Night, the queen of that time had no choice but to exile him from the land. Robbed of his home and society except for the four apprentices who followed him into the wilds, Yuldor vowed revenge and pursued the only artifact powerful enough to vie against the Chromatic Towers of Gladelyl: the Worldheart.

"Though there's no certainty that he ever found it, and Yuldor was never seen again, it was mere decades afterward that the monsters began to come down from the Eastern mountains, and the Nightborn warlocks we call the Extinguished began to twist the politics of the Westreach. Thus the Gladelysh guessed the truth, and decried Yuldor's name as the Enemy behind the war." Falcon shrugged. "Rumor spread like wildfire until it became all but fact, and all living within the Westreach believed Yuldor was a demon, a god risen from the Night's Pyres to plague the World, and only stopped from destroying it by the continued efforts of the Whispering Gods."

Tal breathed long and deep for a moment, sitting with the story, then took a long drink from his wine. "An intriguing tale. But it changes nothing."

Falcon cocked his head. "Why not?"

"Whatever he is, god or demon or sorcerous elf, whether he possesses the Worldheart or not, he's immortal now, and with the Soulstealers and hordes of monsters at his service. The story of his origins doesn't change that the Eternal Animus continues, and we're losing."

"But you don't see it, my friend!" The bard seized his arm in a tight grip. "If he was mortal once, why could he not be mortal again? If we could separate the Worldheart from him, would we not be able to end this ceaseless war?"

Tal wrested his arm from his grip and stood, draining his glass. "No," he said shortly. "It's a dream, Falcon. We struggle to kill the beasts he sends down from his mountains. We can't even kill the Extinguished, for they rise again after every attempt. How could we possibly hope to steal an all-powerful stone from beneath Yuldor's nose?"

Falcon stood as well, gold spinning in his eyes. "Perhaps your songs are over," he said, lips twisting into a mocking smile. "Perhaps the days of glory for Tal Harrenfel are all in the past."

"I hope they are." Tal gripped the bard's shoulder and squeezed. "It was good to talk, old friend. But I've fought too many battles with the East to harbor false hope."

Falcon captured his wrist in his hand. "We must always have hope. And why struggle on?"

"Why indeed?" he muttered.

He tried freeing himself from the bard's grasp but found Falcon's grip too tight. Tal met his gaze. "What?"

"You're hunting one of the Extinguished here, aren't you?" Though he posed it as a question, there was certainty in the minstrel's gaze, and hunger as well.

But Tal wasn't about to feed it. Though his friend might wish to hunt down old tales, he wouldn't land him in trouble for it. Not when Falcon had a daughter.

"No, my friend. Aldric wants something far more ordinary — just to bolster his reign with my good name." Making for the window by which they'd come out onto the roof, Tal added over his shoulder, "Don't hope for more songs from me."

He caught the bard smiling. "I wouldn't dream of it."

Tal tried to ignore the uneasy feeling that spread through his gut as he folded back inside the castle.

SPARRING PARTNER

"So," Wren huffed between thrusts of her wooden sword, "what's he doing here, anyway?"

Garin, gasping for breath, narrowly parried her blows, then caught a swing on his shield. He could barely think, much less come up with the right thing to tell her. "Don't know," he hedged.

The girl feinted to his right, then spun and whacked his left leg. Garin yelped and fell to a knee, but managed to catch her next blow on his shield.

"That's good," she said, mimicking the Master-at-Arms' gruff voice.

Garin wheezed a laugh. "It would be funnier if you hadn't just broken my leg."

"Oh, cry about it. But honestly — what's the great Tal Harrenfel, Defender of the whole bloody Westreach, doing here? Father said he'd retired. And he *looks* like he retired, hair streaked with white, face wrinkled and tired."

"The white is from scars, I think. Scars from sorcery. And he's not too old to fight. We sparred on the way down here, and he moved like a farm cat. Not to mention he and Aelyn took on a tangle of quetzals."

At the memory, he winced. He couldn't quite remember why the monsters had left him alone — all he could remember was how they'd surrounded him, then he'd been falling, and Tal had caught him and dragged him back to safety. More than enough to remember, as far as he was concerned.

Wren stared at him quizzically. "I wasn't attacking him — just noting facts. What's he to you, anyway? He's not your long-lost father or something?"

"No," Garin said quickly. "I'm not his bastard."

Before the words had left his mouth, the girl was attacking him, thrusting her shield forward then jabbing with the sword. He found himself backpedaling, off-balance, until he landed on his rump once more.

Wren grinned down at him and offered a hand. "No shame in being a bastard. I'm one myself."

Garin had already gripped her hand when he froze. "What?"

"Get up! Or do you want Krador to switch us both?" She hauled him to his feet, and they took their distance apart. "Let's practice Fort-Strike-Fort. You remember it?"

"It's in the name, isn't it? I start with a raised shield, wait to block one of your blows, then counterattack, and finally block your returning blow with my shield."

"You're not too daft to learn after all. But are you quick enough?"

She launched her assault, but instead of lashing out with her sword, she bashed forward with her shield again. Garin tried to keep with the Fort-Strike-Fort technique, but when he tried to strike, he found her sword already whipping in and cracking against his arm.

Yelping with pain and rage, he dropped his sword and shield and clutched at his throbbing arm. "What'd you do that for?" he demanded.

Wren stood over him with a small smile. "My mother was a noblewoman my father seduced in Felinan. It caused a great scandal, or so the other players have told me. After she birthed me, she wanted me thrown in the river, so my father stole me, and the troupe fled south that night."

"I'm sorry." The words sounded limp and inadequate even to his ears.

She shrugged. "Just the way it is. Pick up your sword and shield — Krador is headed this way."

Garin released his throbbing arm and snatched up the sword and shield just as the Master-at-Arms reached them.

"Are we chatting or learning how to not get killed?" he demanded, staring between them. His switch was clutched in a white-knuckled grip.

"Trying to not get killed, Master," Garin said quickly.

"That's good. But the way you're going, you'll end up there. Practice Fort-Strike-Fort! If you're not quick and smart enough to stick your opponent, you can at least not get stuck yourself."

Garin obliged by raising his shield, though he wondered if it was any good. Three weeks he'd been coming down here to the courtyard for three hours a day, and though he'd learned plenty in that time, it was rare that he landed a hit on Wren. Little comfort, too, that he seemed to be catching up to the other boys, as they were all at least two years younger than him.

But, he mused as he blocked Wren's quick lash, at least he didn't have to fumble his way through a conversation with Wren. He far preferred to face her sword than the bite of her tongue.

Garin gave Wren the slip after training, as he always did, and found his way to Sister Pond's classroom. Set against only a book for an opponent, formidable as it was, progress was more apparent, and he was already sounding out words for himself and reading whole sentences. Sister Pond radiated approval.

"Never have I had such a quick student!" she marveled. "You have a scholar's mind, my boy! You must keep to your education!"

Garin muttered a reply, then scurried off. The nun's kindly enthusiasm and support always made him uncomfortable, though he couldn't say why.

But he found no solace in his acting practice at the Small-stage, as the rooms the Dancing Feathers occupied were called. With Wren as his tutor there as well, and with no Master-at-Arms keeping them to their tasks, but only her father yodeling loudly from a corner to the raucous laughter of the troupe, he was entirely at her mercy.

She dragged him to the opposite corner, between two different sets of great wooden frames, then turned to face him. "You didn't answer me earlier."

"Answer what?" he asked innocently.

"What the great Tal Harrenfel is doing here! And why he's brought you of all people with him."

He shrugged, mind turning quickly, but finding nothing to say. He didn't want to lie to Wren, but with her forcing the issue, he wasn't sure what else he could do. Tal had been adamant about keeping their mission secret.

That left only deflection. "What are we practicing today?"

Wren grabbed him and pulled him close. "Don't put me off, Garin Dunford. You're going to tell me what he's doing here, or you can count on my making your life miserable."

"Come on, Wren. I promised him I wouldn't say."

"But you can tell *me*. You think anyone could make me tell a secret if I didn't want to?" She arched an eyebrow at him.

"No," he admitted. He hoped the same could be said of him, but at the moment, he wasn't at all sure of it.

"Then what's the harm? Come on. Tell me."

"Why do you want to know so badly?"

Wren gestured at the knot surrounding her father with a

disgusted look. "Nothing happens here! Oh sure, they all seem marvelously happy. But your father—"

"Tal's not my father."

"Whatever you say. The Magebutcher coming to the Coral Castle is the most exciting thing to happen in years. But though he's been here for weeks, I don't know *why* he's here. He just lies around, drinking wine with my father and a bunch of lazy sons of nobles, and does nothing." The gold in her eyes swirled. "Is he actually a hero? Or did Father make up all those stories?"

"He didn't make them up! I told you earlier that he overcame those quetzals. And before that, he scared off bandits by using magic to make a hammer burst into flames."

"Hm." Wren didn't seem convinced.

But Garin's thoughts had caught on something else. "That name you called him — Magebutcher. I'd never heard that in Tal's legends, but King Aldric called him it as well. What's the story?"

The girl's eyes narrowed. "I'll tell you if you tell me why he's here."

Curiosity and loyalty waged war for a short moment. But after all that Tal had done for him, he knew how he had to answer.

"I can't," he muttered, not meeting Wren's gaze.

She lingered for a moment longer, then stalked off, leaving him alone in the dark corner with his guts twisting together.

Ox, one of the troupers, slipped up next to him, moving nimbly for a big man. "Need to sharpen your skills, my boy," he rumbled in his deep voice. "A girl like Wren won't be easy to please."

When Garin stared at him blankly, Ox laughed. "I speak of the highest art in all the lands, Garin! Of mashing one's lips together with a girl — or boy, we're not picky in the Dancing Feathers — in a way pleasurable for both!"

It took a moment longer for comprehension to settle in. "I wasn't—" he spluttered. "That is, we weren't—"

Ox bellowed another laugh and clapped him on the back, sending him staggering forward a step. "Never fear, lad! Falcon isn't that sort of father — he's a lover, not any kind of warrior. Besides, he knows Wren can take care of herself. Now, the secret to a proper kiss is—"

Garin was already running for the door.

THE SONG

As Tal entered the Smallstage, a cacophony of noise welled up to greet him, and he smiled as he took in the scene.

In one corner, Jonn and Ox were showing Garin how to juggle — or attempting to, for the lad didn't seem to have the touch for even three apples. On the stage, other players of the troupe were performing a raucous stomping-and-singing routine, their accents mimicking those of the provincial Nortveld folk to an offensive degree. He could barely glimpse Wren through the door to the backroom as she bent over a project.

His smile widened. For all its royal patronage and expensive costumes, the Dancing Feathers was every bit the same troupe as when he'd left it.

"Practically a menagerie, isn't it?" Falcon appeared from nowhere, not seeming to have lost the stage trick of stepping softly. "I find they're safer viewed from behind bars as well."

"With manacles bolted to the wall, no doubt."

Falcon beamed over the spectacle with all the pride of a parent. But as he looked back to Tal, his smile faded. "Somehow, I don't think you've come to join in the revelry."

"Not today. I need your help."

"My help? Are you sure that's wise?"

"I can't tell you everything. But if you come now, I'll explain what I can on the way."

A smile curled the minstrel's lips. "A mysterious errand. A set-up fit for the stage, wouldn't you say?"

Tal raised an eyebrow. "Don't be too eager. It only involves a case of madness and poisoning nightmares."

Falcon gestured widely toward the door. "Pull the rope already. Your noose is around my neck."

Garin glanced over his shoulder as he slipped into the back-room. Having only just escaped from Ox and Jonn's tireless efforts to turn him into a jester, he felt as if he were only just taking his first breath since entering the Smallstage. Seeing the room was empty, he leaned his head back against the wall and closed his eyes, letting his spinning mind settle.

"Even I think they're a bit much sometimes."

His eyes flew open to find the room not as empty as he'd thought. Wren's head was cocked and her eyes narrowed, wearing an unnervingly similar look as his mother when she was trying to decide which animal to butcher for the Harvest Festival.

Just as he was wondering if he should have said something in response, she spoke again. "Can you keep a secret?"

It was his turn to narrow his eyes. "I suppose so."

She sighed. "It doesn't exactly inspire confidence, but... Silence take it all."

Wren turned toward the back of the room and beckoned him closer. He followed, curiosity urging him forward into the recesses of the dim room.

They passed between rows upon rows of hanging costumes, between half-finished props and parts of backdrops, to the very back of the room. Garin's stomach turned over and over, wondering what she meant to show him, not daring to believe his hopes, unable to do anything but hope.

Reaching the back, she faced a backdrop of a forest that hung from the ceiling like a drape, then brushed it aside and stood back to let Garin see beyond her. He blinked, staring at the object set upon a squat table.

"A barrel?" he asked dubiously.

"Not just any barrel. A tun." The gold in Wren's eyes seemed to brighten for a moment, then she gestured him in, and he bowed in under the backdrop and squeezed by her into the small space beyond. Though they often had close contact while sparring, their proximity seemed far closer there in the back-room than it ever had under Master Krador's watchful gaze.

Garin swallowed as he stared down at the tun. As Wren let the drape fall back, the sparse light from the room beyond was nearly extinguished, so he could barely see her crouch before the keg.

"It's full of Jakadi wine," he heard her say, a note of smug satisfaction to her voice. "Paid a kitchen boy to haul it up here during supper one evening."

"Jakadi wine." He didn't know what exactly made Jakadi wine special compared to any other wine, but he'd heard enough reverent talk of it to be impressed. "No one's noticed it's here?"

"No one who's said anything to me. Here, hold out your hand."

He obliged and felt the cool metal of a cup pressed into his palm. Raising the cup to his nose, he sniffed, and the scent of spice and grapes filled his head. At Wren's urging, he tipped it to his lips. It tasted similar to its scent, only worse, and he was glad for the darkness to hide his expression. Not something he'd have chosen to drink; but then, he supposed it was the same as with Crazy Ean's marsh whiskey: you had to develop a taste for it, and once you did, nothing else could replace it.

He saw her rise, heard her drink, then chuckle. "Still tastes as bitter as doing penance, if I'm honest."

Garin grinned into the darkness. "If I'm honest, it tastes even worse."

Wren clinked their glasses together. "Then we'd best drink it fast."

For once, Garin found his doubts and worries had gone silent, and he tilted his head back and drained the whole glass.

Tal gestured to the door. "You should knock."

Falcon raised an eyebrow. "Why me?"

"Everyone loves bards."

"Everyone except marchionesses with unmarried daughters."

Tal grinned his concession, then knocked.

The butler who answered looked them over with a scrutiny that showed no trace of impropriety, yet managed to look disapproving all the same. When he was through with his examination, he escorted them upstairs to a study where they found the marchioness waiting.

"Gentlemen," Marchioness Nalda greeted them coolly as she rose and extended a limp hand to them. "How very welcome you are in my home."

Tal took her hand and bent low to kiss it, Falcon doing the same after him. "How very welcome you've made us feel, m'la-dy," Tal said with a small smile.

The marchioness supplied her own smile, every bit as cutting as his, as she gestured for them to sit. "I understand you wish to see my daughter, Teline."

Not one to dance around the fire. "Yes, we do."

"About her... incident the other day."

"The very one."

Marchioness Nalda's gaze slid over to Falcon. "As I understand it, you were there that day."

Tal glanced at his companion and found confirmation in his eyes. *So why didn't he tell me before we came here?* he wondered.

The Court Bard bowed his head to the marchioness. "Indeed I was, m'lady. So you must understand why I am concerned and wish to visit Teline and ensure her health is well."

The noblewoman considered him for a long moment, then gestured to her butler. "Show them to Teline's room. They will require but half an hour to conclude their business, I'm sure. Perhaps it will lay to rest some of the rumors haunting this house."

If this is the mother, I cannot wait to meet the daughter, he thought as they rose and followed the butler out of the room.

A short walk down the hall and a turn into a room later, they entered Teline's room, the butler remaining at the door as a not-so-subtle guard. Tal glanced around the room but found nothing remarkable in the opulence. His gaze came to rest on the girl tucked under the canopied bed, her dark eyes wide, her brown hair loose about her pillow and slightly disheveled.

"Hello there," she said, her eyes briefly catching on them, then wandering past.

Tal exchanged a glance with Falcon and found the bard unsurprised. *He knew her state, or at least suspected.* Plastering on a smile, Tal turned his gaze back to Teline and, kneeling, took her hand from the covers, brushing his lips against the cold, clammy skin. "Mistress Teline, what an honor it is to meet you. I am Tal Harrenfel."

The girl, no more than sixteen, smiled back uncertainly, his name seeming to mean nothing to her.

Falcon knelt next to him and took her hand in kind. "An honor for me as well, mistress. Perhaps you don't remember me, but I am Falcon Sunstring, Court Bard to His Majesty."

"The Court Bard." Teline smiled vaguely. "Such pretty songs you played for us at the last ball."

Falcon bowed his head with a smile. "You flatter me, m'lady."

Both of them rising, Tal studied her, his smile planted firmly on his lips. *Some memory loss,* he noted, *but not complete. Absent-minded, as if distracted by something else.*

"Pardon us for the intrusion and impertinence, m'lady," he said aloud, "but we had a few questions for you. Regarding the day you... fell."

The smile fled from Teline's face. "W-why?"

Tal's smile turned apologetic. "I am sorry if the question pains you. We merely wish to understand what happened, for your sake and for others."

The girl's eyes flickered between the two of them, then to the butler standing by the door. "Alright," she murmured.

Tal glanced at Falcon, who looked to the girl. "Lady Teline," the Court Bard said gently, "might you tell us what happened in the corridor that day?"

Teline slowly sat up, hair falling about her shoulders, eyes wide and staring at her covers. "I was near the east tower — why, I can't remember. Everything's so blurry since..." She shivered before continuing. "I was walking down the corridor — to where, I don't recall — when I heard it..."

"Heard what?" Falcon prompted when she trailed off.

"The Song," she breathed.

Tal felt a vague prickling at the nape of his neck.

"A song?" Falcon repeated. "Was it a particular song?"

Teline nodded. "Oh, yes. But it wasn't like any song I'd heard before." Her gaze slid away from them to the wall, but Tal had the feeling she didn't see the stones any more than she saw them standing next to the bed.

"It had no melody, no chords, no rhythm. No instruments played, and no minstrels sang. But all the same, I knew it was a song."

"What did you hear?" Falcon asked softly.

"Birds. The rustling of leaves. The grinding of stone against stone. Water pattering on rooftops. Footfalls in sand." A small smile curved her lips, and her gaze grew yet more distant.

"And what else?" the bard whispered.

Teline's smile turned to a frown. "Screams. The hiss of blades. The thud of falling bodies. The crackle of burning wood and... and..." Her breath was coming quick now, her eyes wide with horror.

Tal knelt before her, taking her hand in both of his. "It's alright," he murmured. "You don't hear it now, right?"

Slowly, her eyes found his, and she seemed to return to the present. She shook her head doubtfully. "I suppose not."

"What happened after that?" Falcon prompted. "After this song?"

Teline startled as if having forgotten the Court Bard was there and looked up shyly. "Then I fell. Mother told me the warlock was the first to kneel by me and care for me, but he said I wasn't injured."

"That warlock? In the east tower?" An uneasy suspicion rose in Tal.

The girl nodded. "Kaleras the Impervious," she murmured.

"My apologies, sirs, but I am afraid I must ask you to leave."

Tal blinked and turned to the butler, who had taken a step into the room. "Now?" he croaked.

The butler nodded curtly. "Lady Nalda's orders were explicit. If you would follow me..."

Teline barely seemed to notice as they bade her farewell and followed the butler from the small manor house. Only once the manservant had closed the door behind them did they exchange a look.

"Do you have any idea what that was about?" Tal muttered.

"Not the slightest."

"Isn't music supposed to be your expertise?"

Falcon's smile was curiously wide as he adjusted the dark

metal bracelet on his wrist, which had slipped from his sleeve into sight. "Not when it involves sorcery. Then it should be yours."

The Song, he mused as they walked back toward the Coral Castle, rising from the hill above them. *A damned dangerous ballad.* He wondered if Falcon was right; if it was sorcery or some other sudden malady. *Or if it is the Song in my book of fables.*

But most of all, he wondered what it meant that the incident occurred so close to the tower where the Warlock of Canturith was presently lodging.

"Why's the World spinning? Silence, Serenity, and Solemnity, won't it stop spinning?"

The words were spilling from his mouth, spewing around his feeble self-control like a cracked ewer patched with parchment. A warmth spread through his limbs, right down to his toes and the tips of his fingers, and a humming filled his head. Almost, he thought he heard whispers of something, vague hints of familiar sounds, but too faint to detect.

Wren giggled in the darkness near him. A giggle — when had he ever thought he'd hear *that* coming from *her*?

"Drank too fast," she said, her words almost as slurred as his. "Supposed to..." She paused, seeming to grasp for words, or perhaps just compel her numb tongue to form them. "...Savor it."

Garin leaned his head back against the stone wall, a grin slack across his face. "Don't know whether to thank you or curse you for showing me your secret."

"Probably both. You haven't been drink-sick before, have you?"

He groaned. "Remind me never to trust you again."

"But if I remind you, should you trust me then?"

They both laughed far too much at that.

"While you're still in a thankful mood," she continued, her tone shifting slightly, "there's something I wanted to ask you again."

He knew there was something to her words he should pay attention to, but he couldn't quite put his finger on it. The pleasant buzzing that accompanied the whirling was making it difficult to pay much attention to anything. "What's that?"

"Tal Harrenfel. I know he's not just a drunk. I know he's up to something. But for the life of me, I can't figure out what." He felt her move closer, close enough to feel the warmth of her body, so close they were almost pressed against each other. "But I know you know."

He was finding it hard to think, and could only manage, "I suppose so."

"Tell me. I won't tell anyone else — I swear it by all the Quiet Havens and Pyres of the Night."

Garin felt the smile slip into a vague frown. He'd sworn to Tal not to speak of it. But what harm could it pose to tell Wren? She wouldn't tell anyone else. This tun of Jakadi wine was proof enough that she could keep a secret.

"Fine."

Now she did press against him, her leg against his, and he had to repress a shiver. "Truly? What is it?"

He leaned closer, close enough he could feel her breath on his cheek. "He's hunting a traitor."

"A traitor? In the castle?"

He nodded, then realized she couldn't see him. "Yes. But that's all I know."

He felt her lean away. "A traitor." Then she was standing on her feet. "We have to find him, or her. Wherever they are, whoever they are, we have to find them."

Garin rose unsteadily to his own feet and nearly fell back over, barely managing to stay upright by holding onto Wren. Once he'd grabbed hold of her, he found he was reluctant to let go. "Shouldn't we leave that to Tal?" he protested weakly. "Or at least wait until the spinning stops?"

Her eyes gleamed again for a moment. "You have to make a name for yourself somehow. And if Tal can make his while drunk, why can't we?"

As she pulled him out from behind the backdrop and back into the dim light of the room beyond, Garin felt there was a flaw in her logic. But with his body feeling strangely warm and light, the vague whispers in his ears, and her pressed close next to him, he found it hard to care.

THE MOONLIT COURTYARD

Tal kicked his heels up and pretended to take another sip from his goblet. "Thank you for meeting me, my dear peers. A man can never have too many companions to drink with."

"Nor too much drink to drink," Falcon added from next to him.

"Hear, hear!" one of the young men slurred, raising his glass and spilling wine down his sleeve.

"Don't act the idiot all the time," another snapped. "You'll show everyone for the fool you are."

Tal leveled his gaze at the foul-tempered nobleman. Their company, gathered in one corner of the castle's grand foyer, consisted of young men from the nearby noble houses, all save Tal himself and Falcon. Between the two of them, they had produced an illusion of constant inebriation during Tal's now five-week tenure at the castle and thus attracted to them admirers of the most sultry sort.

Sir Nathiel Faldorn, the irritable son of a count upon which Tal now stared, was far from his usual preference for a drinking companion. And despite what he'd earlier said, Tal firmly believed there could be too many drinking companions if Nathiel's like counted among them. But he wasn't there to drown his sorrows or relive "days of glory" through drunk reminiscing.

He had a bargain with a king to uphold.

"Funny you should mention fools," Tal said with a genial smile. "Forgive me, but it's an accusation I hear leveled at many young men these days."

Sir Nathiel rose immediately to the bait. "Who's been saying that?"

"Oh, you know." Tal gestured vaguely with his cup. "People. But you know why, I'm sure."

"We didn't lie!" the drunken nobleman protested, eyes wide, glass tipping toward Sir Nathiel. "We saw them, I swear!"

Sir Nathiel shoved his companion's glass back at him, spilling wine down the man's coat and eliciting a round of protests. The count's son didn't seem to notice as he leaned toward his cursing friend. "Don't talk about them so much, and people will forget," Nathiel hissed. "Understood?"

"But we did see them!" the man protested while dabbing at the wine stain on his coat.

Tal watched with a measured smile. Sometimes, a shepherd had to guide his fold. "I believe you," he interjected.

All seven of the young men looked at him.

"You do?" the drunk one asked hopefully.

"You don't," Sir Nathiel countered. "No one does."

"Oh, but I do. Or don't you think I've seen far stranger things than what the rumors claim you have?"

Even the knighted count's son had to mutter agreement at that. They all knew his legend, of course — it was the reason they'd agreed to gather here in the grand foyer, to brag that they'd spent an afternoon drinking with none other than Tal Harrenfel himself. Young men loved to bask in reflected glory, having not gained any for their own. *And these men are unlikely ever to gain any,* he mused.

"But still," Tal continued aloud, "it's intriguing. How did it happen?"

The men started babbling all at once, the drunk one loudest of all, until Sir Nathiel roared, "Shut it!" When the others had quieted, he continued more quietly, "I'll tell you how it was, Harrenfel. And I swear, by the Whispering Gods and by the sword the King knighted me with, that this is the whole, unadulterated truth."

Tal exchanged a glance with Falcon, knowing they must be thinking the same thing. *Nothing marks a lie like insistence that it's the truth.*

"Of course it is," he obliged.

The young man eyed him for a moment longer before speaking. "It was the night of the Harvest Festival, and we were here by personal invitation of the King. Wanting some air, we took our drink to one of the inner courtyards. It was a full blue moon that night, but I didn't think anything of it at the time, not with Toman here making a fool of himself attempting cartwheels."

The other young men laughed, and Sir Nathiel smirked, but the mirth fled as quickly as it had come.

"The hour was late, but the women had just begun to loosen their corsets, and we weren't about to leave. It must have been about midnight when we saw them."

Tal leaned forward, widening his eyes, playing the intent audience. "Saw what?"

Sir Nathiel leaned forward as well. "Ghouls."

For a moment, they both held their postures, each waiting for the other to make the first move. Tal relented, leaning back with a frown. "Ghouls," he muttered as if deeply disturbed by this answer. "You don't say?"

Sir Nathiel seemed heartened by Tal's response and contin-ued. "That isn't the worst of it. King Aldric was supposed to have been out there carousing with us, but he was delayed. If he'd been in the wrong place in the courtyard that night..."

"Did anyone get hurt?" Falcon asked with an air of concern.

"Not a one!" drunken Toman piped up happily. "It was a

close call for me, to be true, but they were still clawing from the stone when we closed the door behind!"

"Unfortunately with you on the inside," Sir Nathiel muttered, to the laughter of those nearest him.

"You didn't see anything else unusual about the courtyard?" Tal pressed.

Sir Nathiel's smirk slipped into a frown. "What else would you notice when fell creatures from the East are rising from the pavers?"

"A sage point." Falcon nodded seriously.

The count's son turned his frown on the minstrel, eyes narrowing.

"I don't suppose you'd like to repeat your rendezvous tonight?" Tal inquired.

"Tonight?"

"Of course! Or didn't you realize it was another full blue moon?"

The young knight was on his feet in an instant. "Is this an insult, sir?" he snapped. "For if it is, I—"

Tal waved his cup lazily. "No insult, my dear Sir Nathiel. Merely a jest."

Sir Nathiel didn't sit again. "Then let me assure you that our harrowing experience was no mere jest. Though they would have posed us little trouble were we ready for battle, we had been deprived of our weapons. As such, we might have died to those foul creatures." He gestured sharply at the other young men. "Come. Let's leave these two old fools to their posturing."

Reluctantly, the other young noblemen followed their leader, Tipsy Toman lurching dangerously behind the rest.

Falcon raised an eyebrow. "*We* were the ones posturing?"

"To be fair, we were." Tal glanced over at him. "Just not like a cockerel in a farmyard."

"A sight that you're no doubt very familiar with."

"Stuff a rooster in it."

The bard smiled. "I assume you'll be going tonight even without our brave Sir Nathiel by your side?"

Tal sighed. "I'm afraid I must. Someone has placed glyphs there in the courtyard, and they'll keep coming every time the Sorrowful Lady is full unless they're dispelled. And unfortunately, they can only be seen — and destroyed — while they're active."

Falcon cocked his head. "A glorious stand against the Nightkin. Seems a deed worthy of a new song."

Tal held his friend's gaze. "If it is, you won't be there to sing it."

The bard hesitated before he ventured, "I have been in danger before."

"Before, yes. But you're old and slow now, and you have a daughter to save yourself for. Wren would never let me live it down if I got you killed."

Falcon seemed to waver a moment longer, then he smiled. "Very well, my friend. But only because I want to spare you from even the thought of Wren's vengeance."

Tal relaxed. He'd thought dissuading his friend would be more difficult; after all, Falcon had always insisted that, as his minstrel, he should be present for his accomplishments. Now that he had that chance, he'd thought the bard would never take no for an answer.

Perhaps he's getting old and cautious, he mused. *Perhaps I should do the same. Devils know my joints would thank me.*

He rose. "Even if you're not coming, you might help me with a few preparations. Some of which may verge on sacrilege."

The gold in Falcon's green eyes began to turn. "Do tell."

Garin jerked awake at the touch on his shoulder.

"It's just me," the shadowed figure said over him. "Tal. Or Bran, if you prefer."

His heart hammered like a carpenter's apprentice at a nail, but Garin forced himself to sit up slowly. "What's happening?"

"I want you to come with me and keep watch while I do something. Can you do that?"

Night had long since fallen, and Garin was warm beneath the blankets. But he knew he'd made his decision as soon as Tal had asked. "Just give me a moment to dress."

A few minutes later, Garin crept after Tal, seeing the hallways in a new way. They navigated by a tiny ball of "werelight" Tal had called into being, like the light Aelyn had used in the Ruins of Erlodan. The werelight caught on Tal's cloak, and threads of silver woven in intricate patterns gleamed across it. *Like the cloak of the Seekers of Serenity,* he realized. He wondered if his on-again, off-again mentor would stoop so low as to steal from a priest, and realized it was no question at all.

Several times, Tal extinguished the light and motioned for them to press against the stone while the orange glow of a guard's torch passed. Garin found himself grinning. Between the thrill of the game and the fear of getting caught, he was nearly giddy with excitement.

By some miracle, they navigated what seemed halfway across the castle without being seen. Tal stopped at a door and opened it to a chill wind. Garin clutched his cloak tighter around him and followed Tal outside onto a balcony.

As his eyes adjusted to the pale moonlight, Garin saw they stood over an enclosed courtyard. The balcony ran along three sides of it. No guards patrolled the grounds, and the only sounds were from the wind spiraling down from above and the fountain trickling below. It would have been a beautiful sight in the sunlight and was hauntingly pretty in the dark.

Tal faced him and pressed something into his hand, a smooth, wooden handle. Garin raised his hand to see he held a silver knife that looked suspiciously like the ones used at dinners to cut meat.

"In case you're wondering, that *is* a meat knife," his mentor said. "But it's sharp and it's silver, so it'll have to do. Besides, I don't expect you to have to use it unless all of this goes sideways."

Apprehension was quickly dampening the thrill that had claimed him before. "What do you mean?"

Tal turned and pointed down at the courtyard. "At around midnight, when the Sorrowful Lady peeks into this courtyard, ghouls should appear. I'll be down there, waiting to meet them, while you'll stay up here."

Part of him wondered if he should insist on going down with him. The smarter half of him knew better. After all, if he couldn't come close to beating Wren in a sparring match, what chance did he stand against a ghoul? The summoned creatures were far from the worst that the East sent into the Westreach, at least from the tales, but Garin doubted he'd be a match for them.

"What do you want me to do?" he asked.

"Watch. Particularly for where the ghouls appear." At seeing Garin's blank look, he continued, "Ghouls are summoned by Nightglyphs, so those are what I must destroy to stop them returning. Wherever the ghouls emerge from, there the glyphs are inscribed."

An involuntary shiver ran through him. "Right. I can do that."

Tal pressed his shoulder. "I know you can. I should mention one other thing, though: if, by some bad luck, guards happen to come out here, run for it. Best not to be caught up in this."

Garin swallowed and nodded, not quite understanding, but knowing that the minutes were dragging them ever closer to the blue moon's arrival.

Releasing him, Tal turned to the balcony and leaned over.

Then, with a swiftness that stole Garin's breath, he vaulted over the marble railing and disappeared.

Garin hurried to the bannister only to find Tal striding toward the fountain in the middle of the courtyard. He stared below him, disbelieving. The drop was at least twelve feet, enough to break a man's legs. How had Tal managed it unharmed?

Then he saw the gargoyle, mounted halfway down the column, and grinned. To most, it wouldn't look like a foothold. But, even though he wasn't in his prime anymore, Tal was light on his feet. He shook his head, wondering if he'd ever be half as daring as him.

From how his legs shook at imagining what was coming for them, he severely doubted it.

Tal drew his sword slowly. As an honored guest of the King, he'd been allowed the privilege of keeping it, though he'd not exercised the right on a daily basis. A fop might wear a sword to impress, but Tal needed no help appearing dangerous. A full goblet in hand and a drunken swagger had better served his purposes.

But now, as the blade flashed mirror-bright in the darkness, he whispered its name like a lover's to the moons: "*Velori*. You have dark work tonight if you're lucky, and I'm not."

The runes on the sword glowed a faint blue, brighter with each moment they remained under the gaze of the Sorrowful Lady.

Looking up, he took in the lay of the courtyard. Fountain in the center; stone benches in a square around it; doors on two sides, but likely watched by guards; the balconies rising above, twenty-five, thirty feet to either side of him. Not much room for fleeing.

Glancing up, he saw the Sorrowful Lady just inching into

the square of the night sky above. When the ghouls first appeared, if they appeared at all, they wouldn't be at their most potent. Well and good for him — he was out of practice and stiff after weeks of self-imposed leisure.

Tal rolled his shoulders, shuffled his feet, and waited, mentally checking the items he and Falcon had secured for the event. The flask of "holy" water from the Solemn Shrine, infused with power through a full cycle under the yellow moon's light; a euphoric for humans and liquid fire for ghouls. The Seeker's silver-threaded cloak about his shoulders, woven by goblins and imbued with protective enchantments against the Night. The cursed mirror from the King's chamber. The silver knife for Garin.

Everything was as much in place as it could be.

"Tal Harrenfel, nervous about ghouls," he muttered to himself. "How the mighty have fallen."

He glanced up at the balcony and smiled reassuringly at Garin, but the lad had a wild-eyed look and was pointing urgently behind him.

Spinning, Tal saw he pointed at the fountain. He edged closer, *Velori* gripped in one hand, the handmirror coming to the other. He saw them now, the pale green glow of the Night-glyphs as they danced beneath the water's surface. As always occurred around magic, the blood in his veins grew hot, and sweat began to bead his brow.

He ignored his discomfort and held up the hand mirror. The glyphs reflected on the glass, burning bright and clear and as legible as if written on paper.

"Seven rounds," he muttered as he read them. "Is that all?"

But his cursory reading swiftly came to an end. As the glow brightened to the point of being painful on his eyes, Tal secreted away the mirror, backed up, and raised his sword.

They burst from the fountain in a foaming spray.

Ghouls were among the ugliest of the Nightkin. Pale-skinned and vaguely human-shaped, with rotten flesh peeling from their bodies and releasing a foul perfume into the air around them, they possessed an inhuman strength and speed and needed no more weapons than their sharp teeth and long, yellowed nails. Their eyes were like pits of charcoal, and thin, black hair hung lankly from their scalp like seaweed.

His blood now boiling, Tal held his sword up by his shoulder, ready to swing. An axe would have served him better here — rather than relying on strategy, ghouls counted on numbers and fury to overwhelm their opponents. And with speed and strength on their side, the method often worked on the hapless adventurer.

Five of them emerged from the fountain, leaping like puppies taken off their chains. As they hit the stone, they shook off the water and took a moment to orient themselves. Each of those coal-dark eyes found him, their pale, wax-melted faces twisting with rage, and they charged him, galloping along the ground like demonic apes.

Tal swung and spun out of the way as the first leaped at him. A shock ran up his arms as the sword cut through the flesh and splintered the bone beneath, and the ghoul fell away in two large parts, its screech fading to a wet gurgle.

The second and third leaped together, tangling midair, and Tal dodged the one and hacked at the legs of the other as they slid past.

The last two approached from different angles, but with the same reckless abandon. Kicking into a forward roll, he heard them collide behind him; then he sprang up, twisted backward, and cut with an upward swing. One head, its mouth spitting with rage, went spinning to splat against the ground, while the other scrabbled with the body like it was still fighting with it.

But even as those remaining from the first round of ghouls regrouped, a fresh round of five emerged. Tal gritted his teeth and backed away, the balcony's shadow falling over him.

The seven remaining ghouls raced toward him, each seeking to be the first to tear out his throat. As they leaped forward, Tal twisted and cut and dodged, and ghoul limbs and bodies went flying around him.

But even for mindless opponents, they were too many. As the last three charged as one, he managed to cut down two of them in a single, shoulder-numbing stroke. But the third jumped onto his back, nails scratching at the cloak for a moment before it released him with a screech. Tal smiled and wasted no time in spinning and cutting off the ghoul's head. The Seeker's cloak had done its work.

Even as he dispatched the second round, a third emerged from the fountain. Tal raised his sword with aching arms, breath hissing in his throat.

As the third wave rushed at him, he knew he wouldn't be allowed a reprieve any time soon.

Garin watched, barely able to breathe, as the man he'd once believed a chicken herder cut down the pale monsters like weeds in a fallow field.

Over forty autumns he might have, but Tal moved more lithely and gracefully than Garin could ever dream of doing. Weaving in and out of the ghouls' reach, he severed heads, limbs, and even torsos as the ghouls threw themselves at him again and again. He was every bit the legend the songs made him out to be.

But even so, Garin wasn't sure it'd be enough.

Twenty ghouls had spawned from the fountain so far, but just as Garin was hoping there'd be no more, another five sprang from the water. Tal finished the last of the monsters from the previous round, then uncorked a flask and held it in one hand, waiting for the oncoming charge, swaying where he stood. Even Tal Harrenfel couldn't last much longer.

Garin clenched his teeth together so hard his jaw ached. He couldn't just watch Tal be torn apart. He had to do *something*.

But what? All he had was a silver knife and barely over a month of combat training. He doubted he could even kill one.

Then an idea sprang to mind that sent shivers running through his body.

Don't think, he told himself fiercely. *Just act.*

Head spinning, feeling almost as it wasn't him doing it, he leaned over the railing and waved his arms. "Oi!" he yelled into the courtyard below. "Up here, uglies!"

Two of the five ghouls stopped their sprint toward Tal and snapped their heads around, their black eyes finding him. The next thing he knew, they were barreling toward the columns.

He backed away, hand aching from clutching his knife so hard. *They can't climb up here. They can't reach me.*

A pale hand reached over the bannister.

Quicker than thought, he lashed at the fingers with his knife. A screech sounded from beyond the railing, but instead of falling away, the ghoul caught the railing with its other hand and hauled itself halfway up. Garin stared the ghoul in its black eyes, saw the red tongue behind the sharp rows of teeth, the skin peeling off from its sickly frame — and whatever mad courage that had filled him abruptly fled.

He turned and ran.

Bursting through the door to the balcony, he tore blindly down the hall. Through the sound of his gasping breath, he heard them behind him — their eager screeching, their claws scratching along the stone. He had no plan, no plan but to escape and hide and hope they'd give up.

And what? a part of him taunted. *Let them find some other prey?*

But he couldn't make himself stop running, couldn't make himself turn around and face them. He was no man — he was a boy, and it took seeing his cowardice to know it.

And what if they find King Aldric? What if they find Wren? How could you possibly live with yourself then?

Garin skidded to a halt and spun, meat knife clutched tight

in his trembling hand. The ghouls were shadows as they passed through the scant moonlight admitted by intermittent windows. Still screaming, they barreled at him — two, three, four, he couldn't tell, for the darkness hid even their pale bodies.

But he didn't run.

"For the King!" he found himself yelling, foolish even to his ears. But even more foolish was how his heart sang: *For Wren!*

"Die!" he shouted as if mere words could make it happen. "Die, all of you!"

To his amazement, the ghouls suddenly stumbled to a halt, toppling into each other and skidding across the stone floor. Garin backed away, wondering if he should have sprung at their fortunate accident, knowing it was too late to take advantage now. Any moment now, they'd rise and charge at him again. At any moment, he'd stare into the Greatdark itself and slip into its cold grip.

The monsters let out mews like injured barn cats. Then they burst.

"Gah!" Garin stumbled back, landing hard on his backside, but he barely registered the pain. Before him, the corridor was strewn with the ghouls' innards, gore and blood and bile. His head felt as light as if it might float off his neck. Thin sounds, almost like a mournful song, echoed in his ears.

Garin shivered violently and clutched his arms around himself. *Die*, he thought he'd said. But when he remembered the sounds that had torn from his throat, he couldn't place them as words. Not in any tongue he knew.

Around him, the castle was awakening. Cries of alarm, guards' armor rattling as they ran down corridors. Toward the disturbance, no doubt. Toward him.

Don't get caught, Tal had told him. And since disobeying him hadn't gone well for Garin so far that night, he figured he'd better start now.

He rose shakily to his feet and stumbled away.

Tal had read the runes wrong.

He'd realized it some time before, when the seventh round of ghouls fell and an eighth emerged. Now, as the fourteenth wave rose from the fountain, Tal could barely lift his sword. A smile plastered itself on his face, his usual mad reaction when the battle grew most hopeless. A devil lived in him, he had no doubt of that.

But even devils grew tired.

"Come on!" he tried to roar at them, but it came out as little more than a hoarse wheeze. "Come and get cut down like the rest of your disgusting kin!" Not his sharpest insult, truth be told, but words were wasted on the likes of these monsters, anyway; most of Yuldor's Brood were stupid, and ghouls most of all.

And now he was going to be torn apart by those moronic monsters.

He'd tried fleeing after the ninth wave, only to find both sets of doors to the courtyard locked — the doing of the Extinguished, he didn't doubt. Guards had pounded on the door after the twelfth wave, but they hadn't broken their way through. And why would they? For all they knew, the ghouls were fighting among themselves. And most men were wiser than to fight them willingly.

The five ghouls that emerged from the fountain charged with just as much abandon as the first wave. Tal set his feet, leaden limbs trying to ready themselves. The Seeker's cloak was shredded to pieces despite the silver threads, and the holy water was all gone, taking with it the ability to drive them back with mere droplets. All he had was his sword, his wits — well, perhaps his sword was all he had left.

But still, he tried for a weary "*Kald!*" as they leaped at him, blade blazing as he cut through two of them. As his gloves again became singed with the flames, he wheezed "*Lisk!*" and the fire extinguished in a burst of frosty mist. He thrust *Velori* through the chest of a third, its skin stiffening with the biting-cold blade, then drove back the other two with a wild wave of his sword.

As he stumbled back, the two ghouls saw their chance and charged again. As Tal cut down one, the other battered him with a violent strike. But as Tal twisted around the sudden ache, he cried out and stuck his sword through the ghoul's neck, working the blade through the flesh until the nearly severed head tipped its body over to the ground.

Tal staggered back, tripped over a stray ghoul limb, and went down hard on one knee. His chin dipped for a moment, but he knew the next wave would come soon. They were slowing, to be sure, but he was slowing faster.

Lifting his gaze again, he glimpsed something from the corner of his eye and startled. A figure leaned over the balcony above. At first, he thought it was one of the ghouls from before, the ones that had fled up the balcony to chase Garin. Then he realized ghouls didn't wear robes.

Hope, like a baby bird feebly rising from its nest, stirred in his chest. Someone had gotten through the locked doors. Someone who might be able to help stop this madness.

He stumbled to his feet again. "Hey," he croaked. "Down here!"

The figure, face lost in shadow, pointed at the fountain, then spoke. But the words that issued forth were in no mortal tongue. They reverberated and pounded against the stone and Tal's ears like the thundering footsteps of a cyclops, and he found himself pressed to his knees again, hands clutched over his ears, eyes narrowed to slits as he stared at the fountain.

As the resounding chant continued, the water in the fountain began to steam, then bubble, then evaporate. Burning mist billowed out from the fountain, flooding the courtyard and hiding the bodies of dozens of disembodied ghouls and stinging Tal's skin.

Then the barbed words ended, and Tal found he could think and move again. Staggering to his feet, he stumbled his way over the happenstance graveyard to the shadow of the fountain barely visible through the steam. As he reached it, he found the air was already beginning to clear, and as he peered inside the basin, he could see the bottom.

The glyphs were gone, only blackened marks left where they'd been.

Tal looked up and saw the figure staring back down at him, features just visible beneath the hood. Then, with a nod, the man turned away and disappeared from sight.

He kept staring up, exhaustion rooting him in place. Perhaps he should have been devising a way to escape the courtyard without being seen, or double-checked that all the glyphs had been destroyed.

But instead, all he could wonder about was why Kaleras the Impervious, the Warlock of Canturith, had just saved him.

The doors rattled behind him, and Tal slowly turned. The small part of himself not deadened with exhaustion registered that the Sorrowful Lady was disappearing above. Sure enough, just as the lock in the doors clicked, the various body parts of the ghouls began to melt, then sink into the stone, leaving behind nothing but dark gray stains.

The doors burst open, and guards poured out, steel bared and faces hard. Krador, the Master-at-Arms, stepped between them, a heavy, double-headed axe in both hands. As he saw Tal standing alone in the courtyard, his scowl lifted slightly, but only just.

"Tal Harrenfel!" he barked. "You're not who I expected to find when I opened these doors!"

What a sight I must make. Cuts bled all down his body. His stolen cloak was ripped to shreds. But though he could barely stand, Tal put on his maddest grin and spread his arms, the tip of his sword dipping down as his arm gave out trying to support its weight. "I just came out for some midnight practice, good master. My apologies if I caused a commotion."

The guards looked uneasily among themselves, while the Master-at-Arms frowned. "Right. Just you then?"

"I don't see anyone else, do you?"

Master Krador grunted, his eyes still scanning their surroundings. "That's good. But warn us next time you're going to screech like a score of demons."

Tal gave a mocking salute. "Consider it done, good sir."

The Master-at-Arms swept another look over the courtyard and pointed at the fountain. "What happened to the water?"

Tal shrugged. "I got thirsty."

"Damned lunatic," one of the guards muttered loudly.

Krador looked as if he might agree. But he just gestured sharply and led the guards back inside.

Tal watched them leave before he sank onto the lip of the fountain, *Velori* resting by his leg. His chin fell to his chest, and his eyes closed.

"Are they ... all dead?"

Tal looked up to see Garin standing before him. He wondered how long he'd been sitting mindlessly on the fountain's edge.

"I'm glad to see you alive, boy. When they chased after you..." He shook his head, realizing how close he had come to meeting down his apprentice. "But they're all gone back to the moons. They can only exist as long as they're in the light of the Sorrowful Lady. Afterward, they melt back to the Pyres from whence they came."

"Oh." The boy's eyes flickered to the shadowed corners of the courtyard. "Then if they went inside the castle, they might... burst?"

Tal frowned. "Not burst, no. They couldn't stay long outside of the moonlight, but even if they stayed away too long, they'd just melt away. Why do you ask?"

Garin turned his back on him. "Nothing."

He shook his head. A mystery for another time. Groaning, Tal rose to his feet and felt every one of his forty years. But, for a miracle, he also realized that though he had many cuts down his body, none of his wounds were deep.

"Let's go, lad," he said, and together, they walked back inside the castle.

PASSAGE III

If I believed in such a concept as fate, I might be tempted to invoke it here. For those of the Blood seem destined to rise to greatness, for good or for evil. But such a theory might be the result of a bias — for how could we hear of those who never perform any acts of significance?

Thus, I satisfy myself with this theory: that these Founts have, through their actions or by chance of birth, a strain of the World's own Blood running through their veins. And it is this that enables their easy mastery of sorcery that the Heart Races must labor to claim.

Yet this Blood comes at a cost. For though many Founts of Blood burn brilliantly, their lives often end tragically and disastrously. And as there is seemingly no origin to their sorcery and few limits, they have threatened, and will continue to threaten, the very fabric of our society.

I fear what havoc these Founts may wreak upon our World.

- A Fable of Song and Blood, *by Hellexa Yoreseer of the Blue Moon Obelisk, translated by Tal Harrenfel*

THE WARLOCK OF CANTURITH

"...Where could he have gone?"

Garin stood near the entrance to the Smallstage, pretending to study the large framed sets, while from the backrooms, the senior players of the Dancing Feathers continued to speak together, their voices heavy with concern.

Wren appeared from nowhere to stand by him, and for once, the fey mood that usually claimed her was absent. "It's Jonn. Ox's partner."

He hesitated. "That's who's missing?"

She nodded. "Since last night. Ox is out searching for him, but things don't sound good. Father was the last to see him, but it didn't seem like he was going anywhere in particular. He's just... vanished."

Garin's stomach churned. *Last night.* He had an uncomfortable feeling he knew exactly what had happened.

Last night, he'd led bloodthirsty ghouls through the castle halls. Who was to say one or two hadn't split off and found a lone trouper wandering the halls?

Wren was watching him. "You know something. I can see it in your eyes."

He wanted to look aside but knew it would only make him

look more guilty. So he watched the gold spin faster in her eyes.

"I don't," he said somewhat truthfully. He wanted to say more, to admit everything, but he'd promised Tal he wouldn't. As close as he was becoming with Wren, as much as he trusted her, a promise was a promise. *And I have to keep at least one of them to my mentor. Or patron. Or whatever Tal is to me.*

She raised an eyebrow, then sniffed lightly and waved him out the door. "Come on. While the adults are distracted, we may as well have our run of the place."

Maybe it was because he already felt guilty, or because it felt like taking advantage of Jonn's absence. But as much as he always wanted to go trekking around the castle with her, Garin found himself hesitating.

Then she took his hand, met his gaze, and the glistening in her eyes banished all of his doubts.

Tal shifted, trying to arrange his clothes so that they didn't pull on his bandages. He knew his scratching and twitching made it seem like a mound of ants crawled up his body, but he couldn't resist. *Let them kill a horde of ghouls,* he thought blackly. *Then they can criticize all they please.*

Even standing before a king, it seemed, his manners rarely improved.

King Aldric stared coldly down at him from his throne. Around the room, the Mutes were chanting again, their Quietude hiding the conversation from those outside the chamber. On the King's right stood the Master-at-Arms, while Aelyn stood on his left. All Tal had by his side was Falcon, but at the moment, grief-stricken as he was from his missing friend, he would be of little use in this interrogation.

"So," King Aldric said at last. "You made quite the spectacle of yourself last night."

Tal painted a sneer onto his lips, adopting his usual performance for the King of Avendor. "You remember the incident those young noblemen had with ghouls last month, don't you?"

"Of course. I was supposed to have been in that courtyard."

Tal just inclined his head, the smile never fading. "Considering the circumstances, the first assumption would be that those glyphs were placed there in a play on your life. But if it was an assassination attempt, it was a clumsy effort."

"It nearly succeeded with you."

"It did," Tal admitted. "A typical summoning of ghouls lasts five waves. From the glyphs I briefly glimpsed in the fountain, these were modified to bring forth seven. To my dismay, over double that number assaulted me."

A smile of his own curled the King's lips. "Then you must have read the runes wrong."

"Perhaps. But there is another possibility — that the spell was amplified." He looked at Aelyn. "Isn't that right, Emissary Aelyn?"

The mage frowned, but he nodded curtly. "Yes. Through human sacrifice."

Falcon shivered visibly, and all eyes turned to him. "Your Highness," he said, a quaver evident in his voice. "One from my troupe went missing last night and hasn't yet been found. Could it be...?"

Tal placed a hand on his shoulder and squeezed it. "We don't know it was Jonn yet," he said softly.

"But it might be," King Aldric said. "Harrenfel, find this missing trouper, then hunt down whoever killed him." He glanced at Master Krador. "You are to help him as he requests, and to search the castle for the trouper."

The Master-at-Arms nodded. "If he's here, my men will find him."

The King straightened and waved a lazy hand. "Krador, Falcon, leave us now."

The minstrel gave Tal a lingering look as he left, his face a mask of misery. *And for once, he's not wearing a mask,* Tal thought. But, his own performance still underway, he kept his face smooth.

After the door closed behind them, King Aldric looked at Aelyn, then Tal. "Have you made so little progress?" he growled as much as his high, nasal voice allowed. "Murder in my castle! Human sacrifice, no less! This traitor must be found and stopped, or Halenhol will be brought low with scandal!"

"King Aldric, I am making great progress with the cursed pendant," Aelyn said quickly. "I trust it will take no more than a few days before I am able to use the artifact to trace it back to the Extinguished."

"I will wait three days, no more," the King warned. "And you, Harrenfel. That mess in the courtyard — what were you damned well thinking? What did I promise the boy a duchy for if you're going to bungle the task?" He snorted. "Some Defender of the Westreach you've turned out to be."

Tal kept the smile firmly planted on his lips. For once, one of the King's barbs had found its way to his pride, and he didn't like its sting. "It wasn't for naught, Aldric. We learned several valuable pieces of information."

"And those are?"

"First, that the warlock is nearby — in Halenhol, perhaps even the Coral Castle."

"And how do we know that?"

Tal raised an eyebrow at Aelyn, but the mage just smiled coldly back. *More than happy to let me flounder, as usual.*

"When a mage bolsters a glyphic spell with sacrifice, they must be nearby. There's not a set distance, precisely, but it should be well within the city. Additionally, we know a trouper went missing last night. It's reasonable to conclude the Extinguished is behind it and is consequently among us. Here, in the castle."

For the first time, fear, true fear, showed through the King's haughty eyes. A moment later, he masked it with a snarl. "You must find him now, Harrenfel! My life is in danger until we do!"

Tal shook his head. "No, Aldric. I don't believe it is."

As the King's eyes threatened to bulge from his head, Tal smiled without humor. "It was made to seem like assassination with the initial placement of the glyphs. But as I said before, it was a clumsy attempt. The Extinguished have many other ways they could kill you if they so desired."

"How reassuring. Then what of last night?"

"Last night makes it seem as if I was targeted for assassination. But I have reason to believe that wasn't the case either."

"And what *reason* would that be?" King Aldric Rexall leaned forward, seeming like a dog straining at a leash.

Tal shrugged. "My reputation, for one thing. Once, even fifteen waves of ghouls would have posed only a moderate threat. But more pertinent is that here in the castle, I had many sources by which to gain aid." He gestured at Aelyn with a smile. "Like our Gladelysh emissary here."

The elven mage's lips twisted into something between a smile and a grimace.

King Aldric considered him for a moment, then turned back to Tal, calmer than before. "Then what is this cursed devil's goal, Harrenfel?"

Tal shrugged. "I'll ask him when I see him. Or her. But for now, I would appreciate you pointing me to where the Warlock of Canturith currently resides."

The King's jaw muscles worked for a moment as if he were imagining chewing through Tal's neck. Then he reached over and grabbed his chalice of wine, nearly upsetting it in the process. "East tower," he snapped, then drank greedily at the glass.

Tal watched him, his smile growing easier. For how early it was in the morning, the King of Avendor was indulging quite flagrantly in drink. *Is it fear? Or guilt?* He hadn't lied to the King; the Extinguished wasn't out to kill Aldric. But Tal could think of only one reason why Yuldor wouldn't take the opportunity to depose Avendor's ruler while he had the chance.

As little as he liked that inevitable answer.

When Aldric set down the goblet, he snapped, "Why are you still here?"

With a brief nod of his head, Tal took his leave.

———

"Where are we going?" Garin asked as he followed Wren down the halls.

"You've asked that how many times and I haven't answered?" Wren gave him a small smile, but it didn't touch her eyes. *Jonn is missing — how could she be happy?*

But despite that, and despite the other thoughts weighing on his mind, he *was* glad to be there with her. It was their first morning free of classes in the five weeks he'd been in the Coral Castle, and he could think of no better way to spend it.

And with no better company.

Some of the servants and guards gave friendly greetings, all of them knowing Wren, while they eyed Garin with a mix of curiosity and suspicion. No doubt most of them knew he'd come with Tal. And with the reputation he'd gathered for himself, it was no wonder people stared. He was a legend turned drunkard, from what anyone could tell, and a madman on top of that as news of last night's expedition spread. The only problem was that it drew attention to Garin, too. And attention was the last thing he wanted.

As much as he tried not to think about it, his thoughts went back to the ghouls exploding, and the strange, discordant sounds in his head. Had he imagined the whole thing? Was he going as crazy as Tal was said to be?

"You're quiet."

Garin shrugged. "Not really the kind of time to be talkative, I guess."

Wren gave a somber nod.

They passed the busiest parts of the castle and ventured into parts he hadn't yet seen. The stone corridors echoed with their footsteps. The suits of armor periodically posted like ghostly sentinels became dustier and lacked the exquisite polish of the main halls. The tapestries hanging from the walls that depicted battles and myths from Reach history became faded and moth-bitten around the edges. But still, Wren led them on.

At length, she pointed to a doorway. "Know where that leads?"

He tried picturing where they were from outside the castle. "A tower?"

She nodded. "Usually, a Magister of the Warlocks' Circle occupies it, to be on hand to advise and assist the King. But right now, it's Kaleras who's taken up residence."

"Kaleras? The Warlock of Canturith?"

"Is there any other? But we don't want to go in there — he'd probably blow us up before we'd crossed the threshold. This way."

The hallway she led him down now was as dusty as any he'd seen and seemed to lead nowhere. But when they reached a wide window, Wren pressed her hands around the edges, found a latch, and swung it noiselessly open.

"Someone keeps the hinges oiled," he observed.

"My father showed me this spot. Look — you have to see the view!"

Garin watched apprehensively as she opened the window wider to a gust of wind and stepped out. Peering out after her, he saw a narrow ledge, no more than two feet wide, just outside the window. His stomach did flips watching Wren slide nimbly out onto it.

She looked back and saw him hesitating inside. "Don't be a cat in a stable! Come on!"

He set his jaw. *If I can face three ghouls, I can step out of a window.* Besides, he knew he'd never live it down if he didn't follow her now.

"Just don't look down while you're moving!" Wren shouted over the wind. "And lean toward the wall!"

Knowing there was nothing for it, Garin held his breath and stepped out. A squall billowed around him, unsettling his balance. For one thrilling moment, he thought it would sweep him from his feet and send him tumbling far, far below. Then he leaned toward the castle and felt the pressure of cold stone beneath his hands and exhaled shakily.

Wren's hand closed over his arm. "Don't worry — I have you."

As she held onto him like a mother her small child, he felt it should have bruised his pride, but he found it hard to mind.

A dozen feet past the window, the ledge widened just enough to be comfortable. Wren settled down, feet dangling over the edge, and Garin sat cautiously next to her. He breathed another sigh of relief and was glad when Wren didn't take her hand away from his arm.

She pointed with her free hand. "Now look!" she said with a wild grin. "Didn't I say you had to see it?"

Garin looked out. Halenhol stretched out in all directions below them, a checkered landscape of red, tan, and orange roofs. Tens of thousands of people — hundreds of thousands, even — lived there below him, all of them with their cares and concerns, with only this city held in common. Miles away, the city walls rose white and gleaming in the sunlight, and beyond that, the gold and green fields of farms were on colorful display. A shining river ran through them, stretching to the distant forested hills where the Ruins of Erlodan hid. The hills receded into a blue haze, then seemed to fall off the World altogether. Above them, puffy white clouds, like giant tufts of wool from the largest sheep ever bred, dotted the berry-blue sky.

"Night take me," he breathed.

She leaned closer to him and spoke in his ear over the incessant gale. "Father would take me here sometimes when the winds had died down. He'd play the lute and sing songs of far-off places. Often, he sang of your secret father. Always was proud of composing his legend."

Garin gave a low laugh. "Tal's not my father."

Despite the scene stretching before him, his mood grew somber as he thought of his actual father. When he'd last seen him, he'd been four, and Father had knelt before him, told him to be good for his mother, then ruffled his hair and left for war. He'd been sure he'd return, sure as only young children could be.

But he hadn't.

"What were you thinking of?" Wren asked.

"My real father. How he looked the last time I saw him." He glanced sidelong at her, conscious of her warmth pressed against his side. "Do you ever wonder about your mother?"

He felt her shrug against his shoulder. "Sometimes. I've asked Father about her twice, but he never had much to say beyond what I've already told you. They didn't know each other well. It was just..." She shrugged again. "An accident."

"Accidents don't have to be bad."

"Oh?" She arched an eyebrow at him. "And was I a good or bad accident?"

Her hand that wasn't holding his arm was resting on the leg closest to him. As he reached to take it in his, he felt braver than he had when he'd stood against the ghouls.

"We'll see," he said with a slow grin.

Tal stopped before the door to the east tower. Long had he loathed stepping foot within towers, and long had he avoided it. Too many dark memories within rooks had led him to skirt around them when he could. But now, he knew it couldn't be helped.

Taking a breath to master himself, he knocked.

The silence stretched for several long moments. He was just about to knock again when a man's voice, aged but strong, called out, "Come in!"

He tentatively set his hand to the handle, half expecting it to catch on fire, and pushed the door open.

The man sat facing the opposite wall, a desk before him filled with an assortment of strange objects. Books with strange drawings. Vials filled with unidentifiable fleshy parts. Glass orbs with white, feathery substances suspended within them. A glance around showed the rest of the tower filled with similarly odd items. Tal's lips curled. If he hadn't already known who occupied the east tower, their surroundings would have been clue enough.

"I'm disappointed," he said to break the silence. "I thought you'd set better defenses than that."

"I did," Kaleras said without turning. "But you've forced me to dismantle them."

Tal stepped further in. Despite the hour of the morning, the tower was dimly illuminated, for Kaleras had drawn curtains over many of the narrow windows. The spiral staircase that ran around the edge of the tower ascended into shadow.

"What is it with magicians and towers?" Tal wondered aloud. "Do they need everyone to not only look up to them figuratively, but physically?"

"The farther we can see, the farther our workings reach."

Tal peered over the warlock's shoulder to see he did nothing more mystical than writing a letter, and in ordinary ink. "A lover's correspondence?" he said, spiking the words with hidden intent.

Kaleras set the quill back in its stand and turned to face him. His hair, once a tawny red mane, had faded to a thinning silver curtain hanging past his shoulders. His face still retained some of his handsome features, but age, scars, and a magician's worries had lined and hollowed it, and his skin hung loosely about his jowls.

"This is a strange way to begin a thank you," the warlock said finally.

"And why should I thank you?"

Though there was no swirl of the elven Bloodline to his eyes, the Warlock of Canturith still had a glare to match any Gladelysh sorcerer. "I never could tell how much of you is an act and how much you truly are a fool."

"I couldn't tell you either. But if you're referring to last night, I'm not sure I have anything to thank you for yet."

"Didn't I save your life?"

"In a manner of speaking. So long as you weren't the one to first endanger it."

They matched stares for a long moment. Though Tal was plenty aware that the man could kill him with a few muttered words — and had come very close to doing so in the past — he found it wasn't difficult to hold his gaze. Anger, cold and long-simmering, had carried him this far.

"If you have an accusation against me, speak it," Kaleras said coldly.

"I have no qualms with you, Magister — or what should I call you, since you were ejected from the Circle?"

"My name never fails."

"Just 'Kaleras'?" Tal shook his head mournfully. "You may just as well announce you've lost all sense of dignity. Regardless, you do seem to have fallen in reputation. Some are beginning to mutter that you're involved with… things. Dark things."

"'Dark things?'" Kaleras laughed, barking and sharp. "Nothing half as much as you know."

"Then the rumors are true? That you've been touched by the Night?"

Kaleras suddenly stood before him. "Is that what you believe? That I'm one of Yuldor's Kin? That the Extinguished have turned me to their side?" His voice dropped lower. "That I am one of the Soulstealers themselves?"

"Why not? You're foul enough for it."

The warlock studied his eyes for a long moment. Then, his mouth twisting in disappointment, he turned away.

"Not all that smells fair is pure, nor all that reeks is rotten." Kaleras raised his hand, the long sleeve falling back from it. In the low light, a circle of dark metal gleamed on his finger, a scrawling script glowing in soft green across it.

Tal laughed softly. "So you haven't misplaced it yet, old man?"

He lowered his hand again, expression spasming with annoyance. "I have worn the Ring of Thalkuun since I took it from you all those years ago."

"Since you stole it, you mean."

Kaleras' eyes seemed to gleam. "Perhaps we shouldn't dwell on old crimes, Magebutcher."

It always stung, that name. But coming from him, he who had witnessed his greatest failing, Tal found himself fighting hard to stay above the panic rising in his chest.

He cleared his throat, and when that didn't do the trick, cleared it again. "Of course not. I wouldn't want you to think your life in danger. But..." No matter how he worked his cheeks, the smile kept slipping away. "Why didn't you kill me that day?" he suddenly asked.

The aged warlock studied him with his hawkish eyes. He didn't ask which day; he already knew. "I couldn't. Not by any moral failing," he added at Tal's raised eyebrow. "The ring protects its wearer from indirect magic as well — magic darts, ensorcelled boulders, the like. It has to be at least two steps removed for it to potentially work around the protective enchantments. When I collapsed the Circle chamber, the ring protected you from harm, but it incapacitated you long enough for me to pry the ring from your hand."

"Yet you didn't leave me in the chamber to die. You dug me

out."

It was Kaleras' turn for a wry smile. "I didn't *dig*, Harrenfel. But yes, I uncovered you." The smile disappeared, and he looked aside. "But not to save you."

"Why, then?"

The warlock studied the wall. "I used you to find the Extinguished who had enthralled you. And after he had cast you aside, I pursued him. And destroyed him."

Tal stared at him. *I should have known. Perhaps I am the fool I pretend to be.* "I was bait. The hook to reel in the big fish."

"In a manner of speaking."

Tal turned away, swallowed, and shook his head as if that could rid him of the thoughts circling his head. He knew he shouldn't open his mouth, knew he shouldn't speak of it, but his iron grip of control had rusted away over the years.

"Do you know?" He said it to the door, not daring to turn and face the warlock. "Did you know then?"

"Know what?"

Was it his imagination, or was there a hint of the knowledge Tal hunted for in his words? Tal smiled bitterly to himself and felt the vault door rolling back into place over that long-hidden hurt.

"Never mind, old man. Just don't fall prey to the Extinguished, would you?"

Leaving explanations unspoken, he sauntered out of the door.

Garin watched Tal stride from the warlock's tower, eyes wide.

"What's he doing here?" Wren whispered in his ear.

He shook his head. "Don't know."

After his footsteps had echoed down the hall, Wren motioned him forward, and Garin crept after her. As they passed the worn door of the tower, he paused and stared at it.

Why *had* Tal visited the Warlock of Canturith? Did he suspect him of being the traitor?

The door swung open.

Garin startled, wondered if he should run for it, but found himself rooted to the spot. In the doorway stood Kaleras the Impervious, staring at him, a scowl etched into his lined face.

"You," the old warlock said. "You came here with Tal Harrenfel."

Garin nodded, his body cold with sweat. Even if it hadn't been common knowledge, he wouldn't have dared to lie to a warlock.

"What are you to him? His bastard, I suppose?" His lips twisted into a mocking smile.

Garin swallowed. "No, uh, sir. We're just friends, I suppose."

The warlock looked as if he would spit, then his eyes seemed to widen and see Garin for the first time. Garin took a step back as the elderly man's deep brown eyes suddenly seemed to have a cast of gold to them. For a moment, he thought he heard a distant clamor, and cold shivered through him.

Then the warlock blinked, and the coldness passed. But the relief was momentary as the mage's scowl returned, more pronounced than before. He turned away but paused before closing the door. "Pass him a message, boy. Tell him to be wary of everyone in the Coral Castle. Even those he feels he can trust."

Garin swallowed and backed away. "Yes, sir."

Without looking around, the Warlock of Canturith closed the door. Garin wanted to double over and gasp for breath.

"What was that about?" Wren demanded in a whisper.

"Don't know." He turned away. "Come on — we'd best not linger outside his door."

But as he walked quickly away from the tower, the clammy stickiness of his palms told Garin he knew exactly what that had been about.

THE BLOODY CIRCLE

"Stop, just stop!" Falcon waved his arms, his irritation permeating the Smallstage with every movement.

Garin halted with the rest of the troupers and stared at the bard, wondering if his foul mood would ever stop. Though, if it had carried on for two weeks, he doubted there was an end in sight. Wisely, the players of the Dancing Feathers bent around the Court Bard's temper, leaping to obey when Falcon demanded that they clear the stage.

Wren slipped next to Garin as he shrugged out of his page's uniform, which fit tightly and loosely in all the wrong places. "He's a bouquet of lemons, isn't he?" she noted.

"Still because of Jonn?"

"That, and Ox is still out there searching for him — he'd have made a far more believable traitor than Mikael. But our performance of *Kingmakers and Queenslayers* isn't making things any better."

Wren slipped off her costume as a young nobleman, unveiling her underclothes with as little shame as the rest of the troupe. Garin quickly looked away, trying to move his thoughts back to safer waters, but they kept straying back to the brief glimpses he'd stolen of her bared skin.

"Why put on a show anyway?" she continued, oblivious to his observations, her voice muffled as she shrugged on a tunic. "Avendor will carry on skirmishing with Sendesh come spring. Why bother with the pretense?"

Garin shrugged. "For the spectacle, maybe. Or maybe King Aldric wants to make use of the troupe he pays for."

She snorted lightly. "Kings and their expectations. Take a coin from a king, and he owns you — that's what Father says, anyway. Funny how he ended up doing it, though."

"Maybe being bound for life isn't so bad."

Wren turned her gold-green eyes on him. "Bound to serve someone else until the end of your days? Is that really the life you want?"

Garin didn't know what he wanted. At the moment, not returning to a certain moonlit courtyard in his dreams every night, forgetting the ghouls spraying their innards across the castle corridor, would have been enough for him.

"No, I guess not."

"Don't sound too sure," she said mockingly. "I know *I* don't. When I'm seventeen and my own woman, I'm going to travel the span of the Westreach."

Hadn't he wanted the same thing, to travel and see the World, just months before? Now, he wondered if he'd seen too much.

Aloud, he said, "That's only two years away."

"Only? It can't come soon enough." Dressed again, she turned and faced him, a hand on her hip. "But you only just got here. You probably still think it's wondrous and all that nonsense."

If only she knew how little I believed that. He tried on a smile. "Something like that. But I guess this castle is as small to you as Hunt's Hollow felt to me. We want something other than what we're used to, I suppose."

She cocked her head. "Is that why you came, then? With Tal?"

"Why else? I felt closed up in my town. Though I thought I'd seen a lot when I first left because I'd visited all the towns in the East Marsh."

Wren laughed — a loud, raucous sound that he found he wanted to hear more of.

"Just wait," she said. "Someday, we'll see far more than that."

His heart tripped over its next beat. *We?* Did she mean by that word what he thought, what he hoped?

She was watching him, lips still curved in a smile. "Who does Tal think the traitor is?"

That was a turn he had hoped they wouldn't take. When he'd woken the day after they'd drunk from the tun, his stomach sour and his head feeling as if it had been stuffed inside too small a skull, he'd hoped he'd imagined his revelation to Wren. But he'd always known it had been a fanciful hope.

Still, the truth was that he didn't know any more than she did. Since the courtyard incident, Garin had wanted nothing more than to stay away from Tal's hunt for the traitor, and not just because he feared running into more ghouls. He had done and seen things, unnatural things. And he had no desire to repeat them.

"I don't know," he muttered.

Wren didn't bother hiding her disbelief. She leaned in closer, and despite himself, he breathed in her scent, earthy and sweet and floral at once.

"Tell you what," she said in a low voice. "You tell me what Tal has learned from his probing about the castle, and in exchange, I'll tell you what makes him the Magebutcher. Agreed?"

Garin only hesitated a moment. It was trading a penny for air, as the saying went. But though he was tricking her, he knew he didn't have to feel bad. After all, it didn't take him long to figure out why she'd questioned him about Tal after filling him up with Jakadi wine.

He shrugged, trying to hide his eagerness. "Fine."

A grin split her face, wide and bright, and under that smile, he found it hard to breathe.

"Then let's go," she said, turning. "Father can orate it far better than I ever could, and telling a Tal story might put him in a better mood."

Following her from the corner, Garin felt a pit forming in his gut, and not for tricking Wren. For some reason, he felt guilty seeking out this story, as if it were a betrayal to Tal. *No more of a betrayal than revealing what I promised him I wouldn't,* he thought wryly.

But the way everyone said that name, Magebutcher… He had to know.

"Father!" Wren had the note of command as she strode up to her father, springy hair bouncing with every step. "Garin hasn't heard the tale of why Tal is called the Magebutcher."

Falcon Sunstring, who had been staring morosely from the set and nursing a goblet of wine, looked up. "Has he not indeed? Come around, then, sit. It's a tale you ought to know, though I can understand why Tal wouldn't want to tell you."

Unable to think of a response, Garin sat on the floor and looked up expectantly, feeling like a child sitting around a fire before an elder's story. Overhearing, other actors began to drift closer, waiting for the story to unfold.

The bard gazed around at his audience for a long, silent moment. Then, without preamble, he began.

"Tal had only just begun to earn a name for himself when he came to the Warlocks' Circle. Only twenty-one autumns old, tales were already circulating about him. How he'd slain Heyl, the demon who had set fire to half of Elendol. How the Queen of Gladelyl had beseeched his aid in tracking down the Silver Vines, a branch of the Cult of Yuldor that had spread throughout the elvish realm. How he had succeeded in infiltrating the syndicate and even killed one of the Extinguished themselves.

"These rumors, however, hadn't reached the Circle by the

time he arrived there. And so when Tal Harrenfel laid accusations of a warlock's murder, a warlock he claimed had been his secret mentor two years before, at the feet of the Cult of Yuldor, and that the Cult had a hold inside the Circle itself, the warlocks were torn between laughing him out and smiting him where he stood.

"The loudest to scoff was Magister Kaleras. Later, Kaleras would break ties with the Circle and rise to become the Warlock of Canturith to hold the Fringes against the East, but at that time he was equal with the rest. He bade that the Circle lock up the young fool until he'd learned to hold his tongue among his betters. But not all agreed with Kaleras, and to Tal's gain, the Elder Magister wished no harm on him. So it was that the old warlock drew him aside, listened to his pleas, and heeded him. Long had he grown uneasy by the growing sympathies of the Circle with the East, and so Tal's accusations struck close.

"The Elder Magister was a cautious man with more than a century to his life, but he knew he could delay no longer. So he told Tal that if he wished to gain justice for his mentor's murder, he must retrieve an artifact that would protect him even from the workings of warlocks: he must steal the Ring of Thalkuun from the Queen of the Hoarseer goblins.

"And so Tal went to the edge of Reach lands, all the way to the Fringes of the East, snuck his way into the Hoarseer Lair, and stole the ring from the Hoarseer Queen. How he did that is another story, and how he earned the name Ringthief. Let it suffice to say that he managed it — but not without great cost.

"For someone lay in wait. The Hoarseer Queen was not allied with the rest of the Bloodlines of the Westreach, but with the East, and a Soulstealer stood as her councilor. Though Tal managed to worm his way into her throne room, he could not escape the influence of Yuldor's servant. Long he struggled, but in the end, he succumbed to the subjugation of the Extinguished."

Garin stared, wide-eyed, wondering if any of this could be true. "How?" he blurted. "How could he have fallen under the influence of the Extinguished and still be alive?"

Falcon turned a sharp smile on him. "Hear the rest of my tale, and you will know."

Wren arched an eyebrow at him, and Garin muttered, "Sorry." But he couldn't silence the anxiety swirling through him, nor the vague sense of doubt.

"As I was saying," the bard continued, his gaze sweeping over the rest of the company, "Tal became a slave to the Extinguished. But the servants of the Night's Puppeteer are clever and cruel, and so he gave him the Ring of Thalkuun to bear back to the Circle, and commanded him to put it on. And though he wore it, and it protected him from all further workings of magic, it couldn't negate the fell sorcery already placed upon him.

"So Tal returned to the Circle, and the Elder Magister, astonished at Tal's accomplishment, gathered the Circle to witness the presentation of the ring. But once they had gathered, Tal drew his sword and slew every warlock there, to the last of them, including the Elder Magister who had believed in him and trusted him."

Garin felt his throat close up. "Magebutcher," he whispered.

Falcon nodded slowly. "So he earned his name. Not all of the Circle had shown for the gathering, however. Kaleras, delayed by an errand of his own, returned to find his peers slaughtered, and Tal, with his sword still bloody, sitting at the Elder Magister's table, a terrible smile on his lips, the Ring of Thalkuun glinting darkly on his finger. Kaleras immediately understood what had happened and knew better than to pit his power against the artifact. Instead, he sealed the doors to the gathering chamber shut and collapsed it, seeking to bury Tal within.

"By what miracle Tal survived, not even he could tell. From what he's told me, his memories of his time under the Soulstealer's influence are hazy. All he knew was that suddenly, everything came into sharp clarity, and he stood outside the chamber, clothes stiff with dried blood and dust, and the Extinguished stood before him. 'How did he take the ring?' the fell warlock demanded of him. 'How did Magister Kaleras survive where the others did not?'

"But Tal could not tell him. He had no memories of the encounter, but when he looked down, the Ring of Thalkuun was no longer on his finger.

"In his rage, the Extinguished sought to make him suffer. And so he told him of all that Tal had done — how he had slaughtered the Circle, down to the old Elder Magister. And though the bodies were buried within the chamber, Tal knew it to be true from the blood upon him. He sank to his knees. 'Kill me,' he begged. 'I can't live with this guilt.'

"But Yuldor's servants are cruel to their cores, and all the more when you have drawn their ire. And so, though death would be punishment, the Extinguished deemed it far worse to let him live, a broken man to be hunted by those who remained of the Circle until the end of his days."

Falcon fell silent. No one stirred.

Garin drew in a ragged breath. "Is that it?"

The bard shrugged. "Hardly. Afterward, he came to us, the Dancing Feathers, his mind feeble and his morals lost. But after another encounter with Kaleras the Impervious, as the warlock became known afterward, he fled as far north as he could in the Westreach. Then came the years when he was a mercenary for the dwarves, fighting the horrors that spawn from the Deep and earning the dwarven name *Khuldanaam'defarnaam*, which means 'He Who Does Not Fear Death, For He Is Death's Hand.' And the years after, when he fought the northern marauders with such reckless bravery and brutality that he earned the name Red Reaver. Years when his name spread, to be sure, but years when he barely knew the face he saw in the mirror."

Garin remembered Tal in the courtyard, chopping ghouls

apart, a savage grin on his lips. *That's part of him*, he realized. *The warrior. The butcher.* He wondered if he truly knew his wanton mentor.

But he hadn't just known him as Tal; he'd also known Bran the Chicken Farmer. Bran, always breaking out a smile no matter how hard the labor, ever making him laugh with obscene jokes. Bran, who slipped him sweets and sent home freshly roasted chickens for his family's table.

The kindness and the killer — they're both part of him. The realization didn't make the man as strange as he'd thought it would. Knowing what demons lay behind that haunted look of Tal's finally made Garin feel as if he was truly beginning to know his mentor.

As he rose, he found Falcon was watching him closely, the fingers of one hand tapping the wrist of the other.

"Thank you," Garin said, uncomfortable under his scrutiny. "For the story."

The Court Bard smiled, but it wasn't soft with his usual humor, but somehow sharp and brittle. "One of the truest I've ever told. And the most illustrative of my old friend, to be sure."

Uncertain what to say to that, Garin turned away. But before he'd taken two steps, Wren had seized his arm and was pulling him out of the door. Only when they were in the hallway did she speak.

"You should have told me!"

"Told you?" Garin asked, perplexed. "Told you what?"

"The King — if Tal is still here in the castle, and he's tracking a traitor for the King, it can only be one enemy." Her eyes were wide, the gold frantically spinning in them, as her voice dropped to a whisper. "He's hunting one of the Extinguished. Here, in the castle."

Garin stared at her, his mouth dry. He'd known there was a traitor. But as he thought over her words, he saw how obvious it should have been now. The visit to the Ruins of Erlodan, the knowing glances between Tal and Aelyn, the King's concern — it could only have pointed toward the worst of Yuldor's servants.

"They can enthrall people to their service," Wren continued, eyes dancing back and forth to make sure no one else was nearby. "They can take on other faces. That means they could be anyone in the castle. And Jonn! Garin, don't you see? The Extinguished must have taken him!"

His head was spinning. "You're right," he said faintly. "You're absolutely right."

But even with the revelation, why did he feel, most sharply of all, guilt?

THE FOX AMONG THE FOLD

His breath hissed through his teeth as he ran yet another lap around the training yard.

"That's twenty!" one of the guards called down from the wall above. "Isn't that your usual?"

"Twenty-five today!" Tal yelled back as loud as he could. His muscles and lungs screamed for release as he forced himself into a sprint again, holding his sword steady at his hip. It was an awkward run, but a necessary exercise. Running without it, after all, wouldn't prepare him for when he needed to do it in a fight.

Tal felt the gazes of the guards following him as he darted past. When he'd first shown up two weeks earlier before dawn broke, they'd worn mocking smiles, expecting another performance such as in the courtyard, the rumors of which had spread across the castle like fire on a summer-dried field. But as the sun peered over the horizon and Tal carried on with his exercises, day after day, their smiles began to slip away. A week in, they were offering to spar with him.

This late in the morning, he'd already beaten all of those on watch thrice each.

Five laps later, he allowed his leaden legs to stumble to a

halt and released his sword's hilt to lean forward, gasping for air. He only noticed the footsteps on the dirt when they were nearly before him, and he straightened to see Falcon wearing an amused smile.

"Not very good for your cover as a drunken dandy, is it?" The bard gestured at him as if his sweat-stained tunic said it all.

Tal shrugged as he gathered enough breath for a reply. "Staying alive is more important than a good cover."

"What's to fear now? You killed all the ghouls, didn't you?"

"But we haven't found Jonn's murderer."

Falcon's jaw tightened, and he looked away. "We should speak," he said softly. "Privately."

Tal nodded and followed him up the wall's stairs.

A few minutes later found them on the ramparts, dozens of paces away from any prying ears and the wind stealing their words in any case. Tal basked in the cool air, even as it began to chill his shirt. "This must be serious for you to leave the comfort of the castle. What is it?"

For once, the minstrel's expression was serious. "I know what you hunt, Tal."

He smiled by reflex. He hadn't told Falcon everything, much as he wanted to. But this task called for secrecy from as many people as possible. Even his closest friends.

"Do you?" he asked lightly.

Falcon didn't return his smile. "Yes. The same twisted bastard who took Jonn. You hunt one of the Extinguished."

His smile faded. *The curtains have closed on that act, then.* "How long have you known?"

"Only a few days — though, as you know, I suspected you were up to something from the beginning." His friend's eyes searched him as if for something he couldn't find. "Why, Tal? You were done with this life. Why come back to it? Haven't you gathered enough scars? And you know I speak selflessly, as the return of Tal Harrenfel can only mean more songs for your bard to compose."

Tal sighed. "I never left the war behind, old friend. While I was in Hunt's Hollow, I told myself I'd hung up my sword and bow, even as I took them down to hunt the beasts that came down from the mountains."

Even as I struggled and despaired of deciphering that ancient, evil tome, night after night, he thought. But that, at least, he still kept to himself.

"But I can't leave the war behind. The war lives within me, now and always. The best I can hope for is a quiet front for a time."

Falcon stared over Halenhol, and Tal followed his gaze, eyes squinted against the wind. The heat of exercise had faded, and now the coming winter's cold was starting to stiffen his sore muscles. But he didn't fetch warmer clothes but looked to the east, to the unseen mountains that always cast their shadow over the Reach Realms.

"Why return now?" the bard asked again. "Aelyn?"

"He was the impetus. But I'd felt the old restlessness stirring in me for some time." He lowered his gaze to his hands. "I found myself thinking of old friends, old mistakes, and scores never settled. Sleep seemed to come less and less often."

"The war never sleeps," Falcon murmured.

Tal glanced at the bard. "How did you find out, anyway? About the Extinguished?"

His friend sighed. "My daughter and your mentee. Garin told Wren about it, apparently, and they've been whispering in corners for a week. I thought it was just the usual youthful sneaking, but it seems they've stumbled onto avenues far more dangerous. It's part of the thing I wished to speak to you about. Why involve the boy at all?"

Tal laughed softly. "The question you and everyone else wants answered, myself included. I've said it once, and Silence knows I'll say it again — I'm not a wise man, and I'm very often the fool."

"Well, what's done is done. All we can do is complete your

task before they find themselves in trouble." Falcon leaned onto the rampart. "I believe we should start with those closest to the matter. Aelyn Cloudtouched — how can we be sure he's not the traitor, or perhaps the Extinguished in disguise?"

For a moment, Tal held back the truth. *But if I can't trust my oldest friend, who can I?* "He's many things, but the Extinguished isn't one of them. For one, he arrived at the castle after these events began. It was one of the reasons Aldric trusted him to fetch me. For another, he would have raised Night's Pyres if the Extinguished had tried taking him."

"And if the Soulstealer ambushed him on the road?"

"It's possible, but I doubt it. I tricked Aelyn into donning a Binding Ring he meant to put on me and bound him not to harm Garin or me. But that night in the courtyard, the ghoul glyphs were reinforced through a sacrifice. It couldn't have been Aelyn doing it — he still wears the Binding Ring, and I would know if he'd violated its magic."

Falcon waved a hand. "Very well. Though I would have liked it to be that damnable elf. Then what of Kaleras? Does he remain as *impervious* as his name?"

Tal tensed, then forced himself to relax. "Also unlikely. He's worn the Ring of Thalkuun ever since he stole it from me two decades ago."

The bard pushed away from the wall and sighed. "Well, at least the wizards are on our side. But it doesn't get us any closer."

"No. And we've searched down the other avenues to no end. The Deliese girl's ravings were odd, but they lead nowhere. The bungling of the supply lines seemed more a clerical error than an act of sabotage. And Jonn is still missing." Tal looked at Falcon askance. "You truly don't remember anything out of the ordinary that night?"

The Court Bard's expression grew drawn, and he shook his head. "If only I could."

Tal sighed. "Then all our leads have dried up. But I always

suspected most of these threads were too tangential for the Soulstealer to be behind them. No, if one of the Extinguished is here, he'll have wormed his way into the heart of Avendor."

The bard raised an eyebrow. "The King?"

"Perhaps. Or his councilors. One way or another, we'll find out soon."

"Will we?"

"Our favorite elven mage claims to be close to cracking the pendant we took from the Ruins of Erlodan. If he can do what he claims, Aelyn will soon be able to find the fox hiding among the fold."

Falcon's eyes gleamed gold in the morning light as he smiled. "Then we'll have ourselves a song."

Tal raised an eyebrow. "I'd settle for a dead devil."

"It has to be him," Wren whispered as they waited in the eaves of the set.

Garin kept his eyes on the scene playing out on stage before them. It was the climax of *Kingmakers and Queenslayers*, and they'd been rehearsing it that day for the better part of an hour. All he had to do was run in, deliver a message, and run off, but it still set him to sweating as he stood in the wings. The performance was in two days, and every hour of rehearsal felt as if he were bent over the block and waiting for the axe to fall.

That one of Yuldor's greatest servants lurked among them, plotting Silence only knew what, did nothing to ease his mind.

"Maybe," he muttered.

"That's it? Maybe? He told you to warn Tal not to trust anyone. I've read, watched, and listened to more stories than I can count, Garin — that line is nearly verbatim from a dozen different plays, and the villain always says it."

Trust no one, the Warlock of Canturith had told him to warn Tal. But Garin hadn't. After all, if Tal was to trust no one, that included Garin. And if he started distrusting him, it might not take his mentor long to discover Garin's secret.

"My cue's coming up," he mumbled.

Wren ignored him as usual. "We have to scout it out. Meet me here at midnight. Then we can go see what that warlock's up to."

"I said—" an imperious voice called with a tinge of annoyance from on stage "—that whoever is knocking may come in!"

With a jolt, Garin realized that was his cue. "Fine," he said hastily to Wren, then scrambled forward, pageboy's tight pants pulling with every step.

When the Sorrowful Lady had long passed by his window and out of sight, Garin crept down the corridors to the Smallstage. Bearing in mind Tal's sporadic instruction in stealth, he wore no shoes, and the stone pressed cold through his stockings, numbing them soon after he'd left his room. He stared wide-eyed into the darkness, expecting at every corner to see black eyes set in pale, peeling flesh over a gnashing mouth. But no ghouls walked the halls, and somehow, he managed to avoid the orange glow of the guards, any noise he made masked by their conversations.

Entering the Smallstage, he found the glow of a candle already awaiting him in the opposite corner. Hesitantly, he approached, hoping it wasn't some other actor out for a late-night rehearsal; or, worse still, Wren's father.

His breath caught as Wren turned the corner, gold dancing in her eyes, features looking even more elfin than before with the shadows playing across her face.

"I was starting to think you'd chickened out," she teased as she stepped up next to him. He was distinctly aware of how close she stood by him and imagined he could feel the heat of her body.

"Easy for you to say," he whispered back. "All you had to do was walk outside your room, not cross half the castle."

"Oh, I don't think my courage is in question. It's not me who's on his ass more often than not in the training yard."

Garin grinned. No point in denying what was true. But as he remembered the task awaiting them, the smile slipped away. "If we're going to do this, we'd best do it soon."

Wren took his hand. "Don't worry," she said softly, the candle's flame reflected in her eyes. "I'll protect you."

He swallowed, a lump suddenly forming in his throat, and hoped she wouldn't notice how his palms had gone clammy. "How could I be afraid now?" he joked weakly.

Wren blew out the candle and hid it, then they crept through the castle toward the eastern wing. She kept hold of his hand, even intertwining their fingers as they went on. Where the darkness had before held horrors, now it brought different imaginings: secret thoughts of finding a dark corner, her lips finding his, her warmth pressed against him...

He tried to banish the thoughts, heart beating fast, wondering how she couldn't hear them jangling in his head.

But at each corner, Wren pulled him forward, and soon the amorous dreams were replaced by fears again. Would they actually sneak into the old warlock's tower? He still didn't know how far Wren would push this. They'd speculated about traps around the door, and from the look he'd given Garin, it seemed more than likely they were in place. Those eyes had pierced right through him, appearing to see the secret shame that Garin kept hidden even from himself as much as he could. A man with eyes like that didn't seem like a man to trust a locked door.

At the final corridor, he pulled her to a stop and whispered, "Are you sure about this?"

Wren's eyes glimmered in the near-complete darkness as she turned back toward him. "Of course not. But if he's a Soul-stealer and no one realizes, shouldn't we find out?"

"Tal will figure it out. He's a living legend, isn't he? And he probably *has* figured him out, one way or another — we saw him leave his tower."

"You don't know that," she said, her voice rising a bit. "But if we get proof, then we can show everyone the truth. Can you imagine their faces when we figure it out before them?"

A game. It was all a game to her, a way to show up her father. For all the stories she'd heard and their daily contests in the training yard, she'd never been in real danger. She didn't realize how quickly she could go from being alive to very much not.

"Wren," he started to say, then yelped and fell back as light flared from the archway.

Wren snarled and spun, a knife held before her as she fell into a crouch facing the figure. Garin, to his shame, had instead sprawled across the floor. As his eyes adjusted, he recognized the old man standing before him, a white ball of light dancing on his fingertips.

Kaleras' lips curled in a sneer, not seeming the least bothered by Wren's bared knife. "Tal's boy," he noted. "And the bard's girl." His gaze traveled over them, his sneer growing more pronounced with each moment. "Put that knife away and stand up."

Wren glanced back at Garin, eyes narrowed, and he nodded to her as he rose to his feet. *Do as he says*, he urged her silently. No doubt the knife would fail to penetrate whatever spells the warlock had about him.

When they stood before him, Kaleras studied them for a long minute, looking back and forth between their faces. "You think you're safe here, don't you?" he said in a low voice. "You think that because you're swaddled away in the castle, no harm could ever befall you. You're young and arrogant and feel a fire to prove yourself. And what's more daring than sneaking into the tower of the famed Warlock of Canturith?"

Wren's teeth were bared in nearly a snarl, but Garin had

gone statue-still. He wasn't sure if he should read into the thinly veiled threats in every word, but he couldn't unhear them.

Kaleras leaned closer, close enough to smell his breath, bitter with some spice that Garin couldn't identify. "But you're not safe here. No one is. And the next time you wander the castle at night, you might find yourselves suffering more than a scolding."

Protect yourself. Kill him.

The warlock's gaze slid over to him, and Garin swallowed, trying to pretend he hadn't heard the strange voice in his head. *Please,* he prayed to the Whispering Gods. *Please, let us go free.*

Kaleras' eyes narrowed, but he backed up a step and gestured sharply down the hall. "Don't let me catch you out again," he snapped. "Especially not in the eastern wing!"

Wren seized Garin's hand and pulled him toward the corridor. They didn't bother waiting until they were out of sight to start running.

When they reached the Smallstage, Wren pulled him to the corner where she'd been waiting and then onto a pile of drapings. He fell like a ragdoll and lay there, heart pounding. *What did he mean?* he thought desperately. *And why did that voice, that voice that sounded both strange and so damn familiar, want me to kill Kaleras?*

Then Wren rolled over, her body pressing down on top of him, and her lips clumsily found his.

Shocked, he lay there, frozen, for half a second — then all thoughts of what had come before fled his mind. His hands found her body, and his lips moved against hers. Was this how kissing was supposed to go? He didn't know, but he could tell she didn't either, and it didn't matter. Her hands ran up his sides, grasping at him, her mouth sucking eagerly at his lip—

A light blazed in his eyes.

Garin scrambled away from Wren and to his feet, standing awkwardly as his trousers pulled uncomfortably. Wren was up nearly as fast as he was, but she appeared unperturbed as she brushed a stray hair back from her face. His heart almost stopped as, for the second time that night, he saw who had caught them.

For once, Falcon Sunstring wasn't smiling. The Court Bard looked between each of them, the gold in his eyes spinning like water sloshing in a bucket, faster and faster.

His gaze settled on his daughter. "I wondered where you'd gone when I didn't find you in bed," the court bard said in too even a tone. "So I thought I'd come and check if you were out here."

"Well, you found me." Wren's cheeks were flushed, Garin saw in the light of the lamp Falcon carried, but she seemed cool and self-possessed as she stared down her father.

"Garin." Falcon looked at him now, and Garin swallowed. "I think you'd best return to your bed. And stay there."

Garin scrambled to obey, only sneaking one last glance back at Wren, heart soaring to see a small smile on her lips. Even the Court Bard's stare after him couldn't dampen his mood as he fled from the Smallstage.

FROM THE SHADOWS

THOUGH THEIR PRACTICE DIDN'T BEGIN UNTIL AN HOUR AFTER dawn, Garin found himself waiting in the courtyard as first light stole over the battlements, watching the door to the courtyard.

He'd barely slept a wink, and not only from Kaleras' threats circling his head. Wren's kiss — it had been messy and warm and like nothing he'd ever imagined. And now all of his imagination was taken up with how it might happen again. He felt like he had in the Smallstage backroom that afternoon Wren and he had stolen away, the World spinning around him, the warmth of wine and anticipation flowing through his body and mind.

But it wasn't Wren who entered the courtyard first, but the Master-at-Arms. "Garin," he said gruffly. "What're you doing up before the sun?"

Garin had been relieved when the Master had taken to calling him by his name rather than just "boy." "Good morn, Master Krador." Garin gave him a warrior's bow, sword-hand clenched in a fist over his chest, the other clasped behind his back. "Just couldn't wait to get started."

Master-at-Arms grunted. "That's good," he said with plain skepticism.

The stout half-dwarf began to turn away, then paused. "Been meaning to tell you. You've done well this past month. Progressed a lot more than anyone else, and you're a fair bit better than most of them. Except for Wren, of course."

Garin grinned, remembering her lips on his. "I wouldn't dream of out-sparring her. Thank you, Master."

Master Krador grunted again and turned away.

"That couldn't have been me you were just talking about."

Garin spun, and there she stood. Wren was dressed in her usual pair of tunic and trousers, her hair in its typical messy disarray — but somehow, everything about her seemed different. Her green-gold eyes; her short, springy black hair; her lips curled into a smile or a sneer, he hardly cared which — each detail was filled with such thrill, such mystery, that he couldn't draw in a proper breath.

Wren cocked her head to the side, eyes narrowed. "Are you going to say anything?"

Only then did he realize how long he'd been staring. "Uh, yes. I mean, no—" He cut off with a sheepish grin.

She snorted and turned away. "Come on. If we're both early, we may as well get some practice in."

His head in a fog, he followed her to the practice weapons rack that the Master-at-Arms had hauled out, then back out to the yard, after which she proceeded to whack him into submission again and again. She'd been holding back before, and now that she wasn't, he knew he didn't stand a chance. Maybe Master Krador had been happy with his progression, but Garin was seeing just how far he still had to go. More startling still was how his feelings were shifting, from dazed and awestruck to sulky and bruised.

"Let me up!" he finally roared when she'd already collapsed his leg, but continued to prod and poke at him.

Wren stepped away, utterly in control, a smile curling her lips. "Finally had enough?"

The other students had long ago arrived, and many paused in their matches to stare. Even so, Garin dropped his sword and stalked forward until he stood barely a foot apart from her.

"What's gotten into you?" he asked in a low voice. "It's like you forgot about—"

She took a step back. "I didn't forget about anything," she said in a normal voice so that all could hear. "Pick up your blade!"

Hell's devils, you didn't, he thought bitterly. He turned and stalked back to his sword, picked it up, and whirled to meet the attack he knew she'd spring.

Two bruising hours later, when Master Krador called the practice to a finish, Garin deposited his borrowed items and followed the other students off of the courtyard without looking back for Wren. But no sooner had he entered through the shadowed archway did he feel a hand on his arm. Wren's hand — he turned and met her gaze, and all his earlier annoyance disappeared. Her aggression had been replaced by something else mesmerizing and strange.

"Meet me again," she murmured. "Tonight at midnight. At the entrance to the Smallstage."

Then, just like that, she was gone, stepping past him and around the corner ahead.

Garin stared, gut twisting, head dizzy, body bruised, wondering what in all the East's evils he'd gotten himself mixed up in, and why he craved her all the more for it.

Tal entered quietly into the Smallstage and stood by the doorway, watching the scene unfold on the set opposite him.

"Away! Away, you spawn of fiends!" the man playing the

king roared. "Away, and never again tempt me with the lust of war!"

The evil advisor, dressed in cream and purple motley, slunk back behind the throne.

The king cocked his head as if hearing something. "Who knocks at my door? Come in at once!"

A pageboy — or a youth too tall to play a pageboy, but forced into the role anyway — ran in, a letter clutched in hand. "News, My Liege! News from the North!"

The king, who had collapsed in his throne, wearily held out his hand. "Give it here, boy. I'll open it myself."

Tal smiled as Garin handed the letter to the king, bowed, then practically ran off stage again. A small part, to be sure, but for all his height, he'd played it perfectly. Falcon had lamented of the boy's ability, but he was sure Garin could fit any role if he set his heart and mind to it.

Wandering around the edge of the room, he flashed Falcon a wink when he glanced over from his seat in front of the stage, then slipped behind the set.

Garin stood near Wren, though they appeared to be ignoring each other. He frowned, wondering what might be between them, but approached them all the same.

"Well done, lad," he said in a low voice so as not to disturb the ongoing rehearsal. "You play the page well."

"Just a small part," the youth muttered, not meeting his eyes, while Wren smirked behind his back.

Tal raised an eyebrow at her, then squeezed his shoulder. "We all start small. Besides, it's the practice that's important, not the part. One day, you may find your training here saves your life."

Garin's gaze shot over to him, studying him as if he'd said something significant. Tal was beginning to wonder if he'd missed more than one thing happening in the boy's life.

"And how have your lessons with Sister Pond been going?" he pressed.

The youth flinched, eyes flickering over to Wren. Too late, Tal realized his error. *Of course he wouldn't tell her.* He hastily amended, "Has she set you right on Solemnity's Path yet?"

Relief was written all over Garin's face. "She's still trying."

The girl's eyes, however, narrowed further.

"Well, there's time yet." He pressed Garin's shoulder again. "I'll look forward to the performance tomorrow night. And what were you playing again?" he asked Wren.

"An upstart nobleman," she replied shortly.

Tal grinned. "How fitting."

Wren sniffed, then, apparently hearing her cue, she turned and walked on stage.

Tal stepped closer to Garin. "I'm sorry, lad. I didn't know you hadn't told her."

The youth gave him a small smile. "It's alright. I probably should have by now."

"I'm impressed you could keep it a secret from the likes of her."

They shared a grin.

"But in all seriousness," Tal continued, "how are your lessons in letters going? Has the nun declared you literate?"

Garin shrugged. "I can write my name and sound out most words, and I'm reading whole passages out loud. Sister Pond is plotting to make me a priest before the year's up."

Tal smiled. For a wonder, his eyes began to grow warm and misty. "We'll see about that. But I'm proud of you, Garin. You've taken to your lessons, grown and learned more than I thought possible in such a short time."

The youth didn't meet his eyes. "It's all thanks to you," he muttered. His gaze darted up. "But what about the real reason we're here? Your, you know, *hunt.*"

Tal sighed. "It could be going better. I've eliminated most of the likely suspects with no further leads. Tomorrow, however, I intend to find out more."

"Tomorrow? How?"

"A plan to draw our quarry out of hiding. Bait so tempting not even a Soulstealer could resist."

Garin leaned in close. "What?"

His wolf's grin stretched his lips. "A king, unprotected, vulnerable to influence or assassination."

The youth's eyes went wide. "How will you manage that?"

"Not through permission, I'll warrant you that." Tal winked. "Just leave the details to me."

But Garin looked far from settled. "Tal, I need to tell you something. Something I probably should have told you before."

That gave him pause. "You have my attention."

"I think Warlock Kaleras is the Extinguished."

For a moment, it was all Tal could do to stare at him. Then he cracked a grin, thinking it must be a joke. "Kaleras? Why him?"

The youth looked far from amused. "I'm serious. The other day, after you visited him—"

"You saw that?" With every word, Tal liked this less and less.

"Wren was — That is, we were—" His face flushed, and he waved a hand impatiently. "Doesn't matter. After you left, we were passing by, and Kaleras came out of his tower. He recognized me as your companion and told me to pass you a warning — to not trust anyone around you, no matter how much you think you should."

Tal studied Garin. There was something more he wasn't saying, and not just about Wren. But what else he held back, he could only guess.

"That sounds like the old warlock," he said with a reassuring smile. "But Garin, believe me when I say I have good reason to trust he's untouched by the East."

The youth's brow furrowed. "What reason?"

Tal looked aside, debating how much he should say. But he'd brought the boy this far into the web of intrigue; he had a right to know and put his suspicions to rest.

"He has an artifact, a magical ring that protects him from others' sorcery."

"The Ring of Thalkuun?"

Tal winced. He'd almost forgotten Falcon had told Garin the story behind the ring and the title he'd gained that day. "Yes. He's worn it for many years. So unless he's been Yuldor's for two decades, the Night hasn't claimed him."

"But didn't he steal it from you in the first place?"

Tal looked away from Garin's accusing stare. "Yes. But if you remember the tale, I hardly deserved to keep it, did I?"

"But you killed all the other warlocks in the Circle," Garin pressed, merciless. "Even if he's not one of the Extinguished himself, wouldn't he want revenge? A warlock never forgets a grudge — that's what all the stories say."

"This isn't a story, though, is it?" Tal found his voice had risen and lowered it again with effort. "This is no legend; this is my life. Things don't work like they do in the stories."

A stubborn set had appeared to Garin's mouth. "That doesn't answer my question."

The answer the youth sought was there, right there, for Tal to tell. Words so simple to say, yet impossible for his tongue to string together.

"That night in the courtyard," he said instead. "He saved me. He stopped the summoning when it would have just continued until I'd been overwhelmed."

But Garin's eyes were as hard as steel and narrow as a knife's edge. "But how did he know to come? Maybe he was behind the summoning, but saved you to gain your trust."

Tal raised his hands. "Believe what you will. But know this: friend or not, Kaleras doesn't take well to being crossed. I'd stay away from him if I were you."

Garin stared at him a moment longer, then shrugged and looked aside. "So you're coming tomorrow night? To the performance?"

He felt his shoulders relax. "Of course. I wouldn't miss the stage debut of my favorite page!"

The youth raised an eyebrow, but his face was coloring. "Whatever you say, old man."

Tal grinned, and the lad reluctantly smiled back.

———

Garin peered either way outside his door. Exhaustion dragged at him, but he couldn't have slept if he tried. The memory of the kiss pressed hard on his mind. Her scent filled his nose; her gold-laced eyes were all he saw. Even fear of the dark hallways, of the warlock's insinuations, couldn't extinguish the yen coursing through his veins.

Again wearing stockings without shoes, he ghosted down the hall, pausing at each creak of a rusty hinge or distant murmur behind a closed door. After standing up to the ghouls, he couldn't call himself a coward, but that didn't stop him from startling at every fleeting shadow. Only he heard distant sounds that didn't make sense in a castle corridor. The clang of a hammer on metal. The hiss of a cat. The roar of a waterfall. And threading through it all was a melancholic note, sustained and droning, whispering in the back of his mind. It formed a quiet cacophony, familiar in some way, and wholly unwelcome.

Not now — any time but now. Garin tried to drown out the vague song, if such noises could be called a song, with memories of Wren once again. And though the song grew louder with every step toward the Smallstage, his eagerness eclipsed it. Soon, her hand would hold his, her lips brush against his, her body warm against his.

He was at the doorway, turning inside, searching for her in the corner where they'd lain on top of the drapings. But as he searched, a sound came from the backrooms that made him freeze.

Her father, was his first thought. *He's waiting.* His feet shuffled back down the hall he'd come from. Though Falcon Sunstring hardly seemed the type of father to harm a young man for kissing his daughter, Garin had no desire to confirm it.

But no matter what his head said, he found himself turning back toward the room and entering through the doorway, drifting on silent feet through the chaotic room toward the entrance to the backrooms, where the strange sounds came echoing from.

Other than hiding a tun of Jakadi wine, the backrooms were used for creating stage props, mending or sewing costumes, applying paints, and crafting other mechanisms of deceit and disguise. This late at night, even the most dedicated trouper would have usually abandoned it for the sleeping quarters further down the hall. One, however, seemed to be burning precious oil to prepare for the upcoming performance. But what they could be doing to make such strange noises — the moans, the almost painful gasps — he could only guess. His cheeks burned hot.

But a dangerous curiosity had hold of him now. Reaching the doorway, Garin found the door slightly cracked. No surprise there — the door had no latch and swung open if something wasn't propped against it. Whispering a silent prayer, he pressed on the door and found it soundlessly opening to his touch. Emboldened, he pushed it open further and cautiously poked his head in.

A single candle illuminated the crowded room, set at the opposite end. Its small flame made the shadow of the figure bent before it dance across the ceiling and the numerous articles that leaned against the walls and were scattered about the floor. Thirty feet away, Garin couldn't distinguish any identifiable features.

Suspicion joined his curiosity now. The man — or so he guessed from the deepness of the grunts — sounded deranged as he labored over the desk. The troupers of the Dancing

Feathers were eccentric, but this went beyond what Garin knew them capable of.

Then a thought came upon him like a blaze of light, and his breath caught in his throat. *The Extinguished*. Why a Night-touched warlock would be here, in the depths of the Smallstage backrooms, he couldn't begin to guess. But he knew that if he truly meant to help Tal and find the Extinguished, he had to move closer and see who this was.

Dizzy with fear and amazement at his daring, Garin stepped through the doorway.

As he once more slipped through the halls of the Coral Castle undetected, Tal couldn't recall a more incompetent body of guards. He'd always respected the Master-at-Arms for being a stolid, dependable sort, but he found his respect for the half-dwarf slipping with each successful late-night rendezvous.

"While the cat sleeps, the mouse feeds," he muttered to himself as he reached the door.

It wasn't his only repeat visit to Aelyn's small workshop. In his hunt for the Extinguished, he'd often dropped by to either taunt the mage for his lack of progress or, if he was luckier, bask in his success. But thus far, he'd mostly been able to make good on the former. Aelyn was usually bent over the desk in the corner, while Tal would settle in his usual chair by the fire and watch him, all the while sipping on a goblet of Jakadi red. A more cramped room had never existed, and the Gladelysh emissary seemed to be molding to it, becoming thinner and more sallow with each visit. It was incredible what failure, a severe lack of sleep, and an all-consuming need to vindicate oneself could do for a body's health.

Now here it was, the night before the Sendeshi entourage arrived, and Tal was sure that Aelyn would have still made no progress.

But as he pressed a hand to the door, he paused. Something sounded from within, a repetitive noise — moaning, he realized a moment later. He hesitated, wondering whether it would be embarrassing or amusing to interrupt whatever Aelyn was doing in there. But, as he'd once told Garin, what was life without the spark of risk?

He pressed open the door, a smile tugging at his lips — then, just as quickly, it fell away.

Aelyn sprawled on the floor, something dark and shapeless looming over him. His eyes told him it must be silhouetted, its features in shadow, but the angle of the light was wrong, the hearth situated so it should have unveiled the figure's face. No — it wasn't in shadow, but formed of shadows, a nameless monstrosity bred of hidden fury and sent in the dead of night.

Once, he'd met a similar monster, and knew that if it meant to kill, he'd be hard-pressed to stop it.

The elf groaned as the shade stabbed its limbs into him, over and over. No blood covered the floor, but Tal knew the wounds went deeper; a Nightborn creature could do far worse than destroy the body.

In an instant, he'd drawn *Velori* and was swinging at the shade, the glyphs on the silver blade shining a brilliant blue. Where the blade passed, the fell creature dissolved into a dark mist, but it reformed immediately after. He hadn't harmed the phantom, only provoked it, for it rose from the prone mage to loom over Tal.

He backed away, sword raised, mind turning through his available cantrips. Raising one hand, he called, "*Fuln!*" and light shone brilliantly from his hand. The shade flinched back, but the werelight did little more than give it pause. If anything, the shade grew even larger, the shadows cast from its black body melding with the rest.

Tal kept up the light, hoping to stay it while he thought of another plan. He could try to draw it away, but as the shade had been sent to kill Aelyn, it would likely go back to leisurely stabbing him as soon as Tal ran. None of his cantrips promised any result, either, and he lacked the equipment for more involved spells, if he could even remember the proper words after all these years.

The shade drifted forward, and a long, black arm formed from it to stab at him. Tal twisted out of the way and held up *Velori* — if it had avoided it once, it might do so again. Sure enough, as the blade intercepted the arm's path, it dissolved into mist, floating back to rejoin the monster.

But three more arms formed now, and the shade thrust forward with all of them. Tal spun the sword in his hand in an arc, trying to hit all three, but one darted through to stab into his shoulder. Cold pain, like he'd been impaled with a knife formed of ice, raced down his arm and across his chest. He gasped with it, his lungs suddenly struggling to breathe, and backed away.

The arm was stiff and numb, though it was quickly coming back to life. The shade advanced, four more arms forming and menacing him. He had to kill it now, or he'd soon be laid prone like Aelyn.

"Tal..."

Tal's gaze wandered to the floor and saw the mage staring at him, the bronze in his eyes stirring sluggishly. The word wheezed through his parted lips.

No time to wonder at it — the shade attacked again, all four arms jabbing forward at different angles. But even with a near-useless arm, Tal was gaining the measure of his enemy. Dodging to one side, he sliced two arms to mist, then the last two as they slowed and curved around to follow him. He was closer to the shade itself now, and without slowing his movement, he chopped at it, again and again.

Like a hot rod thrust into cold water, the sword lashed the shade to steam. Every time the nub of an arm began to form, Tal hacked through it, scattering again into mist. He didn't delude himself into thinking he was harming it. But with his arm almost back to life and the shade on the defensive, he'd take what small victories he could.

Outside, he heard the sounds of feet approaching — the laggardly guards, finally, for all they could do. Sweat beading his brow, Tal gasped, "If you have any advice, you damnable marsh monkey, now's the time to give it!"

Aelyn replied, but it was impossible to hear over the sound of hissing black mist and his exertions.

"Speak louder!" Tal demanded.

Behind them, he heard guards reach the door and burst into the room. By the gasps and clatter of metal, they'd stumbled to a halt when they saw what they faced.

"One of you!" he called behind him, chopping an arm that had almost fully formed. "Drag the mage away and tell me what he has to say! Now!" he added when he didn't hear anyone move.

Finally, movement sounded behind him, and he saw a young, wide-eyed guard duck forward and begin dragging Aelyn out from under the black shadow. He couldn't tell if it was his imagination getting the better of him, but the shade seemed to be expanding so that Tal was finding it harder and harder to reach its arms.

"Anything?" he roared back.

The young man's voice shook as he called, "He says to get the book on the desk and bring it to him!"

A mad grin curled his lips. *The book on the opposite side of the shade — what could go wrong?* He could see it through the dark mist, a book with its pages splayed open, as if it had been hastily consulted.

His left arm coming back to life, Tal shook it out and wielded his sword with both hands. *There's only one way this can end*, he realized. His smile tugged even wider.

"Get ready to catch!" he called back. Then with a wide overhead sweep, he fell into a forward roll under the shade.

Black fog boiled around him, cold and clinging, but Tal

ignored it as he reached the desk and seized the book. Roughly closing it, he swept wildly behind him with *Velori*, then knelt and tossed the book back the way he'd come.

Cold stabbed into his chest, and Tal gasped, falling back. He looked down and saw a black arm extending from it before he collapsed to the ground, all powers of movement lost.

Another cold, stabbing pain in one arm, then the other, then both his legs. Tal hovered inside his frozen body, barely conscious, lips moving in words he couldn't even interpret himself. He clung to his one, thin strand of hope, repeating it in his mind as the arms stabbed the cold deeper and deeper inside of him.

Darkness edged in. He couldn't cling to consciousness much longer. *Rest*, a voice whispered in his head. He couldn't tell if it was his own or another's. *Rest. It will all be over soon.*

"No!" he tried to yell in manly defiance, his lungs filled with a last, desperate effort that would overcome his weakness — but if the word came out at all, it was as the indecipherable wheeze of a bedridden, dying man. He lay there, entombed in cold, only the tomb was his own body, and the lid was sealing closed.

Garin breathed through his mouth, as Tal had taught him, so slowly and shallowly he thought he would faint. Barely able to see in the near darkness, he took each footstep with tremendous care, expecting at any moment something sharp or slippery to be underfoot and give him away.

But halfway across the room, the man still hadn't turned around, his groaning agony only growing louder as Garin neared. Though he had only the voice and the silhouette to go by, something about the man seemed familiar.

Kaleras, Garin thought over and over again. *It must be*

Kaleras. But the Warlock of Canturith had his tower to work his devilry from. Why would he come here?

Unless he needed to be close to the one he worked the magic against.

A fresh wave of fear suddenly flooded him, and he almost lost his balance as he trembled with it. He'd seen Wren with Garin. Perhaps Kaleras meant to get at Tal indirectly by harming the daughter of his close friend. Desperate thoughts scrambled through his head. *You can't just see who it is. You have to stop him!*

But indecision froze him where he was. For one, he didn't have a weapon, not even his belt knife; in the castle, people used the cutlery at the table, not knives they carried around, and only privileged nobles and guards carried weapons. For another, what if he was wrong? What if it wasn't Kaleras, but just the innocent ravings of a madman? And even if it was him, could Garin stab him in the back, killing him in cold blood?

He found he couldn't move forward, but neither could he retreat. The knowledge of what might be happening to Wren at that very moment pounded through him, prodding him to make a decision. Perhaps it was wiser to check if she was well first. Perhaps... unless she was being tortured to death.

Forward or back? Forward or back?

The memory of his previous terror-filled decisions whirled through his mind. At Kaleras' door, didn't he refuse to run away, but instead turned to face the warlock? When the ghouls chased him, didn't he make a stand?

He took another step forward.

Something creaked next to him, items shifting against the wall. As Garin froze, he realized what had happened. Loose cloth, snagged beneath his foot, had pulled something leaning against the wall and shifted it.

Slowly, he turned his gaze back to the hunched figure, reluctant as if by looking, he might make true what he already knew to be real.

The man was a silhouette no more. His face half cast in shadow, Garin knew him still by the gold turning slowly in his eyes.

"Falcon?" he said weakly. Relief and apprehension twisted through him a confusing mix. "What are you—?"

The Court Bard rose swiftly, his face a mask of rage, and Garin stumbled back, tripping again on the props littered across the floor. As he tried to gain his feet, Falcon moved to stand over him.

"Why are you here?" he hissed, his voice suddenly not his at all. "Are you so strongly hers?"

Garin's mouth worked, searching for words. "What do you mean, hers?" he managed to say.

The minstrel leaned down, all his features lost to darkness but for his slowly swirling eyes. But just as Garin started to wonder if he'd taken leave of his senses, Falcon extended a hand out to him.

Taking it as a sign of forgiveness for his trespass, Garin sighed in relief and took it.

His ears burst with a torrent of screaming. He found himself crying out as well, but his yell paled to the roaring in his head. His vision blurred, then went black, and he felt himself falling far away.

"Soon," a voice crooned to him as he drifted into darkness. *"Soon, you will awake, Singer's pet. Then we will see how our master makes you dance on your strings."*

ONE FINAL PERFORMANCE

For a long moment, there was only cold.

Then heat, sudden and searing, spread across his body.

Tal gasped as needles pricked along his skin, his limbs, even inside his lungs. He curled in on himself. The darkness receded from his vision, and the dimly lit room came slowly into focus.

As did the face peering down at him, swirling eyes boring into his soul.

"Gah!" Tal scrambled feebly away from Aelyn and stared at him, chest heaving. When he had sucked in enough air, he wheezed, "If you're going to kiss me, you should ask first."

"I save your life, and once again, all I receive is mockery." Aelyn's voice was hoarse, and his eyes shone fever-bright in his pale face. Like Tal, he was sprawled along the floor.

He crawled to me, he realized. Somehow, it wasn't as amusing as it should have been.

"Saved me?" The initial wave of pain had receded, and Tal pried at the chair nearest him, trying to rise. When he failed, he pretended like he'd been stretching stiff muscles. "As I recall, I ended up like this by saving you."

Aelyn put a hand to the book next to him, its old cover looking more decrepit than ever. Noticing Tal's gaze, he smiled wanly. "Perhaps I would thank you more profusely if you hadn't ruined a priceless book in the process."

"Your life is priceless to me," Tal said with a shaky grin. He tried again to stand and succeeded, righting himself and swaying on his feet.

The guards watched from the doorway, exchanging silent glances. Tal's smile tugged wider. This was too far outside their routine for most of them to process.

"Nothing to clean up here, men," Tal said, losing the smile and adopting the tone his long-ago sergeant had once used. "Report to the Master-at-Arms what happened. And make us sound brave and noble while you're at it, and not..." He gestured at them lying on the floor. "...this."

A few more exchanged glances, then the senior guard nodded and turned sharply out the door.

When the door had closed, Tal looked to Aelyn. "What in the smoldering depths of the Greatdark was that?"

The mage, still sprawled over the floor, gestured sharply. "Help me to the bed."

Tal obliged, grinning at Aelyn's groans as he lifted him from the floor like a child and settled him in the bed. As he stepped back, the mage's eyes promised future vengeance, as if he were purposely humiliating him rather than helping. Tal just gave him a wink.

Aelyn looked as if he might spit, then thought better of it. "And the book."

Once he'd retrieved the tome and settled it into the mage's loving embrace, he finally answered Tal's question. "That was a soulshade."

"Sounds pleasant."

Aelyn's eyes had fallen to the tome. "Not for anyone involved. They're formed from the caster's soul."

Tal frowned. "Not through sacrifice? Every other shade I know requires killing someone or something else."

The mage cast him an irritable look. "Soulshades would be

rather impractical for mages to utilize, then, wouldn't they? But because of their origin, they have limited applicability and intelligence. You saw how ours employed a single attack against you, even if it had several variations. It had been given its command, and it carried it out without a shred of inventiveness."

A grin found Tal's lips again. "Almost killed by it, yet you still find it boring. How frightening it must be inside that head of yours."

"It appears you won't find out today."

"But what caused the devil to show up? Were you plumbing the depths of something you ought not to?"

"You might say that." The bronze in the mage's eyes seemed to dance. "I'm close, Harrenfel. I've almost broken it."

"The pendant?"

"What else?" As quickly as a cat, he turned from jubilant to irritated. "It has put up quite the resistance, to be true. I've worn my way through a dozen of my best books. But just as I knew I would, I've very nearly succeeded."

Tal raised an eyebrow. "Nearly succeeded isn't the same thing as succeeding."

"One night more!" Aelyn snapped. Then his eyelids fluttered, his exhaustion finally catching up to him. "But after I rest."

Tal watched as the mage fell asleep, heedless of him standing over him. Truth be told, he felt he could sleep where he stood.

But the Extinguished still hunted them. He had already sent one creature here to kill Aelyn; if he had the strength, he might send another.

"Legends never sleep, do they?" Tal muttered.

After locking and bolting the door, he sat with a groan in one of the chairs by the fire, stared into the flames, and waited for dawn to come.

Light worked its hard fingers through his eyelids and split open his pounding head.

Garin groaned. He felt every bit as miserable as the morning after his brothers had tricked him into drinking two full cups of Crazy Ean's swamp whiskey. Only this time, he hadn't been drinking.

Sitting up, he fought down his rising gorge and rubbed at his temples. What had happened last night was lost to a fog of pain. He thought he'd left his room, but he couldn't for the life of him recall where he'd gone. It had been a dream, and like a dream, it fled upon waking. But still, he had the nagging feeling he was supposed to have gone somewhere and done something...

But whatever he'd forgotten, Garin knew he couldn't stay abed. Though his usual lessons were canceled, he was far from free. This afternoon, the Sendeshi delegation would arrive, and later in the evening, the Dancing Feathers would perform *King-makers and Queenslayers*. And Garin would make his debut on the stage as a pageboy.

After he forced himself to his feet and stuffed his limbs into clothes, he trudged down the hallway, barely able to resist the urge to slide down a wall and never rise again. He felt like a drunkard, the orientation of the World wavering with every step. *I wonder how drunkards stick to the World when their feet are always falling away.* He snorted a laugh and wondered if Wren would have laughed or scorned him.

The thought brought him stumbling to a halt. *Wren.* His sluggish mind turned around the wonderful, exquisite name. Just thinking it made his stomach pitch and turn anew, but not only in the usual way. He was letting her down, he somehow knew; but however he knocked his head around, he couldn't remember how. Was it just that he wanted to see her? Or was he forgetting something else?

Only one way to know. He tottered his way down the hall.

As he slouched through the door to the Smallstage, a figure popped out from nowhere. Garin yelped and nearly fell over.

Mikael leered over at him, smiling with his sharp, misshapen teeth. "You look terrible!"

"Can't be as bad as you usually look," Garin muttered.

The goblin, who was playing the king's traitor in their production, only grinned wider. "A fair point! But I laid off the rum last night just for the company. After all, the Sendeshi delegation arrives today, don't they? We have a performance to put on!"

"Just what I'd been waiting for." Not wanting to pretend to celebrate the thing that was twisting his stomach into ever more complicated knots, Garin fled to the dressing room.

He found no relief there, however. Everywhere he turned in the Smallstage, the members of Dancing Feathers were cheerfully going about their work, chattering and smiling like it was a festival day. It was almost as if Jonn's disappearance had been forgotten, grins replacing frowns that had been there just a day before.

But they haven't forgotten. He saw it in the way the troupers kept glancing at the spots where Jonn had usually occupied: his chair, his corner, his place behind the stage where he would have been tinkering with the set. Good cheer was just the way jesters dealt with their grief, Garin supposed, and however it grated on him, it seemed a good deal better than drowning in sorrow.

Only Wren seemed immune to the high spirits. When Garin found her mounted high on the frame of the castle setting, fixing some curtains that had torn, she gave him the blackest frown he'd seen from her yet.

"Believe me, I know," Garin called to her. "This din is like nails in my head this morning."

She turned away from him.

His stomach wrenched yet more painfully. "What's wrong? You have a headache, too?"

Wren turned back and leaned over the set so quickly he feared she would tumble to the floor a dozen feet below, but she clung on as the gold in her eyes spun furiously. "No, I don't have a headache. And if you have to ask, you're an even bigger ass than I already knew!"

Garin stared at her, pain giving way before his astonishment. "Did I do something?"

For a moment, he thought she'd spit down on him, the way her mouth screwed up. Then with a furious huff, she pulled herself back up and out of sight.

"Don't mind her, my boy."

Garin whirled, heart thumping, the ache in his head returned in full. Falcon Sunstring stood behind him wearing a strained smile. *He only saw you kiss his daughter,* he tried to placate himself and found it only made his heart race faster.

The Court Bard was studying him, head cocked to one side, gold-green eyes narrowed despite his smile. "She always gets tense on performance days. Nerves and all that. But I'm sure you don't know anything about that, do you?"

"Not at all," Garin said weakly.

Falcon laughed like it was the funniest thing he'd heard all day. "Excellent! First, you play the pageboy; then, who knows what you'll move up to?"

Garin backed away, trying his best to wear an agreeable smile. "Let's just see if I survive this one."

The gold in his eyes seemed to stir. "Yes. Let's see."

Tal jerked around, weary mind sensitive to any movement in the small, stuffy room. But he breathed a sigh of relief when he saw it was merely Aelyn, attempting and failing to sit up in his bed.

"By the devils, I should be stronger," the mage groused, even his voice weak.

"After what that soulshade put you through? By all rights, you should be dead."

He made a sound somewhere between a laugh and a curse as he lay back down. "The pendant. I must continue the work. I'm too close to breaking it."

"The only thing you'll continue is your rest." Tal rose with a groan, knees clicking, back aching, old wound in his side throbbing. He rolled his head around, trying to relieve the soreness that had crept in overnight, though he knew it would do little good. "We're two old and ailing men now, aren't we?"

"Speak for yourself, human." Aelyn managed a small sneer. "I have two centuries yet to see — longer, if I can avoid any more of those abominations we faced last night."

"I'll be surprised if I have a year at this rate." Tal laughed, though even he found little humor in it. "Regardless, there's not a chance in any heaven or hell that you'll be able to finish the job. We're going to need to bring in a new master of the occult arts."

"Who? You?"

Tal rolled his shoulders. "I'm flattered you think so highly of me. But no, not me. The only other magician we can trust within easy reach."

Aelyn's scowl deepened. "I'd hardly say I trust the Warlock of Canturith. Hard to trust a man who abandons his brothers, isn't it?"

"If you can trust a man with as colorful of a past as me, you can trust him." Finishing his stretches, Tal made for the door. "Now, if you can survive for a few hours, I've been holding in a leak that won't stay any longer. That, and our warlock needs fetching."

"I'm sure I'll manage."

Tal flashed him one last mocking smile, then slipped from the room.

Soon after, he stood before the door to the east tower and knocked. A few minutes passed, then the door cracked open. A dark eye peered through the gap.

"You're still alive," Kaleras noted.

As usual, a tumult of conflicting emotions flooded him upon seeing the old warlock, but Tal hid them behind a crooked smile. His eyes wandered to the chain that kept the door from fully opening. "Expecting trouble?"

"Preventing it. Your protege and that minstrel girl have been too inquisitive for their own good." The warlock smiled thinly. "Time was when I'd have let them find out what it means to intrude upon a wizard. I must be growing soft in my old age."

"Soft as a stone, I'd wager."

Kaleras raised an eyebrow. "Much as I'd love to exchange pleasantries, I'm rather busy at the moment. Farewell."

As the warlock began to close the door, Tal jammed his boot in the gap. "Wait a moment. I need to ask something of you."

The warlock's one visible eye narrowed. "Fishing for more ways to insult me, I trust?"

"If asking a favor is an insult. But I think you'll be more than willing to grant me this."

"I'll be the judge of that."

Tal glanced up and down the hall. This far out on the periphery of the Coral Castle, the corridor was deserted, but he still spoke in a whisper. "Aelyn Cloudtouched has been attempting to crack open a pendant. A pendant belonging to a certain adversary we share."

"The Extinguished." He said it calmly as if he'd known all along. *And perhaps he has. Maybe that's why he returned to Halenhol in the first place.*

"If the elf had completed the trace," Tal said, "we'd have located the Soulstealer within the castle."

The warlock raised an eyebrow. "Would have?"

"He was attacked last night."

"Attacked?" Kaleras frowned. "I felt and heard nothing."

"I suspect that's because of the nature of the fiend. A soulshade, Aelyn called it."

"A soulshade?" The warlock's eye narrowed as it wandered to the floor. "No release of energy. Done skillfully, that might have escaped my attention."

Tal rolled his stiff shoulders. "It felt pretty damned skillful. But we managed to banish it in the end. All that to say, now we need you. Will you help?"

Kaleras met his gaze, then nodded sharply. "Give me a moment."

"Take as long as you need," Tal called softly after him as the warlock closed the door. "It's not as if all our souls are lined up for the gallows."

He waited for a moment, listening. But hearing no laugh and doubting that any would be forthcoming, he leaned against the wall and waited.

***

"You wound me, My Liege!" Mikael cried in high drama from the stage, his voice only slightly dampened by the curtains hanging between him and Garin. "You accuse me of disloyalty, of treachery — as if my heart wouldn't break at the barest hint of such filth!"

A few spare laughs echoed from beyond the stage, but they stirred nothing in Garin. He closed his eyes and leaned his head back against the frame. He'd heard every line before, a hundred times, a thousand — or near enough. His speaking line was only a couple pages away when he brought in the missive that overturned the scene, mistakenly exonerating the wheedling duke, whom Mikael was playing, of treachery and accusing the king's own queen — to great tragedy, of course. *Have to give the audience what they came for,* he mused. *Can't name a play* Kingmakers and Queenslayers *and expect every monarch to escape alive.*

He cracked open his eyes and observed Wren standing further back behind the stage, barely visible from where he leaned. After her outburst, she'd hardly spoken two words in his vicinity and refused to even look at him, aside from glares cast across the room when she thought he wasn't looking. What he had done to offend her, he still couldn't say. He'd tried to grope his way past the fog that had settled over his thoughts, like a fisherman casting his line out into a mist-wreathed lake even as his hook came up empty every time. It didn't help matters that his headache had only recently eased, and that he'd had to hold his tongue to keep from snapping at others all day.

But watching her then, he couldn't stand it any longer. He pushed away from the post and steadied himself. He had to know what was wrong; she had to tell him.

Using the soft footfalls the troupers had taught him so as not to make the floorboards creak, he made his way around the other players to halt next to Wren. She glanced at him, but immediately averted her eyes as they narrowed to slits, the gold stirring angrily within the green.

Garin stood for a few moments, trying to find the right words, then abandoned the fruitless effort. "Whatever I did, I'm sorry. I just want to know what it was."

"You can't remember."

He winced beneath the weight of her scorn. "Honestly. I can't remember anything from yesterday. So if I did or said something to offend you, I'm really, truly sorry."

Wren stared at him in silence for several long moments. As the frown lines began to ease away, Garin dared to hope his desperate plea had somehow worked.

"You really don't remember, do you?" She sounded more curious than angry now.

He eased closer. "I remember the night before that, though — how could I ever forget it?"

He'd hoped it would elicit a smile from her, but her brow only creased further. "Then how could you not recall your promise?"

"What promise?"

Wren sighed, eyes casting downward. "After our morning practice, I stopped you in the hallway, and we agreed to meet again. But last night, you never came."

His heart wrenched in his chest as he realized the opportunity he'd missed, the chance that might never come again. "Wren, honestly, I don't remember any of that. The whole day is a blur—"

But she was turning away. "I think I understand. You got cold feet. Maybe it was my father. Maybe it was Tal. Maybe you stole a kiss and had enough. So you didn't come." She laughed, short and bitter. "I guess that's that."

"No, it's not—"

"I have to go." She brushed past him, not meeting his gaze. He wanted so badly to reach out and stop her, but he let her drift past. All around, he felt the eyes of the other troupers on him, all too knowing for his liking.

A hand closed tightly over his arm, and he jerked around to see Falcon Sunstring standing at his shoulder, wearing a pronounced scowl.

A pit formed in Garin's gut. Had he heard? Was he here to make sure Garin didn't hurt his daughter's feelings again?

"Garin," Falcon said, voice hoarse as if he'd recently been yelling. "We have to leave. Now."

"Leave?" This didn't seem about Wren, then. Garin glanced toward the curtains where she'd disappeared. "But I'm supposed to go on soon."

"They'll have to make do without you. There's no time — Tal's in trouble."

"In trouble? Now?" Garin tried to imagine what trouble Tal could be in, and how Falcon expected him to help.

"Yes, boy!" the minstrel practically snarled. His grip tightened on his arm. "We have to go. *Now*."

With his other hand, Falcon pressed something into his hand, and he looked down to see he now held a knife. Fear lanced through him like sharp ice in his veins. He glanced back toward the stage. Strangely, despite how much he'd been dreading it, he found part of him was disappointed he'd miss his debut on the stage.

But Tal was in danger. And if he could do anything to help, he had to go.

He gripped the knife tightly and nodded. "Lead the way."

The bard wore a small smile as he led him toward the door.

Tal stared into the dying flames of the fire. Elsewhere in the castle, the Sendeshi delegation watched Falcon and Garin perform their play. He wished he could see the youth in his role, small as it was. He'd said he would. But just as it had been since he'd brought him to the castle, Garin came second to upholding his bargain with the King.

"Nearly there."

Tal bolted up from his seat and moved to stand by Kaleras' shoulder. The warlock looked out of place in the cramped room, but his air of gravitas had faded as he grew ever more absorbed in the work before him, bending further over the black-gemmed necklace and muttering to himself. Now his eyes glanced up at Tal, the deep brown bright with avidity.

"Nearly there?" Tal asked as he studied the pendant. He saw his face reflected in the gem, fragmented across its dark facets. "Then you'll know where the Extinguished hides?"

Kaleras stared at the pendant again, his hands poised above it. "Yes. I would make any preparations you deem necessary now."

Tal straightened. *Velori* hung at his hip, but the rest of his gear was back in his room. He glanced at the bed in the corner of the room and saw Aelyn's eyes slitted, watching him.

"Don't tap the barrel without me," he said as he moved to the door. "I'll be back in a moment, and I wouldn't want to miss the celebration."

"We wouldn't dream of it," Aelyn's thin voice called after him.

———

Garin stopped short of the castle doors that led out into the central courtyard. "Where are we going?" he asked as he had sporadically throughout their walk down.

Falcon turned back with a scowl. "I told you, boy. Tal needs our help."

Boy? Garin repressed his annoyance. "Out there? Where exactly did he go?"

He glanced down at himself, still dressed in his pageboy costume. But if Tal was in trouble, it was hardly an excuse. He squeezed Falcon's knife tighter in his hand.

The Court Bard finally relented. "He took a horse and went riding out into the city. Now we must follow or risk losing him!"

As Falcon stepped out of the grand double doors, Garin followed him, shivering in the blustering wind outside. Slate-gray clouds covered the sky, killing off the last of the sun's light and making it as dark as a moon-cast midnight. A storm was stirring.

Why would he go out in this? But he knew why. Only one thing could compel Tal to meaningful action and shed his drunken dandy act.

They reached the stables, and Falcon moved from pen to pen, muttering, while he ignored the stablehand's repeated remarks to let him help. Finally, the bard stopped in front of the enclosure of a large, gray gelding. "Ready him!" he snapped at the stablehand, and the boy scrambled to obey.

Garin shifted from foot to foot, glancing back at the dimly lit courtyard. Rain began to patter on the paving stones. Even if they left now, he didn't see how they'd follow Tal. *Where are you going?* he wondered again.

"Garin!"

He turned back to see Falcon mounting the gray gelding, then holding a hand out to him. "Come," the minstrel said. "No time to prepare another horse. You'll ride with me."

Garin hesitated only a moment, then took Falcon's hand. The bard was surprisingly strong for his slight stature, and he easily hoisted him up into the saddle behind him.

As Falcon spurred the horse forward, Garin had no choice but to wrap his arms around the bard's waist, and they left the stables at a gallop, the stablehand scrambling to get out of the way. The droplets of rain pelted his face as they rode hard for the front gates.

"Halt!"

The horse whinnied its protest as the minstrel pulled them to a stop, then whipped his head around, a small smile on his face. Garin turned as well and felt his insides writhe and twist.

Kaleras the Impervious, the Warlock of Canturith, stood in the middle of the courtyard.

"Kaleras," Falcon greeted him. His voice suddenly sounded harsh, like he was playing a goblin in a play. "It's a foul night to be out."

"Let the boy down."

The bard's laugh was short and biting. "And why would I do that?"

The old warlock's face could have been made from wood for all he reacted, rivulets of water running through the furrows in his skin. "I'll only ask once more. Let him down."

Garin's head felt as if it were spinning. Through the sound of the falling rain, he thought he heard distant sounds incongruous with their situation: whispering voices, their words unclear; the roar of distant river rapids; the howl of a wolf. *The Night is near,* he somehow knew. *One of these men is the Extinguished.* And he was certain he knew which one.

Falcon still wore a sneer, but his eyes had gathered a considering look. "Very well, Kaleras. I'll let you have the boy."

Anger suddenly broke through Garin's fear and indecision. "I'm not a sack of potatoes to barter over! And I'm not going with you, warlock. I won't be fooled like Tal, wherever you sent him."

"Tal?" It was hard to tell in the darkness and rain, but Garin thought he saw a flicker of surprise cross the warlock's face. "He's in the castle, boy, not where that man you call Falcon was taking you."

Falcon twisted around to look at Garin, the gold in his eyes swirling rapidly. "Go to him, Garin," he whispered softly. "Obey your Singer. Show me what our Master plans for you."

His earlier anger drained away as he stared into the bard's eyes. Suddenly, they seemed more gold than green, and almost liquid in how the color whirled around his pupils. He found he couldn't look away.

"Our Master?" he muttered. The words needled him, but he couldn't sort out why. The distant sounds were increasing in volume and intensity, and it was growing harder to think.

Obey, Listener.

Hardly knowing what he was doing, Garin swung his leg over and hopped off the horse, landing nimbly on the stones below. The gelding shifted, bumping into him and sending him stumbling forward a step.

Go to him.

"Go ahead, Garin," Falcon encouraged him from atop the horse.

Under the aged warlock's hard gaze, Garin approached him. His body moved as if another willed it like he was no more than a marionette. *Why am I doing this?* he asked himself, and didn't have an answer. But he couldn't stop. He wanted to do as the voice had told him. He wanted to obey.

Stopping six paces from the warlock, Garin stared at him, but Kaleras was looking up at Falcon. "Now," he said. "As for you—"

Protect us. Kill him.

The knife was in Garin's hand, and he was moving forward, but the warlock was swifter, stepping back and raising a hand toward him. Strange, resonant words erupted from his mouth, and Garin felt something hold him tight in place.

But a moment later, he was freed and rushing forward. The cacophony was loud in his ears. Kaleras' eyes widened, flickering down to Garin's hand, and Garin stabbed forward—

A grunt as a jolt ran up Garin's arm. The man before him bent over double. Harsh laughter filled Garin's ears, and he felt the ground slipping from beneath him as he fell far away.

Tal hurried down the hall, knowing what a sight he must make and not caring. His travel-stained leathers on, *Velori* knocking at his hip, his bow strung and slipped across his chest, a quiver at his other hip, a plethora of knives tucked away — he looked ready for war. Guards, who wandered the halls with increased frequency due to the Sendeshi delegation's visit — and perhaps the soulshade's visit the night before — eyed him warily, but none accosted him, the King's orders to leave him be still standing. That didn't, however, stop a pair from following him, though they kept their distance. *Even a king's command can only go so far,* he mused.

He ignored them and, reaching Aelyn's door, pushed inside. The desk was empty, as was the seat before it. Heart knocking against his ribs, Tal strode further in and found Aelyn sitting up in his bed.

"He couldn't wait for me, could he? Where did he go?"

Aelyn's eyes glinted from the darkness. "The warlock figured it out. He knows."

Cold fingers crept down Tal's spine. "Who is it?"

"Did you never guess? In all the hours you spent together, all the confessions you made to each other, you never once suspected him, did you? Blinded by *friendship*." Aelyn said the last word with a twist of his lips as if he were sullied by its utterance.

"Damn you, elf! Speak plainly for once!"

"It's your beloved bard, Magebutcher. Falcon Sunstring."

Tal froze, but his mind kept moving, parsing over the accusation. All he had told him, all he had seen and said… *Falcon? Could it be Falcon?*

"The old warlock has gone after him. Seems that our Soulstealer realized he'd been discovered and was making a run for it." Aelyn looked to be relishing his role as the bearer of bad news, his smile tugging wider.

"Out the front?"

The mage nodded. "Like the man he was impersonating, our puppetmaster seems to have a flair for the dramatic."

Ignoring him, Tal turned and bolted from the room, nearly bowling over the guards who had been lingering outside. "Come on!" he bellowed. "To the front courtyard!"

As he ran, he heard their armor clinking behind him. But he well knew it wouldn't be enough.

Garin stared down at his hand. Dark, it had turned, the liquid slowly dripping down his arm and soaking his sleeve. His hand had been pale the moment before. Now, it was black as a fathomless void, black as the Night's Pyres were said to burn.

I'm going mad.

But he knew this wasn't a delusion. Blood, Kaleras' blood, poured down his arm, down his knife. He jerked away, wet knife still clutched in hand, and stared as the aged man crumpled before him. *It went in so quick and easy. Like he was no more than a pig to slaughter. Like he's an ordinary man.*

Falcon barked a cruel laugh. "Well done, boy! Our Master thanks you. The Warlock of Canturith has long been a thorn in his side."

Kaleras raised his head, teeth bared in a grimace, his face thin and skeletal. "And I will continue to be."

The bard — who was no bard, Garin now saw all too clearly — shook his head. "I think not. That ring may protect you from my direct magic, but you can see I found a way around it. You won't harm the boy — that much became clear when you only tried binding and blocking him, spells against which I shielded. A simple command from my Master again and..." Falcon shrugged and smiled. "The thorn is pulled."

The warlock only raised his hand in response, strange words again on his tongue.

Protect us. Stop him.

The words sang in Garin's head, and he found himself stepping forward again, knife raised. *No!* he cried out in his mind. *Don't!* But he could no more stop himself than he'd been able to the first time. He was a prisoner in his head, watching as his body again advanced on the prone warlock.

"Garin, don't!"

Movement in the corner of his eye, materializing into a familiar figure. *Tal!* he tried to call back to him, but all speech was lost to him.

Yet as the presence that had seized hold of him loosened its grip for a moment, Garin seized back control, throwing himself across the stones and tossing the knife several paces away. "You can't make me!" he cried out, part defiance, part pleading. "I won't do it!"

But as he raised his head, he found Falcon still wore that infuriating smile as he sat atop his gray gelding, staring back toward the castle. "Tal Harrenfel!" he called with a mad cackle.

Garin raised his head to see Tal bolting across the court-yard, his silver sword bared, dandy clothes replaced by travel leathers. Hope warmed his chest. He was here, Tal was here, and they had the Extinguished in their grasp. Soon, everything would be over and done with.

But as Tal stopped short, panting slightly, he looked far from certain. "Where is he?" he demanded.

The Soulstealer who wore Falcon's face was the one with the smile now. "Ah! Tal Harrenfel — long have I awaited our reunion. Or do you not recognize me?"

Recognize him? Garin looked between Falcon's cruel smile and Tal's dawning realization.

"You," Tal said through clenched teeth. "The Extinguished from the Circle."

Falcon laughed softly. "The very one who made you the Magebutcher, yes."

Tal's expression spasmed, but his eyes remained as hard as before. "It doesn't matter who you are. What matters is whose face you stole. Where is he?"

"Your minstrel friend? Alas, I'm afraid he won't be able to join us. You see..." He held up his arm, and his sleeve fell back to reveal the curious, dark metal bracelet he always wore. "His soul is mine now, and his body decays without it. You'd do better to give him up for dead."

To Garin's amazement, Tal wore a small smile, full of sharp promises. "I'd be worrying more about what I'm going to do if you don't hand over that bracelet."

"I don't think that will be a problem. Even if Kaleras is protected from magic, *you* are not."

Tal's eyes flickered to Kaleras. Garin's stomach twisted as he saw him still bowed over the stone, his head sinking lower with each passing moment.

"Alright then," Tal said. "You want to talk. So say your piece."

"I merely wish to extend an invitation. To my lair, shall we say. I believe you're already familiar with it? The Ruins of Erlodan, it's often called."

Tal's smile turned to a grimace. "Flee then, while you still can. Because Silence knows I'll kill you once I catch up."

The Extinguished only answered with a knowing look, then turned his horse and spurred his mount through the open gate.

PASSAGE IV

What is the Song? From whence does it come? Long have I pondered its mysteries, yet I have never uncovered satisfactory answers.

From those tales I have collected and the one Fount I spoke with — not long after which she leveled her village in an inferno that left no others alive — those who wield magic in this manner all hear what they call "the Song." It is not a song as we know it, but made up of all the sounds of the World. Swishes of grass, sneezes over pepper, rotten trees toppling in forests — no sound is excluded.

But though the Song is intriguing, it is the Voice that accompanies it that seems significant. For this "Singer" appears to be a malevolent guide in the working of magic, often supplicating the Fount at times of weakness to give over command of their body so it may provide assistance. Through the guidance of a Singer, the Fount speaks a language they do not know and for which they have no name, and produces effects both marvelous and horrifying. I suspect that, over time, the Fount gives enough of themselves to the Singer as to lead to the complete obliteration of the self.

As to where these Singers come from, and how they come to plague the Founts, I can only speculate. But my theory is that they have always been a part of our World, but known under other guises. Sometimes, they are devils; other times, they are the words a madman hears in his head. Even if Singers aid their Founts in the short term, they inevitably lead to their destruction — and can that be labeled anything but evil?

- A Fable of Song and Blood, *by Hellexa Yoreseer of the Blue Moon Obelisk, translated by Tal Harrenfel*

THE MAN BEHIND THE NAME

"THEY'RE HERE? ABOUT DAMNED TIME. HARRENFEL! NIGHT'S Pyres, you'd best have a good explanation for this!"

At the King's bellow through the doors to his personal chambers, Tal glanced at Aelyn. Though the elven mage swayed where he stood, a smirk curled his lips.

"An odd time for smiling," Tal noted.

"Not when I'm anticipating your head on a pike."

No pithy response came to mind, so he shook his head and entered, the mage keeping pace at his side. The room was opulent and overflowing with even more comfort and riches than the throne room. The audience chamber was only the first of many within the King's personal chambers, with two doors leading off to rooms on either side. Red and orange adorned every surface — crimson carpets, copper tapestries, and a fresco of an enthroned king overhead, perhaps of the first Rexall.

King Aldric Rexall the Fourth, sitting at a table positioned in the middle of the room, was also clad in the Rexall colors, his velvety robe lined with coppery gold buttons as he glared up at them. Despite the late hour, a cup of wine was clutched in his trembling hand.

"What," the King grated in his high-pitched voice, "in Silence's fucking name was that?"

Under the King's fury, Tal found his own anger building. But where Aldric's was fire, Tal's was a cold rage.

"We found your traitor," he said flatly.

"My traitor?" Aldric snorted. "You chased my bard out of the courtyard! And I thought you were friends. If any of you is a traitor, it's that bastard of yours — he stabbed the Warlock of Canturith himself! Though Kaleras must be losing his touch to let that happen."

Tal closed his eyes. *Falcon.* The man he'd trusted most, the man he'd taken for granted — he, of all others, had been the traitor. *Not a traitor,* he corrected himself, *but a prisoner. All this time, the Extinguished hid behind Falcon's smile.*

He felt the King's glare on him and ignored it, thinking over all he'd shared with the man he'd believed his friend. *Some part of me knew,* he realized with a start. *Why else would I conceal what I've been working on for the last five years?* He'd kept secrets all his life, but few he'd withheld from the bard. Falcon had been his confidante and healer when he was broken. Through many sleepless nights, he'd stayed up with Tal, chasing the nightmares away with amusing anecdotes of lovers' quarrels and humorous incidents on stage. And after Tal had recovered some peace of mind, he caroused with him, then began first writing the songs celebrating and exaggerating Tal's accomplishments. Falcon had given him a respite, a home among the troupers. A place where Tal was accepted for no more than who he was.

But for all the time since Tal had returned to Halenhol, he'd been a prisoner of the Extinguished. And Tal had buried his head in the dirt.

Tal opened his eyes again to meet the King's gaze. "It's not like you to pretend the fool, Aldric. You know that the Extinguished steal faces. This time, he stole Falcon's. The bouts of madness, the ghouls, the caravan sabotage, Jonn—"

"Jonn," Aldric interrupted. "That's the murdered trouper?"

Tal kept his face carefully composed. "Yes. All that happened before my arrival and since was orchestrated by the one pretending to be your Court Bard."

Slowly, the full implications seemed to dawn on Aldric. "Sunstring... He could have murdered me."

Indeed, Tal thought. *A shame he didn't do me the favor.*

"But we didn't discover him in time," he said aloud. "He possessed Garin and warded him long enough for the youth to stab Kaleras, then fled. As you no doubt heard."

"Half the castle heard," Aelyn observed with a sharp smile. "And all will know by now."

"Even those damned Sendeshi didn't miss it." The King took a long swallow from his wine, then glared at Tal again. "Well? What are you still doing here? Go clean up your mess!"

Tal watched him for a moment. "You're assuming I know where to go," he said quietly.

Aldric flushed, then took another quick drink of wine before thrusting the goblet toward him, spilling wine on the carpet that no doubt cost the yearly wages of a score of masons. "You'd damned well better, Harrenfel. We made a bargain, you and I. Don't forget its terms."

"Fortunately for both of us, the Extinguished was gracious enough to tell me where he would wait. I'm sure you've heard of it — the Ruins of Erlodan."

The King snorted, his usual blustering attitude recovered. "That haunted old derelict? It's over a week's hard ride away. Best be on your way."

"It's a trap, Aldric. He wouldn't tell me if he didn't want me to come. And he knew I would."

Why? he asked himself. *Why lure me out? Simply to kill me? He could have done it a dozen times over if he'd wished to.* There was a different game at play here, and he had his suspicions he already knew the players' aims.

Aldric waved a lazy hand. "Either he'll take care of you or I will. At least you'll stand a chance against the Soulstealer."

Only a king would be so bold as to threaten with no protection. Aloud, he said, "I'd stand a better chance if you sent soldiers to accompany us. With the Extinguished expecting us, he'll no doubt summon a welcoming party. A contingent of thirty should be enough to deal with them."

The King was shaking his head before Tal had finished. "Send soldiers on this fool's errand? Do you take me for an imbecile? No, Harrenfel — this is your mess to clean up. And you'll do it without my help."

Tal only stared at him for a long moment. Even knowing Aldric Rexall the Fourth as he did, he hadn't expected this. *But I should have. I suspected; now, I know.*

He turned away, hoping he'd hidden all that simmered beneath his skin. "Fine. I'll return before the next full moon for the boy's reward."

Aldric laughed at his back. "I look forward to it, Mage-butcher!"

"You'd have to be a Night-blinded fool to follow him there," Aelyn commented from his seat, the corner of his mouth twitching.

Tal didn't respond. He lifted his gaze slightly to glance at Garin, who leaned, pale-faced, against the opposite wall. The youth had barely spoken a full sentence since they'd brought Kaleras up to his tower. *And who could fault him when he's the cause of the warlock's condition?*

He should have seen it coming, all of it, ever since Garin touched the pendant. He'd seen the signs. But neither he nor Aelyn had believed the Night's influence could linger so long after that brief exposure.

Kaleras paid the price of their arrogance.

"He's probably dead anyway," Aelyn continued mercilessly. Despite his fragile state, his mood was buoyant and soaring higher as his companions sunk deeper into misery.

"He's not!" Wren's shout echoed up the tower as she stood, tight-fisted and trembling, before the mage. "My father's alive! And if you're too coward to rescue him, I will!"

"Calm, lass," Tal murmured. "The King's physician attends the warlock above, and I doubt shouting will improve his health." *Not that the bastard deserves a peaceful rest.* But even as he thought the words, he couldn't put his heart into them.

"Calm? How can I be calm? The Soulstealer took my father's face! All these months, it's been that *thing*, not him, that I—" She cut off, tears gleaming in her eyes. "I'll kill him. I'll kill him for this."

"He's already dead." The harshness in Tal's voice surprised him, as did the bitter smile that sprang to his lips. "It's time you face that."

"He's not!" Wren snarled back. "You said so yourself that the Extinguished had to keep him alive for the illusion—"

"But he doesn't need him anymore. If he's not dead yet, he will be before long. That Night-damned warlock has him, and we can't recover him." He held her gaze, unable to help his mocking smile. "Better to think him dead already."

"How can you say that?" She glared at him, the tendrils of gold in her eyes swirling furiously. "After all he's done for you?"

His smile slipped away. "Done for me? I'll tell you what he's done for me. He's made me a lie — my entire life, a lie. And all for his own gain."

Before anyone could respond, he crossed the tower room to the door. "I need to clear my head," Tal said, then stepped outside the tower.

As the door closed behind him, Garin exchanged a look with Wren, then Aelyn. No one spoke — and what was there to say?

Without Tal, we can't do this. He knew it was true, and he knew the others knew it, too. Aelyn's lips were twisted in a sour pucker as he stared at the wall, his fingers twitching. Wren began to pace, a scowl written across her pixie features.

It was up to him to fix this, Garin realized. After all, he'd been the one to break everything. He'd stabbed Kaleras. Though it had been the Nightvoice that had commanded his limbs, it had been his hand to do it, his will that had been too weak to stop. And it had been his stubborn insistence on entering the Ruins of Erlodan that had landed him under the Night's influence in the first place. Without it, they might have had another powerful warlock on their side, and Tal might still be there with them.

He watched Wren pace back and forth, back and forth. He'd failed her once; he couldn't fail her again. He had to make this right.

"I'm going after him," he said and turned toward the door.

"Why? What could you say?" Wren shot at his back.

Garin shrugged. "I don't know. But I have to try."

He pulled open the heavy door and slipped through.

Tal stood in the hallway just outside, staring out the windows at the darkness outside. His face could have been carved of stone for all it shifted at Garin's approach.

Stepping up next to him, they stood in silence for a moment. Garin looked anywhere but at Tal. Though he'd known he had to come after his one-time mentor, he didn't know what to say. But Garin had done them all wrong. He couldn't let it fall apart now.

Then a thought struck him.

"Follow me," Garin said softly, then set off down the hall. Glancing back, he found Tal following. *Part of him is still with us,* he thought, and hoped it would be enough.

Stopping at the window Wren had shown him, he unlocked

the lever and swung the glass open. A cold wind blew against his face, chilling his skin. The earlier rain had ceased, but the promise of winter kissed the air.

He turned back to Tal. "Ready to lighten your life with another glorious risk?"

The shadow of a smile touched Tal's lips, but he made no response.

Garin stepped carefully out the window and edged along the ledge. His heart pounded hard in his chest, his stomach turned, and his hands prickled at the sight of all the space below them, all the more frightening from how the moon palely lit it. But he swallowed hard and kept edging along until the ledge widened and he could sit, finally breathing a relieved sigh.

Despite having decades on him, Tal was as graceful as a cat as he padded along the ledge to sit next to him.

They looked out over Halenhol, the howl of the wind the only sound between them. Halenhol was wreathed in a low-hanging fog, and only in noble manors and along the streets did murky lights shine. The distant forested hills were hidden from view, and the moons, both yellow and blue, hid shyly behind the thin clouds.

Garin spoke the first words that came to mind. "I followed you here to Halenhol because I wanted to see more of the World. I knew there was so much to life beyond Hunt's Hollow, beyond hoping for rain and chasing the town's girls in hopes of one day settling down on a farm of my own. My father was a soldier, a captain in the King's army, and had seen his fair share of the Westreach, and the stories he told me and my siblings had always stuck in my mind. And beyond those, I remembered all the tales of Markus Bredley, of Gendil of Candor... of you.

"But the World isn't what I thought it would be. I wished for its glory, its wonder — but there's far more to it than I ever wanted."

"I'm sorry." Tal's murmur was almost lost beneath the wind. "I failed you as well."

Garin turned toward him. "No. You haven't failed me, or you hadn't — not until you said Falcon was dead in the tower."

His wanton mentor didn't meet his gaze, but stared up at Cressalia, the yellow moon.

"When I first learned who you were," Garin continued, "I had trouble seeing Brannen Cairn as Tal Harrenfel. After all, I'd spent the last five years around your farm, watching you chase hens in the yard, roll in the mud with pigs, and live in a hovel that was mean even by Hunt's Hollow standards.

"But then I remembered all I'd seen you do. The bandits on the road, and the quetzals. The ghouls in the castle. And even back in Hunt's Hollow, how the Nightkin attacks had ceased for five blessed years. Then I knew it didn't matter what name you went by — you've always been the same man. The same..." Garin shrugged, trying to find the word, then finally settling for, "The same legend."

Tal snorted. "Legend. Falcon made up that legend, Garin, don't you realize that? At the King's behest, to bolster the flagging spirits of his citizens, the bard aggrandized my few good accomplishments and skirted over all I've done wrong. Falcon called me Devil Killer, but I didn't slay Heyl in Elendol. He claimed I single-handedly held off the Sendeshi army at the Pass of Argothe, but that was the moment I deserted the King's own. No mention is made of my time in the caves of the Dwarven Clans, acting as a mercenary and an assassin. No word was written of the true reasons I slaughtered the Yraldi marauders a whole summer long — not to protect innocents, but only to kill or finally die. And Magebutcher — only those who know the truth call me that thrice-damned name."

Garin found impatience building up in him, but he tempered his words. "I know your legend is a lie, Tal. I'd have to be blind not to know that by now."

His mentor's eyes gleamed in the scant moonlight as he glanced over. "If that's meant to cheer me, it's doing a poor job."

"You're missing my point. What I'm saying is that *despite* your legend, you *are* the Tal Harrenfel everyone believes in. Maybe you're not the best duelist in the Westreach, or a slayer of demons. But at your heart, you're a good man, Tal."

A harsh laugh escaped him. "A good man? A good man would never leave his friend behind."

Garin stared at the pale outline of his mentor as Tal again stared up at the moon. After a long stretch of silence, he repressed a sigh and rose. "Just think about it."

He turned away, but Tal's words stopped him. "You were already a man when you left Hunt's Hollow, Garin. But I've never believed it more than now."

Garin didn't turn back. He suspected it wasn't the wind that made his eyes suddenly sting.

He nodded, then skirted along the ledge to slip back inside the castle.

Tal kept an eye on Garin until he was safely across, then leveled his gaze back at the murky face of the yellow moon.

"Cressalia," he muttered. "You damned bitch." She was called the Regretful Sister — which was exactly the kind of company he didn't need right then.

He found himself mulling over the youth's words. He wanted to believe them, desperately wanted to. But they were riddled with holes and flaws. Garin thought he knew him, but he didn't. Tal had kept the worst of his past hidden from him still.

We only ever know the surface of others, he mused. *Only see the face they turn toward us.* Even of those he professed to love, it was true. After all, didn't he keep faithful to a woman he hadn't seen in two decades, a woman who had bound herself to another man and had a child by him? Didn't he keep faithful even when he hadn't really known or understood her then?

But she'd believed in you. Even then, before all of your deeds good and evil, she'd believed in you. She made you feel understood.

To his surprise, a smile creased his lips. Perhaps that was just it. No one could ever know another fully. But to not know and to believe in them anyway — perhaps that was the secret he'd struggled so long to find, the key to the door that led away from his self-imposed solitude.

He'd never been brave. Regardless of how others saw him, Tal had always been struck with fear at violence. Even with the bandits at the Winegulch Bridge, whom he'd been reasonably sure he and Aelyn could kill, he'd been afraid. But Garin had given him courage then. He'd known he would never let him down if he could help it.

And neither would he leave Falcon to die alone.

Tal rose and spared one last glance at the moon. "Regrets don't always make you weak," he conceded to her. "Sometimes, they help you remember what makes you strong. But I don't have you to thank for remembering that now."

Smiling wider still, he found his way back inside.

IMPERVIOUS

TAL PULLED OPEN THE TOWER DOOR. AS HE ENTERED, WREN, Garin, and Aelyn all looked over at him, a mixture of emotions crossing their faces — startlement, fear, anticipation.

"I'm going," he said even before the door closed behind him, the words rushing out before the lingering doubts could stifle them. "I'm going after Falcon, even though I'll likely die. But I have to go." His gaze held Garin's. "It's who I am."

Garin gave him a small smile.

Wren, however, had only a glare for him. "Don't say it unless you mean it."

Tal met her gaze. "I was a coward before. But I mean it now. There's not a man who's done more for me in the whole of the Westreach."

Wren swallowed hard and nodded. "Good. Then it's obvious what we have to do. We have to go to the Ruins of Erlodan."

"We?" Garin pushed away from the wall to stand next to Wren. "What do you mean, we?"

She didn't look at him. "I mean that I'm going."

The youth's eyes looked as if they might fall out of their sockets. "You can't. You heard Tal — you'll get yourself killed."

"I can!" She rounded on Garin. "And no one, not you or anyone else, can stop me!"

Tal rubbed at the stubble on his chin. "I suppose you're right."

Her gaze slid over to him, eyes narrowed. "You mean it?"

He sighed. "Wren, if anyone knows how impossible it is to stop someone from doing what they mean to, it's me. Far better to focus on how to keep you alive."

Garin looked from Wren to Tal and back, then swallowed visibly. "Then I'm coming, too," he said in a small voice.

Tal couldn't bring himself to look at him, wishing his chest didn't warm with pride at the youth's declaration. "If you must. But I think it's unwise."

"But you just said—"

"I can't stop you, true. But if you go, you risk becoming fully possessed by the Night."

Defiance was slowly replacing the fear in Garin's eyes. "I'm going, no matter what you think. And I think there's a way that I can help."

Tal raised an eyebrow. "Do tell."

Garin sucked in a shaky breath before speaking. "The Extinguished was counting on possessing me before, right? He planned to use me to get at Kaleras and did. If I show up at the ruins, he might try to use me again."

"Bait." Tal frowned. "I don't love the idea if I'm honest. It's a great risk for little reward."

"But I can do more," the youth hurried on. "I should have told you before, but... I can command the Nightkin."

Tal found himself sharing a look of disbelief with Aelyn.

"Command them?" Aelyn mocked. "Only Yuldor and his warlocks can do that."

"But I can — I've done it twice. When the tangle of quetzals had me surrounded, a voice whispered in my head, insisting that I let it help. So I did. Then I cried out something in a language I couldn't understand, and the quetzals scattered."

Tal bowed his head, the youth's words stirring buried thoughts. "Go on," he murmured.

"And that night in the courtyard, with the ghouls. I drew some of them away and ran down the castle halls, but I knew they were going to catch me. So I turned and faced them and commanded them to die — only I shouted it in some tongue I didn't recognize. And then they... burst."

Tal winced, but Wren was staring at Garin, mouth open and eyes wide. *The fascinations of youth,* he lamented.

"Convenient for you to only now tell us these hidden powers," Aelyn said with a cruel smile. "Either you were a liar then, or you're a liar now."

"I'm not a liar!" Garin said hotly, then winced. "Well, not now."

Tal moved closer to Garin and put a hand on his shoulder. "I believe you, lad. I understand why you hid the truth; those who are Night-touched are often killed without question. But that won't happen here."

He glanced back at Aelyn as he said the last, and though the bronze in his eyes swirled, the mage only smirked back.

"Why do you believe me?"

Tal looked back at Garin, and the youth met his eyes with a mixture of confusion and hope.

In the end, he thought, *every truth is revealed, and every lie unveiled.*

"Not long before I moved to Hunt's Hollow, I went into the East."

"You went *into* the East?" Garin and Wren exchanged a skeptical look, while Aelyn's brow furrowed.

"Yes. I ventured beyond the Fringes, beyond the mountains, and crossed the borders of the Empire of the Rising Sun. There, I sought a derelict tower, a place where I believed something of great value lay: secrets that Yuldor so feared, he'd killed all of the sorcerers who had resided there, though they had been his loyal subjects."

"This isn't in your songs." Wren frowned at him. "Why would my father not have sung about this?"

"Because I never told Falcon about it. I hadn't seen him until our arrival here in Halenhol, and we had more pressing concerns than writing new songs." Tal sighed. "Fortunately, my reticence has kept this hidden from the Prince of Devils for at least a little while longer."

He hoped that was true. But he remembered the conversation under the stars that he'd had with the man he'd thought was Falcon, two bottles of Jakadi wine drained between them, and he knew he couldn't account for every word spoken. *Silence, Solemnity, and Serenity,* he thought. *If you Whispering Gods watch over us, you'll have done what you do best and kept my tongue still.*

"As I was saying — I entered this desecrated tower, and at great cost, I recovered the tome that had drawn Yuldor's ire. The old book was, however, written in the Eastern dialect of the Worldtongue, what we call the Darktongue. While similar in structure to the Reach dialect, the words differ enough that I couldn't read them at first. Thus, I had to translate it."

"And so you painstakingly translated it for five years when you could have come to me and been done with the task in a month," Aelyn said, eyes swirling, lips twisting.

Tal met his gaze. "I did."

They matched stares for a long moment before the mage looked aside with disgust. "Secrets," Aelyn muttered. "I wonder, do you keep them close from discretion or habit?"

"Anything worthy of being called a secret should be kept hidden until it cannot. And that goes double for secrets close to the heart." Tal couldn't help a mocking smile even as he said it.

Garin opened his mouth but seemed only to speak reluctantly. "What does this book have to do with me?"

"Its author wrote of people who had experienced things very similar to what you described, Garin. Of hearing a voice — what she called a Singer — and a Song composed of all the sounds of the World. Of magic that sprang into people from Bloodlines devoid of natural sorcery."

The youth seemed to slump further with every word, like Tal were stacking each one of them, heavy as iron ingots, on his shoulders. "Did this happen because I took the cursed pendant?"

"Honestly? I don't know. It seems possible, especially since this Singer appears to assist the Extinguished." Tal closed the gap between them to put a hand on his shoulder. "But Garin — it was our fault that you entered the Ruins of Erlodan at all. Well, mostly the wizard's fault, but I'll take a small share of the blame."

"Until you can shirk it again," Aelyn commented.

Tal's smile was brief, especially as Garin's expression grew yet more forlorn. "It's also possible this was always with you but was only brought out by the pendant. The tome spoke of the Song coming to people from all walks of life without provocation. But any way you slice it, lad, this wasn't your fault."

"If you say so."

"Stop that." Wren had stepped forward and stood mere inches from Garin, glaring at him. "You can't feel sorry for yourself now. My father needs aid — because the World knows Falcon Sunstring won't save himself."

Garin opened his mouth, then seemed to think better of it. He resorted to a nod.

"That's better." The bard's daughter looked back at Tal with a raised eyebrow.

Tal turned his gaze to Aelyn. "What do you intend to do?"

The mage's smirk fell away, and his mouth worked as if he'd bitten into a lemon. "You stand little chance of success."

"I know."

"The Extinguished will set traps for you. He will be prepared."

"I'd expect nothing less."

"But still, you insist on going."

Tal glanced at Wren and Garin. "Yes."

Aelyn sighed, the sound as exasperated as it was resigned. "You're a fool, Harrenfel. A fool who will get himself killed."

"Not if you're there to protect my flank. At least, we'll stand a better chance."

The bronze smoldered in his eyes as he glared at him. "You know I have no choice. She'd never forgive me if I let you ride off to your death alone."

His chest stirred unexpectedly. *Decades, kingdoms, and kin-bonds separate you,* he thought with bitter amusement. *Yet still, just the barest mention of her can make you a boy again.*

"Thank you," he murmured.

Aelyn's scowl deepened. "As I said, I don't go for you."

"That's not what I'm thanking you for."

Looking aside, Tal cleared his throat and settled the old memories back into the past. Then he looked around at their small crew. "We'll get no more aid, unfortunately. The King was sad to lose his bard, but not so sorrowful as to spare soldiers for his recovery." A bitter smile twisted his lips. "Perhaps he's too frightened of the Soulstealer."

Or perhaps he has nothing to fear from the East any longer. He kept the thought to himself, too bleak to utter aloud.

"Then it's just us." Garin didn't sound as if he relished the conclusion.

"We'll be enough," Wren said with more confidence than Tal felt. "When do we leave?"

"As soon as we can." Tal started pacing again. "We'll ride through the night and sleep while the horses rest. It's over a week's ride to the ruins, and we won't get there any faster if we kill ourselves and our mounts hurrying."

But he knew any delays meant the Extinguished would have more time to prepare for their arrival and decrease the chance of Falcon still being alive. If he even was now. *He is alive,* he told himself fiercely. It wasn't all wishful thinking. Tal understood only a little of the Night's sorcery, but he'd long ago learned that a person whose soul and face have been stolen had to be kept alive for the illusion to remain intact. At least until the Soulstealer returned to the Ruins of Erlodan, his friend lived.

"Tal Harrenfel."

He glanced up to see the physician standing on the stairs.

"Warlock Kaleras wishes to see you," the wizened woman said.

Tal hesitated, wondering what consequences would follow if he refused. But, knowing better, he swallowed the rebellious feeling and ascended the stairs past the physician.

The room above was bright, with several lamps and the fireplace lit. A bed dominated the room and seemed to swallow the man lying in it. But Kaleras' eyes were as intelligent and intense as ever as they watched Tal mount the last step and stand at the top of the stairs.

"Come closer," the warlock said, his voice weak, but iron in his tone.

Tal reluctantly moved to stand next to the bed. "You wanted me?"

The sheets shifted, and the old warlock's hand emerged, revealing a dull gray ring on his middle finger. Tal stared at the Ring of Thalkuun, its green script seeming to pulse in brightness. When he looked up, he found Kaleras watching him.

The warlock gave him a bitter smile. "Much good it did me in the end."

"This isn't the end for you, old man."

"Perhaps. But the blade was poisoned. I have held the worst of it at bay, and the physician has done her best, but it is a potent poison." Kaleras shrugged, even the small movement seeming to cost him. "Night's End is an aptly named venom."

"Then bring another to heal you."

"A Magister has been summoned. But even if the Circle deigns to aid one who has abandoned their order, they won't be able to heal me." He wriggled his fingers slightly, calling attention to the gray, metal band on his middle finger.

Tal's gaze fell to the ring, comprehending his meaning. The Ring of Thalkuun warded the user against all magic, no matter if it was intended to be helpful or hurtful. "Why don't you simply remove it?"

"If I remove it, I am vulnerable. Which is precisely what the Enemy has been waiting for."

Kaleras' eyes never left him as he worked his other arm free from the blankets and moved it, trembling, to his hand. Slowly, twisting as if it had rusted on, he pulled the band free of his finger, then held it up in his palm.

Tal didn't take it. "Why? Why offer this now?"

The warlock's eyes narrowed. "I told you, Harrenfel. I must remove it to be healed. And it will do me little good anyway while I lay here dying."

"You didn't have any qualms taking it from me and leaving me to die."

"I didn't know you then, boy!" Kaleras meant to roar the words, but they only came out as a furious wheeze. "I didn't know who you—" He cut off and turned his head aside, closing his hand over the ring.

As Tal stared down at the wasted features of the old warlock, long-repressed feelings pushed their way back to the surface. "You didn't know what?" he asked quietly.

"Just take it."

But Tal continued, voice low and cold, the knowledge he'd struggled long and hard to win, that he'd nursed with bitter resentment for decades, finally breaking forth.

"First, allow me to tell you a story. I was born in Hunt's Hollow nearly forty-one years ago. My mother was the daughter of a fletcher, supplying arrows for the outposts along the Fringes and for our kings' endless wars."

"We don't have time for this. You must—"

"One night," Tal spoke over him, "a warlock came through

town on his way to a citadel in the East and saw my mother in the tavern. He took a fancy to her, and she to him — but her fascination, it was said, was to an unnatural degree. After a night of passion, the warlock continued on his way, leaving the woman behind with the present of a bastard—"

"Enough!"

Kaleras had turned as pale as his sheets, his chest heaving with every breath, and he spoke through gritted teeth. "I was young and drunk on my power. I thought myself untouchable — by the evils of the East, by morality, all of it. But I never lost sight of myself so much as to do... what you think I did. Talania took a fancy to me, yes, and I to her. I had charms about me to make folks look on me with a kinder eye, it's true, but warlocks are often killed if they don't take such measures. It was not to... seduce."

As the warlock spoke, Tal felt as calm and serene as a mountain lake, his life and past in sudden clarity. And for once, he saw the blame lay with someone else.

"You enthralled her," he said quietly. "Then you raped her."

"*NO!*"

A gust blew through the tower, the warlock unable to contain the force of his fury. For a moment, his eyes promised further retribution; then his head fell back against the pillows, exhausted.

"No," he repeated, this time in a whisper. "I won't pretend it was love. But it was mutual. She agreed, I agreed..."

Tal found a smile tugging at his lips, though there was not a shred of mirth left in him. "Nevertheless. You don't seem surprised. When did you figure it out?"

The old warlock met his gaze again. "I'd suspected there was something to you ever since we met. A touch of the eldritch in your eyes, but also something else I couldn't quite grasp. Then, after you fled your performance with the Dancing Feathers at that Sendeshi nobleman's manor, I became curious and learned what I could of you. Once I discovered you were from Hunt's Hollow, it was simple to piece the rest together."

Tal searched the warlock's deep brown eyes. Did he see remorse there, in those eyes so like his? Could this man feel enough remorse for it to matter?

He thought back to his childhood. To his mother, a disgraced woman, scrounging to provide a living for him while others spat at her feet as they passed in the street. Working day and night, fletching arrows when they had the materials, scrubbing laundry when they didn't, despair creasing her brow to the last day she lived. He remembered and found himself hardening.

Are you without fault? part of him mocked. *Have you never made mistakes?*

A smile twisted his lips. He had only to remember his many names to recount all the errors he'd made. But he found his heart no softer for the memories.

Tal held out his hand. "I'll take the ring. But giving it to me does nothing to ease your guilt, considering you stole it from me in the first place."

Kaleras' gaze turned to flint again. "You won't forget my mistake?"

"No one seems able to forget mine."

For a moment, he thought the warlock would rescind his offer. Then, with a bitter twist of his lips, he opened his hand and offered the dull gray band again.

Tal took it and held it up, staring at the glyphs. He could read the larger letters, the founding script of the enchantment, but his grasp of the Worldtongue fell away for every fine line that trailed away from the primary runes.

"*Thalkuun Haeldar,*" he whispered. "The One Impervious to the Heart."

A thought flickered through his head as he whispered the words, the vague notion of an idea. But he tucked it away even as he put the Ring of Thalkuun on his middle finger. The shiver of the enchantment pressed over him, and he felt as if he'd stepped into a shadow after standing under the sun's heat.

"Return that to me." Any gentleness in Kaleras' countenance had dissipated entirely. "And be sure you kill the Night-lusting bastard."

Tal stood. "I will."

He turned and began to descend the stairs, but paused and half-turned back, just seeing the warlock from the corner of his vision. "Oh, and Kaleras?"

"Yes?"

Did he hear a note of expectation in his voice? *He needn't have bothered getting his hopes up.* "I have something I'll leave with you in return. Something that might keep you entertained while you're an invalid."

He didn't have to look around to know Kaleras glared at him. "I'm hardly an invalid. But leave what you must."

Nodding, Tal turned back down the stairs, feeling the warlock's gaze on him until he disappeared out of sight.

LIKE OLD FRIENDS

JUST A MOMENT LONGER. ONE MORE GALLOP — ONE MORE — AND another—

Garin struggled to keep his eyes open, but they fought back in equal measure. Had someone told him that he could fall asleep riding a horse at full tilt, he would have laughed them out of the room.

He wasn't laughing now.

Four days, they'd kept up the grueling pace, only resting for the horses while they choked down hard bread and cold, salted meat — then it was back into their saddles again. Despite his complaints about the waste of his talents, Aelyn bolstered the horses' endurance through a steady supply of enchantments. When Garin snidely suggested he ought to spare some on the riders, the mage looked on the verge of showing him a piece of the Night's Pyres then and there.

All of them were nearing their thread's ends — all save Tal. With each mile they neared the ruins, he seemed to grow more vital, more full of life, as if there was no amount of rest or food in the World that could match whatever sustenance awaited him there.

Garin knew the feeling well.

He felt the cursed place drawing nearer, its Night-touched stones calling to him in a faint, ghostly chorus. And no matter how he tried to shut it out, he inevitably found himself straining to hear it again. As much as he feared listening, he feared more its fading.

It's the Night, he told himself, over and over. *It's Yuldor and his kin, trying to lure you to their side.* But though his fascination repulsed him, he couldn't deny it.

So he busied himself worrying over other things. His horse, a dun mare, was loaded with unfamiliar implements of war. A round shield, plain but sturdy. A sword of steel rather than the wooden ones he'd practiced with. Armor of chainmail and padded leather. A crossbow that he'd received with little more than cursory instructions and was still unsure how to load.

Only three months ago, he'd started to learn to fight. And now he intended to take on one of the Extinguished and all the Nightkin at his disposal. But what choice did he have? He'd made a mistake — if stabbing a man between the ribs could be called a mistake — and had to set things right. A man always set things right. Didn't he?

He thought of how his brothers would laugh at him, how his mother would scold, and Lenora would gently ask, *Are you sure about this?* All he had to do was keep riding, all the way to the East Marsh, and he'd be home in another week or two.

His eyes burned, and not just from the constant air rushing past his face.

But every time his courage began to falter, he had only to glance next to him to find it surging again. Wren looked nearly as eager as Tal, though her strength seemed brittle compared to his, like ice cracking under the weight of a boulder. Garin could hardly blame her. The Soulstealer had impersonated her father, had taken his face, his voice, even his memories to mold himself into the perfect doppelgänger. She'd spoken with him, hugged him, confided in him for months, and never known.

But why she would have guilt burning in her eyes, he

couldn't understand. It wasn't her fault this happened to her father. She was as much a victim, and as innocent, as he. But every time he thought to say it during their brief respites, he found his tongue sticking to the roof of his mouth.

Tal held up a hand, and Garin sighed in relief as he slowed his mount to a walk. The evening had bled to dusk, and now even the blue light was fading. Beneath him, his horse panted, its coat sheeny with sweat.

Wheeling his blonde gelding around, Tal faced them. "We'll draw up camp here for the night. The path to the Ruins of Erlodan lies just ahead. Tomorrow morning, we'll find it and make for our puppeteer."

"And my father," Wren said fiercely.

Tal nodded with a small smile. "And Falcon."

Dismounting, Garin blinked away the dragging exhaustion and set to finding an adequate spot for camp off the road. Well-practiced as they'd become, within a quarter-hour they were hidden behind a small grassy knoll, wrapped up in their bedrolls, with full, if unsatisfied, bellies.

As usual, Garin had made up his bed next to Wren. Though they barely spoke, he found it comforting to have her near and hoped she felt the same. He listened to the nighttime noises of crickets, the hum of life surrounding them, just loud enough to drown out the Nightsong, the discordant, rhythmless sounds always murmuring behind his thoughts. Sighing with relief, he began to drift off.

"I doubt he's still alive."

His eyes snapped back open, and he turned to look at Wren. In the moon-lifted darkness, he only saw the outline of her face and her shining eyes staring up into the star-dusted sky. He didn't have to ask who she meant.

"Of course, he is." He didn't sound sure even to his ears. He tried again, his voice stronger. "You remember what Tal said. That bastard Soulstealer would have kept him alive to impersonate him. And besides, he seemed to know we'd come after him. Your father would be far better bait alive than... you know."

Wren gave a doubtful grunt.

Garin swallowed, then said the words he thought she needed to hear, even if he didn't know why. "It wasn't your fault, Wren. You know that, right?"

She shifted, her gaze finding his. Even in the darkness, he detected the faint movement of the gold in her eyes. "Isn't it? I know exactly when the Extinguished took him."

"You do?"

"Three and a half months ago, he went to Gladelyl to research for a song he'd been writing. A song of ancient times, of the forging of the Bloodlines, and of the Worldheart."

"The Worldheart?"

"Never mind that." Wren looked back up at the sky. "The point is that when he returned, he didn't seem right. More prone to anger, less wont to laugh and smile. But I didn't think much of it. 'He'll get back to normal soon,' I told myself. And so I ignored it and pretended everything was fine."

Garin sighed. "That doesn't make it your fault."

"My father has been his prisoner for months. Maybe he's alive, maybe not. But if he is, how could he be whole? His soul..." Her words choked off, then she spoke through it angrily, "That *thing* took his soul. It broke him."

The Nightsong suddenly grew loud for a moment, and Garin spoke so that he didn't have to listen to it. "It's like Master Krador is always telling us — we have to focus on what is, not what might be."

Wren turned back to him, her eyes finding his. "You might be right," she whispered, then gave a quiet laugh. "After all, we don't know that we'll even survive."

His heart pounding a little harder, Garin pulled his arm free of his bedroll and reached out toward her across the cold ground. A moment later, her fingers intertwined with his.

Despite his fear, despite what he knew tomorrow would

bring, he smiled into the darkness, glad at least they would face it together.

Just as gray light began to lift the darkness from the sky, Tal rose from his bedroll, pulled on his boots, and began collecting firewood. He'd built and lit the campfire by the time Aelyn joined him. Unlike on the way to Halenhol, the mage didn't spare any magic to form himself a chair, but sat cross-legged on the ground, back stiff and straight as if he were in council before his queen.

"Finally came down to our level, did you?" Tal gave him a small smile from across the fire.

Aelyn scowled. "Life is one long jape to you, isn't it?"

"And for you, it's one long chore. But never fear, my dour companion. One way or another, our service will be over soon."

"Yes. I imagine it will." The mage looked back into the flames, the firelight making the bronze in his eyes shine even brighter.

First comes the brooding. Then the doubts. Then despair. Tal knew the cycle well, and knew, too, he had to cut it off early lest it spiral out of control. Fortunately, he knew the quickest way to inflate a self-absorbed cockerel like Aelyn: shameless flattery.

"What can you tell me of what our adversary has prepared for our coming?" he asked lightly. "A Nightkin expert like you ought to know."

Aelyn narrowed his eyes, no doubt searching for the insult in the compliment. "Every evil imaginable, I suspect. In a place as Night-touched as Erlodan's Ruins, the Nameless will have access to much more power than he did in the Coral Castle. To make no mention of no longer needing to uphold his disguise as Falcon, which must have taken a tremendous amount of his power to hold so tightly for so long."

"But what specifically?" Tal pressed. "Surely a learned man such as you can say more?"

"A *learned man*, am I?" The mage snorted. "I'm immune to flattery, Harrenfel."

Not flattery, then, Tal decided. *An elf with a rotten heart only needs someone to feel superior to.* He tweaked his expression to look chastened, if still smug.

"But as we're aligned in this endeavor," Aelyn continued with a smirk, "I'll give you the knowledge you seek."

"I'd like nothing better."

Aelyn leaned forward, shadows dancing over his face. "The Nameless will set himself up in the deepest catacombs, weakening us by stages until we reach him. First, he'll cover the grounds with Night-touched mist that will sicken and slow our minds. Then, once we've passed into the upper catacombs, he'll test our strength and probe for weaknesses."

"I'm sure he'll find none of those."

"He'll set Nightkin of every cunning upon us. Quetzals and chimeras will only be the start — ghouls, shades, perhaps even a wyvern if he planned ahead."

Tal snorted. "At least you didn't claim a dragon. Even still, I think we've strayed a little. If even a runty wyrm had roosted in the ruins, fresh rumors would have flown across the Westreach."

"Perhaps so," Aelyn conceded grudgingly. "But there will be manners of evil such as you and I have never seen."

Tal didn't let his smile slip, even if his heart was starting to rattle like a loose wagon wheel. It didn't matter that he knew Aelyn was trying to get a rise out of him; the truth remained that they had no idea what lay in wait.

"So, what are we going to do about it?" Tal asked lightly.

The mage glanced to either side, then leaned closer. "I've been saving something for just such an occasion as this," he said in a low voice. "All we need do is get me close enough to the Nameless and, I assure you, he is as good as dead."

"Or, shall we say, extinguished?"

Aelyn grimaced and leaned back, muttering, "And this is the man I throw my lot in with."

Tal grinned even as he realized why Aelyn had spoken softly. *Garin.* He believed him the pet of the Extinguished still. And not without reason. They hadn't tried cleansing him; only one healer he knew of was powerful enough to attempt it, and she was far out of reach.

"Well, we have as good a plan as we're likely to get. There's just one thing I'm still wondering."

As Aelyn watched him with plain suspicion, he reached back into his pack and, feeling the rough edges of cloth, drew out a covered object, then slowly unwrapped it. Amidst the wrappings lay an old book, its leather cover worn, but the sharp glyphs still legible.

Now the mage looked interested. Rising and drawing near, he stared at the tome like a dog at a bloody bone. "*A Fable of Song and Blood.*" Aelyn looked up with narrowed eyes. "You brought a priceless, irreplaceable book along on a mission unlikely to succeed?"

"Never mind that. You can read the Darktongue — see this passage here." Tal opened the book carefully and pointed a finger above the yellowed page. "What does this say?"

Aelyn narrowed his eyes, but his curiosity overwhelmed his distaste. "'Thus I will come outright and declare my unsavory belief: that the Heart searches for another to possess it.'"

Though the elf tried to read further, Tal drew the book away and closed it. His blood seemed to turn into boiling oil as it pumped through his veins, and his hands shook as he slipped the book back into his pack. "It has to be," he murmured. "That has to be it."

"What in all the Night's Pyres does that mean?" Aelyn demanded. He looked ready to dive after the book and take it by force, the muscles in his face twitching as he stared at Tal's pack. "What 'Heart' is it talking about? What is unsavory about that?"

"Never mind. I only wanted to confirm my translation was sound." Tal cocked a grin, half-hearted as it was, knowing Aelyn would keep after this unless he put him off the scent. "But, as usual, my skills have been found to be prodigious."

Aelyn snorted in disgust and rose. "We don't have time for this. If we're to be up to the derelict fortress and back before sundown, we must start moving."

Tal rose as well and held out a hand. "I don't know if I'd call you a friend, a rival, or a curmudgeon I'd rather avoid. But I'm glad you're here fighting beside me."

Aelyn eyed his hand disdainfully and didn't take it. "I wish I could say the same."

Tal let his hand drop, his smile growing wider. *Even at the end, some things never change.*

THE FICKLE WOODS

GARIN SHIVERED AND PULLED HIS CLOAK TIGHTER AROUND HIM. Though winter had yet to claim Avendor fully, the day was overcast and cold, and the chill inevitably seeped through his clothes as he and the rest of the small rescue party plodded through the bogs surrounding the ruins. They'd left their horses behind and proceeded on foot, knowing the mounts were unsuitable for the terrain and noisier than Tal preferred. Stinking mud spilled over the tops of his boots, numbing his feet and chafing his legs.

But it was the Nightsong growing steadily louder in his head, and the knowledge of where they headed, that posed the worst of his misery.

The unfamiliar scabbard at his hip caught again in the underbrush, and Garin wrenched it free, the shield swinging from where it hung across his back. He ached from the march already, their short rests and long rides already having worn him down to a ghost of himself. *And we have yet to fight*, he thought glumly.

Fight. How could he expect to contribute anything in a fight? He was a novice by any standards, and not a skilled one. He'd barely had the courage to stand up to the ghouls in the

Coral Castle, or the quetzals before that, and only survived by the shame he wished he could forget.

I will protect you.

The words rose from the incongruous sounds of the Nightsong that undercut his every thought. Garin tried not to hear them, tried not to listen, but he found himself tempted by the Nightvoice all the same.

If it helps me survive, he thought, *and saves my friends, can it be so evil?*

But as soon as he found himself thinking it, he repressed it again. This Singer, as Tal had called it, was the same as had told him to stab Kaleras, the same that commanded the Nightkin, the same that served the same Master of the Soulstealer. It was an unholy creature, a devil whispering in his ear, and all the old stories told the same of devils: never accept their deals.

But when he scanned the forest around them and considered what might be lying within the gloom, he couldn't deny that he was tempted.

His companions provided little help in taking his mind off of it. Aelyn and Tal had strayed ahead, their heads bent in conference. Wren trudged beside him, but stared straight ahead, her jaw set, the gold spiraling in her eyes. As often as not, a hand rested on the pommel of her sword, as if she was eager for an enemy to appear so she could cut it down. He had thought she would look as ridiculous as he in their borrowed gear, but instead found it suited her. Shorter and slighter than him she might be, but she was far more the warrior than he'd ever manage.

Tal turned and met his eyes, then stopped and waited while Aelyn continued ahead. As Garin and Wren reached him, he walked between them.

"Wren," he said, his tone as light as if they were making conversation back in the safety of the Coral Castle's halls, but his voice pitched soft. "I've meant to talk to you about something."

Garin hesitated, wondering if he should fall back, but Tal caught his eye. "Stay, Garin. This might be instructive for you as well."

"What do you want to say?" Wren asked abruptly.

"You have elven blood. You know what that means, don't you?"

"Lively eyes and pointed ears?"

Tal chuckled. "There's that. But it also means sorcery should come naturally to you. Today, we will test how much you tend to the Eldritch Bloodline."

Wren glanced at Tal and said nothing, but he hardly seemed to notice, his eyes bright as he gazed at her.

"Have you ever heard of the Worldtongue?"

"My father mentioned it in some of his older stories. It's the language of the World, the tongue that birthed all the tongues of the Bloodlines at their creation. For those with sorcery in their veins, speaking the Worldtongue evokes magic. Or so he said."

"Close enough. Did he teach you any words? Test the strength of your blood?"

Wren shook her head.

Tal grinned. "No time like before a fight to experiment. Speak the word after me — and you may want to stand back."

As Garin and Wren walked a little further apart, Tal raised a hand, then spoke, his voice deep and sonorous. "*Kald!*"

Flames, blue and hot, billowed up from Tal's outstretched hand, illuminating the forest for a moment.

Tal gestured at Wren. "Your turn. But before you try it, bear this in mind: magic must draw from a source. The Worldtongue molds and multiplies the flows of energy, but it must have a starting spark to work from. Minor cantrips like for fire use the body, and you'll feel chilled casting it once. But use it too many times in a row, and you'll be cold as a corpse and likely to end up one soon after. If you have a pressing need for it, though, it's best to alternate it with the cantrip for ice, *lisk*, which will draw heat back in." At the last word, particles of ice filmed his glove, and Tal smiled as he shook them away. "Understood?"

Wren nodded, then held out a hand for her own test. "*Kald!*"

As orange flames reared up in Wren's hand, Garin's gaze caught on something other than her astonished expression. For, as the murky gloom of the forest lifted, he saw shadowy figures all around them.

"Good," Tal said. "Now, Garin, I wanted you to—"

"In the woods!" he interrupted, pointing. "There!"

Tal had his sword out before Garin had finished speaking, and werelights blossomed around him like a swarm of fireflies. The silhouettes appeared again, strangely man-shaped, not the massive monsters that the flashes of shadows had made them seem. All the same, Garin found himself staring, jaw slack, breath caught in his throat, wondering what the Extinguished had thrown their way.

"Draugars," Tal said calmly as he circled Wren and Garin like a wolf protecting its cubs.

"Of course." Aelyn had dropped back to their knot, though he seemed unconcerned by the enemies surrounding them. "I expect they'll be recent revenants brought up from the village graveyards."

"Unless they're ancient bones from the ruins," Tal countered, eyes never leaving the slowly tightening ring.

Aelyn shrugged. "If we're unlucky."

"You going to fight?" Wren hissed.

Garin hadn't drawn his sword or shield. Cursing himself for a fool, he scrambled to do both at once and nearly lost his blade in the bog.

"What are they?" he asked, ashamed that his voice shook.

"Reanimated corpses," Tal replied. "Cadavers brought back from the dead with a singular hate for the living. They have the same strength and speed as a man and, fortunately, die the same as if they were alive."

Garin doubted he could match even a slow man at that moment, much less a living carcass. "We're dead," he whispered.

"Not as dead as they are." Tal grinned at him, and Garin found himself smiling back. A weak joke, perhaps, but somehow, it let him breathe a little easier.

But the draugars were closing in, little more than a dozen feet away. Garin raised his shield and held his sword at the ready, rehearsing all the things he'd learned from Master Krador.

"Wren, use that cantrip," Tal said, speaking fast now. "Burning them can work as well as hacking them apart. Garin, I'm afraid you'll have to do it the old-fashioned way. Too dangerous for you to attempt magic now."

"Great." His breath was coming quick. Draugars stared at him through the darkness, their eyes unnaturally bright, rusted steel glinting dully in their hands.

Then they charged.

All thoughts of maneuver and technique went out of his head as the two closest draugars bore down. He threw up his shield, and as a blade hacked into the wood, his arm went numb to the shoulder. Gasping, he swung at the second draugar, but it dodged and punched a fist forward. Pain exploded from his nose, and Garin stumbled back, flailing to keep it at bay as his vision filled with sparkling lights.

But the draugar who'd struck him suddenly snarled and fell back — someone had chopped at its leg — so Garin stabbed at the draugar still trying to work its blade free from his shield. His sword found a gap in its side, and it shrieked, its cry of fury joining the chorus that had filled the forest. As it tugged away, he almost lost his weapon but managed to keep hold as it withdrew with a sickening squelch.

The remaining draugar had abandoned its sword and drawn a knife, and though one leg was hacked nearly off, still it came on, wasted face contorted with rage. Garin ripped the shield free from his arm and threw it against the dead man, and it caught it in the face, snapping its head back.

He took his chance with a wild swing, but his blade banged into the draugar's rusted pauldron and bounced away, sending him spinning off balance. As Garin tried to steady himself, he felt the draugar bearing down on him, swinging furiously at him with its knife.

The Nightsong welled up in his head, the whirlwind of sounds and senses nearly overwhelming him.

I will aid you, Listener. The fell Singer emerged from the clamor. *Let me protect you. Cede me control, and none will stand before us.*

"No!" he tried to roar, but he had no breath left.

The draugar stabbed down at him, and he threw up an arm as if he still wore a shield. The knife tore into his flesh, glancing off the bone. Red pain surged, threatening to drown him.

Clawing at consciousness, Garin stabbed upward and was surprised when his blade found its way under the dead man's breastplate and slid into its chest. The draugar stiffened and looked down, its features frozen in a furious scream. It almost seemed surprised to find a foot of steel stuck in its body.

Then the draugar looked up and raised the knife again.

Cede to me, or you die! the Singer lashed through his head.

"I don't want to die." It was near a whimper as Garin stared up at the dead man, this impossible enemy, trembling with the knife held aloft, but looking capable of killing him all the same.

Cede to me!

He had no choice. As the draugar brought down the dagger, Garin felt himself let go, and a sudden heat filled his body.

He seized him and twisted his body out of the way. *He* pulled the blade free, dodged around the clumsy draugar, and cut its legs out from under it. *He* stabbed the sword through the neck of the creature as it screamed on the ground, silencing it.

I will protect you, the Singer whispered, then withdrew its searing touch.

Garin reeled, shivering, barely keeping his feet. Only the battle still raging around him kept him from slumping over, curled around his gashed arm. Hovering lights illuminated the forest, showing the shapes of Tal and Wren cutting down the dead men and Aelyn, wreathed in flames, sending them burning to the ground. Turning, he saw more draugars running in from the forest, a score or more seething shadows.

Terror clenched his chest, and his throat seized so tightly it was nearly impossible to speak. Yet he squeezed out the words. "Help them."

Exaltation and triumph flooded through him, and Garin knew it wasn't his own.

"Dead men," Tal wheezed to himself, "shouldn't be able to move so fast."

He'd been counted a skilled warrior in his day, the most skilled by some false accounts. Falcon had once declared that he, Tal Harrenfel, had held off the whole of the Sendeshi army at the Pass of Argothe. The bard had also written that there was no duelist in all of the Reach Realms that had ever managed to touch Tal, much less win against him.

Unfortunately, both of those tales were flagrantly false.

As the draugars flooded the forest, driving at him and his companions, it was all he could do to avoid their rusted blades. In theory, he needn't have bothered; as summoned creatures, the Ring of Thalkuun ought to have protected him from their attacks. But the rules of sorcery were fickle things, and none knew it better than he. He wasn't going to risk being stuck with a sword on a hunch.

For every draugar he cut back into a corpse, three more took its place. He'd lost track of Garin and was barely managing to keep Wren alive, though the youth was holding her own.

"*Kald!*" Tal cried, and swept the blazing blade through three of the enemy at once, sending them reeling backward, blue flames engulfing their bodies. The other draugars faltered for a moment, and Tal risked a glance around. Wren fought two draugars at once, her sword weaving in and out as she parried and riposted. Aelyn made two more of the dead men erupt into blue flames, his lips pulled back into a disdainful sneer.

And Garin? The boy you roped into this mess?

But the draugars were surging forward again, and Tal had no time to look further. He blocked a blade, cut into another on the backswing, twisted out of a stab, kicked the leg out from a third. "*Lisk!*" he called, then "*Kald!*" — again, and again, and the corpses fell burnt or frozen to the ground, the corrupted souls bleeding out of them once more.

But despite the fury of the battle, the constant sorcery was leaving him weak and shivering. As yet more draugars ran at them from among the dark trees, he found himself doubting. *I'm sorry, Falcon, for all the ways I've failed you,* he thought. *You cannot know how much.*

A figure ran past his left, and Tal spun, sword raised. But he stopped short of striking as he recognized the lanky, youthful form running in front of him, straight at the oncoming draugars.

"Garin!" Tal roared and sprinted after him.

There'd been blood smeared across the youth's arm, too much blood, but Garin didn't seem slowed by it. Charging the foremost of the enemies, he stopped and raised his sword. Tal was still several paces behind when the draugars reached the youth. But before they could strike him down, unearthly words cut into Tal's ears. He cringed as the Ring of Thalkuun burned on his finger, and within, his blood surged.

The draugars, however, didn't fare so well. All had stopped fighting and were lined up in a row before Garin, like soldiers presenting themselves to an officer. The terrible words ushered forth from the youth's mouth again, and the draugars moved, twisting their swords around to point at their midriffs.

Then Garin screamed once more, and they thrust the blades into themselves. As one, they slumped forward and collapsed like grass before a scythe.

As Garin turned, Tal could barely meet his gaze. Something else looked out from his eyes, curled his lips into a triumphant smile, made him stand so unnaturally unaware of the deep cut oozing blood from his arm.

You got him into this. Now get him out.

Tal dropped his sword and raised his hands as he advanced on the youth. "Garin," he said softly, speaking as if to a skittish horse. "Come back to us, Garin. The danger's gone; you took care of it. Now it's time to come back."

His expression spasmed, eyes flickering, mouth twitching. Garin's shoulders slumped, but his eyes never left Tal's.

"You will let the blood flow," the youth whispered. "But he will incite the chorus to sing."

Then he fell forward.

Tal caught him and eased him to the ground. Garin groaned, and his eyes rolled up in the back of his head. *He's free.* Tearing his gaze away, Tal scanned the rest of his body and found the most severe wound was on his arm. And what a wound it was, with the flesh torn all the way down to the bone. He'd seen plenty of gore in his day, but he still found his gut twisting at the sight of the boy's injury.

"Garin?" Wren had reached them, and Tal saw her eyes were more panicked than she'd shown during the fight. "Is he…?"

"Get Aelyn," Tal ordered her as he pulled out his knife and began cutting off Garin's sleeve short of the wound. When it was exposed, he studied it. *Clean it, stitch it, bind it.* The old advice from the battlefield infirmaries that he'd worked in as a boy came back to him slowly. It was the best he could do out here.

Wren returned a moment later with the mage, and Tal glanced up from his work. "His arm is cut deep. I need you to purify the wound for corruption."

Aelyn nodded. "I'll require a catalyst — there's one in my pack."

He moved swiftly away while Wren edged closer. The young woman hardly ever seemed uncertain, but now, she looked as wary as Garin had when first entering the Small-stage. "He'll make it," she whispered, and it sounded more like a question than a statement. "He'll make it."

Keep her busy, or the panic will. "Bring me my cloak, or yours," Tal told her. "And my water flask and pack. Quickly!"

She scrambled to do as he'd asked.

Pulling off his shirt, Tal barely felt the cold as he kept pressure on the wound as he waited, his blood hot in his veins. Garin's face was pale, and his lips moved, but only faint, jumbled words came out.

As Aelyn returned and bent before the lad, Tal moved over, letting the mage sprinkle powder from a sack over the wound, then lay his hands over it, heedless of the blood that oozed over them. The mage began muttering just loud enough for Tal to catch the words. He listened intently, hoping he wouldn't need to say them himself, but determined to know them should the need arrive.

A minute later, Aelyn released his arm and stood. "That should have cleansed him of the most common corruptions."

"Then we've got to stop this bleeding."

As Wren returned, she offered the water flask and cloak wordlessly, though her eyes wandered over him, no doubt wondering at the scars and tattoos scrawled across his skin. Tal ignored her and poured the whole flask over the wound, cleaning it as best as he could, then ruffled through his pack. "Cut strips from my cloak," he instructed Wren, and she pulled out her belt knife and set to it.

Finding his needle and gut, he threaded the needle, knotted

the opposite end of the gut, and glanced at Aelyn. "Hold the wound shut."

The mage only slightly scowled as he knelt and pressed the frayed splits of the flesh together. Tal noticed his own hands were shaking. *The performance matters this time,* he thought. But he'd overcome his stage fright long ago, and he inserted the needle through Garin's skin.

Minutes later, the wound was pulled tightly closed with a neat row of stitches, and Tal took the strips of his cloak from Wren and began winding them tightly around the wound. The bottom layer saturated the cloth almost as soon as he'd bound it, but by three more layers, the blood had stopped seeping through. *For the moment, at least.*

Tal glanced at the other two: Wren kneeling next to them, her face pale, Aelyn scanning their surroundings, his scowl growing more pronounced by the moment.

"We can't stay here," Tal said.

"That much is obvious," Aelyn noted irritably. "Unless you'd prefer that more Nightkin find us."

"He can't move!" Wren said fiercely. "Look!"

"I can walk."

Tal stared down in amazement as Garin sat up, his uninjured hand set to his head. A moment later, he came to his senses and pressed the youth back down. "You'll faint if you try and stand now. Wren, could you fetch more water?"

When she returned with another flask, Tal offered it to Garin, and the youth drank it down, reluctantly at first, then greedily. He'd nearly sucked the skin dry by the time Tal pulled it away.

"I'll bolster his strength if I must, but we need to leave," Aelyn said, fingers tapping on his arm.

Wren had stood again, fists clenched at her sides, eyes staring behind them. "Too late," she hissed. "Look!"

Tal whipped his head around and found dark shapes

advancing through the trees. "Yuldor's prick," he groaned. He glanced down at Garin and met his eyes. "Can you walk?"

His face was pale, but his jaw stiffened, and he nodded.

Tal pulled on his bloodstained shirt and his leather jerkin after, and slung his pack over his shoulders. Then he hauled Garin to his feet and, keeping a supporting hand on his arm, his other hand clutched *Velori*. "Warn me if they get too close," he told Aelyn, then set forth, their pace excruciatingly slow.

The mage walked beside him, his eyes still peeled behind. "I don't know that they will," he said softly. "If they meant to attack, they would have charged as the ones before had." His eyes flickered over to Tal, bronze flashing in the fey light hovering above them. "They're herding us."

Tal looked up the hill. "Little wonder where. Still have your surprise ready?"

Aelyn smiled, the pleasure sharp and eager. "Just get me close, Harrenfel, and I'll take care of the rest."

If we survive that long. Even with all the close encounters throughout his illustrious career, Tal was starting to wonder if his luck was running out.

FABLE'S END

In all of their journey of exhausting escapades, Garin had never felt so low.

His head felt so light he thought he must soon float away from the World. His arm throbbed with painful regularity, sending hammer blows up his shoulder and into the base of his skull. The makeshift bandages were already soaked through with blood.

But he ground his teeth and said nothing. No point in complaining; neither he nor his companions could do anything about it. Halt, and the draugars herding them might decide it was finally time to end their march. And always, the incessant Nightsong filled his head so that it felt fit to burst.

All he could do was clench his jaw and keep stumbling up the hill.

As they ascended, a fog thickened around them until the day, already gray to start, became as gloomy as a moonlit night, and their draugar escorts faded to dark smudges. It almost came as a relief when the trees abruptly thinned before them, and high walls loomed out of the flat gray. Garin lifted his head to stare at the mist-wreathed Ruins of Erlodan. *If I had just waited outside the ruins like Tal had wanted, none of this would have happened,* he thought. *And I never would have stabbed Kaleras.*

But as his brothers had often said, regrets weren't worth a fart at the best of times. His gaze fell back to his feet as they shuffled forward amongst the cracked foundations of the time-worn castle.

After some time, he raised his head again and scanned the area. There were innumerable shadows and alcoves in which other Nightkin could be hiding, to say nothing of the fog that pooled in the dark spaces. *But if the Extinguished wanted to kill us, he would have sent in the other draugars.* There was something else Yuldor's warlock wanted, something they could only give alive. But with half the blood in his body leaking from his arm, Garin doubted he'd be able to think it through.

Soon.

The word was faint, less than a whisper, but Garin shivered at it all the same.

Tal pulled him to a halt, and Garin jerked his head up. A courtyard opened before them, but the thickest mist yet filled it so that even the ruined walls surrounding them were nearly lost from sight. Only one shadow, a lone figure dwarfed amid the fog, stood before them.

As comprehension washed over him, Garin felt his legs give way beneath him. Only Tal's grip on his arm kept him upright.

"Stay strong," his would-be mentor whispered to him. "You're stronger than him."

It seemed a funny thing to say when he'd never felt so weak.

"You came." It was Falcon's voice that rang out, echoing unnaturally in the fog, but it sounded wrong. The tone had harshened, and the cruel edge that Garin had begun to glimpse toward the end of the Soulstealer's facade had grown razor sharp.

"Against all reason, all wisdom," the Extinguished continued, "still, you came. As I knew you would."

"We came," Tal called back. "And you know what we came for."

The cruel laugh rang in Garin's ears. "You've grown soft in your old age, Harrenfel. A time was when you'd have sooner cut a man's throat than trust him."

"Time changes men." Tal's voice had changed, too, dropping low and rough. "Sometimes, for the better."

"But not often." The shadow in the fog drifted closer. "Some become bitter, others weepy. And a few become fools."

"Where is he? The man whose soul you stole?"

"Your friend? The one whose daughter you allowed to wander into danger?"

Tal released Garin's arm and stepped forward, and Garin leaned dangerously before someone else caught his arm and pulled him upright.

"I've got you," Wren whispered.

Garin tried for a smile and fell far short.

Tal walked a few steps before the others. He still wore his pack, and his shirt under his leather jerkin was stiff with blood, most of it Garin's. His rune-inscribed sword hung from his hand at his side.

"Give him to us," Tal said slowly, "and you may yet survive this."

The Extinguished laughed harshly again. "I will always survive! Even if you manage to kill this body, my master preserves me for his Path. *My* survival is not in question." The shadow in the fog raised a hand, and the dark band of metal on his wrist was just visible through the bright mist. "Nevertheless, I will give you what you want. If you're certain you still want him."

The stones below Garin's feet began to shake, and he stumbled against Wren as he lost his balance. He glanced up to see the ground split before the Extinguished, crumbling and folding back like a blooming flower until something solid and rectangular emerged from the gap. As it stopped rising, the earth ceased to rumble, and Garin loosened his clutch on Wren. But it was she who now clung to him, eyes wide as she stared at the stone block. *A coffin,* Garin realized.

"Is he in there?" Tal's voice was impossibly steady and sure.

"Yes. Would you like to see him?"

Without waiting for an answer, the Extinguished raised a silhouetted hand and made a sharp gesture. The lid of the coffin groaned, stone grinding on stone, then fell with a resounding thud to the debris surrounding it.

Wren convulsed in Garin's arms, and he hung on desperately to her, worried she would dash forward. But she stayed put, eyes locked on the fog-veiled tomb, straining to see if it was her father's face, whispering, "You bastard," over and over.

Tal made no move forward. "Why give him to us?"

"Why do you think, Tal Harrenfel? According to your legend, you're the cleverest man in the Westreach."

"The man whose soul you stole told many lies about me." Tal paused, seeming to hesitate. "He's no more use to you, true enough. But I never took your Master for a generous man."

"The Peacebringer is many things you little know, *Skaldurak.*"

Garin winced as the word cut through his mind. *Skaldurak* — he knew he'd never heard it before, yet somehow, it seemed familiar. A moment later, he realized how — when the Extinguished had spoken it, the Nightsong had grown louder in his mind, rising like a man greeting his brother.

Glancing over, he saw Tal wince as if he'd felt the same thing. On his other side, Aelyn's eyes narrowed, his lips pursed.

Tal's brow smoothed with visible effort. "I long ago took Yuldor's measure. Name me as he will, it does not make me his tool."

"We are all his hands, whether we will it or not." The Extinguished, just visible through the fog, smiled with Falcon's stolen lips. "We all do his purpose."

"Except you surrendered your soul to be his servant."

The Extinguished laughed. "And I count it a fair exchange still. Look! Do you still not see the extent of my master's power?"

As if it had been called, a wind suddenly gusted into the courtyard, swirling and bearing the fog away, and as it thinned, the silhouettes of the devastated walls around them solidified. Garin stared into the fading gloom, expecting draugars to be encircling the courtyard, but he saw nothing.

Then Wren gasped, and he jerked his head forward. At first, he didn't see anything different. The Extinguished stood in sharper detail, Falcon's face contorted into a sneer. The coffin, though open, was still hard to see inside at the distance, but he could tell there was a man within.

Then the shadows shifted behind the Extinguished, and fear lanced through him, cold and nauseating.

The beast ran the length of the walls, fifty feet long — no, longer, Garin realized, as its tail, ridged with sharp, dusky spines, unfurled and drifted lazily across the broken paving stones. Its wings were folded against its back, but even closed, they covered the whole of its gargantuan body. Its neck was long and sinuous as a snake, and its head was flat as a cobra's. A mane of spines bristled around it, shifting slightly with its breath. Its eyes glimmered gold in the dim light, the black pupils slits. Its legs hung off the wall, the back haunches as big around as three people and as tall, and the visible front foot ending in three sharp, yellowed claws.

A dragon, Garin thought numbly. *He has a dragon.*

The Extinguished laughed again. "Now, you see! The Peace-bringer cannot be resisted, *Skaldurak*. One way or another, you will serve him!"

Tal's blood surged through him, so hot he didn't feel the blistering cold as he stared into the dragon's eyes. In all his days of fighting the Nightkin, among all his other deeds, he'd never seen the greatest of Yuldor's servants, much less contended with one. He'd believed them mere rumor; after all, if the Prince of Devils had servants as powerful as dragons, why had he not long ago won the Eternal Animus between the Empire and the Reach Realms?

But his eyes told him now what his mind refused to believe, and he'd long ago learned the eyes were wiser.

He pressed the Ring of Thalkuun, hidden beneath his glove, with his thumb, thinking, plotting. Knowing that with a single swipe, a spout of its infernal breath, and all his plans would be worth less than the pile of ash he'd be reduced to. *But for all my faults, Falcon's songs got one thing right: I've never cowered from a fight.*

Tal tore his gaze away from the dragon for long enough to glance at Aelyn. The mage was frowning, the bronze in his eyes swirling. For the first time, he looked truly afraid. But though his mouth was set hard, Tal knew whatever surprise he'd had in mind for Yuldor's servant would never be enough for this.

"Behold, *Skaldurak,* the might of our Lord and Savior!" the Extinguished cried out. "Behold the power he grants to his servant!"

The Night-touched warlock pointed at a wall between Tal and him, and the dragon's eyes slid over to spot it. As quick as blinking, the dragon snapped open its jaws and shuddered as it gave a cry both roar and screech. Then flames, blue-hot, flooded over the stone, and the wall wilted like a weed under the summer sun. The heat washed over Tal's face, and he winced at the light blazing from the beast's mouth.

As the dragon bit off the fire, it snapped its jaws and shook its head, as if swallowing a particularly foul-tasting belch. From the sulfuric stench flooding the courtyard and twisting his stomach into knots, Tal guessed that the aftertaste of dragon-fire couldn't be pleasant.

He winced and touched a hand unconsciously to his stomach, then frowned, looking down. Though heat had flooded over him, his jerkin and shirt were still stiff with cold.

"Now," the Extinguished said, Falcon's face still cracked in a wide smile, "I believe we're on the same page. Let us then discuss what you must do if you are to preserve your friends' lives."

Tal glanced at the dragon, still snorting and shaking its head, then looked to Aelyn. The mage's frown had deepened, and his eyes narrowed. Tal's thumb pressed against the Ring of Thalkuun again. Too many questions, too little time for answers. How did the dragon come here? Why did the Soul-stealer still wear Falcon's face? Why show off his might and not just kill them when he had them so wholly in his power?

But he still had a hand to play.

Tal finally met Falcon's gold-bright eyes. "You want something. Something from me. Something Yuldor doesn't want me to have."

"Yes. You stole that which does not belong to you, Skaldu-rak. And now, you will surrender it to me."

Tal forced a smile. "I don't think you understand the situation, so allow me to explain. What could your master fear so much that he'd put you through all this? All this subterfuge, all these traps, luring me out from Halenhol and the King's castle — why bother with any of it? Not to kill me — you had a hundred opportunities if that were Yuldor's aim. Not to destroy whatever knowledge I've acquired — killing me would better serve that purpose. What, then, could he want but to possess my knowledge himself?"

"Our Lord knows all he needs, puppet. What could you possibly offer him?"

"This." Pulling his pack from his shoulders, Tal reached inside and drew out the cloth-wrapped book. Then, slowly unwrapping it, he held it up. "The forbidden discoveries of Hellexa Yoreseer, for which she and her entire sect of sorcerers died. This is what your master needs you to retrieve."

The eyes of the Extinguished narrowed, the gold in them smoldering as they swirled. "You believe you've worked it all out then?"

"Yes, I believe I have."

Falcon's laugh cut through the courtyard. "Very well, *Skaldurak*! Our Lord does indeed wish to possess the heretical book. But do not forget that you are completely in my power here." He gestured behind him to the dragon sprawled along the ruins, one yellow eye never leaving Tal. "You will give me the book now. Then we will see how merciful of a mood I am in."

"No." Tal held up the tome. "I carry something you want, that you can't risk destroying, unless *you* wish to discover how merciful your 'Peacebringer' is feeling."

As the Extinguished glared his hatred across the courtyard, Tal gestured behind him. "You will let my friends walk free and unmolested. You will release your draugars from their thrall and send away your dragon. Then, and only then, will I give you the book."

He watched him, not daring to move a muscle lest his trembling show through. He kept the Soulstealer's gaze, though Falcon's eyes had grown bright enough to burn like he stared into twin suns.

"Very well." The Extinguished waved a lazy hand.

Tal risked a glance back. The silhouettes of the draugars, lingering around the edges of the courtyard, faded from sight. Behind the Extinguished, the dragon shifted its massive bulk, as if readying to move, though not quite making the effort. Tal studied it with narrowed eyes, noting how its claws left no marks along the ruined walls, and how as it shifted, it disturbed no dust or rubble.

Quite the graceful wyrm, Tal thought, a smile tugging at his lips.

"You were to send the dragon away as well," he noted calmly.

"Call it a change of mind. Before I do, you must come to me." The Extinguished gave him Falcon's most biting smile.

"Don't!"

Tal glanced back to see Garin stumbling forward, Wren holding him back. The youth's eyes were wide as he tried to struggle free. "Don't, Tal! Don't trust him!"

Keeping the Extinguished in the corner of his vision, he met Garin's eyes. "Trust is a peaceful man's luxury. Go, lad. Take Wren's father and go."

"He'll kill you!"

Tal gave him a small smile. "I'm hard to kill. Please. You must go now, or we've done all this for nothing."

But Garin's desperation was turning to fury. "You came here planning to die? To sacrifice yourself?"

"Do I seem the type for grand gestures?"

"Yes," Wren said through gritted teeth as she hauled Garin back.

Tal laughed softly. "Very well — call it my preeminent performance. But remember: we came for Falcon. Take him and let me worry about the rest."

"Quickly," the Extinguished said. "Before I change my mind."

Wren, Garin, and Aelyn, wearing a long-suffering frown, slowly walked behind Tal as they approached the tomb. The Extinguished watched him greedily, staring like a glutton at a three-tiered cake. Vicious delight and triumph danced in Falcon's lively eyes. Tal kept his gaze on the huge dragon looming above them, noting how the lingering mist moved strangely with its breath as it snorted.

As Tal neared the tomb, he couldn't help but look down. Over a month of captivity had not treated his friend well. His raven-black hair had thinned over his scalp and balded in patches. His skin was waxy pale, and parts of it had rotted away like the thinning of a well-used blanket. His clothes, once finely tailored, hung soiled and limp around his emaciated form.

His jaw tightened, and he had to look away, fearing he would do something rash.

"His soul. You must give him back his soul."

The Extinguished smiled. "Ah, but that was not part of our deal."

"It must be, or we no longer have one."

The fell mage gestured to the beast sprawled behind him. "I believe I have insurance against that possibility."

Tal glanced back at Aelyn. The mage's mouth was set in a hard line, and his face could have been made of stone for all he betrayed his thoughts.

"Very well," he said as he faced forward again. "You'll give me the bracelet when I give you the book."

The Soulstealer smiled. "It's a bargain."

At Tal's nod, his companions reached into the tomb and began to lift the bard from it. With the tome in one hand and *Velori* in the other, he could do nothing but watch as even Garin pitched in to drag Falcon free, wincing as his friend's slack skin bunched beneath their hands and scraped away against the stone.

Finally, his old friend was free of the tomb, and Aelyn reached into a pouch and began muttering some words. A moment later, a blue glow gathered around Falcon's body, and the minstrel began to float.

"Take your broken bard." The Extinguished sounded as if his patience were quickly fraying. "We have a deal to make good on."

Tal glanced at each of his companions, and only Garin met his gaze. The youth stared desperately at him as he leaned on Wren, his eyes begging for answers Tal couldn't give.

He looked away. *Survival is the best I can give you now, my young friend.*

As his companions began walking away, he turned his gaze back to the Extinguished but watched the dragon from the corner of his eye as the beast swiveled its head after them, its pupils narrow. He knew little of dragons, but when it had breathed fire before, its pupils had dilated. Still, the reptilian stink and remains of the sulfuric cloud filling his nose were enough to keep his heart pounding.

Steady. Choose your moment. You'll only get one.

The Soulstealer raised his hand. "The book, *Skaldurak.* Now."

He held the air in his lungs for a moment, then let it out. Then he held up the tome before him and advanced.

"*A Fable of Song and Blood,*" he said as he closed the final feet between them. "Do you know what it means?"

The Extinguished only held up a hand, ready to accept it.

"It means there are others who can possess the Worldheart. Others who, like Yuldor, may reign like gods. And that means your Peacebringer is nothing more than a charlatan, nothing more than a man with a stone."

The fell sorcerer laughed. "A man with a stone? Even with the knowledge you've gained, you know nothing, Tal Harrenfel."

The worn book held before him, he stood before his enemy. The Extinguished wore a smile as he reached up to grasp it.

The Soulstealer's fingers passed through the book, and underneath his glove, the Ring of Thalkuun burned.

Tal thrust his blade into the Extinguished even as he knew it was no use. Falcon's mocking smile remained on his face as the body toppled, turning ghostly white as it fell, then dissipating into shimmering light.

"Illusion!" Tal yelled, but his cry was swallowed by the dragon's sudden bellow. His breath caught with the sound of it, his ears splitting, but he dropped the tome and whipped out a dagger to send it spinning at the beast. Even as blue flames built in the back of the dragon's open maw, the dagger flew into its mouth and thudded into the flesh. The dragon cut off with a roar, obscuring any other sounds, but even the blue-bright flames couldn't hide the shimmer of white light where the dagger had soared through.

"The dragon is an illusion, too!" he called back to his companions.

But a glance showed his friends were in no position to listen. The draugars had reappeared around the edges of the courtyard and were charging them, at least two dozen strong. But his companions scarcely seemed to notice. Garin, despite his wound and blood-loss, was screaming and lashing out toward Aelyn like a madman, while Wren clung desperately onto him, sword abandoned to the rubble. The mage stared at the youth, a hand digging into a pouch at his waist, distaste curling his lips, ignoring the draugars sprinting toward them. Falcon's prone body hovered nearby.

The sight of the youth hit him like a punch to the gut. *He has him. Yuldor's bloody prick, the Night has him.* But he couldn't worry about that now. First, they had to survive.

"Look!" Tal yelled and started toward them. "Draugars!" He doubted these were illusions; they'd been real before, and odds were they were real now. But before he'd taken two steps, something seized his wrist.

His shoulder felt nearly yanked out of its socket as he was pulled to a halt. Twisting around, Tal held up his sword, ready to strike, but hesitated when he saw the arm holding him came from the tomb.

From seemingly nowhere, a second Falcon rose, a horrible grin stretching his gaunt face. Several of his teeth had fallen out, and something black oozed from his gums. His eyes were dark and hollowed, the gold in them dulled to a sickly yellow.

"Hello, old friend," he rasped. "You didn't think I would trust you, did you?"

Velori was still held poised, ready to stab into the man holding him, but he held back. This Falcon wasn't an illusion; that he could touch him was proof of that. But was he the Extinguished under another guise? Or Falcon himself, possessed by the Soulstealer, while the other Aelyn levitated was an illusion?

Behind him, cries of pain and fury and clashing metal sounded, telling of his companions struggling to hold off the draugars.

As he wavered in indecision, Falcon pulled him closer, demonstrating incredible strength for a man nearly dead, and his other hand flashed forward. Acting on instinct, Tal struck.

Something fell to the ground, and Falcon howled and recoiled. Tal froze, staring at the pale lump on the ground. It had dropped among the debris, fingers curled around the dagger like a dead spider, dark blood sluggishly leaking from it.

"My hand!" Falcon gasped faintly, dulled eyes wide as he stared at the stump on his arm, all menace gone from his voice. "My hand!"

Tal could only watch him in horror. *You can't help him. Being near him only risks him becoming possessed once more.* But he found he couldn't move, couldn't do anything but watch his friend stare at the place where Tal had severed his hand.

His left arm was suddenly wrenched behind his back, and Tal stumbled forward a step. But even off-balance, he managed to twist and stab his blade backward, and his steel found flesh with a jolt. But even as he fell to the ground, the person behind him impaled on *Velori*, something sharp slid against his hand, first cold, then burning hot as if he'd thrust it into a blazing hearth.

A roar of fury and pain tore from his throat as his hand came free from his assailant's grip, and Tal gained his feet, sword-hand still clinging to *Velori's* hilt, his other hand throbbing as he pressed it against his chest. The man he'd stabbed stumbled backward, the front of his dark robes wet and clinging where the blade exited, but still wearing a smile as he held up his blood-smeared hand, something clutched in it.

"At long last!" the Extinguished wheezed. "The Ring of Thalkuun belongs to the Night!"

Tal stared at his enemy's ashy gray hand even as he knew what was clutched in it. His hand throbbed where his finger had been severed, but he barely felt the pain through the burning heat of his blood. *The ring*, he realized. *He has the ring.*

Raising *Velori*, Tal spun and swung it with all his strength at his enemy's neck. But the Soulstealer merely flicked his free hand, and his body seized in sudden paralysis and sent him twisting to the ground.

"You are utterly in my power now, *Skaldurak*." The Extinguished wore no disguise now, and his gray, bare feet moved closer, the skin as flaky as bark burned to ash. From the corner of his vision, he saw the worn cover of *A Fable of Song and Blood* in one of his hands, Tal's bloody finger clutched in his other. "You have done well in Yuldor's service. You have delivered to me Kaleras the Impervious, Aelyn Belnuure, and the Ring of Thalkuun. And you have brought me the heretical knowledge of the Blue Moon Obelisk. For years, I have endeavored to gain these victories for our Lord, and in just two short months, you have helped me accomplish them all. Once again, you have served the Peacebringer well."

Tal tried to shout his denials, tried to fight back, but all movement was beyond him.

The Soulstealer knelt, a hand resting on Tal's arm, his face coming low enough for Tal to see it out of the corner of his eye. Little remained of the mortal he'd once been, the skin pale and flaking, no hair anywhere on it, and the eyes burning orange with the mesmerizing movement of flames.

As he spoke, his voice came out hoarse and high-pitched, as if he'd just inhaled smoke. "Now, we go to Yuldor, and see what else the World's Savior has planned for you."

Tal closed his eyes. Behind him, the sounds of his companions' struggles continued. *I can do this*, he thought desperately. *I can find a way out.*

But even to himself, his lies were growing thin.

Kill him!

"No!"

Garin shouted the denial, or tried to, but he couldn't tell if he'd spoken or not. It was all he could do to throw himself to the ground and refuse to rise, even as the Nightsong rose in a flood and threatened to drown him, and the cold voice of the Singer hissed commands in his head and pulled at his limbs.

You must kill him!

"I won't!"

He had to help. All around him, draugars were hurling themselves at Aelyn and Wren, who stood over him and Falcon in protection. So far, all of the draugars had fallen to the ground and returned to their endless rest, but the Nightkin kept coming; soon, they would be overwhelmed.

Kill him! the Singer thundered, its voice pounding like a hundred drums through his head. *He threatens us — he threatens the Song. You must kill him!*

"Never!"

But despite how he struggled, he found himself rising shakily to his feet. Aelyn had his back to him. So easy to slip his belt knife out and stab forward—

Garin forced himself back down to his knees. "You can't make me!"

You must protect us! You must protect the Song!

With each command, Garin felt his control slipping further away. He had to do something, and fast. But what?

Kill the mage!

Then it came to him. He didn't pause to consider if it was mad or brilliant or stupid but seized hold of the idea. "Fine!" he gasped. "I'll kill the mage!"

As if in disbelief, Garin felt the Singer ease its control on him, allowing him to stumble to his feet. He put his good hand to his belt and worked free the knife, holding it as tightly as he could in his weak grasp.

This is right, the Singer whispered. *This is the way it must be.*

But instead of stumbling toward Aelyn, Garin wrenched his body around toward the tomb.

Even as the sight before him turned his stomach, he forced his leaden feet forward. Tal sprawled on the ground, a man in black robes standing over him. As Garin watched, the man walked toward the legendary warrior and knelt. *The Extinguished.* Though he retained the figure of a man, he barely resembled one with his skin more ash than flesh.

You will take his place, Listener? The Singer seemed curious.

"Yes." Garin agreed blindly, barely knowing what he was saying. But as long as he agreed with the Nightvoice, perhaps it would not stop him.

He stumbled closer as the Extinguished laid a hand on Tal's arm. A man moved within the stone coffin beside them, moaning and clutching his arm to his chest. *Falcon,* some part of him recognized — though how that could be when he'd left Falcon behind him with Aelyn and Wren, he didn't know. He forced his eyes away.

You will bring balance to power?

"Yes."

You will return the Song to the Mother?

"Yes!"

A roar, like the tumult of a thunderstorm, filled his mind. *So the young overcomes the old, and death resurrects life.*

Garin was barely listening. The Extinguished didn't seem to notice him, didn't look up as Tal suddenly writhed under his gray-handed grip. He clutched the knife as tightly as he could in his trembling grasp, moved to stand over the gray man, and raised the knife.

Finally, the Soulstealer looked up, and Garin froze. His eyes burned brighter than Wren's, Falcon's, or even Aelyn's ever had, bright enough to burn at a glance. Those terrible eyes flickered to the knife Garin held aloft, and he smiled with his flat, flesh-less lips.

"Do you think," the Extinguished asked in a high, thin voice, "that common steel can harm me, Singer's pet?"

Garin didn't stop to doubt. The heat of a forge and the force of a stormy gale surged through him. As the Nightsong crescendoed in his head, the distant roar of a terrible beast, he screamed and struck down with all that he had left in him.

His vision blurred, and the knife jarred loose of his grip. Garin stumbled to the ground, blinking, trying to see through his blurred vision at the two figures before him.

The Extinguished stumbled — Tal fell on him, silver flashing forward — then an unearthly scream tore through his mind.

Garin watched, breath rasping in his throat, not having enough energy even to rise. One of the figures rose, a silvery blade darkened in his hand. As he came closer and knelt before him, he recognized him.

"You did it," Tal whispered. Though his face was wrinkled with pain, he wore a smile. "You killed the Extinguished, Garin."

Garin closed his eyes, and the ground fell away, the symphony of sounds swelling up and claiming him.

PASSAGE V

While the previous passages detail tantalizing theories, they contain nothing by which I endanger myself. It is the words that follow that threaten our understanding of our Savior and would be branded as heretical by Imperial law, to be sentenced with death.

Forgive the blots of ink — I write quickly as if I might outpace my fear. But I have committed myself to this; I have outlined the reasons for my concerns; I cannot back away from my duty now.

Thus I will come outright and declare my unsavory belief: that the Heart searches for another to possess it.

How this could be, I do not know. Lord Yuldor has long been the Master of the Worldheart and has forged the glorious Empire that has thrived for centuries. He has performed renowned wonders and manifold mercies for the peoples of the World, regardless of race or birth or worth.

But I can see no other conclusion. Why else would the World's Blood manifest in the bodies of Founts? Why else would its Song reach for others, and its Singers call them to destructive acts? It is the only explanation for this chaos, which increases with each passing year in frequency and severity.

I do not wish to believe it, yet I cannot deny that I do. If I sin, I know I will be punished and accept it. But if I must die for my words, then let me write them in full. If a new master of the Heart is necessary, they will come from one of the Founts, either of Song or Blood.

Though I fear I am right, I hope I am wrong — May He Forever Reign.

- A Fable of Song and Blood, *by Hellexa Yoreseer of the Blue Moon Obelisk, translated by Tal Harrenfel*

A BARGAIN FULFILLED

Tal cradled the unconscious youth in one arm as he looked over the courtyard. *Like the worst of my night terrors,* he thought.

Corpses littered the broken stones. With the death of the Extinguished, the draugars had fallen, their sorcerous bindings unraveling, their bodies emptying into rotting vessels once more. The illusory dragon had disappeared in a shimmering of white light, leaving behind nothing but memories of its heart-stopping roar and searing flames that could not burn. The Extinguished himself had become little more than ashes, the wind slowly scattering them, and the gray, iron bracelet that he'd worn was broken, its links scattered about the ground.

Yet the nightmare was slowly fading. The fog had thinned, and pale fingers of daylight clawed through the clouds overhead, illuminating the ruins and lifting the deep shadows. The unholy influence that had lingered over the Ruins of Erlodan seemed to be dissipating.

But not without its cost.

Aelyn and Wren stumbled over to them. "My father!" the young woman said, her voice rising. "He disappeared! Is he—?"

Then she saw Falcon moaning in the tomb next to them and

dashed over. "Father! Silence, Solemnity, and Serenity, but you're alive! He's bleeding, badly. Someone, help me stem his wound!"

With an arched eyebrow at Tal, Aelyn moved over to help. Tal gently settled Garin onto the ground and rose. The youth almost looked peaceful, his brow smoothed. *Rest*, he thought. *Rest while you can. I fear it won't last long.*

Together, the three of them cleaned and bound Falcon's wound. The bard could do little but moan, for though alive and conscious, he seemed lost in the pain of his awakening. Tal knew it wasn't just from his missing hand. The sorcery the Extinguished had cast over him had largely preserved his body, but his old friend had suffered from his months-long internment in the tomb. He could only hope it had passed as a long, dark dream.

After the bard's arm had been wrapped and purified of corruption, Tal leaned against the tomb next to Aelyn. The mage's hat had been lost during the fight, and some of his hairs had worked free of their braid to stick to his sweaty face. Catching Tal's eye, he nodded at the pile of ashes. "He burned your book."

Tal nodded. Even as the Extinguished had turned to ashes around *Velori*, flames had erupted from his hand to consume the tome. *A Fable of Song and Blood*, the book he had hunted down in the heart of the East's mountains, that Yuldor had so wished to possess that the Prince of Devils had lured Tal from hiding and manipulated him into handing it over, was no more.

"I suppose it's best. At the very least, the Enemy does not possess it." Aelyn glanced at him with a raised eyebrow. "Though I would have preferred to have read it before it burned."

Tal gave him a weary smile. "Never fear, my insatiable friend. Knowledge is never lost so long as one person remembers."

Aelyn watched him with eyes narrowed. "Why are you smiling?"

"Oh, no particular reason. Perhaps I'm just happy to be alive."

The elf snorted. "As if that were any reason. But I have mysteries enough to contemplate here — like that name the Extinguished gave you. *Skaldurak* — do you know what it means?"

Tal brushed back a loose strand of hair. "I may have translated Hellexa's tome, but my grip on the Darktongue is tenuous at best. 'Stone in the' … something."

"For an oaf, surprisingly close — it means 'Stone in the Wheel.'" Aelyn studied him. "But why, I wonder, did he call you that?"

"Because I have a propensity to ruin Yuldor's wagons?" Tal shrugged. "Your guess is as good as mine."

Aelyn harrumphed and pushed upright, swaying in place. "A riddle for another time, for we must now depart. The Nameless is dead, and his minions gone, but the Ruins of Erlodan are no place to linger."

Tal looked over their party. Garin still lay unconscious in the rubble, while Wren leaned over the tomb, holding her father's face in both hands. Falcon's eyes seemed to be focusing finally, and almost a smile touched his lips as he met his daughter's gaze.

"We're hardly fit to travel," he noted.

"And yet, we must." Aelyn's lip curled. "Come, Tal Harrenfel. Don't tell me your name ends here."

Tal sighed. "No, I suppose not. But you'll have to be less stingy with your sorcery if we're going to make it back down."

As the mage scowled, Tal heard a faint call of his name. Turning, he saw Falcon staring his way, and he hurried to him.

"He wants to tell you something," Wren said, beckoning him closer.

Tal leaned over the tomb, trying not to breathe in the putrid stench that rose from it. Preserved the bard might have been, but months in a tomb had still made him stink like the dead.

He gripped Falcon's remaining hand. "We came for you, old friend," he murmured. "You're safe now."

Falcon's words came out as soft as a breath, and Tal had to lean close to hear them.

"You cut off my hand, you bastard."

Tal winced as guilt lanced through him. "Yes, I did. And I'm so sorry, Falcon. But if it's any consolation, I lost a finger."

"A bard's hand is priceless beyond measure, ingrate. I'll make you pay for it a thousand times over."

Tal ignored Wren's disgusted look and said in a hushed voice, "Don't say it. More songs?"

Falcon's lips pulled apart as he tried to smile. "My playing days may be over, but I can still compose. The Legend of Tal lives again."

Tal squeezed his friend's hand even as resignation settled in. *Priceless beyond measure, indeed.* He'd never been more than a man; no one knew that now more than those gathered around him.

But they were alive. And if allowing a legend of lies to be woven around him was the cost, he'd pay it again a thousand times over.

***

Sixteen long days later, Tal stood before the King and fibbed for all he was worth.

"Then I stabbed him in the chest." Tal shrugged. "And that was that."

King Aldric narrowed his eyes. "That was that? You claim to kill one of the Extinguished, as much as they can be killed, then pretend it is of no consequence? It's as if you are reciting one of my bard's songs!"

The King lazily waved a hand at Falcon, who stood just

behind Tal's shoulder. *A truly kingly gesture,* Tal thought, the corner of his mouth twitching. The Court Bard had been entombed for months, his soul ripped from his body, one of his hands severed, and only remained standing by his daughter's support. Yet the King scarcely seemed to notice his return. *Perhaps he was more satisfied with the Soulstealer than a minstrel who can no longer play.*

"I would not say of no consequence." Tal displayed his most conceited smile as he raised his bandaged hand. "I lost a finger, and Falcon a hand. To make no mention that I've fulfilled my part of a king's bargain."

The King of Avendor looked as if his wine had turned to vinegar in his mouth. "So you have. And so must I fulfill mine. After all, a king always keeps his promises."

It's the first I've heard of it. Aloud, he said, "You are quite gracious, Aldric."

"I'm sure." The King took another drink from his goblet, then gestured with it toward Tal's other shoulder. "You wished the boy to have a duchy, didn't you? Which duke or duchess shall I rob of their rightful inheritance?"

Tal glanced back at Garin. The boy looked nearly as pale as he had that fateful day a week and a half before. The wound on his arm had begun to heal under a physician's ministrations, but he'd scarcely seen him laugh or smile during their journey home. Only with Wren did he come close to his normal self, and even then, he fell short.

Tal nodded at the youth, and Garin nodded back. *What we agreed upon, then.*

Tal turned back to the King. "No noble peer will mourn the loss of their ill-begotten estate today. By your leave, I would have Garin sent to Elendol for training, with your purse paying for the travel and boarding of him and his entourage."

"Training? In Gladelyl?" Aldric's eyes had grown small and hard in his large, soft face. "What sort of training?"

His lips twitched. "Dancing lessons."

The King snorted. "Keep your secrets for now, if you must; I will find out before long. But even with your lowly opinion of me, I will maintain my part of our deal. You will have what you wish. Only say — how much of the country do you intend to be part of this 'entourage?'"

Tal grinned outright. "Only myself and the players of the Dancing Feathers."

"No sooner do I recover my minstrel than you whisk him away. Though I suppose he's only half a bard now." Aldric waved his dismissal impatiently, not even noticing Falcon's wince at the casual insult. "Very well, you may go. Just get your thieving fingers out of my pockets before I have the rest of them cut off."

Tal never let the smile leave his lips. "And yours out of mine, my King."

Come, Listener.

The whisper cut through all other sounds. The wind against the high east tower. The now-familiar buzz of discordant noise in his ears. Wren murmuring something beside him.

Come.

He'd tried ignoring it. He'd tried responding. Nothing made a whit of difference. Still, the Nightsong droned on, and still, the Singer told him to *Come, come, come...*

Fingers snapped before his face. "Wake up!"

Garin startled and looked over to see Wren frowning at him, fingers still pressed together. "I'm awake."

Wren lowered her hand, but the frown stayed. "Doesn't seem that way anymore. Not since... you know."

Garin looked out over the city, hazy in the morning light, a light mist quickly dissipating. *Maybe I am asleep,* he thought. *Maybe this is all a dream, a lingering nightmare. Not the first stages of madness.*

Come, the Nightvoice whispered again.

"Not sleeping well," he muttered.

Wren turned her frown out toward Halenhol, but he knew she still meant it for him. "Facing the Extinguished was terrible, Garin. But I was there, too. I had to go through all the same things."

But you have your father back. And you're not slowly turning insane.

"Are you sleeping well then?"

She snorted. "With dead men and dragons staring out of the shadows?"

The wind gusted through the silence that fell between them. Almost, it drowned out the refrain that came again in Garin's mind.

He squeezed his eyes shut and ground his palms into his sockets. There was only one thing he hadn't tried yet. But he wasn't sure he dared to.

"Why did Tal take all the credit?"

Garin looked over at her, his vision blurry for a moment. "He deserved it, didn't he?"

A wrinkle appeared between her brow. Another time, he might have marveled over that crease; now, he barely had the energy to notice. "*Deserve* doesn't matter. *You* did it."

And I've gotten my reward.

Garin shrugged. "He struck the first and final blows. Besides, we talked it over and decided it was best to just say it was him. It was your father's idea, actually."

"My father's? And when did you three sneak off to talk this over?"

"When you were out in the woods at night taking care of your, you know… necessities."

She snorted a laugh, and he glanced up to find her smiling, even if her eyes were still narrowed. "Alright, then. Why was it best?"

A different sort of discomfort came over him now. *A lie is best mixed with nine parts truth*, Tal had said sometimes on the road. The time had come to put it to the test.

"Tal already has a legend, written and sung. A little more fame won't hurt him. Me, though... it would start questions." He feigned a smile. "And I'm not looking for any attention."

He left it there, hoping she wouldn't wonder what kind of questions he feared. But, in her usual Wren fashion, she bulled on ahead. "Does this have to do with the Soulstealer... possessing you?"

Garin shrugged, trying to seem nonchalant. "A bit." *But it has more to do with the devil still plaguing me.*

After a moment, Wren raised an eyebrow and looked away. "I don't care about that, you know. No matter what happened in those damned ruins, you're still Garin to me. Besides, whatever it is the matter, they'll heal you in Elendol."

If I last that long. Though her words stirred him to nervous warmth, the heavy weight remained on his chest. Garin breathed a sigh and stared out to the distant hills.

Come, the Singer whispered once more, shattering the moment's peace as surely as a trumpet's blaring call.

He slumped forward. Only one thing he hadn't tried yet, one thing dangerous and foolish. But he couldn't wait until they reached the elven queendom. He couldn't take it any longer.

"I'll come," he muttered.

There was an exultant swell of the sounds, rising through him like rushing tide so that he had to sit upright and try to draw in a full breath, but he couldn't, he was gasping, drowning —

All fell silent.

"Garin?" he heard Wren ask, hands shaking him, but he could barely register it as he marveled at the sudden quiet within him. *It's gone. It's truly gone.* The Nightsong had fallen silent.

He turned to her with his first unfettered smile in a week and took her hand. "I'm alright. Everything's fine."

Wren looked startled, but she smiled back, gold weaving through the green of her eyes. She squeezed his hand.

Garin looked out over the city again, and the view seemed to have changed somehow, once again marvelous and breathtaking. His grin pulled wider. *This,* he thought. *This is what I left Hunt's Hollow for.*

But he couldn't banish the last shred of doubt, buried like a sliver under his skin.

Tal reached the east tower's door and stopped before it.

For a long moment, he traced the grain of the wood with his eyes. Hoping he would change his mind, fearing he would. The Ring of Thalkuun was clutched tightly in his uninjured hand.

You don't have to say the words, he lied to himself, hoping it would give him courage. But he'd always told the weakest lies to himself.

After several minutes, the pressure to act pressing down hard, he raised a trembling hand and knocked.

"Enter," a voice called from within, almost too weak to hear.

Tal turned the handle and pressed inside. The tower was much the same as before: the same books crowding the shelves, the same werelights dimly illuminating the space. But the man who sat at the desk was changed. Kaleras the Impervious had looked advanced in years before, but he hadn't truly seemed old. Now, though, his every movement was slow and calculated, as if afraid any sudden motion might break him.

The warlock turned slowly around to peer at him with hooded eyes. "I'd heard you had arrived. And your mission?"

"Accomplished. I came to return you something." He approached and held out his hand.

Kaleras didn't move to take it but peered up at him, the light catching in his deep brown eyes. "Did it help?"

"Yes."

Still, the warlock didn't take it. Just as Tal began to wonder, Kaleras slowly raised his hand to his. He didn't meet Tal's eyes as he held open his hand, and Tal dropped the band of dull metal in it, not sure if he was disappointed or relieved.

They both withdrew. Kaleras didn't put on the ring but kept it clutched in his hand, eyes set on the wall. Tal's pulse fluttered in his throat, and he clenched his jaw. *If a job needs doing, do it quick,* he told himself.

"I didn't come here just to give you the ring back. After all, it belongs more to me than you."

"And it belongs more to the Hoarseer Queen than either of us," Kaleras murmured, eyes flickering up to meet his.

Tal smiled briefly at that. "Whichever thief has first claim, I wanted to say that..."

But the words faltered in his mouth. He wanted to say them, tried to — but in a sudden torrent, his childhood swept over him again. His mother, bent over her fletching, working by moonlight because they couldn't afford even tallow candles, then rising before the sun to clean other folk's clothes. The town's children, their faces twisted and mocking, shouting "whore's bastard" at him over and over, shoving him down into the ditches at the side of the road, while his one friend stood by, watching, helpless.

He clenched his fists, his missing finger spreading pain up his left arm. *The pangs of the past never really fade*, he mused bitterly. *And all the more when you cling to them.*

He swallowed the soft, conciliatory words he'd meant to say, the words that might have brought an estranged father and son together after four decades of resentment, and forced out in their place a bitter, twisted smile.

"Well, Father, I must be off to Gladelyl."

Kaleras was looking at him with an intensity that bordered

on anger as if he knew what Tal had denied him. His lips mouthed the word Tal had named him with like he rehearsed a particularly difficult incantation. But all he murmured was, "Leaving again?"

"Yes. Perhaps we will see each other again." Tal shrugged. "Perhaps not."

The warlock's face twisted — in pain or revulsion, Tal couldn't tell. "Listen, Tal. I know your mother meant much to you. That much is clear, for you to take your name from hers. But Talania wouldn't—"

"Don't pretend to know what my mother would or wouldn't." The words came out harsh and biting. "Don't pretend to know her. You gave her one night and a bastard, that's all — let's forget the rest."

Tal looked aside. The hush filling the room was thick, choking — he had to speak. "The boy needs guidance and training. You saw the shadow that falls over him; it has only tightened its clutches since our second visit to the ruins. Only the mages of the Chromatic Towers could hope to get him through this now."

Risking a glimpse at the warlock, he found his barb had gone unnoticed. Kaleras' gaze hadn't shifted, but he stared at him with an expression he'd never seen on the warlock's face, nor wished ever to see again.

He looked aside again. "Before I go, I'll need back the thing I entrusted to you before I left."

A pause. "The pages?" Kaleras asked softly. "Copied from a fell book? I saw the language they were written in, Tal. What are you reading in the Darktongue?"

"Never mind that. I trust you still have them?"

"I do. But, my condition being what it is, you'll have to gather them yourself."

Tal turned and ascended the stairs. It only took a moment of shuffling through his bedside drawers before he found the stack of poorly bound parchment and returned downstairs.

The warlock looked as if he hadn't shifted, staring at the wall as if scrying into the future. *Or, more likely, into the past,* he thought.

Kaleras glanced over as he approached. "Good luck to you. The boy will need it, as will you if you stick by him."

"Perhaps. But that's the difference between you and me, isn't it? I will stick by him, no matter the danger, no matter the cost. No matter that we share no blood."

Not waiting to see the aged warlock's reaction, Tal turned and, the copied pages of *A Fable of Song and Blood* clutched to his chest, exited the door.

As he stepped out, he saw Kaleras had two more visitors. *Who knew the old warlock was so sought after.*

Stranger still was who his visitors were. A young man with a shaved pate and wearing brown robes stood next to a middle-aged monk with even less hair. *Of the Order of Ataraxis,* Tal noted, seeing the eight-pointed star on the dark, iron medallions hanging from their necks, the only ornamentation allowed to the monks.

"Lord Tal!" the younger one said with a nervous smile. "If you could spare a moment...?"

Tal repressed a sigh and shifted his stack of parchment so that his body blocked it partially from sight, then plastered on a pleasant smile. "I'm no lord, but I can spare you two moments if you wish."

"My apologies, L — Mister Tal." The young man quickly gestured at the older monk. "I am Brother Nat, and this is Brother Causticus. If you have the time, my brother wishes to speak with you."

Tal nodded respectfully to the older monk as he looked him up and down. "Well met, Brother Causticus."

The monk didn't answer him but narrowed his eyes, looking every bit as hostile as one of Falcon's former lovers when they caught up to the bard. *A deep admirer of mine, indeed.*

"A thousand apologies again, Mister Tal," the young monk

rushed to say. "Brother Causticus has taken a vow of silence. Since he took it twenty-six years ago, he has not spoken a word but to the Whispering Gods."

"I see." *A Mute,* he thought. *That will make conversation rather difficult.* "How can I help you then?"

The young monk glanced nervously at Causticus, but the older monk just continued to stare unblinkingly at Tal. "Mister Tal, Brother Causticus has dedicated his life to uncovering the facts behind fables. His past work has delved into many of the oldest myths and folktales across the Westreach and beyond and exposed the truths, and the lies, of them all."

Tal nodded, suspecting where this was heading, but content to let the lad fumble his way there.

"Of late, he has turned to modern legends, those formed within our era and particularly within Brother Causticus' own life. So, Mister Tal, you must see how you would be of particular interest to him."

"How's that?"

The young monk was starting to grow flustered, his movements nervous and erratic. "You're the Devil Killer!" he blurted. "The Red Reaver! You're the man who escaped detection from the Circle for years, who has battled the Servants of Night and won!"

Tal's discomfort squirmed in his gut, but he hid it behind a shrug. "So they say."

Brother Causticus had not stopped staring at him. As the young monk began to respond, the older man gestured sharply, and he cut off, though he wore a worried frown.

"By your leave, Mister Tal, Brother Causticus wishes a private moment with you," Brother Nat said, rather stiffly to Tal's ear. "But before I go, I should tell you the King has requested of our abbot that Brother Causticus and I join you on your journey to Elendol, and Father Hush has complied." He gave an uncertain smile.

Tal returned it, though it wasn't for him. *The wheels of the King's machinations never stop turning.*

After another moment's hesitation, the younger monk nodded and turned back down the hall, his wooden clogs clicking on the stone.

When his footsteps had faded, Brother Causticus moved closer, close enough for his odor, stinking of onion and garlic, to fill Tal's nose. But he'd smelled far worse, and didn't flinch away as the monk leaned toward him, lips bare inches from his ear.

"Is it true?"

The monk's voice was dry as aged parchment but sharper than Tal would have expected.

"I'm sorry," Tal said politely. "But is what true?"

Brother Causticus' expression spasmed. His intention was clear, but Tal found himself smiling and pretending not to understand. After all, if the man broke a two-and-a-half decade oath once, he doubted he'd hesitate to do it again.

The monk leaned closer, his voice louder. "What they say of you. Is it true? All of it, to the last claim?"

Tal found his lips curling into his wolf's grin, and he leaned in to whisper in the Mute's ear. "If everyone believes it, does it matter?"

Without a backward glance, he turned and left, Brother Causticus' eyes sharp on his back, his smile pulling wide.

Tal kept a smile firmly on his lips as he was once again admitted to the King's throne room.

King Aldric impatiently gestured at the monks lining the room, and the Mutes began chanting. The magic of Solitude pressed in around him like a smothering blanket by the time he stood before the throne.

"Well?" the King demanded. "You've already robbed me of my troupers and coin. What more do you want?"

Tal stared at him. Smiling. Waiting.

For all his failings, Aldric Rexall the Fourth was no fool. And though he was not a man to pale in fear, he grew pale as he understood Tal's smile.

"What is it?" the King demanded. "Speak quickly, or I'll have my guards throw you out."

"You've made more than one king's bargain recently, haven't you, Aldric?"

A flush returned to the King's throat. "I don't know what you're talking about."

"And 'a king always keeps his promises' — isn't that what you told me?"

Aldric leaned forward and shook one thick finger at him. "I've always been tolerant of you, Harrenfel, as patient as if you were my kin. But keep pushing me, and I swear you'll never feel the sun's light on your face again."

Tal's heart pounded a warning in his chest. Aldric was more than capable of making good on his threats; examples of his steel-edged justice were littered throughout his reign. But though he longed to flee, tail tucked between his legs, he held his ground.

"I am no king," Tal said softly. "I don't have the concerns of a realm weighing on my shoulders. But I do know something of deals with devils."

The King laughed harshly. "I suppose I'm the devil in this scenario."

"Not the only one. I didn't come here to threaten you, Aldric. I came with a warning. Remember: you're nothing more than a puppet. And puppets are easily replaced should they stop dancing to their strings."

"Careful, Harrenfel, careful. Or I may have to snip your threads."

"Do as you must. But remember this: no matter what it may

seem, no matter how my actions may appear, I will always resist."

The King stared at him for a long moment. "Why?" he asked finally. "Why resist? The Night comes after each day. Its shadow falls across the Westreach, longer and deeper each year."

His hands clenched into fists, his gaze wandering to them. "Damn it, Harrenfel, I'm a *king*. No one has more duties than a king! No one has greater decisions and worse options. I've done all I can, the best anyone could — and the Whispering Gods be damned if I need to defend myself to *you*!"

Tal waited as the King burned his fury into silence, then sated the thirst it left in its wake. When the goblet was empty of wine, Aldric slammed the silver chalice back down, bending the stem so that the bowl leaned to one side. The dregs of wine trickled down the bowl, thin streaks of red against the silver.

Only as the King turned his glare back to him did Tal speak. "You ask why I resist, but you already know. It's the same reason why you don't."

"Careful." Aldric's voice went low. "I give you much slack, Harrenfel, but you might still hang yourself from it."

Tal smiled. "We do it for love."

Aldric's eyes bulged from his head, looking at Tal like one of the marsh toads common to Hunt's Hollow. "Love?" he croaked.

"Love for different things, but love all the same. You love being the Ruler of Avendor. You love the power, the wealth, the renown. To you, the sound of your name announced when you enter a room is like the sweetest eunuch's tenor. To you, the fear in your people's eyes as they accidentally catch your gaze is more euphoric than standing atop Heaven's Knoll. You love being King."

Aldric leaned back in his throne, a sneer twisting his broad features as he looked down on him. "And you — you, the Red Reaver, the Magebutcher — what could *you* love?"

Their faces appeared in his mind's eye, some of them surprising him. *Falcon. Garin. Wren. Even Aelyn and Kaleras.* And her, always her, hovering ever in the shadows of his thoughts.

But he shrugged. "What could an unscrupulous rogue like me love beyond fame?"

The King narrowed his gaze, sharp enough to know when he was being mocked. *But though you know how to manipulate love,* Tal thought, *you never could understand it.*

The King of Avendor gathered a cold smile. "My time for games has ended, Harrenfel. Take my bard and his troupe; take my wagons and gold; go to Gladelyl and train the boy you claim isn't your bastard. Only don't return. If you do, I swear by all the gods both good and ill, I'll take your head."

For the first time since they'd met, Tal deeply bowed to his King. "You drive a hard bargain, my Liege."

He turned, and Aldric's high-pitched laughter escorted him from the hall.

THE WAYWARD RETURN

GARIN STARED UP THE UNKEMPT DIRT ROAD AS THE CART BUMPED beneath him. Trees crowded close beside the path and leaned over them, making it hard to see far ahead. But a smile tugged at his lips.

He recognized the way they traveled now.

Soon, the Winegulch Bridge would appear; beyond that, the trees would thin; and soon after, the familiar archway would emerge from the trees, declaring them to be in Hunt's Hollow once more.

Home.

For three weeks, the Dancing Feathers — and their two monk companions — had traveled up the storm-beaten roads to the far reaches of Avendor, braving increasingly wintery conditions. Snow had wafted down on two occasions, but it never stuck, and the cold firmed up the mud to make passage easier. Men and women grown used to the comforts of the Coral Castle pulled their cloaks tightly around them, shivering and complaining to each other of lithe limbs growing stiff and clever hands so frozen they threatened to fall off — though this last complaint was spoken quietly, and only when the one-handed Court Bard wasn't near.

Garin couldn't have felt more the opposite. He barely noticed the cold, and it wasn't from his clothes being any better-tailored than theirs. For one, Wren had warmed his bedroll the past several nights, finally having grown certain enough of her father's health to leave his side. Falcon Sunstring was still no beauty, his skin mending back where bugs and decay had had their way with it, and at the end of his right wrist lay a conspicuous vacancy. But despite it all, he was again smiling, and like spring to flowers, with the reemergence of the minstrel's good humor, his daughter's passion for Garin had rekindled.

His grin felt as if it stretched from ear to ear just thinking about it.

But nights with Wren weren't the only thing warming him. Soon, he would see his family again. He would be the lost son returned, the son who had gone and seen more places than he could count on both hands and would be able to lord it over his brothers. He would feel his sister's arms tight around him, see his mother and her surprised, joyous smile. They would clamor to ask where he'd been, what he'd done, and he would tell them tales they wouldn't believe.

An adventure, he thought. *Just like in the fireside stories.*

His smile faltered a little at the thought. No — his journey hadn't quite been like the tales. The Nightsong and the Singer had been quiet ever since that day atop the Coral Castle's roof, but he knew he wasn't free of them. Like something he'd forgotten, the fell magic niggled at the back of his mind, always there, always waiting. Still, most times, he could forget he'd ever heard them. Most times.

But though he anticipated the reunion, he couldn't help but imagine the farewells. *I can't stay. I have to go on. To see the elves and their sage elders. To...*

He didn't know what reason he'd give. Not the truth; never that. But could he lie? He'd lied many times to get out of trouble as a boy, but that was before he'd become a man. Now, the thought gave him an uneasy disquiet. *What would Father have done?* he thought. *What should a man do? Lie to protect his family? Or tell them the truth?*

It wasn't an argument — he knew better than that. Not even Wren knew the complete truth, and she'd been with him through it all. Aelyn and Tal, he suspected, knew more than they'd let on, and the fewer who knew what he'd become, the better.

I'll come, he'd said, and the Singer and the Song had exalted. *I'll come* — though he didn't have the faintest idea where he was supposed to go.

"I didn't know you slept with your eyes open."

Garin blinked and looked over. Wren, who sat next to him on the cart, was watching him, a small smile on her lips. *Gods and devils, but I love that smile*, he thought.

But his own smile came out strained. "Just thinking."

"Thinking? Don't overextend yourself."

He nudged her, more for the chance to touch her than to silence her, and her smile grew coy. His mouth went dry imagining what that smile dared him to do.

"So when will you introduce me to your family?"

Once again, she'd caught him wrong-footed, and he fumbled for an answer. "Uh, as soon as we get there, I suppose."

Wren raised an eyebrow, the edge of the smile disappearing. "I suppose? Are you ashamed of me?"

"Ashamed? Of course I'm not!"

A laugh burst from her. "You're too soft, Garin! You'd think you'd have grown a spine by now."

He wasn't sure whether to smile or scowl and found his expression caught somewhere between. "Caught me off-guard is all," he muttered.

She patted him on the back. "Don't worry. We'll work on it."

A few hours later, the short-lived daylight was fast dissipating, and though they were close to Hunt's Hollow, a halt was called at the Winegulch Bridge. To Garin's protests, Tal only held up his hands.

"It was Falcon's call," his mentor said, "but it's the right one. No use in getting there early if it costs us a wheel. I know you're eager, lad, but we'll get there tomorrow, never fear."

Garin turned away, trying to hide his disappointment and failing. When Wren asked him what was wrong, he only shrugged and muttered, "Going for a leak," leaving her to frown at his back.

The forest closed around him, the familiar scents and sounds helping to slow his beating heart. Stillness — he'd nearly forgotten what it sounded like, traveling amidst a troupe of actors and musicians. Someone always seemed to be laughing or singing — or both, if the casks of dwarven honey-wine they'd carted from Halenhol were involved.

He untied his britches and winced at the cold, then began to relieve himself. For a moment, the trickling on the dead leaves was all he heard.

Then crunching sounded from the forest behind him.

He glanced back as he quickly began tying up his britches. Most likely, it was just someone from the troupe who'd come to do their business. But he couldn't help a prickling of unease at the back of his mind. Breath coming quick, he stared into the gloom where he'd heard the sound.

More crunching, both left and right. Garin whipped his head each way, a hand falling to his belt knife. Did he glimpse a shadow moving among the closest trees? Were those footsteps, or just forest creatures walking carelessly? He drew his knife, watching, waiting, straining to listen over his thumping heart.

A burst of sound came from behind him, and Garin whirled, then fell back as someone clapped a gloved hand over his mouth. Without hesitation, Garin swung the knife at the assailant's arm, heard him roar in pain, and fought to work free of his grip.

Cold steel pressed against his throat and bit shallowly into his skin. He felt blood trickle down his neck.

"Drop it," the man rasped in his ear, his breath was hot on his skin. When Garin hesitated, the knife pressed deeper, and his hand opened of its own accord.

"Good lad." Someone, large and heavy-footed, emerged from the shadows. In his fear-clouded state, it took Garin a moment to recognize him, and as he did, his stomach gave a painful wrench. The big bandit in charge of the band of deserters, who had waylaid them on their way to Halenhol, was the last man he wanted to see.

The highwayman didn't look pleased to see him either, scrunching up his eyes as he stared at him. "You. I know you. You're that boy who traveled with the man who burned my hammer." The large man stared at him like Garin were a brace of cooked hares rather than a young man with slightly soiled pants. "Burned my hammer," he repeated with a grim smile.

"And he cut my arm," the bandit holding Garin growled.

"Quit your bloody yapping! I don't give a shit if he cut your arm or your prick or your balls — don't whine about it to me." The big man had closed the distance between them and loomed over Garin, half a head taller, even with Garin having grown an inch since the last time they'd met. "Know what I do give a shit about, you little... shit?" He screwed up his eyes tighter, as if debating whether or not to take out his ineloquence on Garin, then continued. "That man who burned my hammer. I've got a score to settle, and you're going to help me. Got that?"

Garin met his eyes and didn't look away. His mind pulsed with a subtle rhythm, sounds that had no cadence drowning out everything else in his mind as they suddenly wove into an urgent chorus. The whining of a fox. The whisk of a reaper through tall grass. The scream of a slaughtered hog. Even with a man holding a knife to his throat, the big outlaw staring hate down at him, and the rest of the band around him, his fear was quickly draining away. Behind the bandit's glove, he started to smile.

The big man moved far quicker than a man his size seemed able, pounding his fist into Garin's stomach. Garin jerked, barely able to keep himself from doubling over and accidentally slitting his own throat.

"Release him, you fucking moron!" the bandit leader hissed. "I need him to talk."

Garin felt the knife and hand pull away, then he was shoved forward and onto his knees. Just as he rose, he was laid flat, his side burning where the highwayman kicked him, lungs struggling to suck in air.

"Well?" the big outlaw demanded as he stood over him.

Garin didn't try to rise again but turned over to stare up at the brigand. Pain wracked his body, and the shallow cut in his neck still dribbled blood. But fear had been replaced by that pulsing, all-consuming Song. He opened his mouth.

The words hissed and curled in unfamiliar sounds even to his own ears. Yet somehow, he knew their meaning as clear as if he'd spoken in Reachtongue.

"*Boil blood.*"

The big man's expression shifted, then he stumbled back a step, eyes widening, staring at his hands. Garin watched as his skin rippled, and his veins bulged, then looked away as the man began to scream. His shrieks cut off in a sudden, wet squelch, and the blood, burning hot, seared Garin's face in droplets.

For a moment, no one moved. Garin opened his eyes and looked around at the bandits. The buzzing still filled his ears, incessant and maddening, like hornets had made a hive of his head.

As his gaze fell upon them, the highwaymen broke, some slinking away into the shadows, others abandoning all dignity and pelting into the forest. In seconds, they were gone, leaving their leader's prone, bloody body on the forest floor.

Garin's eyes fell to what had become of the big brigand.

What you did to him, some part of him corrected, but it was hard to listen with the Nightsong filling his ears, the sharp sounds cutting into him, the soft sounds carrying him away—

"Garin!"

He opened his eyes, and Tal knelt before him, hand on his shoulder, eyes creased with concern. As if his name had been the word needed to break the trance, the buzzing faded away.

"Garin," Tal repeated, low but urgent, "are there any more?"

Garin saw Aelyn standing just behind him, staring with a mixture of disgust and fascination at the remains of the bandit. As the smell of blood suddenly registered, he felt his stomach twist, and then he was bending forward, splashing sick onto Tal's boots.

"Never mind, never mind," Tal muttered, shifting out of the way while maintaining his grip on Garin's shoulder. "You're not the first man to retch at the sight of a corpse."

"Though that one's a good deal uglier than most," Aelyn observed.

Garin sat up and wiped his mouth. *I did that*, he thought, the words cycling through his mind. *I did that.* It was more than the act of it; he had willed it, wished to hurt the man with every shred of himself. It hadn't been the Singer's command that had done it. It was him.

And it was only then that he knew: even when they reached Hunt's Hollow, he wouldn't be coming home. There was no home for the devil he'd become.

Welcome to Hunt's Hollow.

The words were carved into a board raised by two poles that the town's mayor had cobbled together, but Tal supposed it served as an archway. *You certainly know where you are*, he thought.

Home. He wondered if returning to Hunt's Hollow was

coming home. He'd been born and raised within its borders, but he'd left before he'd even become a man. He'd been too many places, seen and done too many great and terrible things, to believe he could call anywhere home.

Yet, in some small way, thinking of Hunt's Hollow as home was a comfort. *And we all need what small comforts we can get.*

He glanced at Garin, who stood staring up at the sign next to him. Wren was on Garin's other side, watching him with a creased brow. He wondered if the boy now felt the same as he did. Ever since the incident with the highwaymen the evening before, he'd barely said more than two words within Tal's earshot.

"Can we enter? I'd rather not waste any more time here than necessary." Aelyn stood at Tal's other shoulder, his nose wrinkled as if smelling something foul. It wasn't just the mage's sensitive nose — the stink of livestock permeated the air, thick and pungent as a duchess' perfume. A sharp-tipped traveler's hat once again hid his pointed ears and shaded his elven eyes.

"You go on," Tal said, "and you as well, Wren. I want a private word with my apprentice."

Wren curled her lips. "Just get me when you're ready," she said to Garin, then went back to join the rest of the troupe as they continued setting up camp behind them.

"Don't keep me waiting," Aelyn said with a strained smile, then went forward to wait under the welcome arch with uncharacteristic patience. *He's more eager for this leg of our journey to be over than I — to make no mention of removing that Binding Ring from his finger.*

He turned back to Garin. "Something's troubling you."

The youth shrugged. "Just the same as before."

"It's a heavy burden. I'm sorry I placed it on you."

"You didn't." Garin finally looked over at him. "I chose to go with you. I pushed to enter the ruins. I knew the risks. Besides, maybe it's just as you said: maybe this devil has always lived inside me." He hung his head. "Anyway, a man makes his own decisions, and he has to live with them."

True enough. Tal looked back toward the village. He knew Garin had grown and matured. He could only hope it would be enough.

"Even so," Tal said, "there's something you ought to know."

He hesitated. *Say the words,* part of him whispered. *You must say the words.*

But the truth often brought far less healing than it promised. Even when it was owed. Even when it was overdue.

Garin was watching him, waiting, his brow creased again. *Perhaps the last time he'll look at you,* another part of him mocked. *Surely the last time he'll want to.*

But no matter the consequences, no matter how it would change both of them, Tal forged on ahead, if only to ease the guilt pressing down on his chest.

"Have you ever wondered why I took you on as my apprentice?"

***

The space between Garin's shoulders prickled at his words. *Have I done anything but wonder?*

"A lot of people asked," he answered, his voice neutral.

The man he'd followed through Night's Pyres and back sighed like he was setting down a heavy rucksack. "Don't mistake me; there were other reasons. In part, it was due to your curious and restless nature, and the fact that you often hung around my farm. But those are the meanest of my excuses." Tal's mouth stretched wide, but it looked like the grin some of the draugars had worn, a corpse's smile. "The truth is... I knew your father."

Garin looked sharply at Tal, his heart suddenly pumping like he were running a race. "You did?"

"Yes. I told you I was born in Hunt's Hollow. Growing up,

most of the other children called me Bran the Bastard on account of my unsavory origins. Your father wasn't one of them. He was a friend, my only friend, in a town that shunned me for being a fatherless, unnatural whelp."

"Friends?" Whatever Garin had been expecting, it wasn't this.

"That's just the beginning." Several hollow laughs joined that stiff smile. "Your father was called back into the King's service before he died, isn't that right?"

"Yes. He was the captain of a company."

Once again, he saw their parting farewell: his mother tearing him away from his father, the hot, incessant tears, his brothers teasing him for crying, his father shouldering his pack and leaving with his band of hardened soldiers.

"He had a mission." Tal's mouth worked for a moment, then he shrugged and said in a falsely light voice, "But perhaps you had best ask your mother for the rest. I am sure Nyssa knew what her husband was sent to do."

The questions flared so hotly in him for a moment it seemed they must come tumbling out. *But do you want to hear it from him, whatever it is?*

The thought stopped him cold.

"Then I'll ask my mother," Garin said softly and turned back to the carts to find Wren.

"A heart-wrenching conversation, it seemed," Aelyn observed as they trudged along the muddy thoroughfare that cut through the town. "Did you tell the boy sharp secrets of his past, I wonder?"

"Not yet," Tal muttered. He wondered if he'd done what was best or simply opted for the coward's way out. *So I didn't have to see his face when he realized the truth.*

"Ah, well. There's always tomorrow. And the past's regrets

never bear fruit in the present, I hear." Aelyn smiled thinly, then swept his arm through the air. "Where, pray, was your humble abode again?"

As they neared his house, Tal was taken aback at the changes. A few short months and already, the marsh had begun to claim his small farm back. The grass had grown long; the fence had broken in several places. No chickens or pigs roamed the abandoned fields, no doubt because neighbors were "taking care" of them in his absence. The house itself looked much the same but seemed comparatively shabby after the opulence of the Coral Castle.

Was I ever content here? he wondered. *Or was I hiding all along?*

"Shall we enter?" Aelyn said, almost cheerily. "And I won't need help over the threshold, I assure you."

Without waiting for a response, he pushed open the door and entered. Heaving a sigh, Tal followed him in.

Under the glow of Aelyn's werelight, the room crowded in closer than ever, absurdly cramped after his rooms in Halenhol, and a perfume of wood-rot and mold filled the room so thickly he could taste it. Even Aelyn's bout of good humor flagged under the assault, his bright eyes watery and his smile strained, but the mage still gestured expansively to the small table that could barely seat one, let alone two, as if it were the King's banquet table. "Shall we?"

Like we're reenacting a scene from a play, Tal mused as he moved around the table to sit in his usual chair while Aelyn took the one he'd sat in before. *Only now we undo what was done before.*

Aelyn pulled off his glove and extended his hand across the table, the Binding Ring glittering on his finger. His eyes never left Tal's face. "Our pact is complete," he said softly, his voice almost a purr. "Now, release me."

Tal held his gaze, hands in his lap. "Did you know?"

Aelyn narrowed his eyes, good humor starting to dissipate. "Know what?"

"That our good and merciful King Aldric is a bought man."

He'd come to think he knew a little of the elven mage, and what he was capable of. But Tal didn't expect him to smile.

"Of course, I did. There's a larger game at play here than you've ever cared to look for, Harrenfel." Aelyn wiggled his fingers, the milky white crystal winking in the werelight. "Now, if you'll release me, I have much to do in my Queen's service and little desire to remain here."

Tal sighed, suddenly feeling every year of his age and then some. "Never cared to look, or I didn't dare to."

But all the same, he removed his glove and reached forward to take the elf's hand. Aelyn's skin was cold and clammy as a fish, and Tal worked quickly, gripping the Binding Ring between his fingers. The band of metal burned cold beneath his fingertips. With one swift movement, he pulled it from the mage's slender finger.

Aelyn shuddered as if doused in chilled water. Then his eyelids fluttered open, the bronze swirling fiercely in his eyes. Tal's spine prickled.

"I've been waiting a long time for this," he said, soft and silky, then shouted, "*Thalkunaras bauchdid!*"

Even as his body stiffened and his mind went numb with shock, helpless amusement washed over him. *As it began, so it ends.* Even before Aelyn pried the Binding Ring from his rigid grasp, Tal knew what would happen, and it felt like the fulfillment of a small prophecy as Aelyn slipped the crystal ring over Tal's finger.

"This I bind you to," the mage said, lips curling, eyes gleaming. "That you will wear this ring until both you and I go to Gladelyl, then return to Hunt's Hollow. That you will never impede or undermine the plans of my monarch, Queen Geminia Elendola the Third of Gladelyl. That you will always obey Queen Geminia's commands, no matter what you may witness in Elendol."

The Binding Ring glowed bright, and Tal already had his eyes closed and his teeth set, braced for the cold wave that shuddered through him even as his blood burned in response.

As the ring dimmed and both the cold and heat retreated, Tal opened his eyes to slits and stared at the smirking mage. "I'm not given to prejudice, but I'm starting to hate elves."

Aelyn smiled the first real smile Tal could ever remember from him. "One man cannot stand for a Bloodline, though I do not think I make such a poor exemplar."

"My name — my Heartname. How did you learn it?"

The smile widened. "There is much I know that you do not, Magebutcher. But if I cannot provide illumination, I can promise this: the sooner we go to the Queen and do her bidding, the sooner you will be free."

"Queen Geminia." Tal snorted a bitter laugh. "Then she is Yuldor's creature as well."

The grin twisted into a snarl, and the mage leaned across the table. "Never! Do not speak such filthy lies about Her Eminence!"

Tal shrugged. "As you say. But you see how it looks suspicious."

"You are a snake, a viper. You cannot be trusted."

"Strange — the same could be said of you."

As the elf glared across the grimy table at him, Tal stood, his legs feeling weak. But the hesitation, the questioning of which course was correct, was gone. *No room for doubts when you're pushed off a cliff, a millstone hanging from your neck.*

"But you did speak one truth," Tal continued. "The sooner we go, the sooner we can return, and I can take my turn again in binding you."

The offense had drained from Aelyn, leaving only his sour smile. "So long as we go, you're permitted any dreams you wish, however unlikely."

Tal lifted his head back and stared at the narrow shafts of pale light streaming through the holes in the roof. *Farewell so soon, my hermit's cottage. The road calls me once more. The road, and all the twists and turns that it throws under my feet.*

He stood abruptly and made for the door. "What are we waiting for? There's walking to be done!"

"We can't wait here all day. We have to go in. Or don't you want to?"

Garin stared at the distant homestead, swinging his feet between the planks of the fence on which he and Wren sat. "Yes," he muttered. "And no."

"No?"

What could he say? *That a demon lives inside me? That I'm not sure if I could look my mother in the eye after what I've done? That I'm not sure if I'll hug them or accidentally harm them?*

And what Tal had told him of his father's death — would his mother know what he said she would? But though he'd always wondered about his father, he found himself reluctant to learn the truth. *He went to the Fringes and was killed by the Nightkin. That's what we were told, and that's the only reasonable thing that could have happened. What could be suspicious about that?*

"I ran away and only left a note explaining why. They haven't heard from me in months." He shrugged. "I'm afraid of seeing the pain I put them through because I was a coward."

To his surprise, Wren snorted. "If that's your reason, you're still a coward. Any suffering your family is going through will be over once they see you, cotton-head."

She kicked off the fence and began walking toward the farmstead. "Come on!" she called over her shoulder. "Unless you want your family to know how much of a nanny goat you are!"

Garin grimaced, then slid from the fence and jogged after her.

The distance between him and the door to the farmstead seemed to last forever, barely coming closer, his dread waxing with every small step. His head felt light enough that even a tiny squall could have knocked him over, his gut so tight and twisted he thought he'd be sick all over the threshold.

Then, all of a sudden, he was in front of it, and Wren knocked on the door. It opened, and his mother stood in the doorway, mouth and eyes wide — then she pulled him toward her and hugged him so tightly he could barely breathe, her face pressed into his chest, sobbing, murmuring his name over and over, saying, "You're home, you're safe, you're home."

She pulled him inside, and Garin reeled behind her, feeling like he had that day Wren and he had drunk wine in the backroom of the Smallstage, the World too bright and happening too fast and his chest so tight with happiness that this couldn't be real. But at his mother's call, the rest of his family poured into the room, all laughing and yelling and running to embrace him. He was crushed beneath the press of his brothers, his mother and sister having retreated to the side to laugh and cry. And in that moment, he'd never felt so loved.

When they separated, and Garin had rubbed at his eyes, pretending he was scrubbing away road dust, he introduced Wren. She was grinning with the rest of them, the gold in her eyes bright, and his brothers all gave him sly smiles and knowing looks while his mother pulled her into nearly as tight a hug as she'd given Garin.

But as the happiness of the greetings subsided, a weight settled back in Garin's gut. Making his way over to his mother, he stepped close to her and spoke under the loud carousing of his brothers, who had produced a small barrel of Crazy Ean's marsh whiskey from somewhere and were taking copious swigs from it.

"Mother," he said, "I know I have a lot to explain. But I have to ask a question first." He hesitated, then pressed on. "I learned something about Father, about how he died. That he wasn't just conscripted to fight at the Fringes, but had a mission."

His mother's smile stiffened, then slid away. "Who told you that?"

His chest tightened so that he felt he could barely breathe. "So it's true? He had a specific goal?"

His mother's gaze flickered to the rest of the family, but Wren was now indulging in the whiskey with his brothers, throwing back a glass to their roaring approval. Only his sister watched them from the opposite corner wearing a slight frown.

"Yes," she whispered, barely audible amidst the ruckus. "He did."

She went quiet for so long a moment that Garin thought she wouldn't continue. But before he could prompt her, she spoke again. "It was a command straight from the King — he couldn't refuse. Your father was to put together a band of a dozen veteran soldiers and go to the northern coast, not wearing Avendoran colors, but traveling as civilians."

"The northern coast. Outside of Avendor?"

She nodded. "To Sendesh. It was the end of the Red Summer, when the Yraldi marauders were coming down from their frozen isles in droves, so they made it their excuse to be seeking work as sell-swords in the fight. But that wasn't what they were sent for."

"Then what?"

His mother stared at the floor. "To hunt down a man your father knew from a long time ago. A man who had gathered another name since the time he lived here in Hunt's Hollow. A man your father had no business ever seeing again, much less trying to capture."

Garin worked his tongue around his mouth. "Who?" he croaked.

"The Red Reaver." She finally met his eyes. "Tal Harrenfel."

———

Tal watched Garin and Wren approach the wagons as they left from the other end of town, passing under a second archway like the one they'd entered under. While the stride of the bard's daughter was unsteady, the young man was certain in his course, his eyes downcast, his arms stiff at his sides.

He knows, Tal sighed to himself. *He knows.* He'd set him on the path. Yet until that moment, he'd dared to hope it wouldn't come to this. *Tal, old boy, you're as much a fool as when you first left your mother's door.*

When they'd nearly reached the wagons, Garin turned to Wren and said something, and she nodded and broke away, weaving her way toward the rest of the carriages, though not without a curious glance back in Tal's direction.

Tal slid onto the end of the wagon as Garin stood before him. For a moment, he watched him in silence, until Garin raised his eyes to meet his gaze.

"I know I have to travel with the troupe," the youth said. "I need the help of the elves. But you... I don't want to talk to you. I don't want you to come near me. If you do..." He looked away, his jaw working, not seeming able to find the words.

"Will you kill me?" Tal asked softly.

The youth whipped his head back up to stare at him. Tal was the first to look away. He'd seen the faces of far too many enemies not to recognize hate.

"Stay away from me." The words came out choked and broken, but there was iron behind them. "For your own good."

"Don't you want to hear what I have to say?"

"No!" Garin nearly snarled the word but calmed almost as soon as he had. Something else flashed through his eyes. *Uncertainty? Fear?*

Before he could say more, the youth turned and staggered away, swaying nearly as much as Wren had. Tal watched him until he disappeared into the rest of the caravan. *So ends my time as a tutor,* he mused. *Nearly as fruitful as my other endeavors.*

"The curse of youth — so much passion, so pointlessly vented."

Despite the heaviness weighing in his chest, a small smile took Tal's lips as he glanced over. Falcon moved like an old man, even leaning on a cane, but seeing him walk on his own at all put some heart back in him.

Tal patted the wagon bed. "Get up here, you failed philosopher, if you can manage it."

"I'll be cavorting and doing cartwheels before you can recite *The Catechism of Silence,* just you wait."

"That prayer is at least two hundred pages long."

The Court Bard groaned as he levered himself onto the wagon next to Tal. "So I've been told. Never bothered with piety myself."

"And you've never spoken a truer word. Though, to be fair, you lie for a living."

They sat in companionable silence for a time.

"So," Falcon said. "Onward to Gladelyl. To the fair Queen Geminia's realm. To the other of my lineage's Bloodlines."

"So it would seem."

"What do you think we'll find there?"

Tal leaned back on his arms, staring up at the dark clouds gathering overhead, promising the season's first, real snow and a long, wintery trek through the marshlands.

"The same things as anywhere else. Soldiers drinking and fighting, priests preaching and fear-mongering, nobles jockeying for position and power. Strife, heartbreak, and the slow extinguishing of hope."

"You make it sound so cheery."

"Perhaps it's the weather." *Or the boy whose father you long ago buried.*

Falcon cocked his head. "Why go if that's all you're expecting?"

Something small and white drifted down from the sky. Tal removed his glove and held out a hand, and the snowflake melted even as he caught it, but his eyes clung to the ring gleaming on his finger. From Falcon's sharp inhale, he knew he'd seen it.

His smile twisted wider. "Because my Queen commands it."

"So the legend of Tal Harrenfel continues. I suppose I'll need to compose more songs." Falcon stared out into the gathering winter storm, his remaining hand rubbing at the stump where the other had been.

Tal's chest tightened, and he looked away. "And I'll need to survive to hear them."

They sat in silence as snow began to fall thicker, blanketing the day and blocking out the sun, beautiful and peaceful and ominous all at once. *Like a new start*, he thought. *The past obscured just enough to pull your cart from the mud and roll onward.*

Tal slid down from the wagon. "I suppose it's up to me to get this sorry fellowship underway. Wish me luck."

"You've never needed luck before."

Tal turned away. "Silence knows I'll need it this time."

BOOKS BY J.D.L. ROSELL

Sign up for future releases at jdlrosell.com.

LEGEND OF TAL

1. A King's Bargain

2. A Queen's Command

3. An Emperor's Gamble

4. A God's Plea

RANGER OF THE TITAN WILDS

1. Ranger's Rebellion

THE RUNEWAR SAGA

1. The Throne of Ice & Ash

2. The Crown of Fire & Fury

THE FAMINE CYCLE

1. Whispers of Ruin

2. Echoes of Chaos

3. Requiem of Silence

Secret Seller *(Prequel)*

The Phantom Heist *(Novella)*

GODSLAYER RISING

1. Catalyst

2. Champion

3. Heretic

ACKNOWLEDGMENTS

A huge thanks to:

Kaitlyn, my wife and first reader, by whose withering critiques this book was forged into something worth reading;

René Aigner, for his fantastic cover illustration;

And *you*, dear reader, for spending your valuable time sojourning with Tal, Garin, and their companions — thank you for coming along.

ABOUT THE AUTHOR

J.D.L. Rosell is the internationally bestselling author of the Legend of Tal series, The Runewar Saga, The Famine Cycle series, and the Godslayer Rising trilogy. He has earned an MA in creative writing and has previously written as a ghostwriter.

Always drawn to the outdoors, he ventures out into nature whenever he can to indulge in his hobbies of hiking and photography. Most of the time, he can be found curled up with a good book at home with his wife and two cats, Zelda and Abenthy.

Follow along with his occasional author updates and serializations at www.jdlrosell.com or contact him at authorjdlrosell@gmail.com.